The Ojanox

Ashes to Ashes

Daemon Manx

Published by Last Waltz Publishing

5 Midland Ave, Pompton Plains, N.J. 07444

All characters in this book are fictitious or used fictitiously with consent. Any resemblance to actual persons living or dead, is purely coincidental.

www.lastwaltzpublishing.com

Edited by Lisa Lee Tone

Original developmental edits by Ben Eads

Library of Congress Cataloging-in-Publication Data

Robert R. Chiossi, 1967-

The Ojanox Series / Daemon Manx

TXu 2-417-807 2024
ISBN 979-8-9868451-9-7

Book Cover by Christy Aldridge (Dark Poppy Designs)

Illustrations by Christy Aldridge and Don Noble

First edition August 2024

Also by Daemon Manx

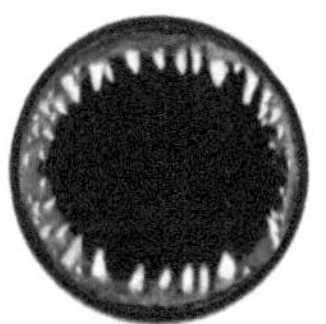

Abigail

Piece by Piece

Drawn & Quartered with Diana Olney

Hacked in Two with James G. Carlson

These Lingering Shadows

Tales from the Monoverse

Arcranium with Mark Towse

Manx-iety: A Collection of Disturbing Stories

The Ojanox Series: I-IV

Scream in the Dark

Ashes to Ashes

All Fall Down

Lonesome Mountain

Praise for The Ojanox

"Every so often, a writer reads a coming-of-age tale that they wish they had written themselves. That's how I felt with Daemon Manx's *The Ojanox* series. Exciting, genuinely nostalgic, and scarier than hell!" –Ronald Kelly, Author of *Fear, The Essential Sick Stuff,* and *Southern-Fried & Horrified*

"In Garrett Grove, the time for evil has arrived, and Manx serves up scares like Halloween candy—the good kind, too ... full-sized, nostalgic, and satisfying to the end."—Gaby Triana, author of *Moon Child;* editor of *Literally Dead: Tales of Halloween Hauntings*

"Daemon Manx has proven in a short time, he is the real deal. And he doesn't mess around. This is a must-read series, and one of the best books I've read this year." –Mike Ennenbach, author of *Cuckoo*

"If you are like me and love horror mixed with great storylines and twisted endings, you must read Daemon Manx. And when you are through, hug the pillow, hide under the covers, and repeat over again, it's only a novel ... or is it???"—Jason Knight - ECW Original

"Written with beautifully descriptive scenes, *The Ojanox* places you directly into the quaint, small town of Garrett Grove during the Halloween season where everything is pleasant ... until it isn't. An ancient, dark entity is accidently excavated and escapes into the world with chilling results. *The Ojanox* is a fresh, original, plot-driven page-turner that I couldn't put down. I highly recommend it and am looking forward to Part Two of this excellent series." – Jeani Rector, Editor of *The Horror Zine*

"Daemon Manx has wrapped up a delicious candy treat that you won't be able to resist gobbling down, razor blades and all. *Scream in the Dark* will put you in the Halloween spirit no matter what time of year you read it. You'll be holding out your plastic jack-o-lanterns for more!" — Jeff Strand, author of *Twentieth Anniversary Screening*

Contents

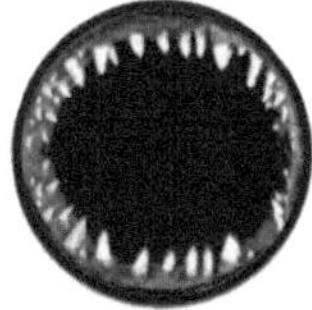

For my fourth-grade teacher, Mrs. Genevieve Smith
A devoted educator with a limitless fountain of inspirational stories

FOREWORD

GAZING INTO THE ABYSS

The year is 1979. A small New York town prepares to welcome the fall season in all the expected ways: young children bicker and boast over Halloween costumes, secret lovers meet in clandestine corners, and a tortured soul plots wicked deeds. All the while, hidden just out of view, patient and hungry ... an ancient evil lurks.

I know, I know. You've heard all this before. You've read the book, watched the film adaptation, and probably even caught the two-part podcast. If you're a fan of old-school horror, like I am, then you'll swear that you know how the plot will unfold. What the primeval horror is. Who will live, who will die, and even in what specific order said deaths will occur.

Hey, I get it. I thought so too.

But I was wrong, dead wrong. You'll probably be wrong too. And, let me tell you, rarely has it felt SO good to be incorrect. To be legitimately surprised. To revisit a hallowed era of storytelling in such a creative way.

Let's be honest: vintage horror is a difficult thing to effectively pull off in today's market. Try too hard and you alienate your target audience, skewing far afield from that elusive "feel". Half-ass it and you're derivative, lazy, or a hefty combination of both.

For anyone who is familiar with his talent, Daemon Manx has, quite unsurprisingly, accomplished something special with *The Ojanox*, making the familiar feel wholly unfamiliar. Pulling us back to the gritty world of late-70s to early-80s horror without stepping on any toes in the process. This is neither an homage nor an emulation. This is a book that could very well have been borne of that halcyon era, resting on some half-askew bookshelf this whole time, just waiting to be discovered. But, as much as *The Ojanox* is a glimpse across decades, it is also a gateway into Manx's mind—one can glean various details about the novelist through the terrors nestled within the typeface.

Much like there are no atheists in foxholes, there are no innocents amongst horror authors. We write from the darkest of depths, from places where light falters and even whispers carry great weight. Yes, the stories we create are ultimately meant to startle, to shiver, and to scare. To invoke those primal sensations of fear and dread. But there is so much more to it than that. We are also, through prose and plot, offering the world a glimpse of our vulnerable sides. Our hopes and fears. The hardships we have endured. Mistakes we've made, and the fallout that followed. From pen to page, our pain is made manifest. Some people suffer for their creations—horror authors put themselves through anguish for their art. And, during this process of composition, this literary baring of souls, we allow ourselves to examine our personal hauntings, be they self-induced or inflicted by others. To exorcise our own demons, keystroke by keystroke. True, we may never completely vanquish the darkness inside us. For many horror authors, those hurts are grafted to our very essence, as much a part of us as blood and bone, woven into the very fabric of who we have become. But, while those shadows may yet linger, we at least get the chance to look our fiends in the eye with an unflinching gaze.

Daemon has never been shy about his personal struggles, of which he has had plenty. I respect both his candor and his fearlessness in facing those dark years. Perhaps that deep well of experience is what gives his writing that extra bit of compelling oomph. Some of us have pint-sized imps on our shoulders, gently reminding us of past indiscretions, tempting us back with honeyed words. Manx has a thousand-pound gorilla clinging to his back, beating its chest and bellowing a mighty roar of misdeeds, yanking at the chains of the past with inhuman strength.

And that, dear reader is what you get with *The Ojanox*. A beast of both the literal and figurative sense. A peek at the demons without ... and those within. This is a massive story, years in the making, touching on a myriad of topics, many of which are just as pertinent today as they were in '79. From a word count perspective (it shouldn't matter, but we're novelists ... it matters) it is an imposing body of work, rivaling the hefty behemoths of the era, as is only fitting. From my first involvement with *The Ojanox*, I have always maintained that Daemon writes like Laymon, but with a more literary bent. This isn't a knock at all: Laymon penned some classics. He was great at concepts, with a knack for the perverse and deft skill at setting a scene. The only place I was occasionally left wanting was with the narrative voice itself. Daemon rectifies that shortcoming with the ease of raw ability, wrangling words in the best of ways. In all honesty, it wouldn't shock me in the slightest to see Manx and Laymon sharing space on bookstore shelves in the not-so-distant future. I am hard pressed to think of an indie author who deserves it more.

But don't take my word for it. See for yourself. Curl up in your favorite space, dim the lights, crack open *The Ojanox*, and step into the town of Garrett Grove. What you find just might surprise you.

Jack Wells

Author of *Jack of All Trades* and the *Monochrome Noir* series.

TRICK OR TREAT

I hope you will indulge me just a little before diving into the book, as the origination of *The Ojanox* is almost as interesting as the story itself. I began the writing process during the spring of 2020 while I was serving my final year of incarceration in a halfway house in Newark, New Jersey. Yes, you read that right. I spent nearly a decade in state prison prior to that. The short story: I made some terrible mistakes because of addiction (rarely are addicts known for making good ones), and that landed me in a very dark place.

But that was only the beginning of my journey because prison is where I finally got clean (Eleven years and four months as I write this today) and it's where I turned my life around. But something else happened while I was serving my days behind the wall. I started writing again. Addiction had stolen everything I loved, and my creative muse was only one of the casualties. But as the fog lifted, my desire to create returned, and it was in a cold, lonely cell where I started to live once again.

By the time I reached the halfway house, years later, I had written dozens of short stories and novellas but had never tackled any larger projects. It was January of 2020, and I had just received permission to leave the halfway house for a few hours a day to attend college in person. I even got a couple months under my belt, and then Covid hit. The house was put under quarantine lockdown, and no one was allowed to leave. Unfortunately, the virus had already found its way into the building.

And that was life for the next seven months. We started out with almost three hundred men in the facility, and that number quickly diminished to less than a hundred. We all got sick during that time, some more than others, and many of the men were taken back to the prison system's medical facilities ... never to return.

To pass the time, I started writing what I thought would be a short story, one that encapsulated the feeling and the mystery of Halloween the way I remembered it as a child. I sat down and wrote the first lines of what is now chapter one, and *The Ojanox* was born. Within a few days, I realized this was not going to be a short story. I had no idea just how massive it would be, but I was about to find out.

I owned a portable word processor called the Alpha Smart 3000, originally intended for my college classes. If you're not familiar, The AS3K is a battery-operated unit with a small screen that allows the user to see three lines of script at a time. There are eight files you can fill with text, but once they are filled, you must transfer the data to a Word doc and zip drive. I would fill the files every night, writing from 6p.m.–11p.m. non-stop. The next day I would use the house's library computer to transfer my work and ultimately free up space for another night of writing.

I should mention that I shared the room with ten other men who were anything but quiet. Who can blame them? We were all stir-crazy. While they were listening to music, playing poker, and screaming to one another in the confines of our 12 x 12 room, I would don my headphones, crank up the tunes, and write, write, write.

And yes, it was like that. I wrote in a fever; the words flowed as if they were coming from somewhere other than me. It was very stream of consciousness, but it was also methodical. During the day, I would map out the next ten scenes in outline, and that night, I would write. Oddly enough, not once did I experience even an ounce of writer's block.

On October 30, 2020, I typed the words *The End* and looked down at a massive file containing 520K words. I had finished the first draft in six months. Seven days later, I was released.

Now would come the hard part. The rewrite. Little did I know, I would be rewriting this beast for the next four years and editing out over 160K words, all for the betterment of the story, I assure you.

Now it's true that this story was created under some very adverse conditions. You could even say it is a byproduct of that suffering. But that's not why *The Ojanox* was written in such a short period of time. To be honest, I have been working on this story since I was ten years old myself. Like Troy Fischer, when I was in fourth grade, I had a Halloween party and built a haunted house in the garage. Yep, you guessed it, it was called Scream in the Dark. In *The Ojanox,* many of the settings, themes, and circumstances are inspired by my memories of Halloweens gone by and my own life experiences as well. However, this story isn't just a tribute to my own childhood but to childhood itself. If I have done this correctly, it is to pay respect to that initial sense of mystery we all felt when we heard our first ghost story, to that chilling fright when we saw our first horror movie.

Although the coming-of-age factor is just a small portion of this story, as *The Ojanox* is pure horror with its fair share of violence, I mention it because that's where it started for me ... when I was a child. My love for horror, that is.

If I got any of this right, I hope you are taken back, if only for a moment, to that innocent time in your life when you set out to grab a pillowcase full of candy on Halloween and returned home with all the peanut butter cups you were hoping for … and more.

Daemon Manx

"A menacing darkness has entered the town, and it knows where you live. It lurks in the shadows, it hides in the woods, waiting for you to take the shortcut through the graveyard."
~ Lois Fischer

CHAPTER 20

Monday

Jared Neibolt turned right onto Sunset Road, making his way into Garrett Grove. He pushed the truck a bit faster than usual and checked his watch to find it was almost five a.m. Right on time. It wasn't the early morning hours he minded; Lord knew there were worse jobs than delivering bread for a living. Still, having to make the arduous trek over Garrett Mountain for only two stops was a royal pain in the ass. The Grove was the most remote destination on his route, and he wished he didn't have to come here at all. But since he didn't make the schedules, there was no point bitching about it. With any luck, he would get promoted to manager in June and his truck driving days would be over. *No more trips into bum-fuck Garrett Grove, and no more hemorrhoids.*

It was still dark at five a.m., with an early morning ground fog making visibility even more difficult. Jared squinted to focus on the stretch of pavement before him, then turned on the high beams, which did little to help. But with barely another vehicle on the road, he relaxed some, pressed the gas pedal a bit harder, and turned up the radio. The sound of the Ramones filled the cab of the truck, making him feel like he wasn't completely alone.

He bobbed his head and sang to the music, unaware he was now doing over forty-five in a twenty-five mile per hour zone. He sailed past the high school and entered a rural stretch with fields and drainage ditches on either side of the street. Then, for one disastrous moment, Jared took his eyes off the road a second time.

It smashed into the bread truck with the velocity of a cannonball, causing the entire vehicle to shudder. Jared jumped in his seat and attempted to slam on the brakes, but it was already too late. He white knuckled the wheel with his heart beating triple time in his chest and his mind racing to figure out what happened. He thought he had hit a deer or a bird had flown into the grill. Then he saw the man's face as it smacked against the front windshield.

It sounded like he had driven into a wet tree. The guy's head bounced off the glass, and for a fleeting moment, time stood still. Jared stared into the man's eyes and watched as life exited his body. There was nothing but darkness left inside him ... cold, blank darkness. Jared fixated on the dead man's stare and wanted to die himself. A second later, the guy was airborne and thrown over thirty feet into a drainage ditch on the far side of the road.

Jared continued to jam on the brakes, bringing the truck to a screeching halt, then exited the vehicle, shaking and ready to vomit. "I killed him. Oh my God, I killed him!" he cried.

He made his way to where the body had landed and looked over the embankment. It was horrible. The man lay face down, half submerged in the muddy water and a tangle of weeds. His body was now twisted in a most unnatural way, and the sight of it made Jared's stomach lurch. He doubled over and spilled his breakfast onto the side of the road.

It's all my fault. What do I do, what do I do? There was no radio in his truck, and Jared had no idea where the nearest phone might be. He had never even been issued a parking ticket, and now he had killed someone.

Jared nearly died a second time when Deputy Kovach turned on the cherries and hit the siren behind him. The officer pulled the cruiser to the side of the road and exited the vehicle. "What seems to be the problem, sir?"

"Thank God! He stepped out of nowhere. I didn't even see him. One minute I was driving, the next he's right in front of me. Oh my God ... I didn't even see him!" Tears streamed down Jared's cheeks, and his hands had begun to tremble.

Deputy Kovach walked to the embankment and looked over to find the body embedded deep in the mud as if it had come down like a meteor. He then led Jared to his cruiser and instructed him to have a seat in the back while he moved the truck off the road. "I need to secure the scene before someone comes along and hits one of us," he told Jared, who nodded but didn't hear much of what he had said.

The fog was beginning to thin, and the sun had just started to rise as Deputy Kovach went to the embankment and looked down into the ditch a second time.

"Poor bastard," he hissed. "And I thought *I* was having a bad day."

CHAPTER 21

Donald Fischer arrived at the quarry long before sunrise and several hours ahead of any of the other employees. He typically enjoyed the early morning solitude but doubted if today would be all that enjoyable. The Museum of Natural History was sending a representative to inspect the artifacts in the cave. The guy's title was Curator of Tribal Antiquities … or something like that, but to Don, that was just a fancy little label for giant pain in the ass. He didn't give a hill of beans what some crusty old geezer from the museum did with the cave or the crap inside it. He needed the old fart to make it quick and leave so he and the rest of the men could get back to work. Production had come to a grinding halt since the recent discovery, and with winter just around the corner, layoffs wouldn't be far behind.

As a geological engineer, it was Don's job to determine and prepare safe blasting formations in the topography of the DuCain quarry. Granted, it wasn't as prestigious as mapping the shift of tectonic plates at Yosemite, but it paid the bills. In truth, he had given up aspirations of getting to California long ago. *That's life: man plans, and God laughs.* Donald Fischer believed God had been getting a good laugh at his expense for some time now.

He opened the office trailer, walked across the scuffed linoleum floor, and put on a pot of coffee. Mark Gold and the other foremen would arrive later, but not before Don had enjoyed the peace and quiet of his first cup of morning Joe. It was all about the small victories, which was exactly what happened last night.

Sheriff Primrose had called the house around nine o'clock with the good news. Robert Boyle and the Richards twins were all doing better, and there was no need to worry about contagion. Don had been cleared to go to work, and Troy was allowed to attend school. Don had been more than relieved. Although he loved his family dearly, he felt another day in the house was more than he could stand. Lois had been on his case more than usual. Everything he did lately seemed to piss her off. He couldn't help that he was needed at work, and she should be able to understand that. *It's this crummy-ass job that puts the food on the table.*

Lois had urged him to have a heart-to-heart with Troy, which had gone well. *Kids are resilient as hell, especially at that age.* Troy had been somewhat pensive, but he wasn't in the sad state that his mother made him out to be. Thankfully, Rob was on the mend, and with any luck, the events of last Saturday night would soon be forgotten. Besides, Don had enough on his own plate to worry about.

The pressing matters at hand had everything to do with the cave and the shutdown of production that sent old man DuCain into a tailspin. It crossed Donald's mind more than once that all their problems could be solved if a pocket of methane actually did explode, taking out the cave and everything in it as well.

Don had even gone inside the cavern himself and taken a look around. It certainly appeared different from the typical cache of bones or occasional tomahawk they usually found. The cavern was huge. Much too big to have gone undetected by his equipment. There was no explanation as to why it didn't show up on his initial readings. It just didn't make sense.

The opening revealed by the blast was large enough for a man to fit into, but it was impossible to determine just how far the cavern extended into the mountain. There were bones in there, a lot of them, not all of which looked entirely human. And the place was loaded with artifacts, including weapons. All appeared to be in excellent condition.

Just thinking about it twisted Don's stomach into a sour knot. He grimaced as he poured a cup of coffee and walked across the narrow trailer, with its scattering of blueprints covering every inch of wall space, and took a seat behind his small but organized desk. He had just taken his first sip and was startled by a knock on the trailer door. His stomach twisted a notch tighter. The other supervisors and quarrymen never arrived before seven, and the guy from the museum wasn't due till even later. The knock came again, soft but deliberate. Don got up and opened the door.

"Good morning." An attractive woman stood in the doorway.

"Good morning," he said, taken aback by her presence. The woman had dirty blonde hair and bright blue eyes. She looked somewhere in her early thirties and wore a toothy smile. Don figured she was either lost and had somehow stumbled across his trailer or she worked for the newspaper and had heard about the recent discovery.

"Can I help you?"

"I hope so. I'm looking for Donald Fischer. Do you know where I could find him?"

"I'm sorry. I'm not allowed to speak to the press about anything yet," he said, trying to be polite but curt at the same time. "You'll have to talk to the people from MNH."

"I'm not with the papers." She held out her business card. "I'm *with* the museum, and I'm supposed to meet with Mr. Fischer this morning. Do you know when he'll be in?"

"I'm sorry." He took the card and examined it. His lips pinched together in a scowl of confusion. "I was expecting—"

"You were expecting a man, probably an old man at that." She smiled and held out her hand. "I take it you're Mr. Fischer."

"Um-Donald Fischer, nice to meet you." He shook it and read the card a second time, **Dr. Stephanie Thompson, Curator DDAH.**

"Likewise, Mr. Fischer." She nodded and offered a look of understanding. "Don't be embarrassed. I get it all the time. No one expects a woman to do my job."

"Um-a, no, it's not that. My boss told me to expect a Dr. Stephen Thompson, so I naturally expected a man. An old one at that."

They both laughed, which seemed to ease the tension. "Is that coffee?" she asked and pushed her way past him through the tight doorway. "I could sure use a cup."

"Do come in." Don's eyes widened as she made her way to the coffee pot, helped herself to one of his mugs, and poured a cup. "Please, make yourself at home."

Had she turned out to be an old geezer, Don would have been put off by the straightforwardness, but Stephanie Thompson had caught him off guard and momentarily disarmed his defenses. She stood no taller than five-two, maybe three, at the absolute most, with a whole lot of spunk packed into a small package.

"My dad had his hopes set on a boy. Wanted to name me after my grandfather. Then I came along. Ta-da!" She held up her hands and took a bow. "So, he changed the Stephen to Stephanie, and well, there ya go." She took a sip of coffee. "This is good, full strength. Well, Dad was the curator for the museum and passed the ambition onto me, his oldest child—not a boy." She finished with a huge smile.

Donald watched as she took her coffee, walked over to his desk, and sat in his chair.

"So, when the museum says Dr. Thompson will be showing up, everyone naturally expects an old man. Then I walk in. And they all react exactly like you are right now, Mr. Fischer."

"Don is fine."

"Great, Don," she continued without taking a breath, "so, what have you got up here? I hear it's quite a find. I'm dying to get a look. When can we go up there?" She had only had a couple sips of coffee and was already bouncing off the walls. Don couldn't imagine what she would be like if she snorted a line.

"As soon as the sun comes up and my engineers arrive. There are strict regulations about working in confined spaces. I realize the relics and contents of the cave belong to the museum, but the cavern is on DuCain property. God forbid there is a cave-in or something. Everyone's safety is my responsibility."

She smiled and nodded her head in agreement. "Of course. I was just seeing how far I could push you." She flashed a smile that made her eyes look even brighter.

"I'll bet that works most of the time."

"You have no idea." She winked and leaned back in his chair.

"Actually, I think I do." Don had been regretting this morning's meeting, but there was something about Dr. Thomson that he liked quite a bit.

"Have you been inside? I hear there are intact skeletal remains. Is that true? Are they intact?"

Don didn't know if they were intact or not, but there were an awful lot of bones in there. He told her as much as he could but still had some questions of his own. How long did she expect the excavation to take? How long would his job site be shut down, and just how many more visitors he could expect to show up?

She told him it was too early to tell. The museum had flown her in from DC and rented a house in town for her and her family to stay. But she expected to be in Garrett Grove for no less than two months.

"Two months! How could it take so long?" His jaw nearly hit the floor.

"If there are as many artifacts in that cave as you claim, I think I could be here much longer."

Donald's shoulders slumped and his chest deflated.

"You should be happy," she said.

"Why on Earth would I be happy? If the quarry doesn't produce, there will be a lot of hungry families this winter."

"Well, Mr. Fischer, as the curator for the museum, I'm authorized to reimburse you and your company for the time and inconvenience this excavation may incur. So, when I say you should be happy, trust me—you should be. Because I have a ledger full of blank checks to help ensure your cooperation." She raised her coffee mug and offered a smile that Don was sure had broken a thousand hearts.

"We've never been offered anything like that before, and artifacts have been turning up for a long time at this quarry."

"Well, let's just say the museum is very interested in that cave and wants to make sure that you and everyone else involved is compensated."

"I've got to say, Dr. Thompson." Don raised his own mug. "I think I like you a whole lot more than some crusty old man."

Sheriff Carl Primrose woke up at six a.m. with a dry mouth and a splitting headache. Thanks to one too many scotch on the rocks, he had a good old-fashioned hangover. After the day he had had ... he deserved it. And Burt had deserved to pay for the drinks. He replayed yesterday's events in his head as he made coffee, then drank two large glasses of water and waited for it to brew.

He and Burt had gone back to the coroner's office and hashed out a plan to solve both of their problems. Carl wasn't thrilled with the idea, but their options were limited. He had become a cop to help people but never imagined that might involve covering up the missing body of a murder victim. Burt had screwed up—big-time—and the old man was his friend. *If you can't help your friends, then what good is the damn badge?* Still, the more he thought about it, the more it gnawed at him.

He sat at his kitchen table, listening to the inner debate rage on. Other than that, the house was silent. The large kitchen with its dark walnut cabinets, the three bedrooms, and two full baths ... all quiet. Carl had never married, and there had been no little Carls running around. At this late point in the game, he highly doubted that either would ever happen.

His breakup with Lois had been difficult, and Carl fully expected to spend the rest of his life pining over her. But life had other plans. And in 1969, he was drafted by the United States Army and sent to Vietnam.

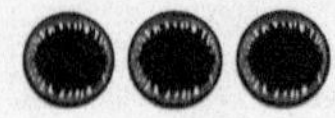

Having grown up in Garrett Grove, Carl had been no stranger to the wilderness. But the jungles of South Vietnam weren't like any of the woods he'd seen growing up. Carl was drafted and shot through basic training like a human cannonball. By the time he found himself in the heart of it, he had a lot more to worry about than Lois Middleton.

He met Ralph Pinkerton at West Point during an eight-week blur that passed quicker than a summer afternoon. The men bonded instantly and were assigned to the same platoon. The training had been difficult, and it wore them ragged. It felt like they were always running, from the time they woke up until they passed out ... mile after miserable mile. But the training had leaned them, hardening the softness that growing up in places like Garrett Grove had afforded.

On one of the rare occasions when they weren't completely exhausted and had managed to stay up late, they'd gotten to talking about girls. What else was there to talk about? Ralph told Carl about his fiancé back in Tempe. He had shown Carl a picture of Kerrie Ann; the guy had done pretty well for himself. "What in the hell does she see in you?" Carl had teased his friend—kind of. Ralph wasn't a pretty boy by any means. He had a large forehead, which made him look slow, and a big nose, which had been broken at least once. The guy sure wasn't going to win any beauty contest, but somehow, he had scored himself a knockout with Kerri Ann. He probably pulled it off because Ralph was one funny son of a bitch. Even with all the shit going on around them, Ralph could always make Carl laugh. Apparently, it had worked on Kerri Ann; the guy must have laughed the panties right off her. Kerri Ann was back in Tempe, Arizona, with a bun in the oven, waiting for the big guy to come home so they could get hitched.

In turn, Ralph asked Carl if he had a girlfriend back in Garrett Grove, and Carl had answered the question with just one word. "No." He didn't elaborate, and he never mentioned Lois's name. Not once during his entire deployment did he ever talk about her. He had managed to push Lois out of his mind as if she never existed—almost. However, there were moments in the darkest hush of night, just before he fell asleep, when he would think about her, sitting in the passenger seat of his Mustang with the moon shining, illuminating the Lenape River like it was the Ganges.

Carl and Ralph's platoon sergeant gave them two pieces of advice when they arrived. The first was to keep their heads down, which was relatively easy to do. The second little tidbit was to keep their socks dry, which was next to impossible. The country was wet. Even when the sun was out. It rained nearly every day, and, supposedly, they were there during the dry season. They had been told it was a jungle. But from what Carl had initially seen, it looked more like a swamp.

That first week, they had been spared from seeing any real action. But their reprieve was short-lived, just enough time to get used to the sound of mortars in the distance. And then it was on top of them.

The concussion of artillery fire was something you never got used to; it rattled your brain and shook the fillings out of your teeth. Survival instinct sent a direct order to the legs: Run! And that's what got most kids killed in Vietnam. The second a greenhorn took off running, the snipers drew a bead and took him out. It was damn near impossible for most to override the flight mechanism. The ability to hunker down and keep a level head was an acquired skill that didn't come easy; it went against every natural urge. But once you learned how to control it, it stuck.

There was one thing that had stayed with Carl more than anything else. It wasn't the molar-rattling concussion of artillery fire. It wasn't the constant battle to keep his socks dry in a place that was wetter than the Great Swamp. And it wasn't the Volkswagen-sized mosquitoes that wanted to carry him away in the night. The thing that stuck in Carl's brain and never left was the nauseating smell of rotting fish.

During one unforgettable day of their deployment, Carl and Ralph's platoon had crossed over the Mekong Delta to find thousands and thousands of dead fish rotting on the surface of the water. The weather had been sweltering, and the fish lay putrefying in the Asian sun. The stench was all-consuming. It filled the men's sinuses, crept into their mouths; it saturated their clothes and permeated the air. It was everywhere, and it wouldn't go away.

That was the scar that stayed with Carl and never left. It had hit him like a fifty-caliber round to the chest. Now, even the faintest scent of fish, cat food, or anything that remotely resembled seafood would render him incapacitated. For most of the men who came back from Vietnam, loud noises or the sound of fireworks brought on that thousand-yard stare. But for Carl, it was the smell of fish that brought him back to the Delta and the memory of all that blood. It had been everywhere.

There were ten men in their platoon, and Carl had taken point. Guys that went by the names of Hacksaw and Tank had been his brothers-in-arms. There was Tennessee and Tucson, who were both from Florida. Then Sergeant Wilkins, followed by Little Joe and Big Joe, which left Goober and Ralph, who were bringing up the rear. The choppers had dropped them in the middle of that mess of fish. It never crossed Carl's mind how it had gotten there in the first place.

They were waist-high in the brackish soup of the Delta with the sun beating down on them like a clenched fist and the stink coming off the water making them gag. The flies were everywhere, and the bastards bit too. The problem was you needed to walk with your M-16 raised above your head when navigating the fish guts, and that left you wide open for the little fuckers to land on your neck and face and gnaw the shit out of you.

The floating carcasses parted like the Red Sea as the men passed through them. Carl had navigated a safe path through the ocean of fish and brought the platoon to land. Nearly every man arrived at the water's edge; they had all stepped in practically the same exact spot that Carl had.

Somehow, they all missed the land mine submerged twenty feet from the bank. All of them except for Ralph. The big guy knew he had triggered the damn thing too. There was just enough time for him to yell, "Loo—"

The water erupted like a marinara geyser where Carl's friend had been standing. A thick mixture of pulverized fish and what remained of Ralph Pinkerton rained down on them, painting the world a nauseating shade of crimson. Ralph never made it out of Vietnam, and he never made it back home to Kerri Ann. She and Ralph's parents had likely received a standard letter from the president, stating how deeply sorry he was to inform them and how Ralph had fought bravely to defend his country. But he hadn't fought bravely; he had stepped on a goddamn land mine. Kerri Ann would be raising the child by herself. No doubt, the kid would come out with a large forehead and a big nose just like his father, a father he would never know. Now, even the thought of fish turned Carl's stomach and filled him with the memory of how it tasted to have Ralph's blood in his mouth. That was Carl's thousand-yard stare. And he never told a soul about what happened that day on the Delta, not even Burt.

Carl found himself sitting at his kitchen table staring at a coffee pot that had stopped percolating ten minutes ago. He grimaced as the taste of dead fish faded to a whisper. Finally, he went to the pot and poured a mug. The magic brew began to work instantly, pushing the hangover to the side and the memory of the Delta back into the shadows.

The house was silent. No wife and no kids for Carl. And that was the way he wanted it, which allowed him to focus on the job—or so he told himself. It was easy to maintain your defenses when you didn't let anyone get too close, and since the death of his father, Burt had been his only real friend. The marriage bug had never bitten him. *You can't miss something you never had.* Carl had even managed to convince himself that he believed it.

It recognized the darkness in the one called Butchie. There was work to be done, and this one would make the perfect soldier. Before the sun had risen, Butchie was dispatched. He smashed the window of Billy Tobin's Charger, then put the vehicle in neutral and pushed it. It had been easy for Butchie, who was much bigger and stronger than he had been less than a day ago.

The dirt lot at Mountainside Park, where the car had been left, sat above a steep slope that ended in a valley of thick woods owned by the state. The car hopped the embankment and was gone. It picked up momentum as it careened down the slope. It bounced over rocks and sailed between trees, then finally smashed into a large boulder at the bottom of the ravine.

There was still more work to be done, but it would be difficult to operate in the light. That had never been its domain; its home was the darkness, and its soldiers were sensitive as well. It could tolerate the great heated orb when it absolutely had to, if it needed to feed or defend. But it was far too dangerous to do so now. First it needed to grow its ranks, to build its army. It dispatched the one called Butchie, and Butchie was happy to be of service.

Margaret Post had drained the last of her gin and fell asleep in front of the TV watching Johnny Carson. She sprawled out in her favorite recliner with the cadence of her snores harmonizing to the static of the television. She was used to Butchie staying out late, and last night had been nothing out of the ordinary. He was usually home in time to make breakfast and to see if she needed anything. Margaret didn't hear the back door creak open or the sound of boots on the kitchen floor.

It stood over the woman, watching her sleep. A lingering sense of affection stirred in the one called Butchie. The presence within appreciated the raw emotion this vessel was capable of. So many flavors and textures. It had tasted Butchie's rage and the hunger incited by the one called Jackie. It knew what Butchie craved to do to her and now possessed the memories of what he had done to others in the past. But the Butchie-vessel was capable of other emotions as well. These creatures referred to it as love, and it was delicious.

Butchie stepped closer to the woman as static buzzed on the television.

She opened her eyes and looked up, still half asleep. "Butchie, is that you?"

"It's me, Mamma," Butchie replied, his voice deep and garbled like it was being delivered through a mouthful of dirt.

He parted his lips and allowed the presence to spill forward. The Ether forced its way inside her, and Margaret Post surrendered to the consciousness.

Chapter 22

Father Kieran McCabe had kept a vigilant watch over the Foothill's woods from his bedroom window at the rectory. The dark presence that had revealed itself after yesterday's Mass initially looked like an enormous waft of black smoke, but Father Kieran recognized it for what it was ... true evil.

He had always been a practical and non-superstitious man; however, he was a man of God above all else, and with that came acceptance for the unexplainable. The Catholic Church trained priests who specialized in exorcism and demonic possession. It was kept relatively quiet, with most of the public thinking it was only in the movies. But Father Kieran knew the truth behind the Hollywood scenario. His mentor, Father Michael, believed it necessary for his young apprentice to learn everything there was to know about demonic possession and the forces of evil that preyed on the weak of faith. He revealed in detail the countless cases of men and women who had received the sacrament of exorcism and been healed by the church. There was a vast library of sacred literature available to the clergy on the subject, and Kieran had made use of the knowledge.

It was easy for him to accept the presence in the woods for what he believed it to be, a demonic aberration. After witnessing the strange smoke-like miasma that darted furtively through the trees yesterday, Kieran had taken up post in his bedroom and watched the woods from behind the safety of his blinds.

There had been more shadows in the trees last night, different than what he had seen yesterday. People were walking through the foothills in the dark, heading somewhere with a particular destination in mind. It wasn't only men and women; there were children as well. Not all of which traveled upright like humans. Some walked on all fours, others hopping like frogs or some type of reptile. Father Kieran had watched the figures as they made their way through the dark woods, and prayed.

"Through my fault, through my fault, through my most grievous fault, I have sinned … in my thoughts, in my words, in what I have done and in what I have failed to do; Father, forgive me."

He had kept his post by the window with his bible in one hand and a wine glass in the other. And by the time the sun started to rise, Father Kieran had been good and drunk. Now he lay in his bed sleeping, turning restlessly from side to side. Strange images filled his dreams and tormented his soul. Godless creatures pursued him through the woods. In his nightmares, he ran from them but kept getting lost in the endless forest. They hunted him, feeding on his fear with an unquenchable thirst and a tireless resolve, and had been dispatched by Satan himself.

Kieran fled until the path before him dead-ended at the base of a great cliff. With nowhere left to turn, he began to ascend the steep incline, his legs growing ever more sluggish by the second. He clawed his way up the rock face as his fingernails bent back and broke against the unforgiving stone. All the while, the creatures continued to close in on him. He struggled to breathe ... fought to breathe. His muscles screamed in pain, and his soul cried out as he desperately struggled to save himself.

Inch by inch, he scaled the sheer cliff wall, blood oozing from his fingertips and terror ripping through his heart. He could hear the grunts and growls of the beasts as he took a lumbering final step and missed his footing. Then ... he was falling. Kieran watched the world rush up at him with the sensation of terminal velocity overwhelming his overtaxed brain. He awoke a second before his body hit the bedroom floor. In the survival flight of the nightmare, he had rolled out of bed in a desperate attempt to save himself. For some time afterward, he lay there crying and shaking, trying to discern what of the previous day had been real and what had been a nightmare. It took him over an hour to convince himself that any of it had happened at all.

Tara Jefferies looked up from her position at the dispatch desk as Carl walked into the station with the brim of his Stetson pulled down to the top of his sunglasses. "Good morning, Sheriff," she said. "Rough night?"

He removed his hat but left the glasses on. "Why are you yelling?" he whispered. "Is the coffee ready?"

"Yep, I'll bring you a cup."

"You're the best," he said, then proceeded to his office. Not bothering to turn on the lights, Carl hung his hat on the rack by the door and sat at his desk. The office, the hat rack, and the desk all belonged to his father before becoming his. He rubbed his temples and wondered how many hangovers the old man had nursed sitting exactly where he was now. Allen Primrose had been a bourbon man, good old No.7. It wasn't to Carl's liking, but on those occasions when he needed a little spiritual guidance, he would sit at his father's desk and pour a glass of Captain Jack. Usually, it helped. Whether it was due to the channeling of the old man's spirit or just the quiet time, he couldn't say. Either way, it was here where he did his best thinking. Probably his best listening as well. Listening to his intuition, his thoughts, but, more importantly, listening to his gut. Carl Primrose had come to respect that cautionary voice he referred to as "his gut". Lord knew it had saved his bacon more times than he could even count. It had gotten him out of Vietnam in one piece, and it had saved his neck as a sheriff's deputy as well.

Carl had drawn his weapon three times during his career. The first time, as a rookie, he'd been called in to help search for a hunter who had gotten lost in a blizzard.

A combined effort of sheriff's officers and volunteer firemen combed the mountain looking for the lost hunter but had no luck finding the man. Carl and his partner, Tim Colbert, continued searching in the knee-deep snow and had ventured out past the abandoned sanatorium.

There were old cottages on the hospital property, connected by an elaborate maze of underground tunnels. The hospital staff had lived in these cottages and used the tunnels to travel back and forth to work. Carl and Tim thought if the lost hunter had made it this far, then maybe he had found his way into one of the buildings.

The place had been deserted for a long time, even back then. The windows had been shattered, and there wasn't a visible surface that hadn't been marked with graffiti. The officers approached the first building, and alarms went off in Carl's head like an air raid siren. His gut screamed, *Something's wrong*, and he listened. He pulled his service revolver and held it in the ready position. A fetid odor, impossible for either man to ignore, saturated the air like a summer storm. There was something inside the building. Judging by the stench, Carl doubted if that something was still alive.

Carl entered the narrow hallway with Tim several steps behind him. Immediately, they noticed the carnage on the floor. Dried blood and animal hide coated the old linoleum. They had discovered the source of the stink, but that didn't set Carl's nerves at ease. He tensed up, walked into the next room, and froze in his tracks. From somewhere in the shadows, a deep growl echoed off every surface, making it impossible to tell which direction it had come from. Then ... in one heart-stopping second, a sizable mountain lion leaped from the furthest corner of the room and propelled itself at the two officers. Carl reacted and fired his revolver three times, putting the great cat down. He had been ready because he listened to his gut, and it had saved both his and his partner's lives.

There had been the other incidents when he had drawn his weapon and even more occasions when his gut had saved his hide. Now whenever it spoke, Carl paid close attention.

Tara entered the room with his coffee. "Here you go, Sheriff." She set the mug on his desk.

"Thank you," he said, taking a sip. "Have you heard from Deputy Forsyth this morning?"

"Not yet. Gary's on the graveyard shift tonight. You want me to get him on the line?"

"No, that's okay. He was following a lead yesterday. I suppose it can wait till he comes in later." Carl considered asking one of the other deputies to handle it, then thought better. Gary Forsyth was one of his senior men, and since Burt had screwed the pooch, it was best to let Gary get to it when he did. Besides, Carl had a better relationship with Gary than with some of his other officers. Deputy Kovach was strictly by the book. And Deputies Rainey and Lutchen were still new on the job. Carl was considering some rather unprofessional measures, which made this a job for Deputy Forsyth's capable hands.

"Who's on patrol this morning?" He took another long sip from the mug.

"Kovach and Lutchen."

"Good, anything on the burner?"

"A call came in from Alice Tobin. She and Will were out of town yesterday. When they got back, they found a note from Billy and Eric. The boys said they'd be home late but never showed up. Alice is worried."

Carl knew Lois's nephews Billy and Eric Tobin all too well. The boys had been giving him a hard time since he and Lois started dating. *Hard to believe it was that long ago.* Carl had been a kid himself when he first met Lois's sister and brother-in-law, Alice and Will Tobin, and their two little terrors, Billy and Eric. Billy couldn't have been any older than six at the time, and Eric had been younger than that. But even at that age, the boys were always getting into something. Eric, the younger of the two, probably would have been okay on his own. But Billy was the alpha big brother and the mastermind responsible for nearly every premature grey hair on Carl's head.

He and Lois had been invited to their house for dinner one Sunday afternoon. It was early December, with a good layer of snow already on the ground, which was easy for Carl to remember. He would never forget the damn snow. He picked Lois up at her house, and they had driven over in his Mustang. The car wasn't great in the slush, but he sure as hell wasn't about to put chains or snow tires on his pride and joy.

Alice and Will welcomed him into their home and introduced Carl to their two little ones, Billy and Eric. They were nice enough kids, not snotty or spoiled, as many were, and appeared relatively behaved for the most part.

If anything, Carl thought maybe the boys were a bit too well-behaved but didn't think too much of it.

Will took their jackets, hung them up somewhere in the house, and returned a moment later to talk baseball with Carl. Both men were diehard Yankee fans, that much they could agree on; however, when it came to the topic of who was the greatest player of all time, they were at an impasse. Will sided that it was Mickey Mantle and could not be swayed despite Carl's every attempt to prove it was Roger Maris. And there was no changing either man's mind, but there was one other thing that they did agree on. They both despised the Boston Red Sox with an equal passion. Alice and Lois had gotten into a conversation of their own that had nothing to do with baseball but had everything to do with getting around the bases. Alice wanted to know if Lois and Carl had started doing it yet. They had, so the women had an awful lot to talk about as well.

That was about the time that Billy and Eric went outside to play in the snow. A fresh layer had recently fallen on the existing six inches already covering the ground, and altogether, there was about nine inches of snow and ice. By the sound of it, the boys were having the time of their lives.

When it was time to eat, Alice called the kids into the house. They came in like a pack of wild dogs, hooting and hollering, dragging clumps of snow up the stairs. They continued to laugh about some inside joke that was clearly the funniest thing either of them had ever heard.

After dinner, Carl thanked Alice and Will for having him and prepared to drive Lois home. Will retrieved their jackets and saw them to the door. Carl kissed Alice on the cheek and extended his hand to all the men in the family. But Billy and Eric were still giddy by whatever had entertained them before dinner. So, Lois and Carl left out the front door, and that's when he realized that the keys to the Mustang were no longer in his jacket. He rechecked each individual pocket, hoping he had just missed them the first time. Then he checked the ignition and under the seats as well. But they were nowhere to be found. Which didn't make any sense since he was a fanatic about that car and never careless with the keys.

Lois went back into the house to see if they had fallen out where Will had put the coats. He had laid them on the bed, but the keys weren't there either. By that point, it was rather obvious what Billy and Eric had been laughing about. Will threatened the boys with a beating that neither of them would forget, and they folded like patio furniture.

Apparently, Billy had gone into Carl's jacket while the men were busy talking baseball. Then he and Eric had gone outside and buried the keys in the snow. However, neither of the boys could remember exactly where they were. The closest that Billy could narrow it down to was somewhere in the backyard.

The property wasn't huge, but it was big enough. And it was useless to retrace the boys' footprints since they had traipsed through nearly every square foot of the backyard. To make matters worse, it had already started to get dark.

So, the search for the Mustang keys began. The four adults started to dig in every possible place the boys might have buried them. The children themselves appeared to feel bad about what they had done, but that did nothing to improve the situation. Carl dug through the snow with his bare hands until his knuckles were raw, imagining how good it might feel to bury both of the little rugrats neck deep and then forget where they were. It had taken over two hours for the four adults to scour the backyard before Will triumphantly stood up with the keys in his hand. By then, Carl had been praying that Will would keep good on his word and beat the tar out of the little brats. That had been his first encounter with the Tobin brothers.

The second time was in '72. Carl had been back from the war for a little less than a year and working for the Sheriff's Department. Billy Tobin must have been around eleven or twelve at the time. Carl had just parked his cruiser in front of the municipal building to monitor the flow of traffic on the turnpike, when from out of nowhere, Will Tobin's station wagon screeched past with two tires on the curb and two in the street. The car jerked hard to the left and bolted into the opposite lane of traffic, then lumbered back into the correct lane—for the most part. Carl recognized the vehicle and thought Will must be drunk. Which would have been a shock because he had never known the man to be a drinker.

"Jumpin' Jesus Christ!" At first, it didn't look as if anyone was sitting in the driver's seat, then it all made perfect sense. He saw the very top of Billy Tobin's blond head, just barely high enough to look over the steering wheel, as the car passed. The little shit had no doubt lifted his dad's keys. *Figures. The kid can't be any older than eleven, and he's already a goddamn car thief.* Billy had decided to take the wagon out for a little joyride and was about to kill himself or someone else in the process.

Carl hit the lights and sirens and took off after him. Billy must have seen the cruiser pursuing him and panicked. Fortunately, he wasn't a skilled enough driver to put much effort into his evasion, and as soon as Carl pulled behind the wagon, Billy jerked the wheel far too hard to the right. The car lurched onto the front lawn of the Lutheran church. It mowed down a large hedgerow of lilacs and rolled to a stop a few feet before crashing into the front steps of the church. It was a wonder the car hadn't been totaled.

Carl opened the driver's door to find Billy Tobin sitting behind the wheel with a shit-eating grin on his face and Eric in the back seat crying his eyes out. No doubt his older brother had forced him into tagging along. Carl wanted more than anything to put Billy in handcuffs just to show the kid what it felt like. And had almost done it too. The only reason he hadn't was because he didn't have cuffs small enough. Will and Alice arrived minutes later to pick up the boys and their car. It had been a close call, and Carl hadn't been amused; it could have easily turned tragic.

As far as kids went, Billy wasn't even all that bad. Lord knew he wasn't anything like Butchie Post, who was just a menace to society. That guy was really going to kill someone one day. If they were lucky, they would get him back behind bars before that happened. Butchie had done an eighteen-month stint in Barre Oaks and come back even worse. Billy Tobin was just too active for his own good. He was into everything and great at getting other kids to follow him. The boy was a master manipulator and a persuasive character ... He was also one giant pain in Carl's ass.

Alice Tobin was forever calling the station. "Billy didn't come home last night. Billy disappeared for the entire weekend." And by the time Carl took the job as sheriff, he was tired of hearing, "Alice Tobin is on the line".

When Billy got older, it became a whole new set of problems. The boy had discovered girls and had damn near lost his mind chasing pussy. He was constantly staying out hours past his curfew—if he made it home at all. Carl had caught him in the act no less than a dozen times. One night he pulled up behind him at the top of Mountain Ave and approached the car to see Billy Tobin's ass pumping away like a jackhammer. Carl had turned his flashlight on the couple. The girl's face turned bright red, but Billy just smiled and gave him a look that said, *Yeah, you caught me again.* So Carl took full advantage of the moment.

"Mr. Tobin," he said. "I just caught you up here last night. When are you going to learn your lesson?" Carl had made it up, but Billy's date didn't know that. The color of her face had gone from embarrassed red to crimson fury. Carl walked away laughing, knowing that Billy wasn't going to finish what he had started unless he took matters into his own hands—literally.

On another occasion, Carl caught him back in the same exact parking spot. He turned the flashlight on the kids to find the young lady with her head in Billy's lap, working extremely hard to please the boy. She almost bit it off when Carl knocked on the window. Billy jumped up as the girl clamped down on his pecker and drew blood. Carl had a difficult time keeping a straight face when Billy rolled down the window. "Mr. Tobin. I'm glad to see that the doctor was able to help you out with those crabs."

The girl looked as if she were about to vomit. But by Carl's count, Billy Tobin was still up on him. It would be some time before the kid was paid in full for the whole car key incident.

"Sheriff," Tara repeated. "I said Alice Tobin called. Billy and Eric never came home last night."

"I heard you, and if I know Billy Tobin, he's out there with his kid brother having a hell of a lot more fun than either of us." *Probably shacked up with a couple of girls and a case of beer.* "Did you tell her not to worry and the boys'll be home as soon as they're done screwing or they run out of beer?"

"Not those exact words, but I told her they would probably be home any minute now."

"Thank you." Carl lowered his head and rubbed his temples.

"Kovach to base! Come in, base."

Tara left the office and headed to the dispatch desk at the sound of the deputy's call. "Go ahead, over."

"Additional units required on Sunset Road, just north of the high school. Over."

Carl jumped up from behind his desk, grabbed his hat, and was out the front door without waiting to hear the rest of the transmission, the voice in his gut screaming at him the entire way.

Donald Fischer sat at his desk listening to Dr. Thompson relive her life's story. The woman had the energy of a three-month-old Labrador pup and hadn't stopped talking since she entered the trailer and helped herself to his coffee. But Donald didn't find it rude and thought it refreshing to see a woman so inspired. She was passionate about her work and had earned the degree, not to mention the endless hours of research. She'd published countless papers, and there had even been an article about her in *National Geographic.*

"I think I remember that article. It was in the rain forest issue."

"So you're the *one* who read it. I'm impressed," she said, working on her second mug. "So, Donald Fischer ..."

"Call me Don."

"One condition. Drop the whole doctor thing. I'm Stephanie or Steph. Deal?"

"Deal."

"So, you're in charge up here. Geosciences?"

"Yep, geological engineering. I was hoping to study tectonic shift and fault lines, but here I am." He shrugged. "You know what they say, all the best-laid plans."

"I don't buy that. Never stop planning and never stop chasing your dreams. If that's your passion, that's what you need to follow. I got to admit, I'm glad to have you here. It's going to be helpful having a geologist on board, especially if the site turns out to be what we hope."

"What are you hoping for?" he asked, a bit more curious than he had been a moment ago.

"I'm afraid I can't tell you that."

"Hmmm, secrets, huh? I got to tell you, Stephanie ... Steph. I'm not a big fan of secrets. Not on my job site. Not when I have to answer for what goes on."

"No secrets." She crossed her heart with her index finger. "I'm just a bit superstitious, and I don't want to say anything to jinx myself. Once we get in there and start looking around, I will tell you everything I can, but until we—"

"You keep saying we. You mean *you* and *your* team, right?"

"Actually, you're on the team as well. Mr. DuCain said he would be happy to lend us his best engineer. I think his exact words were, 'he's at your disposal.'" She fished out a set of papers from her back pocket and leaned across the desk.

Don walked over, took them, and started to read. They were signed by Charles DuCain and stated that he was to assist Dr. Thompson in whatever way necessary to help expedite the excavation. Mark Gold would be covering his position. Everything appeared to be in order, but Don intended to call his boss the first chance he could. However, it did make sense that old-man DuCain would want one of his own men on the inside, acting as a supervisor while the museum folks poked around.

He studied the woman who had stormed into his Monday morning and turned it upside down. He knew he should be pissed off but wasn't. And for some reason, the idea of poking around inside the cave with Dr. Thompson sounded like it might just be the diversion he needed. At least for a little while. Since he was getting paid to do it, who was he to argue? Stephanie Thompson looked at him from across the desk and offered a contagious smile. *Well, I didn't see this coming.*

CHAPTER 23

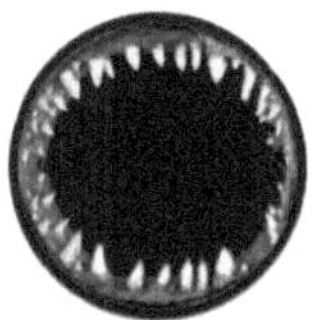

Carl arrived at the scene of the accident only a few minutes before Burt. Although the fog had burned off and the sun had risen, it was still chilly. Their breath hung in long plumes as they exchanged pleasantries.

"You look how I feel," Burt said, still wearing the same wrinkled brown suit he'd had on yesterday.

"Oh yeah? Well, you're about to feel a whole lot worse when you see this." Carl walked with him to the side of the road and pointed over the embankment.

"Oh Christ. Poor bastard." Burt winced at the sight of the body in the ditch. The guy had been thrown and landed face first in the mud with his head and shoulders entirely submerged. His legs and arms were bent at impossible angles, and it looked like Burt's men, Abe and Tony, were going to have a hell of a time getting the body out.

"I hope we aren't going to make this a habit. I don't think I could do this again tomorrow," Burt joked, then realized it probably wasn't a good idea. "I'll check for an ID. Has anyone gone down to see if he's carrying any?"

"Not yet." Carl looked back at the bread truck and cruisers parked on the shoulder. "Kovach had to stay with the vehicles, and the driver is all freaked out."

"I can imagine," Burt said, removing a pair of surgical gloves from his pocket and pulling them on. "Okay. I'll take care of it."

Carl questioned the truck driver and instructed Deputy Kovach to assist Burt and his men with the body. They definitely had their hands full. The driver, Jared Neibolt from Warren, admitted that he had been speeding—a little—but swore he had been wide awake and he didn't drink. "Never touched the stuff." He told Carl the guy had just walked in front of him. "Like he was in a trance or something."

Carl listened to the man's story, took notes, and was fairly convinced it had been just an unfortunate accident. And although he didn't see any reason to arrest the guy, he still instructed Mr. Neibolt not to leave the state in case he needed to get in touch with him for further questioning.

Burt and the other men manage to wrestle the body from the ditch and placed the mud-caked remains on the side of the road. Deputy Kovach checked the guy's pockets and didn't find a wallet or any form of identification. In fact, the man didn't have anything on him at all.

"All right, Abe," Burt said. "Let's get him bagged up and back to the lab. We'll get him cleaned up there."

"Any idea who our John Doe might be?" Carl approached the men.

Burt shrugged, and Kovach replied, "Not yet, Sheriff. He didn't have any ID on him, and there isn't much to go on. I could follow the coroner back to the lab and get some prints once they hose him down."

"That's okay. You stay on patrol. I'll follow them over and grab the prints." Carl bent down closer to examine the body and nearly gagged. "Jeez, Burt. Should he smell that bad already?"

"It's all that shit he's covered in. It gets pretty nasty in those drainage ditches." Burt made a sour face and stepped back while Abe and Tony transferred the body into the large bag and zipped it shut. Once it was placed into the meat wagon, they could all breathe a lot better; the foul stench had lifted some.

Troy sat behind his desk at ten minutes to eight, waiting for class to begin. He fidgeted in his seat, staring at the fourth-grade mascot positioned at the front of the room in the corner next to the blackboard. Henrietta, the full-size human skeleton, wore a long black wig with curls that hung past her clavicle and a yellow button-down cardigan sweater. He smiled, leaned back, and reflected for perhaps the tenth time this morning, not sure what it was about today that reminded him of his first day of kindergarten. Maybe it had something to do with the weather, which was cool and crisp, nearly a snapshot image of that unforgettable moment. It had all stuck in Troy's memory like a wad of bubble gum in the carpet: walking into the strange school for the first time, sitting next to the boy named Robert Boyle, and that solitary tear that defined their friendship for years to come. He had overheard his parents talking yesterday in the garage, and it sounded like Rob was a lot sicker than anyone thought. Then later, his mom told him the good news: Rob was feeling better. With any luck, they would still be able to go trick-or-treating on Halloween, which was now less than a week away.

Before class, the students had gathered at the back closet, as they usually did, hanging up their jackets and putting their lunches away. Today, the hot topics of discussion were the awesome Halloween party and ... Troy and Wendy. The teasing had already begun, which didn't bother Troy as much as it would have only a week ago. He felt like he had changed in some way over the weekend; he felt cooler, wiser, maybe even older. And when Wendy pulled him inside the closet and pecked him on the cheek, he felt even better. Now, leaning back at his desk, with his fingers laced behind his head, Troy couldn't wipe the smile off his face if he tried. He was definitely feeling older.

Scanning the room, Troy noticed that even more of his friends were out sick today. Of course, Rob wasn't there, or Ben and Erin Richards, who hadn't been able to make it to the party either. But now, both Jeff Campbell and Tommy Negal's desks were empty, and they had been fine on Saturday night. He looked back at Wendy, who sat a few seats behind him. She offered a huge smile, making Troy feel self-conscious and nervous. He quickly turned toward the front of the class. *Maybe I'm not that cool after all.*

Then Miss Walsh, the fourth-grade teacher, entered the classroom accompanied by a young girl that Troy had never seen before. She was cute and blonde and hid behind the woman when they walked through the door.

"Hello, class," Miss Walsh said. "I'd like to introduce you to a new student who will be joining us. This is Janis Thompson. She's from Washington, D.C., our nation's capital, and her mother is a friend of mine. So, I want you all to make her feel welcome."

The class knew what was expected of them and responded in unison. "Nice to meet you, Janis."

The whispering started within seconds, mainly from the girls in the class. The boys, however, didn't say a word. They were too busy staring, most of them with their mouths hung wide open.

Janis was pretty, with long hair styled like Farrah Fawcett Majors from the TV show *Charlie's Angels*. She had bright blue eyes, also like the actress, but that wasn't what had all the boys spellbound. They had never seen anything like it before in their entire lives; even Troy found it impossible not to stare. The girl pulled them in with a magnetic power, and the boys were helpless to resist. How could they? Janis was the first fourth-grade girl who had started to grow boobs ... and they were hypnotizing.

Carl finished up at the scene of the accident and headed over to the coroner's office. By the time he entered the building, Burt and his men had disrobed the body, placed it into a large basin, and were in the process of washing off the thick layer of filth. The horrible stench hit Carl like a sledgehammer the second he walked into the morgue, causing the coffee in his stomach to do the Hustle.

"Christ, Burt, that isn't drainage runoff."

The coroner didn't respond; a look of grave concentration etched his face as he focused the spray of the shower nozzle onto the body The pressurized water blasted the muck from the corpse and sent it spiraling down the drain. Burt washed off the man's broken legs and arms and then began the task of rinsing off his torso. The dark filth had seeped through the guy's clothing, soiling nearly every inch of him, but his head and upper body were by far the dirtiest.

Burt grimaced as the silt and slime were jetted away. He aimed the water onto the guy's chest and then onto his neck, dissolving the mud quickly and revealing what lay beneath. He jumped back and nearly dropped the nozzle as the water exposed the area of skin just above the man's shoulders. Burt leaned in to get a better look. "Jesus Christ almighty!" he shouted.

Carl, who had stood back avoiding the overspray, approached the basin to see what startled his friend. The water had revealed a mark on the man's neck: a dark round bruise with several deep perforations along the perimeter and one incision in the center. It was identical to the wound they had seen yesterday morning on Foothills Drive.

"Let me see that." Carl took the nozzle and directed the force of the water onto the man's face, making quick work of the muck concealing his features. First, the jaw was revealed, then the cheeks, and, a second later, the rest of the corpse's face, including his dark black hair.

Burt jumped back another two feet and screamed once again. "That's not possible!"

Carl stared with the world cartwheeling in his periphery. Burt was right; it wasn't possible. There was no way in hell he was looking at what he thought was in the basin. Holding his breath, Carl blinked hard to refocus, then took a step forward. An icy chill raced through his nervous system and settled in the base of his spine. He slowly exhaled and stood over the body. There was no denying its identity. Felix Castillo lay before them, in far worse shape than the first time he had been brought into the morgue.

His face was still recognizable, but it had changed considerably, and not just from the results of getting creamed by a truck. The skin beneath his eyes sagged in loose folds, overlapping his cheeks, and were covered in an almost reptilian texture of lamella-like scales that also peppered the man's forehead and the bridge of his nose. His mouth had grown disproportionately as well and was much wider and longer than it had been only yesterday.

Carl grabbed a pair of surgical gloves from the table and pulled them on. He bent down and lifted the man's upper lip, exposing the most significant change to have occurred. A chorus of gasps filled the morgue. Several rows of small, jagged barbs crowded Castillo's gumline, giving his mouth a threatening resemblance to that of a piranha or a shark.

"Dear God," Carl whispered.

"God's got nothing to do with that." Burt watched from a safe distance. "What the hell happened to him?"

Carl pulled the corpse's lip back even further and jumped when a loud pop escaped from deep within its throat. It happened without warning; Castillo's lower jaw flew open, dropping as if it had dislocated, and an oversized serpent-like tongue slid out of his mouth. It lolled to the side, nearly nine inches long, slender, and black, and tapered to a sharp point that looked an awful lot like a weapon.

The men recoiled in unison. Burt hid behind Carl, whose gut was now screaming. Abe and Tony both retreated from either side of the basin like a pair of synchronized swimmers, and no one said a word. The only sound that Carl heard was the thundering of his heart inside his chest, pumping like a freight train. His palms grew slick inside the rubber gloves, and the muscles in his neck tightened. Listening to the voice in his gut, he instinctively backed away and lowered his hand to the butt of his revolver.

After several tense seconds with nothing further happening, Abe leaned forward to get a better look. He didn't even have time to react. Felix's eyes flew open, and his serpentine tongue rocketed toward Abe like a guided missile. It wrapped around the man's throat and lifted him off his feet. Abe beat at the oil-slicked tongue with his clenched fists and opened his mouth to scream. The only sound to leave his lips was a strangled gurgle. A dark splash danced between them, if only for a second. It looked as if a shadow had been thrown in Abe's direction, but it happened so fast that no one was sure what they had seen. Abe gagged as the tongue tightened around his neck and pulled him closer toward the basin.

Burt made a desperate run towards the office, crashing into one of the lab tables, and Tony tripped over his own feet as he headed for the back door. Carl, who had been listening to the voice in his gut, was the only one who kept his head. He drew his revolver without thinking, instinct guiding his arm. Body on autopilot. Aim, exhale, squeeze.

The first bullet hit Felix in the chest, resulting in an ear-splitting shriek that echoed off every smooth surface in the morgue. The thing in the basin tried to sit up, but the broken bones in its arms and legs made the effort impossible. There was an audible crunch followed by a sickening snap as Felix attempted to right himself. It twisted and writhed when Carl put a second slug into its chest, and then it threw Abe across the room like a wet beanbag. The medical assistant crashed against the wall on the far side of the morgue with a tremendous thud and fell to the floor in a lifeless heap.

The snake-like appendage redirected its attack onto Carl, lashing out at him, snapping like the bands of a slingshot. Ducking to the right, he avoided it by inches and fired a third round into the thing's chest. The tongue retracted, and the body started to convulse in a violent fit. It flipped and slapped against the porcelain of the tub like a fish on hot pavement. Carl pulled the trigger a fourth time, burying the .38 caliber slug into the center of Felix's forehead. The odor of burnt gunpowder filled the air; it combined with the stench of the creature laying in the basin, and the thing that had once gone by the name Felix Castillo finally stopped moving.

CHAPTER 24

I n just a few short hours, Janis became the most popular kid in class. Such a feat had never been accomplished by any other child in the history of Garrett Elementary. At least, the boys were impressed. The girls, on the other hand, felt differently about Janis Thompson. She had disrupted the hierarchy of the pride with one fell swoop of her magical powers. Even Troy wasn't immune. Fortunately, he had the recent enchantment of Wendy's own persuasive influence as a protective shield; however, that didn't make him invulnerable to the occasional peek at the goods.

Mike Barnes and Eric Helmsworth were drawn like iron filings to her strong magnetic presence. The boys gravitated towards Janis during lunch, introduced themselves, and made some valiant—yet awkward—attempts to impress the young lady. But she didn't appear interested and kept looking over at Troy and Wendy, who had gone off to the far side of the playground to eat lunch together. Until only a few hours ago, Wendy had been the new girl in class. She had moved to town just last month, but the overall reaction to her arrival had been far less grandiose.

"What's the big deal? I don't understand why they're all acting that way," she told Troy. "Nobody acts that stupid when a new *boy* starts school."

"Yeah," Troy said through a mouthful of Oscar Mayer bologna. Although he was no fan of the deli meat, he obliged when Wendy asked to trade for his peanut butter and jelly sandwich.

"Boys are so stupid," she said, eyeing Janis's flock of admirers. "Except you; you're different."

Troy didn't think he was all that different but maybe just smart enough to not make a total fool out of himself. He had *definitely* noticed the new girl, but even at ten years old, Troy knew you weren't supposed to stare when your girlfriend was watching.

Is Wendy my girlfriend? They had never actually talked about it, but he figured you didn't get kissed by a girl unless she wanted to be your girlfriend.

As if on cue, Wendy blurted, "So, aren't you going to ask me to be your girlfriend?"

Troy choked on the bologna and swallowed. "I um, thought um—" The truth was he didn't have any idea what he thought. However, Wendy was more than capable to do the thinking for both of them.

"What did you think, silly? Don't you know that you have to ask me? That's how it works. You ask me if I'll be your girlfriend, and then I say, I'll think about it. Jeez, everybody knows that."

Troy felt the heat rush to his face and was sure he had turned a deep shade of red. "Um ... will you be my girlfriend?"

"I'll think about it." Wendy smiled and took a bite of her sandwich with a look of satisfaction smeared across her face.

"I heard there's another *Star Wars* movie coming out next year." Troy changed the subject and hoped he didn't look like a total goof. "Maybe we could go see it."

"*The Weekly Reader* said George Lucas has nine movies he wants to make. That's why the first one was called *Part IV, A New Hope*."

Troy was more than a little impressed that a girl knew so much about his favorite movie. "Really? I always wondered about that. That's so cool. What else did it say?"

"Well, they said it's gonna take a really long time for all the movies to come out. We'll be grownups before they're finished making them."

"Oh man, I don't know if I can wait that long." A shadow cast over the area where they sat, interrupting the moment.

"Hi," a voice said.

Troy and Wendy looked up to find the new girl had left her gaggle of admirers and now stood before them.

"Hi," Wendy replied.

"Hi," Troy managed through a mouthful of bologna.

"Can I sit with you guys?" Janis asked. "Those boys are acting silly."

Troy looked over his shoulder and noticed Mike and the other boys staring in their direction as if something important was about to take place.

"Sure," he said.

Wendy straightened her back and stared at him.

"I'm Janis. What're your names?"

"I'm Wendy, and this is my boyfriend, Troy."

Troy squinted and turned, unsure if he had heard her right. *That was fast. I guess you're done thinking about it.*

"You're from Washington?" Wendy asked as Janis sat down between them.

"Yeah, well, I was born in Florida, then we moved to Washington later, when my mom got a job at the museum."

"Your mom works at a museum?" Troy asked, his interest piqued.

"She's an archeologist and studies artifacts." Janis wore a huge smile that almost seemed to sparkle when she spoke, and Troy understood why all the boys wanted to be around her. It was a smile that made you feel good inside, one that made him want to smile as well.

"No way, that's so cool!"

"We were just talking about *Star Wars*," Wendy said. "Did you see it yet?"

"Are you kidding?" Janis's smile lit up her entire face. "I saw it three times. It's, like, my favorite movie ever."

Troy didn't know why Wendy acted so weird when Janis first approached but noticed a change in the girl when the conversation switched subjects.

"Who's your favorite character?" Wendy asked.

"Princess Leia, of course!" Troy had a feeling Janis would say that.

"Mine too," Wendy agreed. "I liked her because they never make girls the heroes in movies. She was more of a leader than Luke and Han."

"Yeah, that's why I like her too."

"But they had to rescue her from Darth Vader," Troy said.

The girls both turned and gave him a set of looks that made Troy feel like he had said something stupid.

"She was a lot braver than both of them. Han only wanted the money. And Luke was just a kid." Janis turned to Wendy and smiled.

"I guess so." *I should stop talking.* But Troy was unable to control himself. "Wendy said there's gonna be more movies."

"I *said* there were going to be *nine* movies." Wendy's face tightened as if she had eaten a lemon. "At least that's what George Lucas wants to do."

"I read that too in the *Weekly Reader* at my old school." Janis smiled but still appeared distracted by the group of boys who continued to stare at them. "Why are those boys acting so weird?"

"Ignore them. Boys are immature," Wendy said. "My mom says boys mature two years slower than girls."

"The boys in my old school acted like that too. They were fine last year. But when we came back in September, they were different. Like they changed over the summer."

Troy pretended not to pay attention as the conversation shifted. *I know why they're acting funny.* He continued chewing his sandwich and praying at the same time. *Please don't ask me why they're acting funny, please don't.*

"You're a boy, Troy," Janis said, causing the bologna to ferment in his throat. "Why are they acting so funny?"

A cold sweat broke on his brow. *What the heck am I supposed to say now?* He looked at Wendy for support, but there was none to be found. With nowhere else to turn, he looked back at Janis, who only sat there staring at him with her great big trouble-making eyes.

"Um-um, I don't know." He cleared his throat; a piece of half-chewed bologna flew from his open mouth and landed in the grass.

"Well, you sure sound like you know." Wendy narrowed her eyes and stared him down. "Spill it, Troy."

"Come on. You know," he said, nodding at his chest and then looking back at the two girls. He repeated the movement a second time, motioning downward and then up at the girls with his eyebrows raised.

"What's he doing?" Janis asked. "I don't get it."

"Come on, Troy," Wendy said. "Just say it."

He felt it in his face, hot pins and needles spreading across his cheeks like a rash. Certain he was about to faint, Troy scanned the playground, looking for an escape route. The two lionesses had lured him into a false sense of security with talk of *Star Wars* and trapped him. Troy cleared his throat a second time and struggled to think on his feet. Unfortunately, that wasn't one of his strong suits, and he folded under the pressure.

"It's because you have boobs! There, I said it! Are you happy? They never saw a girl in class with boobs before, and they can't handle it!" Troy felt like he had caught on fire and was sure he would pass out any second. *Jeeze, I can't believe they made me say it.* He wiped his brow and braced himself for the backlash.

Wendy and Janis stared at him for what felt like a lifetime without either of them saying a word. Then they turned to each other, smiled, and burst out laughing. Troy didn't understand. He expected Wendy to go ballistic and was sure Janis would have gotten embarrassed or offended.

"What? Why is that so funny?"

"Cause we're messing with you," Wendy said.

"W-what do you mean?"

"Do you really think I don't know about my boobs? Come on, Troy. They're kinda hard to miss, don't you think?" Janis continued to laugh until tears appeared in the corners of her eyes.

"You were so nervous," Wendy blurted. "Every girl in school knows why the boys are acting like a bunch of second graders. Anyway, I'm proud of you. I didn't think you would say anything. Maybe not all boys are as immature as my mom says." She leaned over and punched him in the arm, apparently giving her seal of approval.

Janis stopped laughing long enough to punch him in the other arm. "You're all right, Troy. That was very cool. You're the only guy who was ever honest about my boobs."

Troy felt like he would die if she didn't stop saying boobs. He needed to change the conversation, but once again, that came to thinking on his feet, which just wasn't going to happen. He cracked a smile and let a weak laugh fall out the side of his mouth.

"My mom's working late today," Janis said. "Would you guys like to come over after school for a snack?"

"Sure, but I have to ask my mom," Wendy told her.

Janis gave Troy a look that made him even more nervous than the whole boob conversation.

"I got to ask my mom too-um—probably."

"Great," Janis had taken their answers for yes, and a minute later, the bell rang, calling the children back into the building. Lunch was over. "You can meet my dog, Peanuts. She looks like Snoopy a little."

The three children grabbed their lunch boxes and headed back inside with the eyes of the entire fourth-grade class watching their every move.

CHAPTER 25

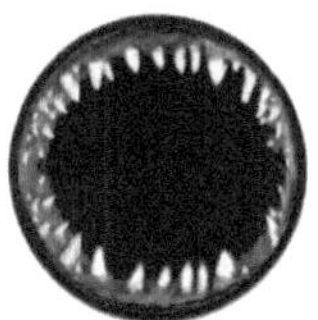

Garrett Grove had been home to the Lenape tribe long before any white man stepped foot on the continent. They lived harmoniously with nature, the spiritual world, and prized peace above all other attributes. Nestled in the foothills of Garrett Mountain, the land had been called Kittatinny by the Lenape, which loosely translated to Endless Mountain; however, Lonesome Mountain was a more accurate interpretation. Their tribal civilization was situated in the valley, flanked by the Lenape River on one side and King Lake on the other.

Still today, there were only two access routes in and out of Garrett Grove. The first was County Road 202 via Route 3, a long stretch of wooded highway spanning the Lenape River by way of the Gables Bridge. The bridge was old and in desperate need of repair; however, a simple patch job wasn't going to cut it. The unfortunate truth of the matter was that the Gables Bridge didn't have many winters left in it.

The other route was even more treacherous. Sunset Road was a twisting, turning, nerve-wrenching stretch of pavement that traversed the south face of Garrett Mountain. With a sheer rock wall towering above the road on one side and a steep drop on the other, it wasn't for the faint of heart. Before the road had been built, the isolated area was even more inaccessible, making the Grove the ideal location for the peaceful civilization.

The Lenape tribe worshiped the Great Spirit and believed in a mystical healing power generated within the land itself. From the mountain, they received their greatest gifts: food, protection, and life. Their tools and pottery were made with natural materials that came directly from the mountain as well.

The Lenape tribe occupied the area longer than anyone could be certain and had vanished before the first colonists arrived. And although archeologists knew the truth about what happened to most of the indigenous people (genocide perpetrated by the European settlers), that hadn't been the case on Lonesome Mountain. By the time the Grove was settled, the Lenape had already disappeared.

There were countless stories of lost civilizations from all over the world. *National Geographic* had published a piece about the subject and included the story of the Lenape in the article. Dr. Thompson, being the chief expert on the subject, was interviewed. She'd been studying the tribe since grad school and was fascinated with the mystery of their disappearance. Although she wasn't inclined to say anything just yet, she hoped that the DuCain expedition would reveal some of the answers to that mystery.

The cavern was declared structurally safe and appeared to extend well past the forty to fifty feet recorded during the initial inspection. Work lights, powered by a generator set up just outside the cave entrance, were installed and now illuminated all but the furthest reaches of the chamber. Stephanie and her team would have to limit their research to the main area until a secondary set of lights were added.

The entire party wore hard hats bearing the DuCain logo, as well as glow-in-the-dark safety vests. Stephanie's team consisted of herself and three coworkers: Joe Hillman, a fellow archeologist; Gail Herd, Stephanie's assistant and photographer; and Barry Knolls, a historian. Don completed the party of five and was the only DuCain representative.

Long shadows stretched out across the cavern floor and danced upon the walls as the men and women passed in front of the work lights. Upon entering, the first details to catch Don's eye were the elaborate cave drawings. Colorful murals covered nearly every inch of the stone surfaces. The vibrant depictions had held up exceptionally well over the centuries. Not only was the vividness of the murals striking but their complexity and size were daunting, with some taking up entire walls. Images of men, women, and children engaged in some type of ritual were illustrated in one of the scenes. Another was decorated with reproductions of various animals, many of which were recognizable; however, some appeared to have been made up.

Skeletal remains littered the floor; many that were intact, while others, nothing more than a random scattering of bones. What could have been some breed of large cat lay next to the skeleton of a child. The proximity of the two suggested to Don that they perished together.

Stephanie, who had finally stopped talking for the first time all morning, focused intently on the murals, pointing out the various details to her assistant. The young girl dressed as if she were going on safari, in tan shirt and fatigues with nearly a dozen pockets in each, all jammed with extra rolls of film and various camera equipment. Gail followed Stephanie's lead, taking pictures at a feverish pace. The sudden flash momentarily blinded

Don, who was looking in the wrong direction. A large white dot filled his vision for almost a full minute before it faded.

"Gail, take a couple shots of this." Stephanie pointed to a figure in the foreground of the first painting. "I want to get these developed as soon as possible." The girl continued to click away, exhausting roll after roll of film.

Don's eyesight slowly returned as he stood behind the women, trying to see what they were interested in. The wall that held their attention extended about ten feet into the cave from the entrance. The mural portrayed the Lenape gathered around one of their own, who was either being buried or honored, it was difficult to tell. It looked like a ritual, possibly a funeral for a chief or a holy man. The man on the ground was dressed in an elaborate gown and headdress.

The following scene showed the same man being buried as his fellow tribesmen cast handfuls of dirt onto him, confirming that the previous scene had been a funeral. Finally, the third painting, which Stephanie and Gail appeared most interested in, showed the same holy man chasing three children. He was dressed in the same gown and headdress from the other scenes, only now it was stained darker—the same color as the dirt he'd been buried in.

The man's eyes were painted black, a stark contrast to their white color in the previous scenes. Something else was strange about him as well: his jaw hung open, disproportionately larger than it should have been. It was hard to make out the details in the dim light of the cave, but to Don, it looked as if the strange mouth was filled with tiny, pointed teeth. Also, a dark cloud of smoke, resembling a wreath, had been painted around the holy man's head, obscuring many of the finer details of the image.

Gail exhausted an entire roll of film on this mural alone before she and Stephanie moved on to the other areas of the cave. They made their way to where Joe and Barry worked, recording information about the bone formations. Joe was the older of the two men, with a horseshoe of unruly grey hair nestled around a perfectly smooth bald head. Barry, on the other hand, didn't have a bald patch on his body. He wore his thick hair on the long side, his beard was unkempt and tangled, and even the hair on his arms looked as if it had erupted from his skin in bristly patches. Don overheard a little of what was being said by the group. *Would you look at that… What do you make of this … See I told you,* was some of it before he moved on to his own investigation. Then something caught his eye.

"Don, just be careful not to disturb anything. We have to inventory every item before any of it can be moved. Thank you." Stephanie didn't wait for a reply, nor did she ask for one.

Don was too focused on the cave itself to take it personally. The flash of the camera had revealed something he hadn't noticed before. He leaned in close to the cavern wall and examined the composition of the rock. *What the hell?* The entire cave was comprised of a massive deposit of lodestone, an iron ore also known as magnetite. It suddenly all made perfect sense, the reason why his equipment hadn't detected the cave before blasting. Lodestone was a natural magnetic ore, known to throw off compasses and interfere with electronic equipment. Don hadn't even considered the existence of the mineral because of how uncommon it was in the area. He felt foolish for having missed such an obvious answer, but it still came as a relief. *Thank God. It wasn't my fault after all.*

Gail took more pictures of the skeletal remains, and as the flash went off, Don turned his head away from the glare. The strobe lit up the area of the cave in front of him, revealing several random shadows. He crouched down to inspect the marble-like objects littering the floor, being careful not to disturb anything.

There were more pieces of the lodestone, only these had been formed into perfectly rounded spheres that resembled musket balls. Don knew the

Lenape had manufactured tools, which was evident from all the arrowheads that had been found in the area, but this seemed awfully sophisticated. He wasn't a historian or an archeologist, but he was familiar with minerals, and he knew it took a great deal of patience and talent to wear a piece of iron ore into a perfect musket-sized ball. The flash went off again as Don got up and walked to where the rest of the party was gathered.

Stephanie and Joe were crouched over two of the skeletons that appeared to be relatively intact, neither of which could have measured any longer than four feet in length. Don figured they were the remains of children. Next to them were several animal skeletons. One looked like it belonged to a large cat and the other from some type of reptile. The jawbones on both skulls were massive and filled with incredibly sharp-looking teeth. What surprised Don the most was how the bones and everything else in the cave had been so well-preserved.

"Are dig sites always in such pristine condition?" he asked.

"Almost never," Stephanie said. "This is an amazing find. I wish my father was here to see it."

"He would be very proud," Barry told her.

"You know, Don, this is *your* discovery. Of course, Mr. DuCain owns the site, but you're the one who told the men to blast here. You're about to become famous."

Not knowing how to reply, Don smirked and shrugged his shoulders. He turned back and watched Barry focus the beam of his flashlight onto the rib area of the cat skeleton. There were several dark objects embedded into the bones and some others scattered on the floor close to the remains.

"What do you suppose these are?" Barry asked, leaning in closer.

"I have no idea," Joe answered.

"Lodestone," Don said.

They all looked up at him. A smile slowly spread across Stephanie's face. "What?" she asked.

"That's lodestone … magnetite. The whole cave is made up of it. Those little guys right there have been shaped into marbles or some kind of musket ball. And I can tell you one thing, that wasn't easy to do."

"Are you sure?" Barry asked.

"Well, I'm sure it's magnetite. And judging by the way they're embedded into the bone, I'd say, yeah … I'm pretty sure they were used as weapons."

"I'd have to agree," Stephanie said. "I told you, Joe. This is the proof we were looking for. Come on, Gail, get a few shots of this."

Gail took more pictures in rapid succession. The constant flashing made Don dizzy, but now that his eyes had adjusted and he could see a bit more clearly, he noticed there were other weapons in the cave as well, all of which appeared to be comprised of lodestone.

"I thought you said that the Lenape were a peaceful people?" he asked.

"That's right; they were," Joe said.

Don surveyed the cave, inspecting the skeletal remains and the random piles of bones that were everywhere. Then he focused on the hoard of weapons stacked against the walls and the tiny musket balls littering the floor, some of which were embedded into the ribs of the one creature. "Well." He rubbed his eyes and took it all in. "You could have fooled me."

CHAPTER 26

Dr. Ziegler arrived at the Chilton Medical Center at twelve thirty-five p.m. He entered through the emergency room doors and passed the reception desk where Head Nurse TenHove was stationed. The grey-haired woman held a clipboard in one hand and the house phone pressed against her ear with the other. She looked up at Ziegler, pursed her lips, and shook her head as if in disapproval. *Looks like someone needs to get laid.* The next thought to enter Ziegler's head was an image of Jackie Gilmartin, who he expected to find at the front desk instead of sour-faced Doris TenHove. He and Jackie had special plans last night, but after working a triple shift, he passed out without even looking at the phone. Then after sleeping late through the alarm, he hadn't had time to call her before leaving for work. Besides, he was anxious to check on the condition of his three young patients. He nodded to the head nurse, making his way through the reception area, and proceeded towards the ICU wing.

"Hello, Dr. Ziegler," a female voice said. He turned to find the young blonde candy striper and quickly checked her name tag. Cyndi, with an i.

"Hello, Cyndi," he said, noticing her full, pouty lips and the inviting blush of her cheeks. "How are you today?"

"Fine, thank you." She smiled, batted a pair of big doe eyes, and that was all it took. Ziegler forgot what he was doing, stopped in his tracks, and looked her up and down. He immediately started doing the math in his head. *She looks too young, but I've seen her here in the afternoon, so she's not in high school. At least eighteen … right?*

"You've been working quite a lot lately." He leaned against the wall and brushed the hair out of his eyes.

"Oh, I took the fall semester off from college, so I have a lot of spare time on my hands."

College girl. Ding-Ding-Ding!

"Oh really." He squared his jaw and tilted his head toward her. "So, what do you like to do for fun? Don't tell me it's all work and no play."

Cyndi fed him a devilish grin and leaned forward to whisper in his ear. "Meet me later, and I'll show you."

The young candy striper turned without saying another word and left him leaning against the wall. She walked off, jiggling in all the right places, and Ziegler was helpless to look away. *That was too easy. Like taking candy from a candy striper.* He watched as she disappeared around the corner, and intended to take her up on her proposal as soon as his schedule allowed.

He remained there for a moment, basking in his glory, then remembered his current objective and headed towards the intensive care unit. He entered the dressing room, washed up, and donned the necessary protective gear.

Dr. Ziegler walked down the hall dressed in a full body gown, surgical gloves, and face shield. He stood before the closed door of Robert Boyle's room, rechecking for any breaches in his clothing. After a thorough inspection and satisfied that he had taken every necessary precaution, he placed his hand on the cold steel of the doorknob and entered. Ziegler stopped as the sound of his footsteps echoed off the back wall of the vacant room. Robert Boyle was gone, along with any sign that he had ever been there at all. The bed was now made, the machines were missing, and the entire place had been scrubbed top to bottom. The lingering smell of industrial-strength disinfectant was the room's only occupant.

Dear God! Ziegler's mind attempted to latch on to any logical explanation but could only come up with one. The child had died. *This is my fault,* repeated in his head, *this is my fault.* He exited and ran down the hall to Erin Richards's room. His heart clenched in his chest as he grabbed the doorknob and pulled. A strangled gasp left his lips. The room was as empty as the first, with no sign of the little girl. *This can't be.* Ziegler couldn't even imagine a scenario as to why he hadn't been notified. Dr. Malcolm would have called him right away if something happened to both children.

Spinning one-eighty on his heels, he bolted toward the room where Ben Richards had been admitted. He crashed through the door and froze. Silence greeted him from the shadows of the empty room. *What the hell is going on here?* Feeling like he had been kicked in the chest, Ziegler returned to the hallway and dialed Dr. Malcom's office on the house phone. He stood there with his mind jumping to dangerous conclusions as he waited for the man to answer for well over a minute.

"Come on!" he shouted, slamming the receiver down. A second later, Ziegler was sprinting down the hall at top speed. He turned the corner and nearly collided with two nurses blocking his path. He swerved just in time, tripping over his own feet but somehow remaining upright, and continued on his way. He barged into the chief's office and stopped short. The lights had been left on, reports were scattered on the desk, but Dr. Malcolm was not there.

"What the hell?" He struggled to catch his breath. The children had been in terrible shape; there was no denying that. Still, Ziegler knew that if even one of them had passed, Dr. Malcolm would have called him right away. And the man would have sent the goddamn National Guard to rip his ass out of bed if something had happened to all three.

He peeled his facemask off and picked up his boss's phone.

"Yes, Nurse TenHove; this is Dr. Ziegler. Could you page Dr. Malcolm for me?"

"I'm afraid Dr. Malcolm isn't here."

"What?! What do you mean he's not here?"

"I'm sorry. I was under the impression you kn—"

"I don't know anything. Where are the children that were in the ICU, and where is Dr. Malcolm?"

"Dr. Malcolm is with them. He called a colleague in Oswego, and they were transported to the toxicology center late last night."

"When did this happen? Why wasn't I notified?" Ziegler shifted on his feet.

"I believe sometime between three and four a.m. I was under the impression that Dr. Malcolm had notified you. Apparently, he made the decision after examining the children last night. Let's see ..." There was a rustling of papers as she paused to look. "Here it is; at three thirty-seven, Dr. Malcolm signed all three of the patients to be transported to the care of the Oswego Toxicology Center for further testing. Dr. Freedman was here as well. I imagine one of them left the paperwork either in your mailbox or in your office."

"Nurse TenHove, don't you find it a bit strange to transport patients at that time of the night?"

"It's really not my place to say. I'm sure Dr. Malcolm had a good reason for doing so."

"Is Dr. Freedman on the floor?" he asked.

"I haven't seen him. But that doesn't mean he isn't here somewhere."

"Thank you." Ziegler hung up and made a beeline toward his own office. He pulled off the rest of his protective clothing on his way, then walked in and found the reports on his desk. There was a cover sheet that had been signed by Dr. Malcolm.

```
Dr. Ziegler,

Sorry not to have called you, but it was late,
and you had already put in a triple shift.
Your test results proved tremendously helpful
and allowed us to narrow down the toxins,
potentially a viper; however, the bacterium
is unknown. There is a toxicology specialist
that has agreed to help. I have accompanied
the children and their families and will be in
Oswego. I will be in touch periodically. Until
then, I trust that Chilton is in safe hands
under the care of Dr. Freedman and yourself. He
is a seasoned vet and won't steer you wrong.
Again, thank you for your dedication to the
welfare of the patients; this is a commendable
attribute that will no doubt look excellent on
your review.

                                    Regards,
                          Dr. John Malcolm
```

Ziegler felt somewhat relieved but still had a lot of questions. He flipped through the pages of reports to find several pictures of what appeared to be puncture wounds. *That can't be.* He had checked the kids thoroughly and hadn't found any marks at all. However, the first image showed the signature bite mark of a viper with bruising around the infected areas. The name on the report said Robert Boyle. It was a close-up of the bottom of the boy's foot. *How could I have missed such an obvious wound?* Ziegler doubted that whatever was making these children sick was any type of snake venom, at least none that he had ever seen. The following photo was the back of Erin Richards's ankle, depicting the same type of wound, a snake bite. The third was of Ben Richards's big toe.

Ziegler didn't consider himself a snake venom specialist by any means, but he had treated plenty of hunters who'd been bitten by timber rattlers and cottonmouths in the past. The children's blood definitely had a toxin in it, but the rest of their symptoms didn't fit the classic mold of hemotoxic envenomation. Surely Peter Gillick or the guys in toxicology would have picked up on that right away. He was desperate for answers and needed to see what Dr. Freedman knew about the late-night transportation.

He called the man's office and got no answer, then he checked the emergency room and didn't find him there either. None of the attending staff had seen Dr. Freedman since earlier this morning; Ziegler figured he was probably catching a few winks in one of the empty rooms.

However, finding Dr. Freedman wasn't the only thing on Ethan Ziegler's plate; he had rounds to make and other patients to attend to. For now, he needed to trust that Dr. Malcolm had made the right call concerning the children. He set off on his rounds and was quickly consumed with the workload.

Felix Castillo's body had finally stopped moving—for the second time, possibly the third—and neither Carl nor Burt were about to give it the opportunity to get up again. With Tony's help, they moved the corpse to a lab table and secured it with a roll of duct tape. Carl tightly wrapped the tape around the arms, legs, and chest, taking extra precaution to cover the mouth and fasten the head to the table. It was the business end for most animals and reptiles and had proven to be the case with Castillo as well. The thing's tongue was long and powerful and had tossed Abe across the room like a dishrag. Carl had unloaded three bullets into Felix's chest, which hadn't done anything but piss it off. The final bullet had hit him in the head, and that one did the trick.

None of the men said much after that. There were no answers anyone could offer, and they were all thinking the same thing: Felix Castillo had been dead Sunday morning. Dead as Dillinger, no question about it. When the body disappeared yesterday afternoon, Carl had been willing to put his badge on the line to cover Burt's ass. Even he hoped it was a prank and that a few kids had stolen the body. Except that's not what happened. Felix had walked in front of a bread truck early this morning, presumably rendering himself dead for the second time. That was until he got up again and killed Abe Gorman, who hadn't even seen it coming.

They moved Abe's body to one of the tables and checked his vitals, but the man was gone. Carl had just finished securing Felix with the duct tape when Burt tapped him on the shoulder. "Um, we all just saw that. Castillo was dead. He was dead yesterday when we found him, and he was dead when he got hit by the truck this morning."

"I know." There was little else he could say. "I know."

"But that's not possible." Burt's voice rose a full octave. "Dead guys can't do that. What the hell was that, anyway? That's like a goddamn frog or snake's tongue. What the hell happened to this guy?"

Carl took a long, deep breath and released it slowly. "I have no idea."

"That thing isn't human. I don't know what happened to him, but he didn't look like that yesterday." Burt's hands shook as he motioned toward the man taped to the table. "It's like he's mutating or something."

"Is there any of that scotch left?" Carl asked.

"Yeah, I think so."

"I need you to go get the bottle, and I want you to take a good shot. You're hysterical."

The old man didn't need to be told twice. He sprinted to his office, retrieved the bottle, and unscrewed the cap. He took a long swig, then returned to the morgue a moment later. He offered it to Carl, who accepted the drink and passed it to Tony. It helped, at least for the time being.

"Look, I'll agree this is something we've never seen before, but there has to be a logical explanation." Although Carl couldn't think of one.

"That's a vampire," Tony blurted out.

"That's not helpful." Carl shook his head. "There's no such thing."

"Then what the hell do you call that?"

"I don't call it a vampire!" Carl shouted. "I'd call it unexplainable. I'd call it a mutation. But I sure as hell wouldn't call it a goddamn vampire."

Burt took another pull from the bottle. "He's right, Tony. That's not helping. We've all seen the movies, and whatever that is, it sure isn't a vampire."

Carl removed his hat and rubbed his temples, thankful that the scotch had relaxed Burt some. "The truth is we don't know anything about Felix Castillo or his background. For all we know, he could have been born with some rare mutation. And that's why you're gonna cut this son of a bitch open, and were gonna get to the bottom of this, right here and now."

Carl watched as Burt's face drained to an impossible shade of white. "Who? Me?"

"You're the coroner."

Tony took the bottle and tilted it back. "Look, this guy started walking around after he died, like a vampire ... I'm just saying, if it walks like a duck."

Carl felt the heat rise in his chest but held back while Tony finished.

"And it just killed Abe. I mean, shouldn't we tape him down too? Just to be sure."

Carl and Burt looked at each other for a brief, tense moment. Burt shrugged his shoulders, and Carl raised his eyebrows. "That's not a bad idea," Carl said, grabbing the duct tape. Together, the three men proceeded to bind Abe's body to the gurney, taking extra care to secure his mouth.

CHAPTER 27

Troy, Wendy, and Janis set out after school with the eyes of the entire class on them. Boys who had been enchanted by the new girl found it unacceptable how she had bonded with Troy so quickly. And the girls in the class watched and whispered as well. Janis and Wendy noticed them gossiping and found it exciting, although Troy was oblivious to what was going on. He was also unaware that his innocence and ability to remain unaffected had somehow proved him worthy in the eyes of his two new friends.

As they made their way across the parking lot, Wendy handed Troy her *Brady Bunch* lunch box. "The man is supposed to carry our things," she said, taking Janis's *Starsky and Hutch* container and handing it to him as well.

Troy struggled to find a comfortable position, now juggling three lunch boxes—including his own with a picture of the Fonz on the front—and nearly dropped them all in the process. Then Wendy took both her and Janis's notebooks and dumped them into the pocket of his knapsack. The extra weight set him off balance, but Troy straightened his back, stood tall, and managed to exude a little extra bravado. *Jeez, I had no idea being someone's boyfriend was such hard work.* With the straps already digging into his shoulders, he gritted his teeth and prayed that the walk to Janis's house wasn't all that long.

They made their way past the municipal building where the sheriff's department and courthouse were located, then cut behind the first aid squad/firehouse. A baseball diamond sat perpendicular to the buildings, with a path etched into the grass just beyond centerfield. The route then cut across the railroad tracks and led the children to the small community called the Village. From there, it was just a few side streets to Janis's house.

When they arrived, they found Janis's aunt in the driveway and two moving men carrying a sofa. She saw the children approaching and abandoned what she was doing. "Well, what do we have here?" she said with a smile. Troy thought the woman looked like an older version of Janis, with dark blonde curls and a contagious toothy grin.

"Aunt Lynn, these are my new friends, Wendy and Troy. They're in my class. Can I show them my room?"

"Nice to meet you, Wendy, Troy." She shook both their hands. "Sure. Are you guys hungry? I think we have some chocolate chips and milk?"

"Yes, please." It was unanimous.

"Your mom won't be home for a while, hon. Try not to get in the movers' way, and I'll bring up some snacks in a few minutes."

"Thanks, Aunt Lynn," Janis replied and headed toward the house with her blonde curls bouncing as she went.

"Thank you," Troy and Wendy added as a small white beagle with black spots bounded out of the house and intercepted them, its tail wagging so hard it looked like it might throw out a hip.

"Hi, Peanuts." Janis bent down to let the pooch lick her face. "How's my good girl?"

"She really does look like Snoopy," Troy said.

The dog greeted him and Wendy with equal enthusiasm. They took turns petting and scratching her ears till she rolled over on her back in the grass, exposing her belly, clearly in heaven. A second later, Janis entered the house, and the rest of them followed.

The place was filled with cardboard boxes and stacks of furniture wrapped in blankets. There weren't any pictures on the walls or plants hanging in the windows, and the children had to zigzag around the maze of clutter just to get to the staircase. They carefully stepped over the piles of books on the steps and made their way up to Janis's bedroom. Troy gasped at the immaculate state of it. Janis's bed had already been set up, and the room looked as if she had lived there for years instead of just a few days.

"My aunt got here last week, but my mom and I didn't come till Saturday. So, this is my new room." Janis threw her hands out as if she were revealing a magic trick.

Troy's attention shot to the *Star Wars* movie poster hanging on the wall above her bed. It was the big one that had been used in the theaters.

"Wow, that's so cool!" He gawked at the size of it.

"Thanks." She walked over to a bookcase. "Check this out." The shelves contained all the *Star Wars* action figures. The princess stood front and center, flanked by the rest of the characters on either side.

"Oh my gosh," Wendy said. "You have every figure. I only have the princess. You're so lucky."

"Na." Janis shrugged. "My dad buys me lots of stuff since my parents got divorced. I don't really see him much, so he sends them to me." She took one of the figures from the shelf and handed it to Wendy. "Here, you can have this one. I got a couple."

Troy had almost dropped the lunch boxes several times along the way, and then again coming up the stairs. His arms trembled from the strain as he released his hold and set them to the floor. Then he wiggled out of his knapsack and placed it down as well. Peanuts didn't miss a beat and inspected each item thoroughly, making sure to sniff every square inch of the lunch boxes.

"This is super cool for a girl's room," he said, trying to work the cramps out of his hands and shoulders. "I mean, it's not all girly and stuff."

"Thanks ... I guess." Janis took a case off her shelf and placed it on the bed. She unfastened the snaps and lifted the lid. Troy let out an exaggerated gasp when Janis revealed the treasures inside. Within the case were over a dozen separate compartments lined with cotton. Inside each chamber sat individual arrowheads, spearheads, and smaller objects that looked like sharks' teeth.

"No way!" He leaned in closer. "Where did you get all of those?"

"My mom gave them to me. She works for the museum and finds this stuff all the time." The children focused on the box of artifacts, noticing the perfect condition of the arrowheads. Labels were inserted into the compartments as well, depicting where each item had been found along with a date and name of tribe.

"Your mom found all of these?" Wendy held on to her action figure as she studied the arrowheads.

"The woods in town are called the foothills, and you can find arrowheads there too. Scott Cole found one on a class trip. I go there with Rob all the time, but we still haven't found any yet." Troy told the girls about his adventures, trying to sound impressive but doubting there was much of a chance. Not with all the cool trophies Janis already had. Her reaction caught him by surprise.

"Really? Maybe we could all go together. As long as you don't mind looking for arrowheads with a couple of girls." Janis flashed an exaggerated smile.

"I don't mind; that would be cool." Troy had no idea that at just ten years old, Janis had already figured out how to get exactly what she wanted from the men in her life and been practicing on her dad since her parents got divorced. "I'll show you guys anytime. Maybe Rob will feel better and can come with us." Which gave him a great idea. "What are you both dressing as for Halloween?"

"Princess Leia, of course," Wendy said, rolling her eyes. "You already saw my costume, silly."

"I bet you look exactly like her," Janis said.

"You should have seen her. She looked awesome," Troy agreed, causing Wendy to blush and shove him.

"You missed Troy's party. He made a haunted house in his garage that was so scary. Oh my God, even the boys were scared. Tommy Negal was crying," Wendy said. "There was one room that was full of rats. You could feel them crawling on your feet. But my favorite room was the one with the strobe light." She winked at Troy.

"That sounds like a lot of fun. I wish I saw it."

Troy stood a little taller with his newfound confidence swelling within. "Well, I was supposed to start taking everything down, but I wanted to wait for Rob to get better. You know, so he could walk through it one last time since he helped build it. I bet my parents would let me show it off again if you wanted to see it. I call it Scream in the Dark."

"Scream in the Dark," Janis repeated. "That's so cool. I want to see it."

"I'll ask my mom and dad tonight and see what they say. Oh no!" Troy blurted. "I forgot to call my mom. Can I use your phone?"

"Who wants a snack?" Janis's aunt entered the room with a tray of chocolate chip cookies and a pitcher of milk, causing Peanuts to jump up with her tail beating like a windshield wiper.

"Yes, please," Janis answered for all of them. "Can Troy use the phone to call his mom?"

"Sure." Lynn set the tray down on the nightstand. "Right this way, Troy." She led him out of the room and left the girls with the cookies and milk. They dug in.

"How long have you and Troy been boyfriend and girlfriend?" Janis asked with half a cookie in her mouth.

"Well, we kinda liked each other since I moved here last month, but—" Wendy leaned in and whispered. "I kissed him at the party, and today he asked me to be his girlfriend."

"You did?" Janis bounced where she stood. "He seems nice, not stupid like the other boys."

"Yeah, that's what I like about him too. I mean, he still gets a little stupid every now and then but not as much as the other boys. He's different, probably because he spends more time with his mom than his dad. You're gonna like Mrs. Fischer; she's cool. Too bad you weren't at the party. She told us a scary story; it was far-out."

It was Janis's turn to lean in and whisper. "Did you guys really kiss?" Wendy nodded yes. "What was it like? Were you scared?"

Wendy giggled, then looked over her shoulder to make sure they were still alone. "I was at first. I didn't really know what to do. So I did it again."

"Oh my God!" Janis's voice jumped an octave, and she covered her mouth. "You did it twice?" She started to giggle as well.

Wendy smiled and nodded her head. They were both laughing when Troy walked back into the room but stopped as soon as they saw him.

"What's so funny?" he asked.

The girls exchanged a quick glance. "Nothing, just girl talk," Wendy told him and shoved a cookie in her mouth.

"Have some chocolate chips," Janis offered, and Troy didn't need to be told a second time. They were Chips Ahoy, his favorite. Apparently, they were Peanuts's favorite too, who waited patiently underfoot for any crumbs to fall. "We should all go trick-or-treating and dress as the characters from *Star Wars*. Troy, you can be Luke, and Wendy is already Princess Leia."

"Don't forget Rob. He can be Han Solo if he feels better," Troy added.

"Who will you be?" Wendy asked.

"That's easy." Janis opened her closet door and poked her head inside. She rummaged around for a few seconds, rearranging and searching within until she appeared to have found what she was looking for. She struggled for a moment and then popped her head out and jumped toward Wendy and Troy. She growled at them with a full-size Chewbacca mask covering her head.

"Oh my God, that's the best!" Wendy shrieked.

Troy couldn't control the excitement brimming within him and felt as if his smile were too big for his face. "We're going to look so cool! Don't forget the costume contest at school on Friday. We'll definitely win."

He turned his attention to the collection of arrowheads and finished his last cookie. "Janis, what are those little things on the bottom row?" He pointed to the perfectly pointed triangles that looked like tiny arrowheads.

"Those are teeth." She picked one up and handed it to him. "My mother said no one really knows what they belong to. There was a Native American colony that disappeared in the 1400s."

"Back in the time of Columbus?" Wendy asked.

"I think even before that. It was named Cokia, or something like that. It's called America's forgotten city, and it was a huge civilization in Illinois. Then, one day, they disappeared, just like that ... vanished."

"What happened to them?" Troy asked.

"No one knows for sure. But my grandfather was one of the archeologists on the excavation, and he told my mom everything about it."

"Really, what does she think?" Wendy studied the tooth in Troy's palm.

"She never really said. But the museum she works for found a whole bunch of these weird teeth and some strange animal bones."

"Maybe they got eaten," Troy said.

"That's what I think too."

"What kind of animal is it?" He flipped the item over in his palm, noticing how it resembled a piranha or a shark's tooth.

"An Ojanox," Wendy said. "That's definitely an Ojanox tooth, if you ask me."

Troy looked at her and shook his head. "Come on, my mom made up that story." He turned to Janis. "She's a great storyteller ... usually. She was trying to scare us at the party, so she made up a Halloween story. It was pretty good too, until she made up a dumb name for the monster. She called it an Ojanox."

"Sounds pretty scary to me," Janis said, taking a closer look at the tooth herself. "Looks like it could be an Ojanox tooth, if you ask me."

"I told you, Troy. Don't disagree with the girls," Wendy said. "Everyone knows girls are smarter than boys."

Troy was smart enough not to disagree. He kept his mouth shut and smiled. *Man, it's hard being a boyfriend.* It took a lot more practice and patience than he'd imagined. Now he knew why the other boys in school didn't have girlfriends. It was a full-time job.

Although he wasn't consciously aware of the occasion, it had been a pivotal day in Troy Fischer's life. He learned just how different boys were from girls and how hard it was to look cool in front of them. He struggled to say the right things and not act immature because if there was one thing his new friends were focused on, it was how fast girls matured compared to boys. It wasn't like he could forget since Wendy had made it a point to remind them, more than just a few times. It made Troy feel like a traitor to have to agree with them, but given the audience, he didn't think he had a choice.

Troy couldn't wait to tell Rob everything that had happened. In one action-packed Monday, he had become Wendy's boyfriend and met the new girl in class. He had already decided that Janis and Rob would become instant friends when they all went trick-or-treating on Halloween. He couldn't believe how cool Janis was. *Whoever heard of a girl collecting arrowheads and teeth and even having a Chewbacca mask?* Troy wouldn't have been surprised if his new friend had the entire costume hidden somewhere in her closet.

When it was time to go, he told the girls goodbye and set off with plenty of time to spare. He didn't want to get home late after being allowed over to his new friend's house for the first time and hoped to go back to see what other cool things she collected. Janis thanked him for coming, told him she would see him tomorrow, and Wendy decided it was time to leave as well. Together, they walked to the end of the block, where Wendy needed to turn left and Troy to the right. He knew it was customary to kiss your girlfriend goodbye but still wasn't comfortable with the practice. Again, Wendy proved that girls really did mature faster than boys and kissed him on the side of the mouth. Then she spun on her heels and quickly walked away.

"See you tomorrow," she said, and skipped off in the other direction.

Troy headed home with his chest inflated and a new spring in his step. He swung his lunch box in long arcs, feeling like the first man to climb Mt. Everest. Taking in his surroundings, he checked out the Jack-o'-lanterns on the front porches, the fake cobwebs in the windows, and the spooky decorations set on nearly every lawn. Freshly fallen leaves of every color danced across the grass, adding a soundtrack to the seasonal displays. Troy had always loved autumn, with the sense of mystery and wonder that it brought. But today, it felt as if a whole new element had been added to the mix. He figured that had something to do with his new friends ... the girls, who had somehow enhanced the mystery of the season. There was something taboo about the way Wendy made him feel. Troy had no idea he wasn't the first boy to become enchanted by the fairer sex. He couldn't describe the way he felt, and had it been 1679 instead of 1979, he might have called it witchcraft, which wasn't that far from the truth. Still, for Troy, it was a wonderful surprise accentuated by the coming of fall. The wind appeared to sense his mood and tossed his hair just as he crossed over the railroad tracks and cut across center field.

He passed the municipal building and backtracked his way to the school. From there, he needed to zigzag through a couple side streets to get from the Turnpike to the Boulevard. Instead, Troy opted for a more direct route and cut through the graveyard behind the Lutheran Church. He usually walked this way with Rob, the two boys noticing the dates and names on the headstones along the way. One of the oldest ones they had seen dated back to 1806, although many were too worn to read and could have been much older.

Troy and Rob had been walking through the graveyard when they first decided to use the names I.P. Daily and Bob Frapples on the headstones in their haunted house. He remembered that day well and laughed under his breath, then quickly stopped, remembering where he was. As if sensing his thoughts, the wind picked up and the temperature felt like it had suddenly dropped several degrees. Troy continued on his way past the old burial markers; David Swift, Beloved Husband and Father 1824-1878. Another one read, In Loving Memory Abigail Rosewood 1912-1965. He zipped up his coat to block the wind and stopped in front of a grave he hadn't noticed before. The inscription read Sheriff Allen Primrose Loving Father 1922-1976. *That must be Sheriff Primrose's dad.* Troy wasn't sure if he remembered him.

Another gust of wind raced between the headstones, causing a branch to snap somewhere in the distance. Troy jumped and turned in the direction the noise had originated. The tree limbs now bent back against the strong breeze, and the leaves had started to turn themselves inside out. He scanned the area behind him, checking the gravestones, and caught the slightest flicker of motion, as if someone had ducked behind one of the large mausoleums. A cold wind raced a shiver across his scalp, and Troy was overcome with a sense of vulnerability and an unshakable notion that he was being watched. The sky above him grew darker, looking as if it might rain any second. He started to walk again, faster now, with the feeling growing stronger with every stride. He'd heard the stories of what happened to kids who walked through graveyards alone but always thought it was something grownups made up to keep them from trespassing. Troy quickened his pace, using all his willpower to not look back over his shoulder once again. He could see the fence that bordered the main road and double-stepped his way toward it.

He heard another noise behind him, as if someone had coughed or shouted, only this time it was much closer. Now Troy was certain there was something behind him and it had started chasing him. Fear sizzled in his blood like boiling oil, making his face tingle with pins and needles. His legs threatened to cramp and glue him in his tracks, but survival kicked in, and Troy broke into a full sprint. The second he took off, it screamed—an agonizing bellow that sounded like a howl mixed with a shriek. There was a flash of movement he saw in the corner of his eye, of something running parallel on his right. It darted out from behind the tombstones and disappeared behind another. Then he noticed something else moving on his left. *Oh God, there's two of them.* They were trying to pin him in the graveyard and cut him off before he could reach the gate. He couldn't tell who or what was trying to ambush him, thinking maybe they were dogs or even a couple of men, but he wasn't about to stop to get a better look.

Troy had never been the most athletic kid in school, but he was a ten-year-old in good health, and he had a plan. He knew if he ran straight for the gate, the men, or whatever it was, would edge him out and catch him. Instead, he dodged left and headed toward the part of the fence closest to him. Troy prayed he could get there before the assailant on that side could reach it; he also figured this would throw off the one on the right, who was even closer. He pulled the straps on his knapsack tight so the contents wouldn't shift and throw off his balance. Then he tossed his lunch box into the air and over the fence, which prompted another horrifying shriek. That sound hadn't been made by any person, and now Troy was positive there were wild animals after him. Which made it that much worse. *Who knows how fast these things can run?* Lightning flashed, and a second later, the sky turned dark black as the first drops of rain started to fall.

Troy could almost make out the figure on his left, cutting through the graveyard and heading straight toward him. He also sensed the presence of another one close behind. Focusing only on his escape route, Troy zeroed in on the large oak tree closest to the fence and sprinted as fast as his legs would allow. The shrieks were much closer now, howling and growling from multiple directions, and Troy wondered if there were even more than two pursuers on his tail. Taking a running leap, he grabbed on to the lower limb of the oak and pulled himself up to the next branch. He scrambled from limb to limb, then swung his legs out over the wrought iron spikes and dropped to the grass on the other side. Without thinking, he ran into the street, across the Boulevard with his heart screaming and tears in his eyes. Troy was suddenly halted by the sound of screeching tires and looked up just in time to see the grill of the vehicle barreling down on him.

Deputy Ted Lutchen slammed the brakes of the cruiser, stopping less than a foot in front of Troy Fischer. He hopped out of the car and ran to him. "Are you crazy, kid? I almost killed you."

"They're chasing me!" Troy cried and fought to catch his breath. His heart thundered in his temples like a marching band.

"Who's chasing you?" Deputy Lutchen looked toward the graveyard where the boy had just come from.

"I-I-I dunno. They're fast, howled ... screamed." Troy bent down and put his hands on his knees.

"I don't see anybody. It was probably just some kids messing with you. Are you sure you didn't just get freaked out?" Another flash of lightning lit up the sky and was followed by a low rumble of thunder. Then the heavens opened.

"Hop in, kid. I'll give you a ride home. You live around here?"

"Pine Street," he told the deputy and jumped into the backseat.

The cruiser sped down the Boulevard with several sets of dark eyes watching from the shadows of the graveyard. The owner of one of those sets had seen the boy clearly. It dug its newly formed talons into the granite headstone and let out a strangled cry that could have passed for human ... almost. The mournful noise the creature made sounded as if it had screamed a single word. "*Troooyyyeee!*"

CHAPTER 28

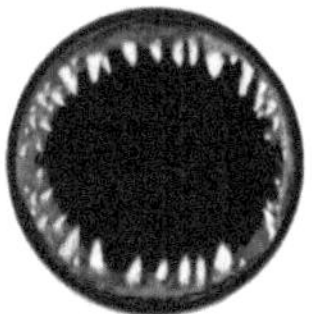

The rain came down heavy and sudden, and it was already dark by the time Burt started the autopsy. There was no such thing as vampires, on that they were all in agreement. Everyone except for Tony, who stood at the back door, chain-smoking one Pall Mall after another. However, they were also in agreement that Felix Castillo had exhibited some very vampire-like qualities. He had mysteriously defied death more than once. First, from a neck wound that resulted in a total depletion of his blood. And although it couldn't be determined, Felix appeared to have turned into something similar to what killed him. Which only supported Tony's vampire theory and pissed Carl off even more.

Still, it was a regular bullet to the head that put Felix down for good. Not holy water, a crucifix, or a wooden stake through the heart. The fact that the first three shots hadn't even slowed him down was more than troubling. It was possible that the bullets had missed the man's vital organs; unlikely, but it was possible. However, the one to the head had sealed the deal, the same as it would to any normal human being.

For no other reason than to cover his ass and ease his mind, Burt had taken the crucifix from around his neck and pressed it to Felix's forehead. Everyone, including Carl, held their breath, half expecting the thing to start thrashing about and smoking. But nothing happened; there was no smoke and no reanimation either.

"Try Abe," Tony said from the safety of the back doorway. "Go ahead, try it on Abe. You'll see."

Burt shrugged and took the cross to where Abe was secured to the gurney. He held his breath again, then placed the cross on the man's forehead. Nothing happened.

"Thank you, Dr. Van Helsing." Carl exhaled. "Do you think we could get on with cutting this guy open already?"

The thing on the table that entered the world as Felix Castillo had left as something entirely different. Burt first checked the man's eyes. His pupils had tripled in size, blacking out the irises and corneas. It appeared that, for whatever reason, they'd developed to adjust quicker and more efficiently to darkness. At least that was Burt's immediate theory. Transparent flaps resembling a second set of lids were visible as well, which also supported that postulation. The man's skin was waxy and grey and hung loose as if he had lost a great deal of weight or there was just too much of it. And Burt wasn't about to examine the mouth or the tongue, at least not yet.

The smell that saturated the room when he cracked open Felix's thoracic cavity was so putrid that Carl and Tony had to step outside while Burt removed the organs. "Dear God! Carl," Burt called from the lab. "You have to see this."

Carl returned to find his friend removing a muscle as big as a horse's heart from the man's chest. "That can't be his heart!" He stared at the massive organ.

"It can't," Burt said, "but it is. Also, his lungs have shriveled away to nothing. I can't explain that either, but it looks as if he no longer needed oxygen to survive. Judging by the size of this heart, I'd say he still needed blood—and a lot of it. I see where you shot him, missed the lungs completely. Not that I think it would have mattered if you hit them. They're desiccated, all dried up and useless." Burt removed a tissue sample and placed it in a stainless steel basin next to the one containing the heart.

"Have you ever seen any of these conditions before? Is there a disease that can do this?" Carl asked.

Burt looked at his friend as if he had asked him to set his lips on fire. Then he stepped away from the body and began preparing slides. "I've never even heard of *anything* that can do this. As crazy as it sounds, this guy looks like he's turning into some type of lizard or reptile."

Carl leaned over the body and squinted. "I hate to agree, but that's exactly what it looks like."

Burt cut a small section from the tissue, set it on the slide, then he placed it on the microscope and turned on the light. He stared into the lens for a long time, focusing and refocusing. Finally, he stood up, rubbed his eyes, and swayed on his feet as if he might pass out. "What the hell is it, Burt?" Carl asked.

"We better call Dr. Malcolm—right away."

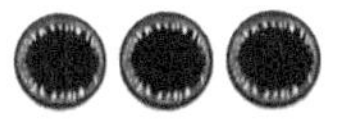

Lois Fischer answered the door to find Troy and Garrett Grove's youngest deputy, Ted Lutchen, standing on her front steps looking like a couple of drowned kittens. Even in the heavy rain, she could see the tears streaming down her son's face and the stern look in the deputy's eyes. She threw open the door, and Troy rushed into the house and wrapped his arms around her without saying a word. Lois started to speak, then stopped and turned her head to Deputy Lutchen. Ted looked back at her and raised his eyebrows. Lois braced herself for what she was about to hear.

She let the deputy inside while doing her best to comfort Troy, who appeared to have relaxed some, now that he was back home. When the tears finally subsided, Lois lifted his head by the chin and looked him in the eyes. She smiled and kissed his cheek.

"Why don't you go dry off, honey. We can talk when you're ready."

Troy nodded, then headed upstairs and made his way to the bathroom. When he was out of earshot, Lois turned to the deputy and lowered her voice. "Wha—?"

"Your son is fine, Mrs. Fischer," Ted said. "But ... he was running across the Boulevard, and I almost hit him with my cruiser." Lois's hand reached to cover her mouth. "He said something had been chasing him ... in the graveyard. It's possible maybe some older kids were messing with him, but I didn't see anyone else."

Lois felt the color drain out of her face as the deputy explained. "Thank you for bringing him home. Can I get you a towel to dry off, or a cup of coffee? You must be freezing."

"No, thank you. I have to get back to work; we're a bit understaffed today." Ted turned to exit the house, then lowered his voice as well. "Just one thing, Mrs. Fischer. Your son said *something* was chasing him, not *someone*. I thought I should mention that."

Lois thanked him again as he left out the front door and ran across the lawn into the downpour. She rushed up the stairs and joined Troy where he stood before the bathroom mirror drying himself off. He looked terrified, which was more than worrisome. Troy didn't scare easily; he was a horror fanatic and had spent much of his time building the haunted house with all its frights and surprises. *Maybe all this scary stuff is getting to him after all.*

"What's going on, kiddo?" She smiled and mussed his hair.

"They chased me, Mom. I was walking through the graveyard, and there were at least two of them. God, they were so fast." His voice grew shrill, and he looked as if he might start crying again.

"You know I don't want you in there."

"I know, but me and Rob walked through there before and nothing ever happened." Lois had a good idea what was really going on. Troy wasn't fine, despite what his father insisted. Her son had recently found his best friend close to death, and that was a lot for anyone to deal with, especially a ten-year-old boy.

"Promise me you won't do anything like that again."

"I promise. I'm sorry." Tears welled up in the corners of his eyes and spilled out onto his cheeks. Lois hugged him and drew him as close as she possibly could.

"Th-they were so f-fast, Mom. They almost got me. I-I had to climb over the fence."

"Who was chasing you, baby?" She lifted his chin again and looked in his eyes.

"Animals. I only saw them f-for a second. They ran kinda like dogs, but they h-hopped too."

"Do you think they were coyotes? They've been coming down off the mountain a bit more lately, or maybe someone's dogs that got loose."

"It wasn't coyotes or dogs. They screamed, and I think they were hunting me."

"That sounds scary." Lois didn't know what to think but knew that Troy believed every word of it. "I would have been scared too, honey. Would you like some hot cocoa? You're freezing."

He nodded and buried his head into her bosom again. "Mom?" His voice sounded impossibly small.

"What is it, baby?"

"You know that story you told us at the party?"

Lois had to think. Although it had only been two days, Saturday night felt like a lifetime ago. Then she remembered the ghost story she had told the kids. It was something she had written back in college, some of it at least, the rest she had made up on the spot. "Why do you ask?"

Troy pulled his head away and looked up at her. "I think that's what it was, the things that chased me. It was just like you said; it watches when you walk through the graveyard, waiting for you to fall. I think that's what it was. I think it was the Ojanox."

Carl rubbed his eyes and looked into the lens of the microscope a second time. No matter how hard he tried, he couldn't get it to focus and finally quit in frustration. "Christ! Will you just tell me what I'm supposed to be looking at?"

"That's a bacterial infection!" Burt said. "If I had to guess, I'd say it's parasitic."

"Like in the children?" Carl's eyes focused on the old man.

"I don't believe in coincidence. This guy died in front of the Boyle kid's house. And all three of those kids live less than a block from each other. Dr. Malcolm needs to confirm if this is the same infection. But I'd bet my prick on it." Burt removed a hypodermic from a drawer and approached the gurney where Abe's body was secured. He watched the man as he took the blood sample.

"What are you doing?" Carl asked.

"Following a hunch. With Abe's help, I think we'll find out how this infection is transmitted." Burt prepared a slide with Abe's blood and transferred it to the microscope. He stared through the aperture and jumped back a second later. "Bingo!"

Tony pitched his cigarette out the back door, where he stood a safe distance away from the bodies. "Is it the same?"

"Identical," Burt said. "Same cellular pattern exactly, except ... What the hell?" He refocused the scope, then changed the magnification level.

"What is it, Burt?" Carl asked.

"These cells are still active. His white blood cells are attacking the red. That shouldn't happen, not in a body that's been dead for over an hour. This blood is alive." All three men turned to the body duct taped to the gurney. Burt's cross still sat on Abe's head where he had left it.

"That's not possible; we checked his pulse," Carl said, making his way toward the body. He leaned over and touched the man's wrist. There was no pulse, but the body was warm ... too warm. "Christ, Burt! He's still hot."

Tony shrank further back until he was almost standing in the parking lot. They all focused intently on the man secured to the gurney, watching for the slightest twitch or warning sign. Half a second later, Abe's eyes shot open as if they had been spring loaded. Large black pupils zeroed in on the men, then Abe began to buck and twist, struggling to free himself from his bindings. The tape held fast—for the moment—but the man continued to flail about on the gurney, nearly tipping it over in the process.

Carl pulled his revolver and pointed it at Abe's head; dark, toxic eyes fixed on his every move. Satisfied that the duct tape was indeed holding, Carl lowered the weapon. Then an awful noise erupted from Abe's mouth, filling the morgue with a repulsive shriek that bounced off every metal surface in the place. Carl pictured a dozen razor-sharp teeth exploding through the man's gums.

Grabbing one of the stainless steel basins, Carl threw it over Abe's face. Then he took the duct tape and fastened it to his head and to the gurney as well. *Better safe than sorry.*

"Get me the phone, Burt."

The coroner ran to his office and came back a second later pulling the phone along with a mile of cord.

Carl picked up the receiver, dialed, and looked to the back door. It stood open, but Tony was gone; he had run out into the storm.

"Yes, this is Sheriff Primrose. Could I speak with Dr. Malcolm, please?" He paused. "He what? Oswego? I thought he said the children were doing better ... uh-huh ... uh-huh, yeah, I'll hold."

"What's going on?" Burt asked.

"Malcolm's in Oswego. Left last night and took the kids with him. Some toxicology center or something."

"Just like that? What did he find out?"

Carl shrugged and motioned for Burt to hang on one second. Then a familiar voice came on the line.

"Hello, this is Dr. Ziegler."

"Hi, Doc. This is Sheriff Primrose. I didn't know Dr. Malcolm transferred the children."

"I just found out myself. Happened around three thirty this morning, which struck me as odd."

"That doesn't sound right, not without alerting you or myself first. You were working on the lab results. Dr. Malcolm said you suspected a possible toxin or a bacterial infection."

"To be honest, it's nothing I've ever seen before," Ziegler continued. "Dr. Malcolm left a report on my desk indicating the possibility of snake venom, which seems unlikely, if you ask me."

"Snake venom?" Carl and Burt turned toward the mutated body of Felix Castillo.

"It didn't sound right to me either. But Dr. Malcolm is the chief of medicine. Besides, there wasn't anything I could do."

"I think we may have a related case, Doctor. Would you mind looking at something for me?"

"Are you sick, Sheriff? You aren't showing symptoms, are you?" Ziegler's voice wavered.

"No, I'm fine. I think it would be better if we just show you."

"We?"

"I'm with Burt Lively at the coroner's office. Is there any chance you could swing by here?"

"I suppose I could sneak away and be there in about half an hour. What's at the lab that's so important it can't wait?"

"Like I said, Doctor, I think it would be better if you looked for yourself."

"Is everything all right, Sheriff?"

"I'll see you in a half-hour." Carl hung up the phone and turned to Burt. "Is there any of that scotch left? I think we're going to need it."

CHAPTER 29

Carl and Burt congregated under the awning at the rear entrance of the morgue. It had started to rain even harder, and the dull glow of the yellow lamp hanging from the building did little to illuminate the parking area. Occasional flashes of electricity etched the sky, casting long shadows across the slick blacktop and the men's faces. They exchanged a tentative look when Dr. Ziegler pulled into the lot. Moments later, the young doctor opened the car door and stepped out into the deluge. Ziegler spotted the men and ran to where they stood; he was soaked by the time he reached the back entrance.

"Hello, Sheriff, Mr. Lively. I must say you have my curiosity piqued. What's this all about?" He shook their hands.

"Thanks for coming, Dr. Ziegler." Carl said. "Before we begin, you need to promise you won't tell anyone what you see here. No one but Dr. Malcolm."

"If this is a medical concern, I am sworn to secrecy."

"It is," Burt said. "But you better hold on to your stethoscope."

Ziegler turned to the coroner and furrowed his brow. "Gentlemen, if this is some kind of a joke, *now* is not a good time. I have patients that requi—"

"It's no joke, Dr. Ziegler," Carl said as they entered the morgue.

The first thing Ziegler noticed was the overpowering stench of decay that hung in the air like a wet blanket. He covered his mouth and nose to try to block it out.

"Dear God! How many bodies do you have in here?" he asked. "Are they supposed to smell that bad when you work on them?"

"No, Doc," Burt said. "Definitely not after only thirty-six hours."

They approached the lab tables, and Ziegler immediately spotted the body of Felix Castillo where it lay putrefying beneath the bright fluorescent light. Then he focused on the duct tape that had been used to fasten him down. Sudden movement on the other side of the room drew his attention to the man on the gurney. A stainless steel basin had been secured to his head, and he was bound as well. The man struggled to free himself from his bindings.

Jesus Christ! Ziegler's heart raced into overdrive, and his flight instinct kicked in. He ran for the door, but Carl slammed it shut before he could reach it. "Not so fast, Doc." Ziegler spun on his heels and tried to take off in the other direction, but before he could, the coroner jumped in front of him and blocked his path.

"What the hell is going on here?!" Ziegler turned again and came face-to-face with Carl, who seized him by the biceps and held him fast.

"I need you to calm down, Doctor. We're not going to hurt you."

Ziegler motioned to the man on the gurney. "Who the hell is that, and what have you done to him?"

Burt approached the frightened doctor and placed his hand on his shoulder. "Doc, if you would just take a look at the slide on the microscope, I'm sure this will make much more sense."

Carl loosened his grip and walked Ziegler to the counter.

Seeing that his options were limited, Ziegler bent over the instrument and peered into the lens. He studied the sample for a moment, then let out a long gasp. "Where did you get this? It's identical to the infection we found in the children."

"That's what I figured," Burt said. "Dr. Malcolm mentioned you believed the infection was a toxin with a bacterial signature?"

"Yes, and that's what you have here as well. If I didn't know better, I would say they were taken from the same subject."

"I found this infection in both of these men," Burt said.

"Dr. Ziegler." Carl addressed him in a calm, deliberate tone. "I need you to keep an open mind for what I am about to show you." He led the doctor to the dissected body of Felix Castillo.

Ziegler noticed the abnormalities immediately; a Y-incision revealed the open chest cavity. *Dear God. That's not possible.* The man's lungs were shriveled and had wasted away to nothing. Then he saw the enormous heart in the basin. *That couldn't have come out of this guy.* Ziegler leaned in closer to focus; the skin on the man's face sagged and hung loose, almost as if he had at one time been obese and then lost a tremendous amount of weight.

Burt pried open the man's eyelids. "Look at this, Doc."

The subject's eyes were entirely black.

Ziegler gasped but remained silent.

Then Burt used a pair of tweezers to reveal the translucent folds that had grown over the man's eyes. They looked like a secondary set of lids.

"Dear God, what happened to this man?"

"He died, Doctor," Carl said flatly.

"Obviously."

"No, this man was found dead in the middle of Foothills Drive yesterday morning." Carl looked to Burt to fill in the blanks.

"I inspected the body, and the only wound I found was this." Burt lifted the tape, revealing the strange punctures on Castillo's neck. Ziegler creased his brow and examined it as Burt continued. "The man's blood and body fluids were depleted when we found him, and there wasn't a drop at the scene."

"His name is Felix Castillo," Carl said. "He was transported here around nine o'clock yesterday morning. At eleven o'clock, the body went missing. This morning, a delivery driver hit Mr. Castillo on Sunset Road."

"How did the body get there?" Ziegler shook his head, not sure if he was following.

"It walked." Carl held up his palms. "Just stay with me a little longer. The guy was covered in mud, so we didn't know it was Castillo. But we sure noticed the stink. We brought him back here and washed him off. That's when he woke up. He opened those giant black eyes and stared at us like we were a couple of late-night snacks. Then this ... thing shot out of his mouth and killed Abe."

"That's Abe Gorman? The medical assistant?!" Ziegler suddenly noticed the scrubs the man was wearing. "What happened to him? Let him go!"

"That's not a good idea," Burt said as the body on the gurney jumped and twisted against the tape.

"Would you both take a few steps back?" Carl produced a pocketknife and approached the body of Felix Castillo.

"I don't think you should do that," Burt said. "You saw what that thing did to Abe. What if it wakes up again?" He took several steps away, pulling Ziegler along with him.

Carl positioned himself at the back of the table behind the man's head. He held on to Castillo's chin with one hand to keep the mouth from opening and then sliced the duct tape with the knife. Ziegler gasped when the face was revealed. The dead man's mouth had transformed into something straight out of a horror movie; it had grown longer and more circular, with flaps of extra skin that now hung loose like silly putty.

Carl nodded to Burt, and the old man pushed Ziegler back several more steps. Then the sheriff pried open the man's mouth and plunged the knife inside. He fished around for a moment, then began to pull his blade upward. *Dear God.*

The sheriff lifted his knife and revealed the hideous appendage attached to the business end. It looked like an eel, slimy and black and pointed at the end. It stretched out as if it was made of rubber, unraveling from some unlimited source like clowns exiting a tiny car. Carl continued to remove it from the man's mouth as Ziegler watched with his heart doing the Hustle and his sanity threatening to jump off the rails. When he was finished, Carl had revealed a tongue that measured over three feet long.

Ziegler swayed, feeling like he might pass out. The next thing he saw was the bottle of scotch that Burt shoved into his hand. *Oh, thank God.* Ziegler unscrewed the cap and took a long slug of the liquor.

"What the hell is that thing?" Ziegler said, wiping his eyes.

Carl let the tongue retract into Felix's mouth and went to work with the duct tape. "I was hoping you could help us figure that out."

"Are you telling me this all happened after he died?" Ziegler took another healthy swig.

"It used that ... tongue thing to grab Abe," Burt said. "Tossed him around the room like a goddamn puppet and killed him. Then Abe woke up, and he was just like it."

Carl approached the gurney where Abe was bound. He cut the tape securing the basin to the man's head and slowly lifted the pan covering his face. Abe immediately reacted and started bucking and twisting to break free. He stared up at them and focused on Ziegler with a pair of coal-black, lifeless eyes. Carl replaced the basin a second later, which appeared to relax the thing on the gurney.

"This is impossible, all of it!" Ziegler shouted.

"I think whatever killed Felix Castillo infected him with your parasite or bacterium." Carl folded the knife and slipped it in his pocket. "And when he attacked Abe, he passed it on to him."

Ziegler held on to the bottle and listened as Carl continued.

"This toxin, or whatever the hell it is, got these men up and walking after they died, like some kind of freaking zombies or something. If those kids have been infected by the same thing, we need to get to them right away."

"But they've been transported to Oswego. The toxicology center."

"You said Dr. Malcolm suspected some type of snake venom?" Burt asked. "This doesn't look like that to me."

"I didn't think so either. But I had no way to question him about it. When I arrived this morning, he was gone."

"Vanished in the night, huh?" Burt nodded.

Ziegler pointed to Felix's forehead. "That looks like a bullet wound."

"It was the only way to get him to let go of Abe. I shot him three times in the chest first; didn't do much. But that one did the trick."

"I should take a look at Abe," Ziegler said. "If there's any way to save him, maybe I can help."

"What exactly do you have in mind, Doc?" Burt asked. "Whatever you do, you do *not* want to get too close."

"Dr. Malcolm blew this year's budget on some new equipment that's supposed to change the way we look at the human body. It's called MRI, short for magnetic resonance imaging. Cutting-edge stuff, really. We have a technician specially trained to operate it, but I've watched him a few times. I'd like to get Abe into the chamber and take some pictures, see what's going on in his brain—but we'll need to secure him to a wooden plank. There can't be any metal at all. It'll interfere with the imaging and probably destroy a million-dollar machine in the process."

The thing on the gurney thrashed about as if in response to what he had said. The stainless steel basin covering its head wobbled like a capsized ship, and the men were helpless not to stare at it.

"Is there any other way?" Burt asked. "Like an x-ray or something."

"I'm afraid not. The metal from the gurney and the basin would also interfere with an x-ray. To see what's really going on in the soft tissue, it's got to be the MRI machine."

"Well, if we're really going to do this, I have an idea." Carl removed the radio from his hip and depressed the button. "This is Sheriff Primrose to any available officer. Come in."

A squelch of static flooded the tiny speaker. "This is Deputy Rainey, Sheriff."

"What's your twenty, Rainey?"

"I'm behind the station. I was just about to start my patrol."

"I need you to grab the riot gear from storage. The body armor, the helmets, and some of those large cable ties? I want you to bring them to the morgue."

"Could you repeat that, Sheriff? It sounded like you said bring the riot gear and cable ties to the morgue?"

"Roger that. Come to the back entrance. I'll meet you there." Carl waited for a reply.

"Ten-four, Sheriff."

The body on the gurney twisted and arched its back against the restraints. The duct tape did its job and continued to hold it securely in place ... for the moment at least.

CHAPTER 30

Although the worst of the storm had passed, it continued to pour well into the evening. Occasional whips of lightning sliced the ozone like a machete through silkweed, followed by the rolling growl of thunderheads clashing in the distance. Deputy David Rainey exited the cruiser and stepped out onto the rain-slicked blacktop behind the morgue. Petrichor emanated from the earth and fused with the dark odor seeping out the back door of the building—damp and crisp tainted with a dash of pestilence. He spotted the three men standing at the rear entrance, looking like they were about to blow the charge on a bank vault. The suspicious movements of the men made him even more apprehensive than he already was. *What the hell is this all about?* Rainey was still a rookie, just a few months longer on the job than his younger coworker, Ted Lutchen, and had never travelled further than fifty miles from his hometown of Garrett Grove. In fact, he still lived with his parents and kid sister, Kelly, in the three-bedroom Cape Cod he had grown up in. He took another apprehensive look in the men's direction and made his way to the back of the cruiser. For the life of him, he couldn't imagine why the sheriff needed riot gear at the morgue.

Sheriff Primrose approached the cruiser with Burt Lively and Dr. Ziegler from the medical center behind him. He went straight for the riot gear and started to distribute it. "I need you to put these on," he said, passing out the helmets and body armor.

"Am I missing something, Sheriff?" the young deputy asked.

"We don't have time for questions right now," Carl said. "I need you to gear up and help restrain a suspect. Follow your orders to the letter, and I'll brief you later."

Rainey did as instructed and donned the riot gear while the other men did the same. After they had strapped up, the sheriff inspected each man's vest, helmet, and face shield, then gave them the go-ahead. Carl ran into the building, Burt and Dr. Ziegler followed close behind, and Rainey brought up the rear.

The overwhelming stench of death smacked Rainey in the face the second he entered the morgue. He gagged as the contents of his stomach shifted and felt his heart cramp inside his chest. Then he saw the man bound to the gurney. The figure writhed in a most unnatural fashion and struggled to break free from the duct tape securing him. *What the fuck?* A shiver sliced through Rainey's groin like an arctic blast at the sight of the stainless steel basin taped to the man's head.

On a table adjacent to the gurney sat a wooden stretcher with leather straps wrapped throughout its handles. Rainey knew right away that the sheriff intended to transfer the body from the gurney to the stretcher, then bind it in place. Sheriff Primrose quickly positioned himself over the man's head while the doctor and coroner ran to either side and grabbed his arms.

"I need you to hold his feet, Deputy. And for God's sake, don't let go, no matter what happens." The sheriff held a pocketknife in one hand and used the other to remove the basin.

What in the name of—? Rainey stared down at the thing laying before him. Its giant dark eyes darted around the room and focused directly on him. Rainey was helpless to look away. The man strapped to the gurney was Abe Gorman, the meat wagon driver. Except it wasn't exactly Abe ... not anymore. Something terrible had happened to him; his face had distorted and grown grotesquely disproportionate. Rainey felt the bile rise in the back of his throat and swallowed hard to force it down.

He grabbed Abe's legs as instructed and froze, unable to do anything but stare into the endless sea of black. His pounding heart echoed in his temples as he struggled to digest what he was seeing. Abe's face contorted and twisted in an aggressive fit of rage. And his eyes—*dear God*—were huge and dark and all-consuming. They stared back at David Rainey and penetrated him. He shifted his gaze to avoid looking directly at the awful obsidian eyes until it started to hiss, breathy and slow like a serpent. A second later, the most God-awful sound spilled out of the creature. The unbearable shriek filled the room and gnawed into the deputy like nails on a chalkboard. His head began to swim, then he started to feel queasy. Rainey bit down on his bottom lip and fought to regain his composure.

David ... the voice echoed from inside his head.

"You got him?" The sheriff gripped Abe underneath his chin, and the coroner produced a wide leather muzzle from his pocket.

"Here we go. You ready, Rainey?" Carl shouted. "Are you okay, David?"

"Fine, Sheriff. Ready," he said, and the voice spoke again.

David ... relax.

Carl cut the tape securing Abe's head to the gurney, then ripped it free, exposing his mouth. Burt passed one end of the leather strap under the man's neck and looped the other across his jaw. Together, they worked to secure the muzzle while Abe heaved and bucked as if he'd been thrown into a fiery pit. Ziegler grabbed the stainless steel basin a second before it was knocked off the gurney onto the floor.

Abe continued to writhe, with every muscle in his body screaming to break free. The men struggled to subdue him but were halted by a sudden tearing sound as Abe ripped through the restraints securing his legs. He kicked wildly and bucked against the table, then the tape securing his torso began to loosen as well. Rainey gazed into the creature's bottomless pits of black and was lost.

"Dammit, Rainey!" Carl shouted. "Hold him down!"

The deputy released his grip and stepped away from the gurney. Carl looked up to find himself facing the barrel of a service revolver. He froze as Deputy Rainey leveled it with his head.

The creature continued to thrash while Burt and Ziegler fought to control it. But their hold on it was waning, and it was getting loose.

"Deputy Rainey, lower your weapon!" Carl screamed. "That's an order!"

David ... shoot himmmm.

The voice was cold and intrusive and bore into him like a drill. Rainey pulled back the hammer of his revolver, sensing the pressure of the trigger against his index finger. It was heavy ... so heavy, and the urge to squeeze was impossible to resist. Moreso, he wanted to do it; he wanted to pull the trigger.

David ... Now!

David closed his eyes, stopped fighting, and squeezed.

Ziegler raised the stainless steel basin like a broad sword and brought it down with a sickening *thwack!* It connected with the deputy's hand a second before the gun went off. The slug passed less than two inches to the right of Carl's ear, breaking the air like the crack of a whip. The deputy's weapon was knocked from his hand and sent flying across the room. Ziegler raised the basin a second time and slammed it against the deputy's helmet, cracking the faceplate and knocking the man out.

Carl didn't wait; he cut the remaining tape binding Abe to the gurney as the doctor and coroner clamped down. Together, the three men lifted and transferred him to the stretcher. They fastened the straps around the body, restraining his arms, legs, chest, and head. The leather proved far superior to the duct tape and prevented the man from moving almost entirely. Finally, Ziegler replaced the basin over the thing's head and stepped away.

Panting and out of breath, Carl walked across the room, picked the deputy's gun off the floor, and stuck it into his waistband. He took the cable ties from his back pocket and handed some to the other men. He secured Deputy Rainey's hands together while Burt and Ziegler went to work on Abe, fastening the man directly to the oval openings in the plank.

"What the hell was that?" Burt's voice cracked.

"He was going to kill you." Ziegler fought to control his breathing. "That wasn't your deputy. Did you see him?"

Carl had seen it and knew Ziegler was right. Somehow, the thing on the table had taken control of Deputy Rainey and had almost killed him. *What in the hell are we dealing with here?*

CHAPTER 31

Night fell an hour after the storm started. The sound of thunder and the drone of the constant downpour helped suppress most of the screams that would have otherwise alerted the citizens of Garrett Grove. Tommy Negal had returned home late Sunday afternoon after spending most of the day in the foothills' woods with his friend Jeff Campbell. Both boys had gone to bed early, feeling feverish and achy; neither had made it to school. Tommy had stayed in bed ... listening. A gnawing voice spoke from within him; he was unaware as it ransacked his consciousness. It took what it needed, and then ... it left a little something in return. Everything that Tommy knew, every thought he possessed was sorted and filed away.

It was a gatherer, a consumer, a collector. A reaper of emotions and flesh. Ojanox was the last word on the boy-creature's lips. It was as good as any name it had been called in the past. It didn't matter what they called it. It was power, it was thought, and it was eternal. It had dominated this rock since the dawn of time. Now, there was so much more to feed on, knowledge to consume, fear to devour, and desire to satiate its hunger. There was so much food!

Tommy lifted his head in the darkness of his bedroom with a mind full of thoughts no longer his own. He got to his feet, leaving most of his hair on his pillow, and entered the hallway. The visitor watched through his eyes as he descended the stairs and walked into the room where his parents sat with their backs to him.

The boy lifted his head and opened his mouth, allowing the ear-cracking shriek to escape from his throat. Sarah and Otto Negal turned to find their son's black eyes fixated on them ... then they noticed his teeth.

Sarah tried to scream but was silenced when Tommy sprang like a panther onto her. He buried his face into the woman's neck and bit down. Sarah's eyes rolled back in her head as the child ripped a mouthful of flesh from her throat. Her arms flailed for a second, then fell limp at her side.

Otto was helpless to react and stared for far too long. Finally, he lunged at the boy and attempted to pry him off his wife. Tommy jumped up, landed on all fours, and snarled at his father with Sarah's blood covering his lips. Then he threw his head back and howled through a mouthful of tiny razor-sharp teeth. Otto managed only a feeble moan before Tommy hushed him for good. The child tore into his father like a chainsaw while the voice in his head screamed with pleasure. None of the neighbors on the block heard a sound; what little noise there was had been masked by the storm.

The area behind Wilson's Diner tended to flood when it rained. Roger, the dishwasher, ran into the heavy downpour with a bag of garbage in each hand. He splashed through a large puddle, soaking his foot all the way to the ankle. The entire lot was several inches deep, and by the time he made it to the dumpster, he was soaked from head to toe. He tossed the trash and allowed the metal lid to crash back into place. A sudden blur leapt from the shadows and onto the dumpster, causing Roger to jump backward. At first, he thought it was Scraps, the alley cat that always hung around, but he knew cats hated water and he dismissed the idea. Then he noticed the size of the figure before him, which wasn't any cat. This thing was huge.

Stumbling backward, he tripped as the shadow launched itself into the air and landed in front of him. It was dark and impossible to make out any of the its features, but it was obvious that it was a person. A strangled cry escaped his lips as the figure crawled towards him. Crouching like a gargoyle, it hobbled closer on its spindly arms and legs, then Roger noticed the bra and panties. It took another step forward, and Roger could see that it was a woman and she was practically naked. *Dear God.* He recognized her. *It's Mandy!* Only she had changed.

The waitress had lost almost all her hair, and her body looked as if it had withered away. Her bones were visible beneath her tight skin, which looked almost grey in the darkness of the storm. Mandy crab-walked across the blacktop at full speed and charged toward Roger. He turned and sprinted through the puddles toward the door but was stopped in his tracks when a tidal wave of rainwater erupted in front of him. A second figure splashed down, lowered its head, and sized him up. This one looked like Mandy's roommate, the nurse at the medical center, but not exactly. Something awful had happened to her as well.

Roger backed away, and the creature closed in on him, propelling itself forward like a spider. *What in the name of God?* He blinked against the driving rain and struggled to focus on the impossible vision. An extra set of arms protruded from the woman's ribcage. Only they didn't look much like arms. The appendages were black and hairy, as if she really was turning into some type of spider.

The air was knocked out of him as Mandy landed on his back and drove him to the pavement. Her taloned fingers sank into his skin as Roger landed face first in the dirty water. Struggling to breathe, he fought to shake the girl off him, but the other one was on him before he could do a thing. He choked on a mouthful of dirty water while the girls held him down and ripped into him. They consumed pieces of his flesh and then dug into his head to feast on the good parts. Before he surrendered, Mandy lowered her awful mouth to his ear and spoke in a gravelly voice, just loud enough to be heard above the pounding rain. *"See anything you like?"*

Jeff Campbell discovered his mother and father preparing dinner in the kitchen and decided to share something with them. It was the very same something that Tommy Negal had shared with his own mom and dad. One thing was certain, neither of the boys or their parents would ever have to worry about such menial diversions as cooking, going to school, or watching TV ever again. When Jeff was finished, he left the house and scurried across the street to where his classmate Mike Barnes lived. The light was on in the boy's second-floor bedroom. Jeff crouched in the driveway, then using the newly developed muscles in his lower legs, he propelled himself ten feet into the air and landed on the garage roof. He clawed his way up the ridgeline to the boy's window and peered inside to find Mike seated at his desk doing his homework; a Batman comic sat on his opened textbook.

Mike jumped at the sudden noise. It wasn't much more than a tap against the window, but he had been engrossed in his comic and not expecting it. He looked up from his desk and was met only by his reflection against the darkened pane. *Just the storm.* He leaned back in his chair and turned the page. The second time it happened, Mike was a bit more prepared for the faint clicking at the glass, as if the wind had kicked some debris and tossed it against the house.

Click ... Click ... Click

It happened again, sounding like someone throwing pebbles.

Click ... Click ... Click

Mike set the comic book aside and got up from his desk. He walked to the window and strained to look through the darkness and pouring rain. He pressed his face against the glass.

Click ... Click ... Click

Mike unlatched the lock and lifted the lower pane. He squinted and drew in closer to the screen to get a better look. Then he saw it. Just the outline at first. There was something outside on the roof. *Oh, my Go—*

The thought was silenced in a heartbeat. Jeff tore through the screen and seized Mike by the head, his hands clamped around his friend's neck, and ripped into his skin. He yanked the boy out of his room and pulled him into the night as if he weighed no more than a throw pillow. Mike landed on the wet shingles and began to slide down the slick incline of the roof. Before he could think, Jeff was on top of him, and they were both falling. By the time they hit the driveway, every thought the child ever had was consumed and added to the collective. Now it knew everything about the one called Mike. It knew his sister's name was Melissa. It knew that Melissa was downstairs. It also knew that the back door unlocked.

The creature that had once gone by the name of Robert Boyle waited outside, watching the house. It crept on all fours like a massive beetle, making its way to the side of the garage. This place ... Scream in the Dark. It drew upon the catalogue of memories and came to a vision of the two children working together, building. Troy ... It had come close to taking the boy earlier in the graveyard and had tasted the child's thoughts. Now, it craved to possess him, to add the one called Troy to its collection. It yearned to savor his fear. Nothing satisfied its hunger like fear.

A blinding light illuminated the creature where it hid; it quickly retreated behind the building. The vehicle stopped, and a man exited. It was the one called Fischer, the boy's father. As the man approached, the creature inched slowly from the shadows to the edge of the house. It made its way closer, ready to pounce, ready to feed. Lightning flashed, casting a brilliant aura, momentarily freezing it in its tracks. It no longer looked anything like Robert Boyle, the boy it had once been. Its features now far more primal, hunched and reptilian; its dark eyes seeing everything in the darkness as the man entered the house. It waited ... it watched ... it hungered ... Troyeeee.

Father Kieran sat in the kitchen of the rectory with a glass of wine in front of him and the good book opened to the Revelations of John. He read from the Scripture every day and typically favored the Gospels for his after-dinner meditation. However, tonight he believed that one of John's other books was a bit more fitting.

The shadows in the woods had stopped moving shortly before daybreak, just as Kieran knew they would. *For the light is the Lord's domain; there is no evil that can prevail in the light.* But now that the storm had arrived and the sun had set, the creatures were traveling once again. Some of their numbers walked much like humans, upright and on two legs. But there were many that didn't resemble anything even remotely human. They leaped from shadow to shadow, traveling swiftly on all fours like beasts. *They are Satan's Imps*; he knew it to be true. *The children of the Dark One have come to Garrett Grove to test the flock.* He prayed for guidance and waited for a reply. His only answer was to immerse himself in the word of the Lord.

"And I saw, coming out of the mouth of the dragon and out of the mouth of the beast and out of the mouth of the false prophet, three unclean spirits like frogs."

Father Kieran blessed himself. He had witnessed these very creatures last night as he watched from behind the curtains of his bedroom window. *Dear Lord, tell me what you would have of me.* He made the sign of the cross and continued reading.

"And they assembled them at the place that in Hebrew is called Armageddon."

There was a sudden noise at the back door, causing Kieran to jump. His breath stopped, causing his lungs to tighten and clench within his chest. It sounded like something significant had fallen outside, just beyond the threshold. Father Kieran waited and stared at the doorknob, expecting it to turn at any moment and the beasts to burst through. He listened with an icy sweat breaking on his brow and the book trembling within his grasp. Again, just over the sound of the wind, he heard a rustle. And then the voice of someone outside.

"Help."

It was too soft and weak to be real, but Kieran was certain he had heard it.

"Thy will be done, Lord," he said as he got up from the table and approached the door. He held his breath, reached out, and took the handle in his hand. Kieran pulled it inward and froze. He gasped at the sight of what lay before him.

"Help me, Father."

He rushed into the night without concern for his own safety. "Dear Lord, what happened, my child?" he asked.

Dr. Stephanie Thompson arrived home late from work, thanks to an exciting first day at the DuCain excavation. Her daughter and sister had dinner ready and waiting. Together, they sat on the floor eating tuna sandwiches and drinking Kool-Aid, with a houseful of unpacked boxes and plastic-wrapped furniture towering around them. Peanuts performed her doggy-duty to the letter, scarfing up even the tiniest of crumbs that happened to fall to the floor, while Janis told her mom everything about her first day at the new school and the cool friends she had made.

"You already have new friends?" Stephanie set her sandwich down and leaned forward. "That was quick. Tell me about them. What are their names?"

"Troy and Wendy. They came over after school. They want me to see the haunted house that Troy made in his garage. It's called Scream in the Dark, and it's supposed to be really scary. Wendy and Troy are boyfriend and girlfriend, and they have another friend named Rob, but he wasn't in school today. We're all gonna go out trick-or-treating ... if that's okay."

Stephanie felt her smile grow wider by the second as Janis relived her entire day without taking a single breath. *Is that what I sound like?* She knew that she did but imagined most people didn't find it quite as adorable on her as when it came out of a ten-year-old. Janis was the spitting image of her mother, just a miniature-sized version. In fact, all three women who sat together looked incredibly similar, with the same wavy blonde hair hanging in long ringlets past their shoulders and the same exact shade of pale blue eyes. "You had a big day. Did you have any time for school, or was it just one big party?"

"Oh no, we got to hear about the guy Tolkien, who wrote a book called *The Hobbit*. Miss Walsh said she was going to start reading it to us." Janis took a large gulp of the red Kool-Aid and continued. "Oh! I showed Troy and Wendy the arrowheads you gave me and the little teeth from Cokia."

"Cahokia, sweetie," she said.

"Cahokia, and Wendy said that they were from an Ojanox."

"Where did she come up with a name like that?" Lynn asked.

"Troy's mom told them a story at the party about a monster that only comes out at Halloween. It hides all year long and only comes out in the fall; it's called the Ojanox."

"Well, honey, no one really knows what those teeth belong to, but I'm pretty sure there's no such thing as an Ojanox. I bet it was a good story, though." Stephanie brushed a long curl of Janis's hair and tucked it behind the girl's ear.

"Yeah, I know." Janis took a bite of her sandwich.

"I was telling the movers where to put the couch," Lynn said. "Then here comes little Miss Social Butterfly walking up the street with her two friends. I gave them milk and cookies and let Janis show off her toys."

Stephanie smiled and tossed a piece of crust to the dog. "You said Troy and Wendy are boyfriend and girlfriend? I hope you aren't thinking about things like boyfriends yet. You're only in fourth grade, and you know how I feel about that."

"I know, Mom. Don't worry. The boys at school are dorks. They were all staring and acting dumb because I have boobs."

Stephanie nearly choked on her sandwich, and Lynn just escaped spitting Kool-Aid through her nose. The girls shared a very open dialog in the household, and Janis's early development had been a topic of many conversations.

"Yes, baby. Boys can be very immature. They are two years behind you when it comes to maturity. They can't help it, though; they don't know any better."

"Except Troy. He's different than the other boys." Stephanie gave Lynn an apprehensive look as Janis continued. "We were talking, and I asked him why all the boys were acting so weird."

"You did? Well, what did he say?"

"At first, he got really embarrassed, but me and Wendy kept asking him, and finally, he said, 'They're all acting stupid because of your boobs. They've never seen a girl in class with boobs, and they don't know how to act.'"

Stephanie felt like her eyes might pop out. She worked to control her expression for several seconds before she started speaking again. "He did? It sounds like Troy is different, all right. I'd like to meet Troy and Wendy next time you guys get together."

"Okay. Troy's going to ask his parents if me and Wendy could come over and see Scream in the Dark before he takes it down. Maybe you could meet him them?"

"Wendy and I." Stephanie said. "And what can you tell me about your friends' parents, anything?"

"I'm not sure about Wendy's parents, but I know Troy's mom tells scary Halloween stories and his dad works at the quarry."

Stephanie paused again; she hadn't told her daughter that her current assignment had taken her to the quarry. "What are your friends' last names?"

"Wendy Sirocka and Troy Fischer."

Stephanie's cheeks hurt from smiling so much. It had truly been a day for surprises. Troy was Don Fisher's son. *I bet Troy is different than most boys. Like father, like son, I guess.*

CHAPTER 32

The meat wagon pulled up to the rear entrance of the medical center with Sheriff Primrose, Dr. Ziegler, and Burt Lively crowded together in the front seat. In the back was something that could no longer be described as Abe Gorman, tethered to the wooden stretcher, and Deputy David Rainey, who lay bound and unconscious on the floor.

Carl backed the van up to the loading dock. He turned off the engine and scanned the area for activity. "Looks like the coast is clear."

"Okay," Ziegler said, grabbing the door handle. "I'll check inside. If I'm not back right away, just hold tight."

"Hey, Doc." Carl grabbed his arm. "You might want to take off the body armor first."

Ziegler looked down at the vest and the rest of the armor he still wore and shook his head. He removed the protective gear and discarded it onto the floor. Then he exited the van and let himself in through the back service entrance of the medical center.

Carl and Burt watched the man enter the building and offered each other a tentative look. The parking lot was quiet ... too quiet for Carl's liking. And sitting there in the dark made him feel more like a criminal than the town's sheriff, even though it wasn't unusual for the meat wagon to be parked in the loading area, where it was used to transport bodies.

"How do you suppose we're going to get this thing in there without drawing attention?" Burt asked, removing his vest. Carl shrugged and continued to scan their surroundings. They stripped off the rest of the riot gear and waited till the back door swung open and Dr. Ziegler stepped outside. The man gave them the *all clear* sign and waved to them.

"Here we go," Carl said, tapping his fingers against the steering wheel. "Showtime."

They exited the vehicle and met the doctor at the rear of the van. Burt opened the back door, and together, he and Carl removed the stretcher, leaving the unconscious deputy lying on the floor. Then Dr. Ziegler led them inside to a gurney he had placed near the entrance. They set the stretcher down, and Dr. Ziegler covered Abe with a large sheet that almost made him look like just another patient—almost.

The men wheeled the gurney down the hall with Ziegler leading the way, first taking a right down an adjacent corridor and then following the doctor to the left. They arrived at a large steel door without running into a single staff member. Ziegler ushered them in and turned the lights on in a small reception area. They quickly maneuvered the gurney into the room, and the doctor closed the door behind them.

"That went well." Sweat beaded on the doctor's forehead. "Follow me."

Ziegler led them through the only other door in the reception area. They entered a room that looked to Carl like something straight out of a *Star Trek* episode. He had never seen an MRI machine before or even heard of one. It was ominous and threatening, a beast of a mechanism that took up the entire room. A massive cylinder that resembled a giant torpedo tube fixed with keypads and dials surrounded a flat table where the patient was intended to lay.

"Is he secured enough for this thing, Doc?" Carl asked.

"It will have to do." Ziegler check the straps and bindings that secured Abe to the wooden plank. "Doesn't look like he's able to move much, to me. Hopefully, this will give us some answers."

"If you say so, Doc." Burt stared at the thing on the stretcher. "But I got a feeling it's too late for that."

They transferred the wooden plank onto the table of the machine. Carl rechecked the cable ties and nodded to Ziegler, satisfied that the man was bound securely. The leather strap around Abe's face, the bindings, and ties all appeared to be doing the job. Carl felt reasonably confident they would hold and were almost safe enough to remove the basin that still covered the face—almost.

Ziegler told them it would take about twenty minutes for the imaging to register. Shortly after that, they would see the results. Hopefully, the MRI machine would reveal much about the changes that had occurred in the man's organs and soft tissue.

"If you'll both follow me." Ziegler pointed to an adjacent room with a large glass window that resembled a recording studio.

He led them through a thick, padded door into the next room. Carl was the last man to leave the chamber; he grabbed the basin covering Abe's face and wheeled the metal gurney into the room. The overhead light came on automatically, revealing a tight space that looked even more like the inside of a spaceship than the chamber itself. A large instrument panel took up the area in front of a window overlooking the machine. A sea of dials and buttons covered the entire back wall of the room. Carl examined the staggering amount of equipment packed into the cramped quarters and gasped. *This shit probably costs more than every house on my block combined.*

"Would ya look at all this stuff. Do you know how to operate this thing, Doc?" Burt asked.

"I've got a pretty good idea. I guess we're about to find out. Besides, once it's on, it does all the work itself." Dr. Ziegler flipped a large switch on a circuit panel and proceeded to turn on the smaller sub-circuits. Lights began to flash across the board and on the instruments covering the back wall. The entire room began to buzz with electricity as Ziegler turned a large dial on the board and depressed a button beneath it. The MRI machine in the adjacent room came to life; small yellow lights flashed on a panel near the top of the cylinder. The sound of a churning motor could be heard above the noise of the other instruments.

Ziegler turned another dial, and the table retracted into the heart of the cylinder. Abe's body was swallowed by the circumference of the imaging system. The only parts of the man that remained visible were his shoes.

The intensity of the motor grew louder as the instrument cycled to operate. Carl and Burt exchanged an uneasy look and waited for the process to begin. The noise the machine made was unnerving. From inside the room, a loud, sporadic thudding began. There was a jarring buzz, followed by more of the thunderous thudding.

"Is it supposed to do that?" Carl asked, watching for any movement from within the chamber.

"It's fine. We just have to wait. About twenty or so minutes." Dr. Ziegler exhaled and wiped his brow.

A horrifying shriek erupted from the chamber, loud enough to drown out the thudding of the instruments and cause each man to jump. The thing inside the machine screamed in anguish.

"What the hell is going on?" Burt shouted.

Ziegler pressed his face to the window to get a better look. Abe began to buck and twist violently inside the cylinder. The man shook with such great force that the stretcher itself began to shudder against the table. The next sound that erupted from the man sliced through the air like a lance and threatened to pop the soft membranes of their eardrums. Dr. Ziegler lunged for the instrument panel and proceeded to power down the machine. Carl saw what was happening inside the chamber and stopped the doctor before he could.

"Don't do that. You need to see this!"

Ziegler looked up through the glass to see what the sheriff was talking about and immediately stopped what he was doing. A dark cloud had begun to permeate the inside of the chamber. It rose from Abe's body and appeared as if it was seeping out of his pores. The man continued to struggle against his restraints, shrieking and howling, as the cloud grew thicker and took on more density.

"For fuck's sake!" Burt cried, but no one could hear him over the tormented wail of the thing inside the MRI machine.

The stretcher crashed against the table. The dark mass that had formed above the body darted forward and was halted as if it had hit a barrier. Half a second later, it was pulled backward into the heart of the machine. Carl focused on the strange cloud; it looked like it was attempting to escape from the chamber. But the smoke was unable to breach the outer edge of the cylinder. Abe howled with such insane intensity, Carl was certain the man had shredded his vocal cords. Then the cloud folded in on itself, collapsed, and vanished. The body of the man inside the chamber stopped moving.

Carl, Burt, and Dr. Ziegler stared through the glass, trying to see where the strange substance had gone. There was no sign of it anywhere. "I think it's dead," Burt said.

Ziegler cycled down the machine and retracted the table from the chamber. He turned off the main power at the control board, which resulted in a most unnerving silence. The body on the stretcher lay motionless. A dark black fluid ran from its eyes and ears.

"Any idea what that was, Dr. Ziegler?" Carl could still hear the sound of the man's screams echoing in his ears.

"Whatever it was, it's also in the children." Burt's voice cracked. "That's your poison right there. That machine just sucked the infection out of Abe and killed him in the process."

Ziegler opened the door to the imaging chamber and walked in to inspect the body. Carl followed. They approached the side of the table with Burt bringing up the rear. Abe was dead ... for good this time. A tar-like fluid ran from his open orifices and pooled on the table beneath his head. Ziegler examined the man's eyes to find their original shade had returned. He checked for a pulse, looked at his watch, and recorded the time of death. "Eight fifteen."

"I suggest we get this body out of here and go check on my deputy. Then we can discuss just what we think we saw here tonight." Carl looked at Burt and then at Ziegler to see if they had anything to add. No one did. "Okay then, let's get out of here." They transferred the body to the gurney and let themselves out the way they had come in. Carl didn't feel like they needed to operate in secrecy anymore. Now they really were just transporting a dead body.

Deputy Rainey regained consciousness sometime later. He held an ice pack to the side of his head but could recall little of what happened. Tilting his head back, he took a slow pull from the bottle of scotch. "I don't remember any of that," he said.

The four men gathered in the lab, recounting the night's events. The dissected corpse of Felix Castillo lay just a few feet away; next to it rested a black body bag containing Abe Gorman, the man who had once driven the very vehicle he had been transported in.

"You pointed your gun at the sheriff," Burt said. "You were going to kill him."

"Try to remember, son." Carl sat across from him, holding his hat in his hands. "We were getting ready to move Abe, then something happened. What can you tell me?"

"I'm not sure." Rainey squinted. "I remember an itch. You know, like the kind you get in the back of the throat. Except, it was in my head. I know it sounds crazy."

Carl leaned back. "Like a headache or something like that?"

"Not exactly." The deputy paused and took another sip. He stared at the floor in front of him as if the answers might be lying there. "I remember someone calling my name. Next thing I know, I woke up in the van."

"You discharged your weapon." Carl pointed to the bullet hole in the freezer door.

"I-I would never try to hurt you." The deputy's voice wavered, and he appeared on the verge of tears. "I'm sorry, Sheriff."

"I forgive you, son," Carl told him. "In fact, I don't believe it was you who tried to kill me tonight. I think that thing got in your head and made you do it."

"Why would it only affect him?" Burt started to pace the floor.

"Well," Ziegler said, "I could think of several possible explanations. Now, it didn't happen until the sheriff took the basin off its head. And when he did, the deputy was looking right at it. That's when he started acting crazy."

"That's right!" Rainey shouted. "I looked up, and it was staring right at me. That's when I heard someone call my name."

Ziegler nodded. "Also, the deputy was the only man who was armed, other than you, Sheriff. It saw you as a threat. You're the one who killed Castillo, after all."

"Well, Doc." Carl stood up. "Why wouldn't it just jump into my head, make me shoot myself or something?"

"Not sure; it's just a theory, really. But I'm guessing you're not easily influenced. No offense, Deputy."

"Yeah, he's right about that, Carl," Burt said. "That thing probably got a taste of your sour ass and spit you back out."

Carl cracked a half smile and met the doctor's stare. "You need to get in contact with Dr. Malcolm immediately. If he's with the children, he is in way over his head. We've seen how it spreads, and if even one of those things got out ... Christ, if that truck hadn't come along and flattened Felix Castillo, there's no telling how many we'd be dealing with right now."

"That's what worries me, Sheriff," Ziegler said. "Castillo disappeared a full day before that truck hit him. What if he got to someone already?"

The sudden hush that fell over the men was broken by a blast of static from the radio on Carl's hip. Andrea's voice crackled through the tiny speaker: "Dispatch to Sheriff Primrose. Come in, Sheriff Primrose."

Carl's gut clenched as he reached for the radio. The other men stared at him with the same look of apprehension on their faces.

"Go ahead, Andrea."

"Sheriff, we have a few situations. There's a house fire at Sixteen Poplar, the Barnes residence. Also, Deputy Forsyth never made it in. I called

Deputy Kovach to cover for him, but there's no answer at Forsyth's house, and I can't seem to get in touch with him."

"I'm on my way. You said Sixteen Poplar?"

"10-4 Sheriff. Sixteen Poplar. Oh, one other thing." Carl braced himself. "The Tobin boys still haven't come home. Alice is really starting to worry."

"Roger that, Andrea. Deputy Rainey is with me, and we're on our way. Over and out." Carl replaced the radio to his hip and started to move. "Doc, I need you to get in touch with Dr. Malcolm as fast as possible." He turned to Burt. "I want you to burn these bodies, pronto."

"Abe too? Wouldn't his family—" Burt stopped in mid-sentence as if he thought better of what he was about to say. "Yeah ... it would probably be best if no one saw them. I'll take care of it right away. Oh ... Carl?"

"Yeah?"

"Be careful out there, for Christ's sake."

Carl put his hat on and nodded to his friend. He bent down to adjust his sock and came up with a small-caliber pistol in his hand. He handed it to the coroner. "You too, old man." He left the office with Deputy Rainey at his heels.

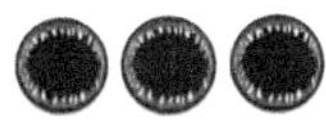

Donald Fischer walked through the front door to find Lois and Troy sitting at the kitchen table. He could tell right away that something was wrong, something far more serious than him being two hours late for dinner ... again. Tear stains were visible on Troy's cheeks, and his eyes were bloodshot. However, Lois's eyes told a completely different story, one that Donald was certain he didn't want to hear.

"What happened?" He rushed up the stairs and into the kitchen.

Troy lifted his head to his mother but didn't say a word. Lois kissed him on the cheek and then turned to Don. "We had a little scare this afternoon. Troy was almost hit by a car."

"What?" Don raised his voice. "Didn't you look both ways?"

"I-I guess not." Troy took a ragged breath and wiped his face. "I cut through the graveyard on my way home."

"You did what!? We talked about this. You know I don't want you guys walking through there, even if it is a shortcut." Donald felt Lois's laser-bolt stare sear into him from across the room and decided on a different approach. "Why were you guys walking through the graveyard?"

"It was just me." Troy's voice shook as he spoke. "I went to a friend's house after school and cut through the graveyard on the way home. There was something in there ... following me, like an animal or something. Th-then ... I heard them, and they started chasing me. I ran, Dad, but they were so fast, and-and-I don't know. I was so scared; I ran into the street, and I guess I didn't look." By the time Troy finished telling the story, a stream of fresh tears coursed down his face.

Don got down on one knee and hugged his son. He looked up at Lois and lifted his brows. She shrugged her shoulders in reply; apparently, she didn't know what to make of Troy's story either.

"Hey, kiddo." Don released him. "What do you think it was?"

"I don't know, Dad. I-I didn't get a good look." His tears ebbed to a trickle.

"Okay, kiddo." Don knew it wouldn't help any to interrogate his son. "Just promise me you'll stay out of the graveyard from now on. Okay?"

"I swear. I'll never go in there again."

"Say, I got some news you might think is cool." Don figured he'd try changing the subject. "We were blasting on the north face last week, and we discovered an old cave."

Troy's eyes widened. "Really, was there anything inside it?"

Lois went to the oven, removed a plate of left-over roast beef and pota-toes, and set it on the table for Don.

"That's why I didn't say anything before." Don nodded to Lois. "In fact, there are *a lot* of artifacts in there. I couldn't tell you because we were waiting for the archeologists from the Museum of Natural History to arrive."

"That's Janis's mom! I was at her house today." Troy's face brightened a full shade.

"You mean Dr. Thompson?" Don asked.

"Yeah! Wow, Dad, you should see all the arrowheads and teeth she gave Janis. They're so cool."

Lois cut in. "Dr. Thompson from the museum is *Janis's* mother, and she is working at your job?"

"Well, it isn't *exactly* my job. It's a DuCain job, and the museum is working in the cave. It's my responsibility to make sure they don't get in the way so everyone else can get back to work."

"What's in the cave, Dad? Come on." Troy fidgeted in his chair; he appeared to be feeling much better.

"You wouldn't even believe it. Everything looks as if it could have been left there only a few years ago, except for the bones, of course."

"There's bones?"

"Oh yeah, lots of them, human and animal. There are murals on the walls too. So colorful and vivid. But you know what's really amazing? The entire cave is comprised of lodestone, which is another name for magnetite. It's a magnetic iron ore used to make magnets. The Lenape tribe made weapons out of it. They sanded the stone into these little balls, like the kind you'd use in a slingshot or a musket."

"That's radical. You don't think they would let you take us up there, do you?"

"I doubt they'd let anyone in who doesn't work for the museum, not until they finish what they need to do first. They're still taking pictures and making a list of everything in there."

"And you were in the cave while they were doing all of this?" Lois asked.

"Well, yeah. Mr. DuCain wants me to represent the company and make sure his interests are considered. I am the go-to guy for the museum personnel," he boasted and messed Troy's hair.

Lois folded her arms as Don began to eat his dinner. "You're working with Dr. Thompson then, in the cave?"

He took a bite of the roast beef. "Uh-huh, but I tell you what I'll do. I'll tell the doctor that you're interested in artifacts and see what she says. Who knows, maybe she'll let you and your friends see the pictures. I don't think it hurts that you're friends with her daughter." He shoved another forkful into his mouth and grinned at Lois.

She turned her back and walked to the fridge.

"Want some pudding, kiddo?" she asked.

"Yes, please." Troy smiled. "Do you think I could wait a couple days before I tear down Scream in the Dark? I know you need the garage back, but Janis wants to see it, and I was hoping she and Wendy could come over so I could show it off one last time."

Lois and Don exchanged a look and nodded to one another. They had always been good at reading each other, even though they weren't all that good at talking.

"Your mom and I will discuss it. Okay?" Don leaned over his plate, a bit more curious than a moment ago. "*Both* of your friends are girls, Wendy and Janis?" *When the hell did this happen?* Troy hadn't expressed an interest in girls yet, not that he knew of.

"Yeah," Troy squirmed a little more, "but it's cool. As soon as Rob gets better, I won't be so outnumbered. It's really tough hanging out with two of them."

"You don't say?" Don coughed and almost spit his dinner onto the table. He looked up at Lois again. "How do you mean?"

"I dunno. You really got to think about what you say. It's easy to look stupid. It's like they're testing you all the time … ya know?"

Lois rubbed her son's head and placed a can of pudding in front of him. Donald swallowed and leaned in closer. "Get used to it," he whispered. "It's gonna be like that for the rest of your life."

Troy picked up his spoon and dug in. "Oh man! That sounds exhausting."

"It is, kiddo, it is."

Lois turned toward the sink and ran the tap. She lifted the window an inch and started to wash the dishes. It had finally stopped raining, but occasional sizzles of lightning continued to light up the sky. She smiled and listened to the Fischer men talk about the great plague that had suffered the male species for centuries, the great scourge of women.

CHAPTER 33

Garrett Grove's volunteer fire department responded to the house fire at Sixteen Poplar. Both the ladder truck and the pump were at the scene when Carl and Deputy Rainey arrived to see the billows of thick grey smoke still lifting into the air. The entire block was a beehive of activity. Firefighters continued to fight the blaze from every angle, and it looked like they had it under control. The sheriff exited the cruiser and spotted Deputy Kovach, who had taken point on crowd control by securing the perimeter and keeping the on-lookers at bay. Carl made his way across the street and approached him.

"We couldn't get inside. The entire place was lit up by the time we got here. Neighbors called it in." Deputy Kovach had soot marks on his cheeks and hands. "No sign of the family. Christ, I hope they weren't inside."

"Andrea said this is the Barnes residence." Carl scanned the gathering crowd. "Any of the neighbors see or know anything?"

"There isn't anyone home across the street," Deputy Kovach checked his notepad, "the Campbell residence. The other neighbors seem to think the Barnes family was probably home at the time."

"All right. Well, see what you can find out from the other neighbors. Deputy Rainey!" Carl shouted. "Give Kovach a hand questioning the crowd." Carl walked toward the house and entered the driveway of Sixteen Poplar. Firemen were in the process of soaking what remained of the smoldering structure, and the last of the flames appeared to have died out. However, radiating heat still poured off the burnt timbers, and the smell of charred, waterlogged wood filled the air. Carl surveyed the damage from where he stood and prayed that no one had been home at the time. He walked up the drive, stopping at the two cars parked near the garage, and knew there was little chance of that. His stomach somersaulted with the realization that the Barnes family had more than likely been home when the fire started. He feared there would be some grizzly discoveries once the smoke cleared.

He was alerted by the commotion as two firemen kicked in the front door and entered the house. They dragged a hose from the pump truck and sprayed the interior as they walked inside.

Carl checked the vehicles to find nothing out of the ordinary. He then followed the driveway to the garage, where a litter of broken glass peppered the asphalt. He inspected the windows and noticed that all the panes on the garage door were still intact. Wondering where it had come from, he backed up and looked on the roof. The reflection of the streetlight glinted as if it were caught in a thousand tiny mirrors. Slivers of broken glass spread out across the wet shingles in a wide pattern. Carl strained to see the single window on the gable side of the house. It had been smashed; the torn screen hung from the frame along with a portion of the window itself. It looked like it had blown outward or something had jumped through it.

Maybe someone got out after all. But there was no sign of survivors, at least not in front of the house. *Better check out back.*

"Hey," he called to the group of firemen gathered on the lawn. "Did you guys knock that window out?"

An extra-large fireman in full protective gear removed his helmet and face mask, revealing a boyish face and thick handlebar moustache. It was Bob Jones, the chief; Carl knew him well and genuinely liked the giant man. "Howdy, Carl. We haven't been up there yet."

"Your men didn't break that window, Bob?"

"Wasn't us. Maybe someone got out."

"Okay, thanks." Carl left Bob and the rest of the crew to finish their work and made his way to the back of the house. He pulled a small flashlight from his belt and inspected the lawn as he proceeded. The grass hadn't been disturbed, and there was no broken glass as far as he could tell. He continued around the house until he came to the back screen door.

It hung open with the top hinge ripped off. Carl approached the entrance and stopped. It was still too hot to enter without proper protection; he would have to wait for the place to cool down before he could go in tomorrow with the fire inspector and look around. He backed away from the door and bumped into a stone statue set on the top steps. Turning around, he cast his light onto the small figure and froze. Carl leaned in closer. Something on the stone surface shimmered in the beam. He touched the circular stain and noticed it was still sticky. He examined his fingers in the light. *Blood ...* A small drop had come to rest on the statue. Someone had either come out of the house bleeding or they had gone in that way. Carl's gut told him what he already suspected. They weren't going to find the Barnes family inside the house after all. In fact, no one was going to find them, and if they did, they were going to wish they hadn't. Felix had infected at least one person before getting hit by that truck. If he had walked out of that morgue at three on Sunday afternoon and hadn't been found until five the following morning, he had been out there for fourteen hours. *Fourteen hours ... Jesus Christ!* If they were lucky, Felix had only infected one or two and not dozens. At the moment, Carl Primrose wasn't feeling very lucky at all.

The Thompson family continued to share their day's experiences with one another. Stephanie was more than thrilled that Janis had gotten on so well and prayed they would be able to stick around long enough for her daughter to finish out the school year in Garrett Grove. Lord knew they'd been bouncing around a lot lately. She hated uprooting the family repeatedly, but that was the job and she had to go where the museum sent her.

They talked and they laughed until it had gotten late. Stephanie knew tomorrow would be a busy day for all of them and told Janis it was time to wash up. The girl was still excited but tired from an eventful day; she kissed both her mother and aunt goodnight and went off to bed. Stephanie said she was exhausted as well and went to her room once she and Lynn finished cleaning up the remnants from the meal.

However, she hadn't been as tired as she let on; there was something she had been curious about since the afternoon. Her bedroom was still littered with unpacked boxes, and after raking through a few of them, she found the one she was looking for. Cracking the packing tape and digging through the contents, Stephanie came across the large binder. She opened it and flipped to the picture on the first page. It showed a cave painting, far more primitive than the murals at the DuCain site. The hands that created the art belonged to a race that had vanished long before the Lenape had crafted their own designs. Still, the subject matter was oddly familiar.

The picture revealed a dark-skinned woman being tended to by the members of her clan; she appeared to be suffering or sick as the healers of her tribe treated her. The photograph on the opposite side of the page showed a secondary scene. The same dark-skinned woman had undergone some type of trauma. Her features had transformed into something grotesque and inhuman. She looked as if she had de-evolved into something primitive. This was evident by how she chased after her healers on all fours. And although it wasn't an exact replica of the murals they had seen today, the likeness was uncanny. Tiny pointed teeth lined the woman's mouth, similar to the ones depicted in the murals at the DuCain site. The skulls that Stephanie's team had found today also contained mouthfuls of those same awful teeth. She focused closer on the picture. As the mutated woman pursued her healers, a strange shadow appeared to follow her. It looked as if it originated from her body, as if she was expelling it.

Stephanie flipped to another set of pages titled "Cahokia." There were photos and newspaper clippings that dated back to the 1920s. They showed a massive excavation that had taken place. The Cahokia civilization was one of the countless unexplained mysteries that archeologists loved to speculate on. Stephanie's father had been fascinated with America's forgotten city and devoted much of his life's work to finding an answer to the strange disappearance. Stephanie followed in his footsteps and wrote the thesis for her doctorate about the archaeological evidence found at the colony's site.

There were several working theories as to what led to the disappearance of nearly 40,000 people. Cahokia was a thriving centralized hub of religion and politics by the year 1000. It also went by the name The City of the Sun and, by all rights, could be considered a kingdom. It had been the largest

North American civilization, spanning from the Great Lakes and covering much of the southeastern region of North America. Some historians believed environmental impact played a major role in the disappearance of the tribe. Evidence of previous floods and periods of drought could possibly explain a mass exodus, but that evidence was inconclusive. Still, something had occurred near the year 1200 that started a catastrophic chain of events. Lack of resources, including food and wildlife, led the nation into war and an increase in ritualistic sacrifices, which ultimately resulted in the extinction of the people. By 1250, Cahokia had fallen, and by the 14th century, the great nation was nothing but a memory.

But Stephanie didn't subscribe to any of those theories and neither had her father. They both believed that the correlation of the die-off in the area's wildlife revealed more about the period than anything else. The evidence indicated that nearly all biological life had disappeared in the area somewhere between the years 1200 and 1300. And there had been some valuable clues left behind, clues that only senior members of the dig team had been privy to. Dr. Edgar Donavan, the lead archeologist of the expedition, had shared that information with his oldest daughter, Stephanie.

The next page in the binder displayed two photographs. The first had been the source for much hypothetical speculation and controversial disagreement from Stephanie's peers. The photo depicted what appeared to be the jawbone of an animal. The same small, razor-sharp teeth lined the bones of the animal's jaw, much like the teeth depicted in the cave paintings. The jawbone was found during the Cahokia excavation and appeared to be somewhat canine in nature. Only not exactly canine; there were qualities of the bone that looked prehistoric reptilian. And there were other anomalies as well. In fact, there were at least three distinct biological features found within the singular bone. But that wasn't what had perplexed the original scientists the most. The back molars of the jaw appeared to be human; not only did they resemble human molars but it was almost certain that they were. Two of the rear molars contained gold fillings. A rudimentary dentist had drilled out cavities in the teeth and packed the malleable alloy into the holes. There was no reason to suspect that a dentist would perform this type of procedure on an animal, certainly not one as strange as this. Stephanie believed that the jawbone had belonged to a human, one that had undergone a drastic mutation and changed its physiology.

Other excavations had led to similar finds, revealing hybrid fossils of human and animal remains combined. In most cases, it looked as if the bones were in the process of mutating into a creature that had never existed. At least no creature ever documented by paleontologists. Stephanie believed the reason they had never been documented was because they were a combination of species from different periods. It was evident in the jawbone that human, canine, and Jurassic qualities had been somehow fused together. These weren't anomalous findings either. Fossils exactly like the jawbone had turned up all over the world from myriad cultures. The Lenape cave was the most recent of these findings, and Stephanie hoped it would prove to be her Rosetta Stone. *This could be the discovery that ties it all together.* The secret was in the murals. They were in far better condition than any of the other cave paintings they had inspected in the past.

If only you were here to see this. Her father had inspired her to continue the search, and he had been right. All those years ago, he had been onto it and been so close to the truth. Stephanie touched the book that had once belonged to Edgar Donovan. "Oh, Dad, you should be here," she said.

The last picture in the book finally made sense. She hadn't been able to understand the significance of it before. But after today, thanks to Donald

Fischer, she understood much more. The picture was taken of several weapons discovered during the excavation. There were a few arrowheads, a dagger, and several spear tips. All the weapons had been fabricated from the same material ... magnetite, an iron ore also known as lodestone.

Lois picked up the telephone and dialed Karin Boyle's number. She'd been reluctant to bother her at home after everything she and her family had been through in the past few days. But Carl had called last night and said that Rob and the other children were on the mend; however, Lois hadn't heard a thing since.

She let the phone ring, waiting for Karin or Bob to pick up, but no one answered. She waited a bit longer, hung up, and then dialed the center.

"Chilton Medical, how may I direct your call?" a woman's voice greeted her.

"Hello, this is Lois Fischer. I brought a young boy into the emergency room on Saturday night."

"Yes, Mrs. Fischer. I was here Saturday as well. What can I do for you?"

"Well, I was wondering how Robert is doing. I was concerned, and I haven't heard anything since yesterday."

"Well, Mrs. Fischer, I am really not supposed to give out that information to anyone who isn't family."

"Oh, I see." Lois waited for the woman to continue.

"But I know how worried you were about the boy." The woman lowered her voice. "So ... don't tell anyone I told you, okay?"

"Of course," Lois said.

"Well, late last night, Dr. Malcolm transferred all three of the children to a toxicology center in Oswego."

"Oswego. Why on Earth did he do that?"

"Apparently, he believes that the children may have come in contact with the same toxin. He mentioned something about snake venom."

"Snake venom? I thought Robert was being treated for a bacterial infection."

"I'm not sure, Mrs. Fischer. In fact, that's all I really know."

Lois thought for a moment, then continued. "I suppose both Karin and Bob made the trip with Robert. I tried to reach them at home, but they weren't there."

"Yes, I would imagine they did."

"Is there any chance I could talk to Dr. Malcolm? If he isn't too busy."

"Oh, I'm sorry, but Dr. Malcolm accompanied the families and is in Oswego assisting with the patients." The woman paused to clear her throat. "I think Dr. Ziegler is in his office. He may be able to answer some of your questions. Would you like to talk to him?"

"If I may. Thank you."

"Remember, Mrs. Fischer. I didn't tell you anything."

"Of course. Thank you for all your help." Lois waited to be connected, and after several rings, the doctor picked up.

"Dr. Ziegler," he answered.

"Hello, Dr. Ziegler. This is Lois Fischer; I hope I am not calling you at a bad time."

There was a pause before the man replied. "Not at all, Mrs. Fischer. What can I do for you?"

Dr. Ziegler was Troy's physician and had known the family since he started working at Chilton. Lois trusted him and thought he was a good doctor. "I was concerned about Robert Boyle. He and my son are good friends, and well ... we brought him in the other night to the emergency room."

"Is Troy feeling all right? I know he was in close contact with Robert."

Lois's pulse quickened at the man's reaction. "I was under the impression this wasn't contagious like Dr. Malcolm originally believed. Sheriff Primrose told us there was a possibility of quarantine and that we should stay home yesterday. But then he called later and said that Robert was somewhat better and there was no need to worry."

Ziegler cleared his throat on the other end. "Yes … that's exactly right."

"Oh, because the way you asked about Troy, it sounded like you might be worried about something serious." Lois thought carefully about what she would say next. "Dr. Ziegler, are Robert and the other children all right? Should I be concerned for my child's safety?"

"Dr. Malcolm transferred the children to a toxicology center up state. I was just about to call and check on their progress."

The man's voice had changed. *What are you hiding, Dr. Ziegler?* "You didn't answer my question, Doctor. Should I be concerned for my child's safety? Is there a chance that Troy could catch what Robert has?"

"Mrs. Fischer." He cleared his throat and paused again. There was a rustling of papers on the other end of the line, and Lois could tell he was more than just uncomfortable. "I can tell you with one hundred percent certainty that if Troy had what Robert has, he would already be showing symptoms. There would be no hiding it; you would know."

"So, you believe it *is* contagious and *not* a snake venom or some type of poison?" She had no choice; she had started down this line of questioning and couldn't stop until she got an answer that satisfied her. Ziegler was hiding something.

"Um, who told you that?" he asked. "Where are you getting your information from, Mrs. Fischer?"

Lois cursed herself for overplaying her hand; she thought about her next move and hesitated for a moment. But if there was even a chance that Troy was in danger, she was prepared to do whatever it took. "Well, Dr. Ziegler, I've known Carl since before he had to shave. I spoke with him earlier, and he recommended I call you. And as Troy's doctor, I trust you have my son's best interests in mind." She knew she had crossed the line by using Carl's name and there would be repercussions, but she had no choice.

"I assure you, Mrs. Fischer, there's nothing more important to me than the welfare of *all* my patients. And since Robert and the other children have been transported to Oswego, you have nothing to worry about."

"Hmmm-mmm, let me ask you this. What if Robert and the other children weren't in Oswego? What would you tell me then?" Troy didn't know how right he had been when he told his father that men had to think fast around women, and Lois Fischer knew Dr. Ziegler was no exception to the rule.

The doctor paused for a long moment; there was another sound of papers moving and the rattle of a door, as if the man had checked outside his office. He returned a moment later and lowered his voice even more. "Mrs. Fischer, if that were the case, I would suggest that you and your family strongly consider going on vacation. I hear Florida is lovely this time of year."

Lois felt a massive lump well up in her throat and almost dropped the phone. Had she heard him correctly? *Did he just tell me to get the hell out of town as fast as possible?* Lois Fischer had pushed it as far as she dared with the good doctor and knew there would be backlash from Carl for her manipulation of the man. But she had all the information she needed, at least for the moment. "Thank you very much, Dr. Ziegler," she said, her voice trembling and on the verge of tears.

"Mrs. Fischer," Ziegler said more directly. "This conversation never happened." He hung up.

Lois's heart throbbed as she remained clutching the phone like a baseball bat. She struggled to wrap her head around the words he had said. *Florida is lovely this time of year.* But Carl had told her the children were improving. *Just what the hell was wrong with them, anyway?* Surely, she and Troy had been exposed to whatever Rob had. Ziegler said he would have already started showing symptoms. Lois tried to think if Troy had appeared sick in any way. He seemed fine, but there had been the incident in the graveyard. That was odd behavior, but he had only been scared. He didn't seem sick. The phone started to beep in her hand; she hadn't realized she was still holding it long after the doctor had hung up. She laid the receiver on the cradle.

Lois walked down the hall to her son's room and peeked in on him. He was in bed reading a comic book, nothing strange. Then she passed the den where Donald was busy looking over some paperwork he had brought home. She didn't want to tell him what Dr. Ziegler had said; it would only lead to a conflict. Lois knew exactly what she had to do, but she would have to wait until tomorrow. *I need to talk to Carl and get to the bottom of this.*

CHAPTER 34

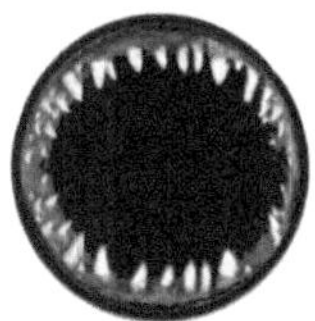

Father Kieran had carried the boy into the downstairs bedroom of the rectory, where he remained unconscious, looking as if he had lost a fight with a mountain lion. The priest did everything he possibly could for him, but the child was dehydrated and in shock. Kieran offered him a few drops of water at a time but didn't want to overdo it at first. Surely the boy needed the liquid, but too much too soon would cause him to choke. Kieran slowly offered him a bit more.

The boy moaned and shivered while some violent nightmare plagued his dreams. There was no telling how long he had been wandering the woods or what evil he might have encountered out there. Kieran could only imagine that he'd been lost in the woods for a couple days, judging by the state he was in. Large punctures tore into the material of the boy's jeans, leaving dark crimson stains that traveled from his hips to his ankles.

He had lost a lot of blood. Most of it had already dried; however, some of the deeper wounds appeared fresh. Kieran took a large pair of shears and slit the leg of the boy's jeans.

"Dear God." The priest let out a gasp as the wounds were revealed. He exposed the boy's other leg. On the table beside the bed, he gathered what medical supplies he could find in the rectory. A large pair of tweezers and some disinfectant, along with bandages and rolls of gauze, were assembled neatly within reach.

The kid was in bad shape; his legs had sustained massive puncture wounds and deep lacerations. Father Kieran immediately discovered what had caused the injuries. He used the tweezers, grasped at the object, and pulled. It came out easily, though it had been lodged a good three-quarters of an inch into the boy's flesh. Kieran examined the massive thorn; the tip was covered in blood. It was much bigger than the thorns that grew at the base of Garrett Mountain, and Kieran suspected that this one had come from somewhere deep in the woods, where it had been growing wild for ages. He dropped it into a bowl, making a sound like a penny being tossed into a dish at a carnival, then went to work on the other intruders that impaled the child.

The boy moaned while the priest removed the massive splinters from his legs. Fresh blood oozed from his open wounds and stained the sheets he lay on. Once Kieran had removed all the thorns he could find, he cleaned the wounds with disinfectant and bandaged the worst of them, wrapping the child's legs with the gauze.

He offered the boy more water, allowing him only a few sips at a time. *Thank you, Lord.* Kieran believed it was a good sign that he was taking in fluids. Still, he knew that infection would be the real threat. The boy was going to need antibiotics and proper medical attention, but ...

Father Kieran rechecked the window. *Dear God, there's so many of them.* Now the creatures were traveling in two directions, some toward the mountain and some headed into town. He knew it best not to call an ambulance or the authorities for the risk it might put them in, not with the beasts so close to the rectory property. He opted to tend to the child himself rather than put anyone else in harm's way. *We will wait it out together, my son.* The boy stirred and moaned in his sleep.

"Help me," he said, his voice sounding cracked and dry.

Father Kieran rushed to his side and leaned in close. "Tell me, son, what is your name?"

The boy opened his eyes for a moment and allowed the weakest gasp to slip through his lips. *"Billy,"* he said.

Evading the truth didn't sit well with Dr. Ziegler. In the past, he had exercised discretion and avoided certain particulars to maintain an air of professionalism. But he had never outright lied before—or, in this case, withheld the truth from a patient or their family. Having to dance around Mrs. Fischer's questions left his stomach feeling sour, like he had swallowed a peach pit. He told himself he had given the woman enough information to use her own discretion. After all, he did warn her of the potential danger without exactly spelling it out. But telling himself that didn't make him feel any better about it.

Ziegler finally found the number to the toxicology center in Oswego and dialed the phone. A man picked up on the second ring.

"ECHO Toxicology, this is Adrian. How may I direct your call?"

"Hello, Adrian, my name is Dr. Ziegler. I'm calling you from Chilton Medical in Garrett Grove."

"Hello, Doctor. What can I do for you?"

"Well, my chief of medicine, Dr. John Malcolm, is there, and I was wondering if you could find him for me?"

There was a long pause, and for a moment, Ziegler thought he had been disconnected. "Hello, Adrian. Are you still there?"

"I'm sorry, did you say Dr. Malcolm?"

"Yes, that's correct. He would have arrived sometime yesterday with the children we transferred."

"Could you hold for one moment, please?"

Ziegler was put on hold before he could answer, and after about a minute of waiting, another voice came on the line.

"Hello, this is Dr. Klein, the chief administrator. You are Dr. Ziegler. Am I pronouncing that right, Doctor?"

"That's right. I'm calling from Chilton Medical in Garrett Grove."

"I'm sorry, but my assistant was a bit confused; he said you were looking for a—" There was a rustling of papers, then the doctor replied, "Dr. Malcolm, is that correct?"

"Yes. Dr. Malcolm, he transferred three children to the care of your facility. They would have arrived early this morning sometime."

"Dr. Ziegler." The man paused. "There's no Dr. Malcolm here, nor have we had any patients transferred from your facility."

Ziegler's heart jumped into his throat and stagnated. His mouth went dry as he attempted to speak. "A-are you quite certain?" He nearly choked on the words. "The children's names are Robert Boyle, Erin Richards, and Ben Richards. All are ten years old and have been exhibiting cellular degeneration caused by a potentially unknown bacterium."

"I'm quite sure I would have remembered any patients exhibiting symptoms as extreme as that. ECHO Toxicology is more of a research facility, and we have very few patients on the premises at any given time. Perhaps your chief of medicine transferred the children to another facility."

Ziegler had a pretty good idea that Dr. Malcolm and the children weren't going to be found in any other facility. He didn't need to inquire any further.

"I'm sure that's what happened," Ziegler said. "I'm sorry to have bothered you, Doctor. Thank you for your help."

"You're quite welcome, Dr. Ziegler. Sorry I couldn't be more helpful. Goodnight."

"Goodnight." Ziegler hung up and stared at the phone. *Oh God, this is my fault.* He had no idea what they were dealing with when the children were brought in. *I should have listened to you.* Dr. Malcolm had been right all along. Quarantine would have been the correct course of action, and he had talked the old man out of it. And for what? So hé could get laid.

Things may have turned out the same regardless, but at least it wouldn't have been on his shoulders. Ziegler believed the worst thing he could do was allow a contagious variant of the flu loose in Garrett Grove, but he had ended up releasing something much worse.

There was no doubt; the infection that attacked the children was the very same bacteria that had mutated Felix Castillo and Abe Gorman. The result would also be the same for the children as it was for those men. But for some strange reason, the transformation had taken much longer to manifest in the three ten-year-olds. Now, it was only logical to assume that Dr. Malcolm and the children's parents had been infected as well.

This is bad; this is so bad. Only a few hours ago, the laws of medicine and physiology applied. He had been trained that everything could be explained with scientific method, that through research and observation, a logical conclusion could always be concluded. But Ethan Ziegler had seen things tonight that changed all that. He could no longer trust what he believed to be the truth. Dead bodies didn't get up off the table ... or did they? He raked his hands through his hair, clenched his fists, and racked his brain for an answer. *Come on, man ... think.* But no matter how hard he tried, there was no logical answer to be found.

He had been staring at the phone for almost twenty minutes before he finally tore his eyes away and looked up at the bulletin board. Several notices were held in place with large red ladybug magnets. He studied the colorful design on the back of the bug, bright red with black dots. The circular patterns of black reminded him of Abe's eyes just before they had put him into the MRI machine ... just before it had killed him. Ziegler wondered if Dr. John Malcolm now had eyes that resembled the dots on the backs of the ladybugs. Big, black, lifeless eyes.

Chapter 35

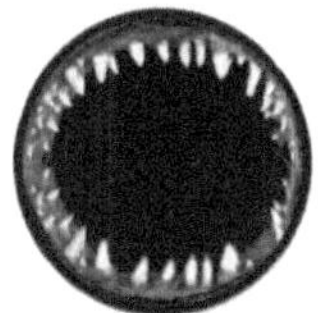

Tuesday

Donald Fischer arrived at the quarry at five-thirty a.m. to find Dr. Thompson sitting on the steps of his trailer with two Styrofoam cups in her hands.

"Good morning, cowboy," she said, handing him a cup. "I brought the coffee today."

"Bright and early, I see. Kind of figured you would be." He skirted past her up the wooden steps and unlocked the trailer door.

"Big day," she said and followed him inside. "It's hard to sleep in when you've got the discovery of your career just sitting there."

"I can imagine." Don turned on the lights, approached his desk, and took a seat. He motioned for Stephanie to join him. She pulled out a nearby chair and sat directly across from him. "My son said he met your daughter yesterday. She made quite the impression."

Stephanie laughed. "I heard nice things about Troy as well. Janis said he made a haunted house in your garage."

"Yep. He calls it Scream in the Dark. He did one hell of a job too."

"He did that all by himself? Quite the motivated little man. Must run in the family."

"He had some help from his friend ... Rob. Known each other since kindergarten. Unfortunately, Rob caught the flu, so Troy had to finish it up. And to be fair, he's a lot more motivated than his old man. Doesn't take much to run a quarry. I know it looks glamorous, but I assure you, once you get past all the dirt, dust, and guys named Rusty, it really isn't."

Stephanie laughed and threw her head back. "You're modest ... That's a good quality. But don't be so hard on yourself. Nobody's life turns out exactly as planned. Unless, of course, your last name's Rockefeller or Kennedy." She tilted her head and made a face. "Even then, it's not guaranteed."

Don laughed and nodded. "True, although it looks like it worked out pretty well for you—pursuing your dream and all."

She took a sip of coffee and leaned back in the chair. "It did, but this wasn't *my* dream. It was my father's. I only picked up where he left off and ended up finding a passion for it."

"Really?" He placed his elbows on the desk and folded his hands under his chin. "Well, don't keep me in suspense. What was it? I'm guessing you wanted to be an astronaut, no wait, an Air Force pilot?" He laughed.

"Not even close, funny man. If you must know, it was ballet. And I was damned good at it!" She twirled her arms at her sides and mimicked taking a bow.

Don had been doing his best keeping his eyes off her legs as she sat across from him but could no longer help himself. She had worn shorts to work again, despite the chill in the air. "I could see that," he said, trying not to stare. "You're strong and petite and look like you'd be easy to pick up." He realized what he had said and felt the heat rush to his face. "I-I didn't mean it like that. I meant … you know, as a dancer. I'm sure it helps to be small so the guy can throw you around." *For Christ's sake, just stop talking.*

She smiled and watched him squirm. "You're not very good at talking to women, are you?"

"No," he said, taking a quick sip from his cup. "Not at all."

"Actually, it's kinda cute." She leaned in and lowered her voice. "The truth is, I *am* easy to throw around." She winked at him and smiled.

Don choked on his coffee and almost dumped the Styrofoam cup in his lap. He made a valiant effort to recover, sitting up straight and wiping his chin, but Stephanie was already busting a gut.

"Relax, cowboy. I'm just messing with you. My God, you should have seen your face. I wish I had Gail's camera. Talk about a Kodak moment. Speaking of, I told the team to be here by seven. I was hoping to get started right away. Is someone else taking over the daily glamour of the quarry while you babysit me and my guys?"

Don still hadn't fully recovered, but he felt a bit better. The woman was a pistol, and he appreciated her energy. "Yes, Mark Gold will cover me while I play in the dirt with your team."

"So, aren't you going to ask me what happened?"

"Why did you never become a dancer?"

Stephanie leaned back in the chair and kicked her foot up onto his desk. Don's eyes followed the slope of her calf all the way to the curve of her thigh. Then she twisted her leg, exposing the inner side of her knee and a great deal of the rest of her as well. An angry scar lined with a severe number of stitch marks formed a circular pattern around her kneecap. "Torn ACL," she said. "I had the lead in *Swan Lake*. It was a big deal. And when you're small like me, it's easy for the anchor to, I believe you said, 'throw you around.' Well, I landed wrong and tore my ACL, and that was the end of my dancing career. It healed fine, but it was never strong enough to dance again. Besides, who wants a dancer with a big, ugly scar on her leg?"

Don felt hypnotized and found it impossible to pull his stare away from her perfectly toned thigh muscle. "It's not ugly at all." He finally looked up to find her staring at him.

"Why, Mr. Fischer, you *do* know how to talk to women after all." She slowly removed her leg from his desk, taking her time and never breaking eye contact.

Donald felt the heat flushing his face again but managed to handle it better this time. "So," he said. "Now that you've seen what's in the cave, is it everything you were hoping you would find?"

"Everything and more." She looked down at the floor and folded her hands in her lap. "These murals are in pristine condition, and the artifacts—the preservation of the site is impeccable. I've never seen anything quite like it before."

"Really? What makes this site different from others?"

"Well, there are many factors that could explain the unique preservation. It doesn't appear as if the elements were able to penetrate the cave; that's a big one. Also, geographic location, the summers aren't too bad in this part of the country. And who knows, maybe it has something to do with the rock itself. You said the cave was made of magnetite. That's got to be rare."

"It's usually found in smaller deposits in Asia and on the west coast. You'll hit a vein here and there, but never an entire cliff face. Not like this, not in the northeast. It makes me wonder why the Lenape chose this location in the first place."

"It makes sense when you think about the lifestyle of the tribe. They were a spiritual and mystic civilization. They used crystals and stones to stimulate the chakras. I'm sure you've heard what people are saying about the healing powers of magnets. Maybe the Lenape knew something we don't."

Don didn't know about that. He was a man of science and had never been into all that cosmic idealism. Still, as a geologist, he had to admit there was something about the makeup of many geological formations that defied logical answers. There was Stonehenge, for one, and the crystal skulls left by the Toltecs in Lucasio, Mexico. Also, numerous civilizations had discovered the magnetic quality of lodestone and utilized it. But he had never heard of anyone using an entire cave of the ore as a burial site, if that's even what it was.

"Is the cave a burial site? I mean, it looks like it, but I thought they typically used mounds."

Stephanie raised her eyebrows. "That's the million-dollar question. Obviously, some type of ritual took place in that cavern, but I'd be lying if I told you I knew for certain. I'm hoping to find out an answer by getting in there and digging around."

"I've been thinking about the pieces of lodestone found in the ribs of the skeletons," Don said. "What do you think that's all about?"

The smile on Stephanie's face dropped for a fraction of a second, as if she were searching for a quick answer. "I'm not sure of that either."

Don studied her face, looking for a chink in her armor. *Did she just lie to me?* He checked his watch. Stephanie's team would be arriving soon.

"Well, I guess I should put on some more coffee. I think we're gonna need the energy." He left his desk and walked across the trailer.

"Sounds like a plan, cowboy," she said.

Miss Walsh entered the classroom and stopped in the doorway with her mouth hung open while she studied the room. More than one-quarter of the seats were empty. She checked the clock above the blackboard just to make sure she had the correct time. Eight o'clock on the nose. She'd heard there was a flu bug going around, and it wasn't only her class that had been affected. The fifth-grade class was missing six students yesterday, and the third-grade class had just as many absentees. It was too soon for flu season to be hitting so hard. It was still only October.

Miss Walsh took a seat at her desk and asked Scott to lead the class in the Pledge of Allegiance, followed by "America the Beautiful." Afterward, it was time for show-n-tell. "Who would like to go first?"

Troy had completely forgotten that Tuesdays were show-n-tell day. He looked around the class and noticed that Rob was still out. *Aw, man.* Erin and Ben hadn't made it back to school either, along with Tommy and Jeff. And now there were even more kids out sick. Mike Barnes wasn't in his seat and neither was Beth Doran or Terry Wallen. *Jeez, I better not catch the flu. I don't want to miss Halloween.*

Troy had woken up a little later this morning than usual and rushed out the door after breakfast. His mom seemed a bit preoccupied as well and burnt his Eggos on the first try and had to make him a second batch.

The other children hadn't forgotten that today was show-n-tell. Even Janis had brought something to show the class, and it was only her second day. Troy turned around to Janis, who had been given the seat behind him, and whispered, "I forgot to bring in something for show-n-tell. I'm so stupid."

The little blonde girl shrugged her shoulders and smiled in reply. Troy turned back as Caroline Smith made her way to the front of the class and revealed an x-ray of her father's arm. While cleaning the gutters, Mr. Smith had fallen off the roof and broken the bone between his wrist and his elbow.

Troy felt a tap on his back and turned around to find Janis holding a Luke Skywalker action figure. "Here," she said. "I was gonna give this to you at lunch to help you make your costume, but I guess you can have it now." She handed the small figure to him.

"Oh my gosh, thank you. That's so cool!" He looked back to where Wendy sat, held up the action figure, and smiled. Wendy's face pinched tighter than Troy thought was possible. Her lips pressed together, and she shot him a look he had seen countless times in the past. *That's the look that Mom gives Dad.* He had an idea he had done something wrong but hadn't a clue what that might be. He turned around quickly, scared he might do something else to earn another one of those looks. It was getting harder to be a boyfriend by the minute. *I'm not ready for this.*

When it was his turn for show-n-tell, Troy proceeded to the front of the class and displayed the action figure. He looked at Janis and then looked at Wendy, then back at Janis, and then at Wendy again, and then ... he started to panic. The little blonde girl brimmed with pleasure when he told the class how his new friend had given him the figure to help him make his costume for Halloween. But this brought out an entirely different reaction from Wendy. She looked pissed. *Jeez, what the heck did I say?* He cleared his throat and told the class about their plans to dress up as the characters from the movie and how he hoped Rob would be better by Saturday so he could be Han Solo. His eyes darted from Janis to Wendy, with his heart racing like a soap box car. Troy's palms started to sweat, and even his fingers felt slick, and for a second, he was sure the small action figure would slip from his grasp. He held on to it tighter and finished up by saying they were going to win the costume contest on Friday because he had seen Wendy's Princess Leia outfit and she looked exactly like her. Wendy's face softened, and a bright smile quickly spread like a case of the flu. Troy exhaled, feeling like he had been granted a stay of execution. *Man, I'm so confused.*

At recess, the trio retreated to a corner of the room for a little pow-wow. Wendy walked up and punched Troy in the arm, which he took as a good sign. Apparently, what he had said made Wendy forget about giving him dirty looks.

Janis had worn a baggy sweatshirt to school, and the boys appeared to settle down a few notches. In fact, the whole class seemed a bit more subdued than they had been the day before, maybe because so many kids were out sick.

"I asked my parents about showing you guys the haunted house, and they said they were gonna talk it over," Troy said. "That's usually a good sign. I'll ask them if tomorrow night is okay."

"Great." Janis smiled. "Did you get started on your costume yet?"

"Um, no, I had a little situation on the way home yesterday. Oh, I almost forgot, my dad knows your mom. The cave they found at the quarry is the one she's working at."

"Really, that's weird. She didn't say anything about it. And we were talking about you last night."

Troy wondered why Janis and her mother would have been talking about him. He didn't know, but for some reason, it made him feel good. He smiled and turned to Wendy, who was definitely *not* smiling—not even a little. Troy felt his own smile falter, then fall to the floor.

Wendy's face had pinched up again like she'd just eaten something sour. "What do you *mean* you had a little situation yesterday?"

Troy's hands started sweating again. "I um … I was walking home and cut through the graveyard. It was getting dark and started to rain. Well, it felt like someone was following me. Then I heard this scream and these things started to chase me." Janis's big eyes focused on him as he retold the story, and Wendy's mouth hung open. She didn't look mad anymore. "I started running, but they tried to cut me off. They weren't dogs, and they weren't kids either. So, I ran for the big tree by the fence. I climbed it and threw myself over. I was so scared, I ran into the middle of the street, and Deputy Lutchen almost hit me with his car. He had to drive me home because it was raining so bad."

The girls stared at him for a tense moment. "Are you kidding around and trying to scare us?" Wendy asked. "'Cause it sounds a lot like your mom's ghost story. You know, the Ojanox?"

"That's what I thought too. I asked my mom about it, and she said she made the name up. But I don't know if I believe her. It felt like she wasn't telling me the whole truth."

"Was it one Ojanox, or maybe a couple of them? Do you think that's what was after you?" Janis asked.

Troy didn't want to admit that he thought the stupid made-up monster from his mom's story really had chased him through the graveyard. He knew that wasn't the way you impressed girls.

"I don't know what to call it. Ojanox sounds about right, though. All I know is they were after me, and they weren't friendly."

"Do you think they're still there, in the graveyard?" Wendy asked.

"I don't know, but remember what my mom said? It comes around this time of year. So, it might be here for a while. I was so excited about Halloween and dressing up as *Star Wars* that I didn't even think what could happen if those things are still here on Halloween. We could be in big trouble."

"Not just us but all the kids in town," Wendy said. "Troy, swear that you're not lying to us. If you're lying, I'll tell the whole class that you let us put makeup and a dress on you."

"Whoa," he yelled. "I'm not lying. It really happened, just like I said."

Janis leaned closer and lowered her voice. "I think you should both come over after school. I have to show you something."

Troy wondered what other surprises the new girl had to show them. Janis had certainly turned out to be an interesting individual with her arrowheads and *Star Wars* toys and Chewbacca mask.

"I don't know if my mom will let me after what happened yesterday. I'll see if I can call her at lunch to ask, but I doubt it," Troy said.

"What do you think?" Janis asked Wendy.

"Yeah, I can go."

Troy already felt left out and decided he would do whatever it took to get to Janis's house after school. Exactly how he would pull it off was another problem altogether. When Miss Walsh called the children back to their seats, the three agreed to talk later.

"Not a word to anybody," Wendy instructed them.

It was exhilarating, and Troy felt as if he had been accepted into a secret club. He especially loved the attention.

Lois hadn't slept well and woke up with too much on her mind. She burnt Troy's breakfast on the first try and forgot to put the coffee in the percolator. She didn't even realize it until she poured herself a cup of hot water and ended up having to drink tea instead.

Dr. Ziegler's words continued to resonate in her head. *Since Robert and the other children have been transported to Oswego, you have nothing to worry about.* She had used Carl's name to manipulate the doctor. And it worked like a charm. But Dr. Ziegler said something else that had kept her awake most of the night. He said if Rob and the other children were in town, it would be a good idea to consider taking a family vacation. *I hear Florida is lovely this time of year.* In other words, Ziegler had told her to get the *hell* out of Dodge.

She couldn't talk to Donald about it. It was hard enough to talk to him as it was. There was only one person she could talk to, and that was Carl Primrose ... her ex. If anyone knew what was going on, it was Carl. She didn't want to jump to conclusions but found it impossible not to. There was something in Ziegler's voice. He had been hiding something; that much was obvious. But there was more than just that ... The man had sounded scared.

Lois had finally managed to feed Troy breakfast and get him to school. Unable to control herself any longer, she drove straight to Carl's house, only to find his driveway empty. He was already at work. Lois tried the front door, just to be sure. She mustered her nerve, walked up the steps, and knocked.

There was no answer. Lois knocked louder and waited. "Damn," she said under her breath and considered heading to the station to talk to him. She checked her watch, saw it was eight thirty-five, and thought better about bothering him at work. She decided to come back later and drove home, running through every possible scenario of what might be wrong with Robert and the other children. *What the hell do you know, Dr. Ziegler?* She needed to find out.

CHAPTER 36

Shortly after eight-thirty a.m., Sheriff Primrose met Bill Hamilton, the King County fire inspector, and Bob Jones, the fire chief, to inspect the house fire at Sixteen Poplar. Bob's men had battled the blaze and brought the fire under control late last night. The pump crew remained on the scene to continuously douse the ashes and watch for any flare-ups. Now, just a few hours after sunrise, the embers had cooled, and it was safe for the men to walk the ruins of the house. Bob Jones had already canvassed the scene last night, but this was the first time the inspector and sheriff were able to see the place themselves.

After finding the blood near the back door, Carl was concerned about what discoveries they might find inside the house. But he was more worried they'd find nothing at all. And it was beginning to look like the Barnes family had not been in the home when the fire broke out.

Chief Jones led the men through the front door and brought them down a hallway to the kitchen. "This is where it started." Bob showed them to the stove. "It looks like the burners were left on. Apparently, they were cooking dinner. But you'll be able to tell us if that is correct or not."

"It looks that way from what I'm seeing." Bill Hamilton pulled a pair of Clark Kent-framed glasses from his coat pocket and examined the dark flash points near the back of the stove. "But we'll get it all straightened out."

"I take it you didn't find any bodies?" Carl asked.

"None at all, Sheriff. Not even a family pet," the large fire chief said. "My men turned the place upside down, and there isn't anyone here. Good news. Strange they would start supper and then leave the house."

More than strange. Carl knew how unlikely that was and wondered if either man thought the same. Sure, the family could have escaped once the fire started, but wouldn't they have run to a neighbor's house or been outside when the fire department arrived? Nothing about that scenario sounded plausible.

Carl followed Bill and Bob through the rest of the house, assessing the damage. The place was totaled, the furniture, the contents, and the structure. It had been a family's home just yesterday. One of the many families that Carl had taken an oath to protect. The children had done their homework at the kitchen table, they had played Candy Land on the living room floor, and they watched Bob Hope on the family television set. Carl's heart ached as if it had been skewered with an ice pick. He knew in his gut that the Barnes family would never know they had lost their home and everything in it. Which was hardly a consolation. They had met a far worse fate.

Carl removed his hat and rubbed his forehead, feeling the lump growing in his throat. He needed to talk to Ziegler and see what the man had found out. Hopefully, he had gotten in touch with Dr. Malcolm and had an idea of what they were dealing with.

Dick Wilson stood at the grill with a scowl on his face. He flipped an omelet and slapped it down hard, as if the egg and cheese concoction owed him money. Mandy hadn't shown up for work and wasn't answering her phone. He had called his only other waitress, Amy Sterling, but the girl was unable to cover Mandy's shift. Typically, Mandy's absence would have been nothing short of a catastrophic event, and even though it had set Dick into a tailspin, it could have been far worse. Of all days for the girl to go AWOL, she had picked the slowest day the diner had seen in years. With only one table occupied and a few seats taken at the counter, Wilson's Diner looked as if its usual patrons hadn't bothered to get out of bed.

Dick's nephew Josh finally agreed to come in and lend a hand. He busied himself while Dick sneered and barked out orders from his position behind the grill. Josh approached the counter and refilled the mugs for a few men who worked for Con Edison, the power company. "Can I get you guys anything else?" he asked.

"Yeah," joked one of the men. "You can get Mandy. I sure as hell didn't come in for the coffee."

"You and me both." Josh nodded and smiled. "She didn't show up, and we haven't sold one slice of peach cobbler all morning."

"And you're not gonna if *you're* serving it," another man chimed in, spurring a fresh fit of laughter from his coworkers.

"The garbage isn't going to empty itself!" Dick shouted. "Do something about that, will ya?"

Josh set the check on the counter in front of the men. "Whenever you're ready," he said, then grabbed the garbage bag and let himself out the back door into the lot. He was met by a breeze that smacked him in the face and sent gooseflesh rippling down his arms. The area near the dumpsters tended to act like a wind tunnel, catching the breeze and swirling it around between the buildings and the back fence.

Josh checked the lot and looked down the alley, trying to locate the stray cat Mandy had more or less adopted. She'd fallen in love with the poor thing and been feeding it for months now. The little guy was never going to leave and had no reason to, not with the constant supply of leftover greasy food that the diner's employees provided.

He pulled out a plastic bag containing a few pieces of ham. He threw the garbage into the dumpster and checked the area again, not seeing Scraps anywhere. Josh emptied the meat onto the ground near the wheel of the dumpster, then headed back to work. *Where are you today, kitty?* He thought maybe the cat was like the men in the diner who would only eat peach cobbler if Mandy was there to serve it. Scraps was really *her* cat after all.

Josh crossed the lot and was about to open the back door when he heard a rustling behind him. He turned back to see Scraps had poked his head out from underneath the dumpster and was munching away. The cat paid no attention to him and continued to devour its meal. "I guess you were hungry after all," he said and went back into the diner. Dick was already barking a new set of orders the second Josh walked in the door.

Doris TenHove attempted to juggle not only her job as head nurse but the duties of three other staff members who had not shown up for work that morning. To make matters worse, not one of them had bothered to call in. Nurse Gilmartin was perhaps the most surprising out of all the no-shows. The girl was always punctual and dedicated to the job, even though lately she appeared a bit preoccupied. And Doris had an idea why. She suspected that Jackie and Chilton's resident ladies' man, Dr. Ethan Ziegler, had started playing doctor together. Not that Doris could blame the young nurse. *Damn, if I was twenty years younger, I'd teach you a thing or two about anatomy myself, Dr. Ziegler.*

Doris called Jackie's apartment repeatedly but was unable to contact her. In addition to Nurse Gilmartin, Kate Wallen was scheduled to be in at seven, and there had been no answer at the girl's home either. Kate still lived with her parents and her kid sister, Terry. Surely someone should have been at home to answer the phone. The other missing girl was Angela Shupp. Doris heard there had been a fire last night on Poplar Ave. That was practically next door to where the Shupp family lived. She prayed that the fire hadn't affected Angela's house. It was more than peculiar that she should get no answer from all three girls' homes.

Angela had been scheduled to work pediatrics, and Kate was slotted to cover the reception desk, where Doris busied herself answering phones and pulling her hair out. She continued trying to find someone to cover the girls' shifts but had no luck. Many of the nurses were unable to come in, and a large percent of the ones she did call hadn't answered either. To make matters worse, Jackie was one of her top ER nurses, and her presence was urgently needed.

There had been a bad car accident this morning on Route 3, and the occupants of the vehicles were currently being treated in the emergency room.

Doris looked up in time to see Michelle Marks and Joseph Santos preparing to exit the building. Both Joe and Michelle worked the paramedics unit for the center and had responded to the car accident. Doris waved them over to the reception desk. "Are you both still on call?"

"Yeah. What's up?" Joe asked.

"I have three nurses who never showed up, and I need help. Is there any chance you could lend a hand for a little while?"

Michelle nodded. "Of course, just tell me where you need me."

"No problem," Joe said.

"Great!" Doris felt as if she had been thrown a life preserver. "Michelle, could you report to Pediatrics? And Joe, you're needed in the ER. Thank you so much." As if on cue, the phone at the reception desk started to ring on three separate lines. Doris suddenly wondered if her life preserver had been made of lead.

Baxter ran from one side of the kennel to his empty water dish and stared at the bowl, panting. He had been barking for the past two hours, but no one showed up to feed him or to fill his water. He looked toward the house, then jumped against the fence and let out several loud barks.

Baxter belonged to Tommy Negal. He had become a member of the family when he was just a ten-week-old German Shepherd puppy and been a loyal companion ever since.

He sensed there was something wrong last night and whined and howled with concern. He struggled to escape from his pen and even tore one of his pads on the fence in the process. But Baxter had been unable to free himself and been upset all night.

Now he was hungry and thirsty and knew that something terrible had happened to his family. He continued to pace across the pen and flipped his water dish, hoping to find a drink. When he finally got tired of running in circles, he laid his head down on the cold concrete and let out a mournful whine. He missed Tommy.

CHAPTER 37

Donna and Angelo Franco lived just a few doors down from the Barnes residence at Ten Poplar Ave. The newlywed Italian couple were younger than most people on the block and had moved in last year. Donna was the first one to call the fire department last night. She had looked out her front door to see flames wicking out of the Barnes's kitchen window. Hoping to help, she and Angelo ran to their neighbor's house before the fire trucks arrived and pounded on the front door. Angelo even tried to get inside, but the blaze was already out of control and made it impossible. The young couple watched in horror along with the rest of the neighborhood as the home was consumed by the inferno.

It hadn't occurred to Donna last night amidst all the confusion, but this morning, she realized she hadn't seen Beth or Jerry Campbell among the crowd of concerned neighbors. Beth and Jerry lived directly across the street from the Barnes house. Donna knew the two families were close, and their boys were good friends. It was odd they hadn't ventured out of the house.

After Angelo left for work, Donna got to thinking. She was worried sick about what had happened to one family on the block and now wondered if she had reason to be concerned for another. She looked out her front window and noticed the Campbells' Buick was still in the driveway and had been there all night.

She tried to mind her own business, but the more she thought about it, the more it bothered her. Unable to contain her concern any longer, she threw on one of Angelo's sweatshirts and walked out the front door. The air smelled like burnt wood and wet smoke, thick and overwhelming. Donna crossed the street, walked up the driveway, and knocked on the Campbells' front door. There was no answer; she knocked again, harder this time, and waited, but there was still no answer.

"Oh well. In for a penny, in for a pound," she said, walking around the side of the house and into the backyard. Donna froze in her tracks as if gripped by a sudden frost. Her heart stopped, then fluttered, and a cold sweat slicked her palms. The screen door had been left open; it caught the autumn breeze and swung back and forth in lazy arcs. "Hello," she called out, loud enough to be heard.

She took a step forward and approached the house with caution, as if she were walking up on a sleeping hornets' nest. The interior door was open as well, and from where Donna stood, there appeared to be no one inside.

"Hello," she called again, rapping her knuckles against the doorjamb. She poked her head in and yelled out, "Hello, it's Donna from across the street. Is anybody home?"

There was still no answer. She looked through the open door into a dark, quiet living room and took a step inside. There was a smell in the air, one she couldn't quite place. It was deep and thick like metal, but there was something else to it as well. It reminded her a little of burnt toast but not exactly. Donna took several more steps and was overpowered as the odor knocked her over the head. *God, what is that?* She covered her nose and mouth with her hand.

The living room opened into a hallway that led up a small staircase. Donna tiptoed up the stairs, and the odor grew stronger with every step. She could see the kitchen just over the rise of the stairs. The lights were on, and it had suddenly started to feel much warmer in the small stairwell. By the time Donna reached the second to last step, she could feel the heat pouring out of the kitchen in waves.

"Hello," she called as she topped the staircase and entered the kitchen. *Dear God!* She gasped at the state of the room. A frying pan lay face-up on the floor along with whatever had been cooking in it. A bowl of salad had been discarded and scattered across the floor as well. The food rested atop a dizzying pattern of long, dark smears that had dried to a dark crimson brown. *My God, that's blood!* The stains looked as if someone had been butchered and then dragged across the tile. Dozens of footprints had tracked through the blood while it was still wet and led into the living area of the house. Donna's head swam; she could feel the heat rising inside her and was certain she would either pass out or vomit. The burnt toast smell was now all consuming, and the heat was unbearable. Then she saw it. Flames flickered on the front burners of the stove. The oven had been left on as well; the dinner within it had burnt away hours ago. Her heart pounded in her temples, and she started to hyperventilate. She knew she should turn off the oven and the burners, and running out of the house as fast as possible felt like a solid plan as well. But the fear crippled her, and no matter how desperately she tried to take that first step, Donna found it impossible to move a muscle.

Please, God, help me.

Donna couldn't think straight and knew if she didn't react soon, she never would. She held her breath and forced herself to count down from five in her head. When she got to one, she skirted around the blood on the kitchen floor and turned off the gas. Then she ran through the kitchen, tore down the stairs, and burst into the living room. She flew out the back door like a cannonball exploding from the deck of the Jolly Roger. Donna ran home before the first tears hit her cheeks. But by the time she reached her house, she was hysterical. She smashed through the front door and fell to the carpet, unable to call the police or even her husband. It was forty-five minutes before Donna was able to pick up the phone.

Deputy David Rainey arrived at the home of Gary Forsyth to check on the whereabouts of his fellow officer. He immediately noticed Gary's pride and joy sitting in the driveway, a black Camaro Z28. Rainey exited his cruiser, walked up the drive, and laid his hand on the hood of the car. *Cold.* He proceeded to the front door and rang the bell. The chime sounded from inside the small hallway, and Rainey waited nearly a full minute before he rang it again. There was no reply.

"Hey, Gary. Are you in there, buddy?" he called up to the second-floor window. Again, there was no answer. Rainey tried the knob, which clicked open, allowing the door to swing inward. "You home, Gary?" He stepped inside and stood there for a moment listening. The place was silent.

Rainey had seen some crazy shit in the past twenty-four hours and wasn't about to go off half-cocked. He pulled his service revolver out of his holster and held it pointed toward the ceiling. "Gary," he called again.

He took several slow steps across the burgundy-tiled foyer and poked his head around the corner with his gun leading the way. He headed to the staircase and ascended them two at a time. A muffled noise echoed from somewhere on the second floor. There was a soft thud and then a rustle, like something had moved in one of the back bedrooms. Rainey swallowed and stood motionless. He heard it again, the sound of someone walking across a wood floor.

He eased back the hammer on his revolver and crept down the hallway, one step at a time. The noise was coming from the bedroom at the end of the hall. He reached the door and paused outside, listening to the furtive movements within.

Another thud, louder this time, almost caused him to discharge his weapon on the spot. There was definitely someone inside. Rainey took a long breath to steady his nerves, raised his foot, and kicked as hard as he could. The flimsy door flew inward, and Rainey rushed into the room, pointing his gun at the intruder. "Don't fucking move!" he shouted.

The woman screamed and dropped the lamp she had been holding, along with the dust rag she had been using to clean it. She raised her arms to shield herself as splinters of wood from the shattered jamb were thrown her way.

"Who are you? What the hell are you doing in here?" Rainey shouted at the now hysterical woman, who continued to shield her face and cry. Then he noticed the headphones on her head and the radio clipped to her waist.

He lowered the weapon and raised his arms to show he wouldn't hurt her, then pointed to his own ears. The frightened woman got the gist of what he meant and removed the headphones; loud music blasted from the tiny speakers.

"Who are you? What are you doing here?"

"You scared the shit out of me," the girl cried. "I'm Claire … Claire Rizvi. I clean the place for Gary. You can call him. He'll tell you." The girl looked about nineteen or twenty years old, with long, dark hair pulled back tight into a single braid. She dressed almost completely in faded blue denim, with the exception of her Pink Floyd concert T-shirt.

"Gary didn't show up for work today. Have you seen him?"

"No. I saw his car out front and thought he was home; my boyfriend dropped me off. There was no answer, so I let myself in. I have a key, see." She held up a house key to show him.

"So, he wasn't here when you got here? Did you notice anything strange, anything out of the ordinary?" he asked, holstering his weapon.

"Everything looked the same as usual."

"Okay, I'm sorry I frightened you, Miss Rizvi. Let me help you clean that up." He motioned to the broken lamp on the floor.

"It's okay, I got it. That's what I get paid for anyway; next time just yell or knock or something."

"Actually, I did. You didn't hear me with the headphones on. You might want to turn them down a little bit."

"Cool, isn't it?" She unclipped the radio and held it out to him. "It's a Walkman, they just came out. Now I can listen to Floyd everywhere I go."

Rainey had seen the commercials for the Walkman and planned on picking one up for himself at the Radio Shack in town or the Crazy Eddie's up in Warren. And even though he wanted to show his interest, he was on the job and fought the urge. "If you don't mind, I'm going to take a look around. I'll let myself out when I'm finished. Sorry again for startling you, Miss Rizvi."

"It's cool," she said. "See you around, Deputy"—she looked at his name tag—"Rainey."

He searched Gary's house and found nothing out of the ordinary or peculiar in any way, then let himself out and called base. "Deputy Rainey to dispatch."

"Go, Deputy, over," Tara answered.

"It was a no-go at Deputy Forsyth's place. The maid is here, and she hasn't seen him either. His car is in the driveway, but there's no sign of him."

"That's strange. I hope he's okay. I'll relay the message to the sheriff. Thank you, Deputy Rainey, over."

"Roger that, Tara, over and out." He started the cruiser and backed out of the driveway. Rainey had a feeling that something bad had happened to Gary Forsyth, and no one had been there with a stainless steel basin to save his ass either. Of course, it was just a feeling, but it was a strong one. *Christ, I hope I'm wrong.*

Tara Jeffries terminated the communication with Deputy Rainey and prepared to radio Sheriff Primrose just as the phone rang. "Sheriff's Department, how can I help you?"

"P-p-pllee." The words were impossible to understand, but the voice was female.

"Ma'am, please calm down," Tara said. "Take a deep breath and tell me what's wrong."

"M-m-my n-name is Donna." The woman continued to cry and stutter.

"Yes, Donna. What seems to be the problem?"

Tara could hear the woman forcibly drawing in a long-exaggerated breath and then expelling it on the other end of the line. Finally, the woman sighed and sounded like she had regained an ounce of her composure. "I think someone's been killed. Th-there was so much blood; it was e-every-where."

"Okay, Donna. Where are you? Who do you think was killed, hon?"

"My neighbors, Jerry and Beth Campbell." Donna's breaths hitched on the other end of the line. "Th-They live at Fifteen Poplar. There's blood all over the kitchen. I-it was everywhere."

"Okay, Donna. Where do *you* live? You said they're your neighbors?" Tara wrote the information on the blotter in front of her.

"I live at Ten Poplar."

Dear God. Right next door to the house that caught fire. "I'm sending an officer right now." Tara was about to radio in the report when a second line started ringing. "I have to put you on hold for just one second, Donna." But the woman on the other end had already hung up. Tara answered the second call. "Sheriff's Department, how can I help you?"

"Yes, this is Alice Tobin." The woman was also crying but controlled herself a little better than Donna had. "Billy and Eric still haven't come home. I know something's happened. Please help us?" She sounded defeated.

"Yes, of course, Mrs. Tobin," Tara said. "I will send a deputy over right away. Just hang in there, ma'am. I'm sure we'll be able to locate them."

"Thank you, the address is Seventeen Garden Drive."

Tara was about to disengage the call when a third line started flashing. *What the hell is going on here?* "A deputy will be right over, Mrs. Tobin."

"Thank you," the woman said and hung up.

"Sheriff's Department. How can I help you?"

"Yes, this is Brian Miller. I live on Stanhope Road. My neighbor's dog has been going nuts since late last night. Ordinarily, I wouldn't call, but the poor thing sounds like it's in distress, like something's wrong. I knocked on the door, but no one is home. The dog is in a pen in the backyard. He's one big German Shepherd, and there's no way I'm going near it without the family around. I thought you might want to check the place out. They love that dog. There's no way they would leave it alone all night."

"Sure, Mr. Miller. What's the address?"

"One Thirty-Three Stanhope Road. It's Otto Negal's house, and I live at One Thirty-Two."

"I'll send a car over as soon as I can."

Tara turned to the radio and waited for the phone to ring again. When it didn't, she spoke into the mic. "This is base to any available unit. Come in, over." As soon as she finished the transmission, the phone started to ring once again.

Dr. Ziegler had spent hours trying to locate his chief of medicine and the missing children by calling every toxicology center in the state. He struck out with every attempt; none of them had ever heard of Dr. Malcolm. Ziegler knew he was in over his head and needed to contact Sheriff Primrose as soon as possible. But by the time he finished with his phone calls, it had been well past three a.m. and he was beyond tired. He didn't bother to drive home. Instead, he found an empty room on the second floor, sat in one of the chairs, and racked his brain trying to figure out just what the hell was going on.

Ziegler had been on a rollercoaster since the Boyle kid arrived Saturday night, and it felt like every move he made since was the wrong one. He had been sure that using the MRI machine was the only way to see what was going on inside Abe and how the infection had affected the soft tissue. But the man had died during the procedure. *Just what the hell happened in there?* None of them could explain the strange dark cloud that had permeated the interior of the chamber. Whatever they were dealing with was powerful and able to control Deputy Rainey without even touching him. It almost killed the sheriff and would have killed the rest of them if it had been successful. Something had been inside of Abe. *Was that cloud the infection? Can an infection be visible outside the host's body?*

Ziegler asked himself a thousand questions and fell asleep in the dimly lit quiet of the room on the second floor without finding a single answer. He ran his brain in circles till it finally turned itself off. He didn't open his eyes until an orderly woke him Tuesday morning.

"Dr. Ziegler, I'm sorry. I was hoping I might find you," the orderly said.

"What time is it?"

"Just after nine. Nurse TenHove and Dr. Freedman have been looking for you. They're a bit understaffed this morning."

Ziegler jumped up, shaking off the sleep. "Thank you," he said and headed to the bathroom to freshen up.

He had intended to contact the sheriff immediately upon awakening but stepped into a beehive instead. Many of the staff had not shown up for work, and those who did were overwhelmed. He located Nurse TenHove, and she immediately sent him to help Dr. Freedman in the emergency room with the victims from the car accident. Several of the patients were in critical condition. Ziegler dove in and focused on the job at hand. His call to the sheriff would have to wait till later.

Burt arrived at the morgue early Tuesday morning to dispose of the ashes of Felix Castillo and Abe Gorman. He had left the office shortly after the incinerator finished running its cycle, with the interior of the giant oven still too hot to open. He started his day with a strong cup of coffee and the glamorous job of removing the remains, using a large steel dustpan to scoop the ashes into the trash. Despite what most people liked to believe, there was nothing sacred or dignified about death. It was messy and oftentimes humiliating. Burt knew that better than anyone. It had been his bread and butter longer than most marriages lasted these days.

Old Smokey, the morgue's incinerator, was an amazing piece of equipment, capable of reducing the human body to a pile of ash. Often, there were some bones and teeth left behind on the first go-round, but nothing fully intact. Most of the time, they, too, were rendered dust in the wind. Burt scooped up an undignified panful of cinders and paused as something hard rattled against the steel. *What the hell?* He sifted the ashes into the trash, waiting for the harder items to surface. Burt gasped as the lighter dust fell away and he found himself looking at what remained in the bottom of the pan. The small triangular-shaped teeth that filled Felix Castillo's mouth had withstood the incredible heat of the incinerator and remained unfazed.

"That's impossible," he said, examining the small objects. Burt had run the incinerator two full cycles to make sure nothing was left behind. He transferred several of the specimens to a container and examined them as yesterday's events replayed in his head like a crappy disco tune. Burt tried to wrestle with logic and reason, but after seeing what happened to Castillo and what Castillo had done to Abe, he was having a hard time of it. Something inside those men had changed them, and it sure as hell wasn't the flu. It was a lot more contagious than influenza and made the Black Plague look like a case of the sniffles.

The thing inside Abe had controlled the deputy and used the man like a tool. Burt hated to keep thinking it, but the damn thing had some very real vampire traits about it. *Look into my eyes.* He let out a nervous laugh. Being a Catholic, Burt had always imagined that Satan probably looked a lot like Nosferatu.

The big question that kept getting snagged in his head was *What the hell happened in the MRI?* It looked as if the machine had somehow extracted the infection from Abe and killed him in the process. If that was the case, then the answer lay in the inner workings of the machine itself. Unfortunately, Burt didn't know Jack-squat about an MRI machine, other than it extracted pictures of the body's soft tissue using magnetic resonance. And anyone who went to medical school could tell you that much.

It continued to eat at Burt how Dr. Malcolm could suspect snake venom. There was no way the bacterium that infected Felix and Abe was any type of reptile toxin or anything that even resembled one. Burt's next thought sent an icy shiver up his back. *What if it got Dr. Malcolm like it did the deputy?* If this thing was powerful enough to manipulate a deputy and make him try to kill the sheriff, then couldn't it control an old doctor and make him do just about anything? It could make him pick up the phone and lie about his patients, and it could feed the staff and the sheriff any false information it wanted to. It could also allow the children to simply walk out the back door. *Dear God.* Burt realized he had just given this thing a consciousness, and dammit if it didn't make sense. He needed to get in touch with Dr. Ziegler immediately.

Burt picked up the phone and dialed. A frantic woman on the other end answered. "Chilton Medical, please hold."

"Wha—" Chilton was never so busy you got put on hold. Burt could remember it happening maybe twice in the past. And those rare occasions had been under the most extreme circumstances. One time involved a four-car pileup on Route 3, and another happened the year the Lenape River overflowed the King Dam and flooded the south end of town. The early thaw combined with heavy rains swelled the watershed, and the county hadn't released the flood gates in time. Those who were caught in the frigid water succumbed to hypothermia within minutes. It had been a nightmare.

Finally, the woman came back on the line. "Thank you for holding. How can I help you?"

"Good morning, Doris. This is Burt, could I please s—"

"Oh, thank God," she said. "Burt, I am in a real pickle here. I have three nurses out sick, my lab tech never showed up, and about a half dozen other staff members decided to take off from work as well."

Burt listened with an impending sense of dread swelling within him. That many employees being sick on the same day, he doubted it was a coincidence and was almost certain his concerns for Dr. Malcolm had just been validated.

"If you aren't too busy this morning, I could really use an extra set of hands." Burt could hear it in Doris's voice; she was in over her head.

He told her he would be right over since there was little left to do at the morgue. Besides, he had known Doris for years and still held a man-sized crush for the woman. He also needed to talk with Ziegler as soon as possible. He hung up the phone and started to run out his office door, then grabbed the small jar of teeth he had collected earlier and stuffed them in his coat pocket.

Father Kieran struggled to keep the boy's fever down throughout the night. The child had started to shiver, and the heat continued to radiate from his body. He needed medical attention, but with the creatures still roaming the woods, it had been too dangerous to risk it. Kieran had placed two ice packs under the young man's armpits, checked his dressings, and wrapped him in a blanket, but he wasn't sure any of what he was doing was the correct way to treat the boy.

He had said his name was Billy. The boy was clearly in shock and suffering from exposure, and there was little that Kieran could do. However, there was always one thing that helped more than anything else. Father Kieran made the sign of the cross on the boy's forehead and on his own as well, then he opened the bible to the Gospel of James, rested the gold-bound book on the young man's chest, and prayed.

"And the prayer of faith will save the one who is sick, and the Lord will raise him up. And if he has committed sins, he will be forgiven."

Father Kieran kept a vigil over the boy until the cloak of night was pulled back like a shroud. The sky grew increasingly brighter with the morning's first light, and Kieran knew he was in the presence of the Lord. The darkness had passed, and the child stopped shivering. It felt as if his temperature may have dropped a little as well.

Kieran ran to the window to find that most of the creatures had vanished into the woods. In another hour, the last of them would be gone as well. The priest knew he couldn't risk putting another soul in danger and would have to take the boy himself. The child had already been spared once from the creatures, and Kieran had the Lord to protect him. He started to turn from the window when a sudden movement from the opposite direction caught his eye. The beasts had been traveling north towards the mountain, but what Kieran now saw was headed south. He watched as a family of raccoons darted from the woods and crossed the church parking lot. They were followed by no less than two dozen squirrels. "What on Earth?" he whispered. A large black bear stumbled out of the woods accompanied by a pair of mountain lions. Kieran gasped as possums and badgers joined in the parade and ran across the rectory parking lot. There were chipmunks, and groundhogs, and even a few wild boars. The animals were running as if they were being chased, fleeing from whatever it was that had invaded their home. They were trying to get as far from Garrett Mountain as possible.

Father Kieran again made the sign of the cross on his forehead and prepared himself for the work at hand.

Carl entered the station just as Tara hung up the phone. She shot him a look of wide-eyed panic, then picked up the second line that had been ringing. She gave him the universal sign for stop as he prepared to enter his office; the affirmative palm of her hand told him something was wrong. He watched as she wrote something down and told the person on the phone that a deputy would be along shortly. He took his hat off and walked around the counter to the dispatch station to find a shopping list of calls she had fielded.

"Thank God you're here. The whole town has gone insane." Carl braced himself, knowing it was bad. "Possible homicide at Fifteen Poplar. A neighbor called and found blood on the kitchen floor but didn't stick around to see if there were any bodies. She was too freaked out."

"Jesus Christ, I was just over there." *That's right across the street from the Barnes place.* Carl's gut twisted. "I'm on my way. Call Deputy Rainey and have him meet me there."

"10-4, Sheriff. Also, the Tobin boys never made it home. It's officially a case of missing persons now. Mrs. Tobin is frantic."

Goddammit, Billy, what are you up to now?

"Okay, send Kovach; he'll know what to do." Carl threw his hat on and attempted to exit the building a second time.

"There've been a few other calls as well, Sheriff."

"Anything life-threatening?" He was halfway out the door.

"Not exactly."

"Call Ted in and send him to the most important one first, have him work his way down the list." As Carl descended the front steps, the phone started ringing again. "Call me on the radio if you need me," he yelled and jumped into his cruiser.

Carl hit the cherries and siren and sped out of the municipal parking lot just as Lois Fischer was pulling in. He didn't see her as he sped down the Garrett Turnpike towards the south end of town. And by the time Lois had turned the Impala around, he was already gone.

CHAPTER 38

Sheriff Primrose and Deputy Rainey arrived at the Campbell residence within seconds of one another. They exited their vehicles and noticed the man and woman approaching from the opposite side of the street.

"Hello, Sheriff." The man wore a black silk shirt, unbuttoned enough to reveal the chain and gold crucifix that hung to the center of his chest. "I'm Angelo Franco. My wife made the call." He held on to the woman, who appeared visibly distraught, with fresh tears in her eyes and her hair knotted in curly black tangles.

"What happened?" Carl asked.

"Donna was worried about the neighbors and went over to check on them. The back door was open ... Said there's a lot of blood. She called me at work, and I came right home."

"Okay, I need you to go back inside and don't open your door for anyone other than me or my deputy. We'll be over soon," Carl instructed them.

"Of course, Sheriff." The man led his wife across the street and back into their house.

Carl nodded to Rainey with a look of understood risk, then turned toward the house and drew his weapon. Rainey followed his lead and did the same. "I'll take the front, and you take the back. And for God's sake, David, don't shoot me."

The deputy feigned a halfhearted smile. "Don't worry, Sheriff, that was a one-time thing." Deputy Rainey crept around the side of the house and proceeded to the back door while the sheriff checked the front, only to find it locked. Carl tested the door, rocking it slightly in its jamb. It didn't feel all that solid, and he figured it would only take one forceful push in the correct spot.

He pressed his shoulder against the door and backed up. Then Carl threw himself against the oak with the full force of his body, and the jamb splintered at the latch. The door swung inward as he rushed into the house.

Carl smelled the blood right away; it was strong, acrid, and overpowering. He heard Rainey ascending the back staircase like a Muskox in heat. "Front hallway clear," Carl yelled.

"Back room clear," Rainey answered.

Carl made his way up the front steps and met Rainey in the kitchen. Mrs. Franco hadn't exaggerated. The blood was everywhere. Judging by the look of it, there had been a struggle; the family had most likely been ambushed while they were preparing dinner. Food, cooking utensils, and gore littered the floor. There were tracks from several different prints, one of which was barefoot and led out of the kitchen down another hallway. Carl motioned for Rainey to follow him. They entered the living room, where the struggle had continued, judging from the mess. Someone had been dragged into this part of the house and bled onto the carpet before moving on.

More tracks led down the main hallway to a closed door. Carl followed the trail towards the room with the deputy on his heels. Silence consumed the house. All was still except for the intrusion of their footfalls on the carpet and the sound of the officers breathing. Standing at the bedroom door, Carl counted down from three. When he got to one, they burst into the room, with Carl sweeping left and Rainey covering the right. The bedroom was empty.

A large king-sized bed sat in the center of the room, where a massive pool of blood had soaked into the mattress. It looked as if someone had been laid out, bled to death, and then been removed sometime later. The paisley-printed curtains covering the windows suddenly ruffled inward from the force of a breeze entering the room. One of the windows had been left open. Carl pulled the curtain to the side and looked down at the windowsill, where several bloody handprints remained. "Jesus Christ!"

"They left through the window?" Rainey asked.

"That would be my guess."

They continued to check the rest of the house but were unable to find anything, including a body or a weapon. Then Carl radioed Tara and sent Rainey across the street to interview the couple who reported the incident.

"Sheriff Primrose to base."

"Come in, Sheriff, over."

"Tara, could you get in touch with Burt and see if he could meet me out here on Poplar?"

"Sure, Sheriff. I'll do that right now, over." Tara picked up the phone and dialed the medical examiner's office. She let the phone ring until the answering machine finally picked up.

"I didn't get an answer, so I left a message."

"Okay. Did you send Kovach to talk to the Tobin family?"

"I did, and Deputy Lutchen is taking care of the other calls. I think we got everything pretty much under control. How are things out there on Poplar?"

"Well, it's just as Mrs. Franco reported; there's a lot of blood, but there aren't any bodies." He didn't want to say anything else to his dispatcher, not just yet.

"Oh my, Sheriff. It sure has been one crazy week."

You have no idea.

Deputy Kovach had just finished interviewing Alice and Will Tobin when Deputy Ted Lutchen arrived at the Negal residence to investigate the neighbor's noise complaint. There was no answer when he rang the front doorbell, but he could hear the dog howling in the backyard. He rapped hard against the wood frame with his knuckles and waited. "Hello, Sheriff's Department. Is anybody home?"

The dog continued to carry on as if its ass was on fire. After waiting several minutes without an answer, Ted proceeded around the side of the house and let himself into the backyard through a large wooden gate. He first came to an oblong-shaped above-ground pool that had been covered for the fall. Then he noticed the pen and the giant German Shepherd pacing back and forth within. The massive dog locked eyes with him, stopped barking, and began to wag its tail.

Ted approached the pen as slow and non-threatening as he possibly could. "What's all the fuss about, buddy?" The Shepherd stood up against the pen on his hind legs to greet the deputy, his long, pink tongue hanging from the side of his mouth.

Ted noticed the two overturned water bowls and that the concrete beneath them was bone dry. "How long has it been since you had a drink?"

The dog reacted, wagging his tail even harder. *Poor thing, you're thirsty as hell.* He scanned the yard and located a garden hose attached to the house.

He walked over, turned the water on, and dragged the hose to the pen. The Shepherd jumped against the fence as Ted squirted the water directly into its mouth; it lapped and slurped it up as if it hadn't had a drink in years.

"Damn, I guess you were thirsty. Where's your family?" Ted read the tag on the dog's collar. "Baxter," he said as the dog gulped down the cool water. "Where's your family, Baxter?"

Once Baxter had drunk his fill, Ted threw the hose to the grass and approached the back door. The Shepherd let out a few disapproving barks and returned to pacing in his pen.

"Easy, boy, I'll be right back." Ted knew he was a bit of a softy when it came to animals and already liked this dog, a lot.

He ascended the steps and looked through the back kitchen window. At first glance, the place appeared to be in order ... Then he saw it. Pressing his face against the glass, Ted scanned the first-floor living room and noticed the television had been left on. His internal warning system red-lined. Less than two feet from the television, a recliner had been upended. The cushions lay next to it on the floor. He couldn't be sure, but it looked as if the cushions from the sofa had been thrown about as well. "This is Deputy Lutchen requesting backup," he called into his radio. "I'm located at One Thirty-Three Stanhope Road."

"Roger that, this is Deputy Kovach responding."

"10-4, Deputy Kovach." Tara's voice came over the radio. "Deputy Lutchen, Deputy Kovach is en route to your position. Copy that? Over."

"10-4, Lutchen out." Ted backed away from the door and prepared to kick it in. He hesitated and then tried the knob. It turned easily in his hands, allowing the door to swing inward. "Sheriff's Department! Is anyone home?" he shouted into the solitude of the empty kitchen.

The house remained as silent as a corpse while Baxter continued to raise holy hell in the backyard. As Ted prepared to enter, the distant echo of a siren reassured him that Deputy Kovach's approaching cruiser was only minutes away. Feeling it was safe to enter with backup en route, Ted proceeded into the house.

The kitchen was empty, and nothing appeared out of place. The counter was clean, and the small Formica table surrounded by its cushioned vinyl chairs all seemed in order. He walked into the living room, where the recliner lay tipped over on its side. The cushions were tossed, and a bowl of popcorn lay scattered on the floor like New Year's confetti in Times Square.

Something happened here. Deputy Lutchen took extra care not to disturb anything as he tiptoed around the popcorn and fallen furniture.

The sound of the cruiser's siren grew louder and then cut off. Ted looked out the front picture window to see Deputy Kovach getting out of the vehicle. He opened the front door for his partner and let the man into the house.

"What do you have?" Kovach asked.

Lutchen pointed to the state of the living room as Kovach entered. "A neighbor called and reported the family dog had been barking up a storm since last night. I checked, and the poor thing hadn't had any water in a long time. I gave him some from the hose."

Kovach nodded and pointed to one of the cushions on the floor. From what Ted could see, it looked like the underside was either wet or stained.

Kovach removed a ballpoint pen from his pocket, leaned down, and carefully used it to tip the cushion over. The opposite side revealed a dark scarlet stain in the shape of a handprint, smeared at the fingertips. The edges of the stain had dried and turned brown.

The men looked at one another, their hands dropping to their guns simultaneously. Not only had something gone terribly wrong in the house, but there was a chance that the perpetrator was still inside. They scanned the room and surveyed the exits. A hallway ran past the kitchen to a staircase leading to the second floor.

They remained still for a moment, listening for anything out of the ordinary. Ted stared intently at Kovach as one of the floorboards above their heads creaked ever so lightly. Frozen in place, they continued to listen. It came again, the faintest creak; something was moving upstairs. Whatever it was couldn't be big, either that or it was being cautious. *Creak!* A third time. Ted felt his heart rise into his throat and prayed that Kovach, his senior officer, wasn't half as freaked out as he was.

Deputy Kovach moved towards the staircase, and Ted pushed himself to follow. Slowly, they ascended each riser, trying not to alert whoever was hiding upstairs. The top landing opened onto a bathroom with bedrooms on either side. The door to the left was open, and upon quick inspection, there appeared to be nothing out of the ordinary inside. However, the door on the right was closed, and that was where the noise had originated from.

The officers took position on either side of the door with their weapons drawn. Kovach put his hand on the knob and waited. He gave Ted a nod of acknowledgment and, in one motion, turned the handle and pushed the door forward. The men swung their weapons in on the empty room. Ted prepared to yell "freeze!" but held back at the last second.

There could be no doubt that the owner of the bedroom was a little girl. The entire place was pink, from the paint to the bedspread and even the curtains. It reminded Ted of cotton candy.

They stood in the doorway for a moment with their weapons at the ready. *Creak.* It was soft and barely audible, but one of the floorboards on the far side of the room had shifted as if under stress. There was something underneath the bed. Ted felt his throat tighten and go dry with the realization. He waited for Kovach to take the lead.

"Cover me," Kovach said with his weapon trained on the floor. The senior officer took a step forward and approached the small, twin-size bed that could only belong to a child. Then, holding his weapon in one hand, he used his other to take hold of the bed. He nodded to Ted and flung the mattress and box spring with ease. It overturned quickly and fell against the wall, exposing the small figure that had been hiding beneath.

The child screamed and backed away, clutching what looked like a board game to her chest. A scatter of dolls and toys littered the floor where she hid.

"Whoa, easy, easy," Kovach said. "We're not going to hurt you. We're sheriff's deputies."

The girl screamed and buried her face behind the board. She trembled and screeched like a feral cat as she clawed herself further away from the men. Her hair was tangled and matted, and her clothes were stained. Ted could see the poor girl had urinated on herself. There was no telling how long she had been hiding underneath the bed.

Kovach reached out and tried to grab the child, but she lashed out at him. Ted shook his head and holstered his weapon, then slowly entered the room. Scanning the area, he took notice of a picture frame on the child's dresser, a family portrait of the girl with her brother and parents; the name engraved on the frame read, Dawn.

"Hi, Dawn," Ted said, lowering himself onto one knee in front of her. The girl's eyes widened in response to the sound of her name. "My name's Ted, Dawn. That's your name, right? Dawn? That's a pretty name."

Kovach watched as the rookie stepped in and took control of the situation.

"You know how I found you?" Ted smiled as she shook her head. "Baxter told me. He was worried about you. So, he called me over to find you."

"Baxter can't talk," the little girl said in a voice as small as a tear.

"Well, he was barking, so I went into the backyard. Then he started looking at the house. That was his way of telling me to go find you. Baxter's a good dog, isn't he?"

"Y-yes."

"Do you want to go thank him and bring him something to eat?"

She slowly nodded, her head barely moving at all.

Ted extended his hands and offered his kindest eyes. Dawn reacted and allowed him to take her in his arms. He carried her out of the bedroom past Deputy Kovach.

Cradling Dawn against his shoulder, he hid her face from the mess in the living room and headed straight to the kitchen. He filled a glass of water from the tap and offered it; she eagerly sucked down half the contents. "Are you hungry?" Ted grabbed a box of donuts from the counter and handed her one. Dawn accepted and shoved it into her mouth. Then Ted opened the door to a large pantry and found a jumbo-sized bag of dried dog food, which he scooped up with one hand as he transported Dawn with the other and exited the kitchen.

The girl's demeanor brightened at the sight of her dog, and Baxter lit up like a Roman candle when he saw her. He started whining and running in circles around his pen.

"Baxter won't bite me, will he?" Ted asked.

"No." She smiled. "He's a good boy."

Ted put Dawn down and let her stand on her own as she opened the pen. The enthusiastic dog bound from the kennel and proceeded to lick the girl's entire face. After slobbering on nearly every inch of her, he sniffed her up and down and whined, apparently concerned about the smells coming off her. But it appeared the dog was most interested in the bag of dog food. Ted watched Dawn upright the bowls and begin filling them herself, managing to spill only half of the bag as she overflowed Baxter's dish.

The dog didn't seem to mind. Baxter tore into the kibbles like a Hoover attacking an army of stray dust bunnies.

"Wow, he sure was hungry. You must have been hiding for a long time?" Ted knelt to meet the child at eye level.

Dawn looked at him and nodded. Her big eyes welled with tears.

"Can you tell me what happened, Dawn?" He didn't want to push but needed answers.

"It was Tommy."

"Tommy, is that your brother?"

She stroked the back of the dog as he polished off the rest of the food.

"What happened to Tommy?"

"He killed them. He killed Mommy and Daddy." Dawn latched onto Ted and buried her face into his neck. Baxter whined and looked up for a minute, concerned but not enough to tear himself away from his food. He hadn't eaten in a very long time.

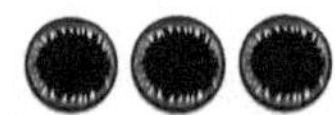

Don Fischer instructed four of his men to set up a second generator outside the cave and snake an extra fifteen hundred feet of electrical cord through the six-foot opening. An additional arsenal of high-powered floodlights was carried in along with the rest of Stephanie Thompson's own personal gear. Once the last of the lights were set in place and the generator was fired up, searing illumination penetrated the furthest reaches of the endless chamber, dispelling every shadow.

The original area where the team worked yesterday extended deep into the earth, far beneath the bedrock of Garrett Mountain. This initial chamber was the widest portion of the cave, although now it appeared to be more like a tunnel. The expansive cavern narrowed as it stretched back and sloped gradually downward into the earth; there was no telling just how far it went.

Don also set the team up with an array of portable lanterns and flashlights. The cave, now free from shadows, was as bright inside as it was out, allowing Stephanie to point out the nuances that had gone unnoticed in the darkness. Gail followed her lead and began taking pictures of the elaborate murals.

Joe and Barry once again gravitated to the skeletal remains and dove right into the process of cataloging and recording. But for Don, the big mystery was the cavern itself and the presence of the lodestone. Now that he was aware of the magnetite surrounding him, he felt more in tune with the subtle pull it influenced upon his metallic equipment. Holding his flashlight close to the rock surface, he noticed the way it was tugged toward the wall. He could feel it in everything from the buckle of his belt to his steel-toed boots.

Yesterday, they had only been able to see so far into the darkness. But now, with the unlimited visibility, Don was able to safely navigate his way toward the back of the cavern. The walls were decorated with even more murals. Scene after scene, there appeared to be a chronology to them, a progression that was noticeable. It was apparent the Lenape had been telling a story through their art. All of it struck Don as familiar in some way. *Where have I seen this before?*

He resumed his trek into the endless tunnel within the rock. The ceiling dropped, and the walls drew in closer, but the cavern continued to stretch on and on. Nearly a half dozen more murals covered the walls on either side as he made his way inward. It was impossible to say how far he had traveled or just how deep below the surface the cavern extended. Feeling his ears pop, Don knew he had descended at least a full atmosphere's worth in pressure. He ventured a bit further until he found himself in front of an opening in the rock wall, slightly smaller than the one at the entrance to the cave. A blanket of endless night stared back at him. Don cast the beam of his flashlight into the darkness and leaned forward. On the other side was another great chamber; this one was massive, far bigger than the one he just walked through. The weak beam of light was all but absorbed by the suffocating black of this new chamber. From what Don could tell, the void was endless. Somewhere in the murky distance, the faint sound of water dripping off the rock surface echoed back at him. He cast the light onto the floor and didn't find one. It was impossible to know if there was a safe passage through the chamber or a bottomless drop. This was one of those places that killed both the skilled and the foolish alike.

Donald turned to leave and bumped into Stephanie. He jumped back, finding himself face-to-face with her. "Christ, you scared the crap out of me."

"What are you looking at?" she asked, not bothering to back up.

"I was surveying the cavern to see how far it extends and noticed all these murals." He cast his light against the walls, but Stephanie didn't bother to look.

"I think you know how dangerous it is to go off on your own in a place like this?" she said with a smirk on her face.

"I do. There's a chamber on the other side of this opening, and I don't see a floor. It could be a very far drop."

"Really?" She attempted to poke her head inside to get a better look, but Don stopped her.

"Nobody goes in there without my guys checking it out first, even then, not without the proper gear. The last thing we need is for this to turn into a rescue situation or, God forbid, something worse."

Stephanie stood there for a moment longer before turning back toward the entrance. "Fair enough, Mr. Fischer. Maybe you could bring your flashlight over here and show me the rest of the murals you found?"

They left the entrance to the great chamber and proceeded to the relative safety of the main chamber. Don noticed the flashlight as it trembled in his hand; he had been shaking. He was certain it had more to do with his proximity to the dangerous drop-off and nothing to do with how close he had been standing near the young doctor.

The second Burt Lively entered through the emergency room doors, he was flagged down by Doris TenHove and put to work. Joey DeStefano, who worked in phlebotomy, had been one of the many employees who hadn't shown up, along with Dean Childers, one of the lab technicians. Doris let Burt decide which position he felt comfortable filling. Naturally, he opted for the lab.

"Thank you for coming over so quickly." Several lengths of Doris's grey curls had come undone and hung loose from her nurse's cap. But to Burt, the woman looked as lovely as ever.

"Well, maybe you could make it up to me and let me take you out for dinner on Friday." He leaned over the counter and raised a pair of bushy eyebrows. They had been playing the flirting game for years without it ever developing into anything. Both were married to their jobs, but Burt was more than just a little interested. Doris was close to his age and carried a few extra pounds in the back, an attribute Burt was defenseless against.

Doris fixed her hair and pretended to blush. "Why, Mr. Lively. I'm afraid you couldn't handle me if you got me. I might give you a heart attack."

"I couldn't think of a better way to go. Come on, give an old man a break, or do you want me to beg?"

"I tell you what, old fool. If you hustle your buns down to the lab and get to work, you might not have to buy me dinner. I might just give it to you right here on the counter."

Burt choked and almost swallowed his tongue. He felt the heat rush throughout his body and turn to steam. Doris TenHove dangled the goods under his nose, leaning over the counter while he stared with his jaw hung slack. Then she gave him the shoo sign by waving her hands, indicating he was dismissed. Burt left the reception desk grinning like a fool. At sixty-two, he had no more resistance to the powers of the feminine sex than a fourth-grade boy.

Burt passed through the ER on his way to the lab with his mind somewhere in the clouds and not on where he was going; he nearly ran right into Dr. Ziegler.

"Burt, what are you doing here?" Ziegler asked.

"Looks like you're a little understaffed today. I told the pretty nurse I would pitch in and lend a hand."

Ziegler looked at the reception desk and spotted Doris TenHove. He raised his brows, and his eyes widened as he opened his mouth to speak.

"I-um-a, I'm glad you're here. We really must talk." The doctor checked his watch. "Unfortunately, it will have to wait. Meet me in the cafeteria at one o'clock."

Burt looked around the emergency room. There were at least four occupied beds, which was unusual. Not only was there an absence of staff, but there appeared to be an influx of patients. Burt tried to push what he was thinking to the back of his mind, but it was impossible. *So, this is how it starts.*

CHAPTER 39

Sheriff Primrose instructed Deputy Kovach to tag and log all the physical evidence he could collect at the Negal residence. Similar instructions had been given to Deputy Rainey regarding the home of Beth and Jerry Campbell, but without the assistance of the medical examiner, there was only so much that could be done. The absence of victims at either scene prevented the events from being filed as murder investigations; however, there had been a witness at the Negal place. Dawn Negal had seen something, but the girl was in shock and only five years old. Ted Lutchen was able to bring her around somewhat, but her condition was delicate, and there was no way she could be subjected to rigorous questioning. The sheriff was hoping they might coax a little information out of the girl, but first she needed to see Dr. Ziegler to make sure she wasn't suffering from something a bit more serious.

Carl pulled into Chilton's parking lot just as Ted opened the back door of his cruiser and lifted the child out. He cradled her in his arms and approached the sheriff.

"Sheriff, this is Dawn Negal." Her tiny fingers dug into the collar of his uniform. "Want to say hi, honey?" She shook her head and clung for dear life. Ted shrugged his shoulders and nodded.

"Looks like you found a friend. Hi, Dawn. I'm Sheriff Primrose. The doctor is going to take a look at you."

The girl began to squirm and cry.

"Do you want Deputy Lutchen to stay with you?"

The answer appeared to be yes and seemed to calm her down.

"Okay, then."

They entered the medical center to find the place a flurry, with nurses and orderlies running every which way. Carl made eye contact with Dr. Ziegler as he emerged from behind a drawn curtain. He rushed over to where they stood.

"You must be Dawn. I heard how cute you are. I guess they weren't kidding." Ziegler produced out a lollypop from his lab coat pocket. "You look like a cherry girl. Am I right?"

Dawn nodded as Ziegler pulled the wrapper from the candy and handed it to her.

"Do you think you could do this in a quiet room? She's been through a lot," Carl said to Ziegler, lowering his voice.

"Sure, if you'll just follow me." Dr. Ziegler led them down the hall away from the bright lights and commotion of the ER. He opened the door to an examination room and showed them inside. Dawn continued to suck on the lollipop but latched on to Ted's collar when he attempted to place her on the exam table. However, she did allow the deputy to sit down with her on his lap, and even remained still as Ziegler checked her heartbeat and looked in her eyes. Carl waited and held his breath.

Father Kieran loaded the boy into the backseat of his Buick and transported him to the medical center. It had been difficult, but he prayed for strength, and the Lord had provided. *Praise God.* The child continued to moan and stir in his unconscious state as Kieran pulled up to the emergency room entrance and laid on the horn. Having been alerted to the commotion, two orderlies rushed to the car, pushing a gurney. Kieran directed them to the boy in the backseat, then stood back as the men lifted and transported him inside.

The child was whisked away to an open bed in the ER, and the priest was directed to the desk, where an older nurse worked. He gave her all the information he could about the boy, omitting how long he had waited before bringing him in and not mentioning a word about demonic apparitions.

The only thing Father Kieran knew about the boy was that his name was Billy. He wasn't a member of the parish, at least not recently. Maybe when he was younger. But it was difficult to remember every child that walked through the doors of the church, even in a town as small and isolated as Garrett Grove.

Doris told him that the young man looked familiar but couldn't place his name. More than half the teenage boys in Garrett Grove saw the inside of the emergency room at one point or another, whether it was for a broken arm, a couple dozen stitches, or something a bit more life-threatening. And without proper identification, there was only so much they could do, so the young man was admitted under the name William Doe.

Lois drove down every side street in a vain attempt to locate the sheriff. She'd heard police sirens multiple times throughout the morning but had always been too far away to follow them. Finally, she returned home just before noon to use the restroom and refuel. She was heating a bowl of clam chowder when the phone rang, and she picked it up immediately. "Hello." She half-believed it might be Carl calling.

"Hi, Mom," Troy greeted her.

"Honey." Lois's heart fluttered, and she clutched the phone in a death grip. Her thoughts went straight to worst-case scenarios, assuming something was wrong. "Is everything okay? Why are you calling in the middle of the day?"

"I'm okay. The principal let me use her phone. I wanted to see if I could go over Janis's house after school."

"Oh, I don't know if that's such a good idea." After Troy had nearly been killed from running into the street, Lois felt she had every right to be a bit frugal with her son's extracurricular activities.

"Aw, please, Mom. I promise I won't walk through the graveyard. Janis lives right by the school in the Village. I don't even have to go that way, really."

Lois considered his request, which wasn't all that unreasonable. He would be with two other children, and the Village was only a few blocks from the school. "I guess so, but I'll come pick you up at five. I don't want you walking home alone, and I want to meet Janis's parents."

"I think her mom will still be working with Dad. But her aunt will be there. You can meet her."

Lois felt the muscles in her back tighten at the mention of Janis's mother and Don working together. If she didn't know any better, she might have mistaken what she was feeling for jealousy. *That's ridiculous.* She and Donald didn't have that type of relationship. It was hard to say what type they actually did have. They had only stayed together for Troy. Everything she had ever done had been for Troy. He was her entire world, and she hated to deprive him of anything that brought him happiness. So, Lois acquiesced to her son's request, as she knew she would, just like she always did.

"You said she lives in the Village. What's the address, kiddo?"

"Twenty-Two Village Road, right around the corner from Wendy."

"I'll be there at five on the dot."

"Thanks, Mom. I love you."

"I love you too, kiddo." She was about to hang up and added, "Be careful, honey."

"I will, bye."

Lois sat in the kitchen alone. She had gotten used to being alone throughout the day. Ever since she had taken Troy to his very first day of school. The house had felt so empty without him there. But as time passed, she learned to deal with the unnerving silence and even managed to block it out.

Troy had been such an animated child, as most children were. But Troy was hers, and he was her only one. Every first experience for him was a new one for Lois as well. His first taste of ice cream made her feel as if she had never savored the decadent treat before. His first step, his first words, she had seen it all as if through his eyes. Donald missed out on most of those firsts, and it hadn't even fazed him. It didn't even occur to him that Troy had mastered enough of the English language to put a sentence together until one unforgettable night. It was late, and Lois had spent most of the day chasing Troy around the house. She was exhausted and didn't even stir when the boy started crying. Donald walked into Troy's room to find his son toddling in his crib, waving a bottle that had been drained dry. "Fill 'er up, Pop," a one-year-old Troy had said, and Donald nearly pissed his pants.

He later returned to bed and woke up Lois. "I think if he's old enough to say, 'Fill 'er up, Pop,' then he's old enough for us to take away the goddamn bottle."

That had been a funny one; Lois could always count on Troy for a good laugh. And Donald had been furious, which made it even funnier. Maybe if he had been around more or paid closer attention when he was home, Donald would have known that his son had been talking for nearly two weeks by that point. But even when Donald was around, he was never exactly present, and that had always been the biggest problem in their marriage. He had almost choked on his roast beef last night when Troy said he had spent the day with two girls.

Lois felt as if her little man was growing up way too fast. Just four days ago, she figured out that Troy and Wendy had been kissing, and now he was spending his afternoons at another girl's house—with them both. At this rate, she couldn't imagine what his high school years would be like. Lois thought about the day she told her parents she was pregnant and envisioned a similar situation involving her son. *Don't you dare do that to me, Troy.*

The sudden sound of police sirens cut through the silence like the slamming of a door. Lois tried to discern their location but realized they were somewhere on the other side of town. There had been an awful lot of police activity this morning; this had to be the third time she heard sirens. *Carl's really got his hands full.* As if on cue, her mind started to wander into the land of *what if,* as it frequently did. It was always the same questions she asked herself. *What if I hadn't gone away to college? What if I stayed in Garrett Grove and married Carl? What if I never broke his heart... What if?* They were questions she would never know the answers to, but still, she continued to ask them almost constantly. The ultimate answer to all of them was always the same. If she had done any of it differently, she might never have had Troy, and that was a blessing she wouldn't trade for anything, not even for Carl.

Her concentration was shattered by the sound of the phone ringing on the counter. Lois jumped and answered it. "Hello."

The voice on the other end was hysterical but clearly recognizable. "What is it, Alice? What's wrong?"

"Oh God, Lois. Billy and Eric are missing. The police just left. Th—" Alice broke down, unable to finish what she had been saying.

"What?" Lois thought back to Saturday night, the last time she had seen her nephews. They had helped Troy with the haunted house. It seemed impossible what her sister was saying. Surely there had to be some type of mistake. "Slow down, Alice. I don't understand. What happened to Eric and Billy?"

Her crying continued, but Alice managed to control herself enough to form a coherent sentence. "The boys. Will and I went to visit his brother, and when we got back, they left a note. They said they would be home late." She nearly lost what little composure she had but was able to continue. "They never came home Sunday night, and then we never heard from them yesterday. Oh God, Lois, the police just left."

Lois attempted to get her mind around what her sister was saying. Her nephews had been missing since Sunday, and she was just finding out about it now.

"Why didn't you call me sooner, Alice? Why did you wait so long?"

"You know the boys. I kept thinking they would be home any minute. And the police said they couldn't do anything until they were missing for forty-eight hours."

"You've got to be kidding me! You should have called me. Carl would have come right over, I'm sure of it."

"Oh, Lois, I don't know what to do." Alice broke down and sobbed into the other end of the phone. Finally, Will came on the line.

"Hello, Lois?" he said.

"I'll be right over." Lois slammed the phone down, grabbed her purse, and was doing twenty miles over the speed limit before leaving her block.

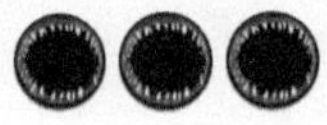

Wendy and Janis waited for Troy near the tire swings while he called his mom. The girls passed the time talking, mostly about boys, and of course, Troy's name had been mentioned more than once. The story he told them about his walk home yesterday was a major topic of discussion.

"Do you think Troy really saw something in the graveyard?" Janis asked.

Wendy had come to school with her hair styled similarly to how Janis wore hers. Now the girls could easily pass for a miniature version of two-thirds of Charlie's Angels. "If Troy said something chased him, you can bet it did. He doesn't lie, not like other boys. He's just not good at it." The girls looked up as Troy exited the back doors of the school. "I don't know what he saw, but if it scared Troy, it had to be really scary."

Janis listened while her new friend applied reason and rationale to help understand their problem.

Troy jogged over to the girls with his lunch box in hand. "My mom said yes, but she wants to pick me up at five. So, whatever we do, we gotta be done by then." He sat down next to them and dug in. "I got peanut butter 'n jelly. Mmm, grape too."

Wendy opened her lunch box and removed an egg salad sandwich, which Troy spotted out of the corner of his eye. He hated egg salad more than getting a haircut and prayed that Wendy wouldn't want to trade again.

"Here you go." She handed him the egg salad and ripped the PB&J from his tightly clenched fist.

The look of defeat must have been written on his face, as Janis smiled and held out a sandwich in her small hands. "I have salami and cheese, Troy. Do you want to trade?"

He didn't know what to say. Had she really just offered him salami and cheese, the holy grail of the deli sandwiches? It was too good to be true.

"Sure." He accepted the trade-up, fully expecting a negative reaction from Wendy. However, the PB&J had had a calming effect on the girl, and she didn't seem to mind.

It was nearly a full minute before any of them spoke. Troy imagined they were all probably thinking the same thing but no one wanted to be the first to bring it up. He was just happy he didn't have to eat egg salad.

A few mouthfuls later, Wendy broke the silence. "If you had to guess what they looked like, how would you describe them?"

Troy had given it a lot of thought since yesterday. And although he hadn't gotten a good look at either of the creatures, he had caught a glimpse of the one on the left. "It was really weird. They were fast but not too big. Maybe a little smaller than a kid, or about the same size. It kinda ran like those African dogs with the big shoulders."

"Hyenas," Janis said.

"Yeah, like hyenas. Only, they ran a little, and then they kinda hopped too, almost like a frog. I never saw anything like that." He took a bite of the salami and chewed as fast as he could.

"Hmmm," Wendy said. "Why do you think they were in the graveyard? Do you think they live there?"

Troy thought about it as he chewed the delicious meat and swallowed. "I don't know ... maybe. But I doubt it. I think something like that needs a lot more room. I think they would get bored in the little graveyard."

"That makes sense," Janis said. "Predators need a large hunting ground. Something like that would probably need a lot of land, like a park or the woods."

"The foothills!" Wendy slapped Troy in the shoulder, almost knocking the sandwich from his hands in mid-bite. "There's no bigger woods in town than the foothills. If they live anywhere, I bet that's it." The look of satisfaction that crossed her face suggested she was pleased with her deduction. Troy thought it made her look smart and admired how Wendy was able to figure things out so fast. It had only taken her a few seconds. He was glad she was on his team.

"That makes sense." Janis took a small bite of her egg salad and set it to the side. "Do you think they live on the mountain and came down because they were hungry?"

"I guess," Troy said. "But there's a lot to eat on the mountain, and the mountain lions hardly ever come into town. These things were brave." Troy noticed Janis wasn't eating the sandwich and started to feel bad. He wondered why she had traded in the first place if she didn't like egg salad. It didn't make sense.

"Maybe they don't eat animals," Wendy stated. "I mean, they chased you. If they ate animals, they could have gone after a squirrel or a cat or something. Maybe they preferred boys and girls. You know like the ... Ojanox."

"I need to show you something in one of my mom's books. It has to do with those little teeth, you know, the ones I have in my case?"

Troy had been thinking about those dangerous-looking teeth ever since yesterday, and if he had to guess, he would have said that Wendy was right. Those things that chased him probably had teeth just like that.

And it was as simple as that. It wasn't even a consideration that the teeth in Janis's case might belong to an animal that had gone extinct eons ago. The children had their own mystery to solve and had each concluded a correlation. Something had chased Troy through the graveyard, Janis's mother had given her teeth from some mysterious creature, and Mrs. Fischer had recently told them the story of the Ojanox. The connection was elementary. The teeth obviously belonged to an Ojanox, and that was what had chased him. Garrett Grove had an Ojanox problem.

The big question was: what do you do when you have an Ojanox problem? Janis was the one to make the suggestion. "In her book, there are a bunch of pictures of those teeth, and then there are other pictures too. Pictures of weapons. I think that's what you need to use to kill them. I don't think you can use just anything."

"You mean like a werewolf?" Wendy said.

"Or a vampire?" Troy added.

"Yeah, that's what I think. I want you guys to look and see for yourselves."

The bell rang to call the children back into the building. Troy watched Janis wrap up the rest of the sandwich and place it into her lunch box. He figured if he got the chance, he would ask her why she had traded in the first place. The second bell rang as they beelined back into the building. The other children had been watching their pow-wow. However, there were now fewer eyes to watch than there had been yesterday.

Perhaps the quietest place in the medical center was the lab where Burt Lively sat working alone. How could he say no to Doris TenHove? He'd been playing cat and mouse with the woman for the better part of a decade now, and she'd always dismissed his advances and acted uninterested. But today he just might have melted the old girl's icy heart, even if it was only just a little. She'd been pleased with his eagerness to lend a helping hand and promised him a good time in return. Either she was finally coming around or just sick and tired of turning him down. Whichever it was, Burt would take it; there was nothing wrong with accepting a little pity sex.

There was a saying that guys Burt's age came to respect as gospel: *Never trust a fart, and never waste a boner.* If Doris TenHove was willing, he damn sure wasn't going to waste that boner.

The lab was quiet except for the occasional doctor checking on the status of their tests. Burt pushed through a mountain of work that had piled up since yesterday, which was nothing more than a stack of files. The results of several biopsies, an array of blood samples, and an abundance of reports. Nothing all that taxing, but it felt good to get out of the morgue and be around the living. The only human being Burt had a semi-healthy relationship with was Carl, and that was often debatable. Before that, it had been Carl's father. He had been friends with Allen Primrose for years, but Burt had been a different man in those days. He and Allen grew up together in Garrett Grove. They went to school together, played cowboys and Indians on the trails of the foothills, and when the world went to war for the second time that century, they joined the army to go kill Krauts together.

However, they were soon split apart. Allen was a born soldier and found himself an infantryman; he was sent into France and then on to Berlin to aid in the liberation of the city from the Nazi regime. Burt, on the other hand, already had a few years of medical school under his belt and became a corpsman for the Army. He ended up in Poland. Burt's division swept through Auschwitz as the last of the Nazi generals were choking on their cyanide pills. The ones that remained were rounded up by Burt's platoon and executed on-site ... the lucky ones, that is. Those that weren't lucky enough to have eaten their own bullet or one issued by Uncle Sam found themselves corralled and set loose into the same cages they had used on their captives. The platoon released the Jewish prisoners and let them do with the German soldiers as they pleased. It was a bloodbath, and the prisoners showed no more mercy than they had been shown themselves.

It affected Burt horribly. Though he had initially joined the Army for that very reason, to kill Nazis, he didn't have the heart for it. Burt was a healer and wanted to help the German, Austrian, and Polish Jews they had found emaciated and at death's door in Auschwitz. Sadly, Burt's division were unable to help those poor people and had ultimately been responsible for killing a great deal of them as well. The prisoners were starving. Burt had never seen how bad the human body could look when it was deprived of nourishment for such an extended time. He instinctively did what the rest of the American medics were doing and gave the prisoners food. They gave them whatever they had available. The rich, filling food that had fed the Nazi generals was there for the taking, and these people were close to death. Burt's platoon liberated the stockpiles and distributed it amongst the emaciated faces with their outstretched hands. They needed his help, and he had given it to them, and it had killed them by the truckload.

The men, women, and children had been starving for longer than any American soldier could even imagine, and their bodies had undergone tremendous physiological changes. Their stomachs and digestive tracts had grown used to being empty. Their organs had shrunk and been in a state of shock. The rich food that the Germans had eaten, as well as the American's own rations, acted no less effectively than the gas chambers. Some of the prisoner's stomachs burst and ruptured due to the strain of over ingestion. Others grew violently sick and developed acute colitis and gastritis. The results were the same, and they died just as horribly, if not worse, than at the hands of the Nazis. Burt had joined the army to kill people, and he'd gotten his wish.

Allen returned home to tell stories of the people he freed in Berlin and tales of German women who had shown their appreciation to the American soldiers. Burt returned with a darker view of humanity and a terminal disinterest in life. He no longer felt fit to pursue the field of medicine. How could he trust himself to diagnose a patient and treat them properly after the devastating mistakes he and the other men had made in Poland? It had been a dark time for Burt. While the world was celebrating the victory and America was patting itself on the back for saving the day, Burt was receding into himself. He damn sure didn't feel like a hero. Shit, even the Russians had done a better job, since they were used to starvation. Stalin had prepared them. They saw the people in the concentration camps and had tossed them a single potato—"Here you go, make soup."

Allen helped his friend through it and forced Burt to get out of bed on days he would have simply hidden away. He drove Burt to class and forced him to finish med school. Burt still didn't believe he had what it took to become a doctor, but he was willing to pursue what he started. Allen forced him to go on double dates, and when Allen met Carl's mother, it was Burt Lively who made the toast at the wedding. Allen had brought Burt back from a darkness that easily could have consumed him, and Burt owed the man a lot more than a few kind words on his wedding day. He owed him his life.

It was Allen who suggested that Burt become a medical examiner. He was at the top of his class when it came to lab work and discerning abnormalities of the various systems. If he didn't want to be a diagnostician, at the very least, he should consider forensics. He would make one hell of a specialist. It was settled, and the position of medical examiner proved to be a place where Burt found himself comfortable. At least he didn't have to worry about killing anyone. That was an off-color joke he told only Allen … every now and then.

Burt watched Carl grow up and took to the boy as if he were his own. Allen let young Carl tag along quite a bit, and it was obvious the kid would one day follow in the old man's footsteps. Then Carl himself was sent to war … a very different war. One that was on the television and wasn't pretty. Not that war ever was. Still, there were some things the public didn't need to see and never needed to know. The media had filled a lot of people's heads with images that changed the way America looked at the young men who went to Vietnam. And the soldiers got nothing like the hero's welcome that Burt's generation had received.

Carl returned in one piece, making it home just in time to say goodbye to his old man. Allen died the following year, and Burt delivered the eulogy at his funeral. Suddenly, he and Carl were the only family either one had left. Carl's mom had passed away young, and Burt never found the right gal to settle down with. He looked at Carl as a son, and that son grew to be a friend—a damn good one, at that.

Burt arched his back and listened to his joints crack. He opened another file and went to work transferring data to the blood catalog. Checking the clock, he noticed he still had some time before his meeting with Dr. Ziegler. Lord knew they sure had a lot to talk about.

CHAPTER 40

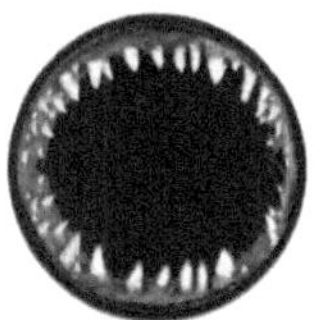

Dawn Negal had spoken briefly to Ted Lutchen at the crime scene but withdrawn into herself and grown silent once again. Carl didn't want to push the child but was desperate for answers. She was the closest thing to a witness they had. It was apparent that something horrific had taken place in the house, yet somehow, the girl had managed to survive.

Dr. Ziegler checked her vitals and gave her something he called apple juice to drink, although what he had given her contained far more vitamins and nutrients than regular apple juice. He asked routine questions as he examined her, but she still wasn't talking. It was possible there were too many men in the room. Carl whispered in Ziegler's ear, then said something to Ted. A moment later, he spoke up. "Dr. Ziegler, do you mind if I have a word with you outside for a moment?"

"Sure," the doctor answered. They stepped out of the room and waited by the door. Ziegler lowered his voice. "If I sense this is going the wrong way, I will end it."

"Of course," Carl said.

They listened outside the door as Deputy Lutchen began to speak.

"Don't be scared, Dawn. I won't let anything happen to you." She wrapped her arms around his neck like a cat about to be thrown into a bathtub. "Whoa, that sure is a tight grip. I didn't know you were so strong. You must eat a lot of spinach. Is that it? Do you like spinach?"

She shook her head and shoved her thumb in her mouth. Ted didn't have children of his own, but he knew it couldn't be a good sign. It had probably been years since she last sucked her thumb, and to suddenly revert to the habit was concerning.

"Oh, you like thumbs better than spinach?" She let out a noise that could have been a laugh. Ted rocked her in his arms and continued to talk.

"I bet you're still hungry, aren't you?" She nodded again. "What if I found us some ice cream? Would you like some ice cream?" She raised her head and nodded, looking at him through eyes that were slightly brighter.

"Yeah, I could go for some ice cream too," Ted said loud enough to be heard by the men on the other side of the door.

Carl got the message and looked to Dr. Ziegler, who pointed in the direction of the cafeteria. He took off down the hall like an Olympic runner.

"I saw all the toys in your room. You sure have a lot. Did you know my favorite color is pink? What's your favorite color?"

"Pink," she said, her voice a little more than a whisper.

"No kidding, we both like pink. What else do you like?"

"Drowsy," the girl said with her thumb still in her mouth.

"Drowsy, are you tired, honey?"

"No, silly." She removed her thumb. "Drowsy is my doll. She can talk."

"Oh, I see. What does Drowsy say?"

"She says, 'Kiss me goodnight,' and 'I want a drink of water.'" Dawn perked up with the discussion of the doll.

"Were you in your room playing with Drowsy last night?" Ted steered the conversation.

"No."

"No? You weren't in your room last night?"

"I wasn't playing with Drowsy. I was playing with my stick-ums."

He didn't know exactly what she was talking about but thought he might have an idea.

"Oh, you mean like color forms, peel and stick?"

"No, stick-ums are magnets. You put them on the stick-um board and move them around. There's teddy bear stick-ums and flowers and one that looks like Baxter. I have a lot."

Ted remembered seeing the board she had been clutching and the collection of magnets scattered around her when Deputy Kovach upended the bed.

"Oh, so you were playing stick-ums in your room last night." He paused, unsure about how to lead into what he wanted to say next. "Did you hear anything while you were playing stick-ums?"

She nodded her head and stared up at him.

"Can you tell me what you heard?"

She clutched him tighter. "Animals in the house ... monkeys, maybe. Then Mommy and Daddy yelling."

"What were they yelling, honey?" Carl had returned and listened outside the door with Dr. Ziegler.

"They yelled 'Tommy, no; Tommy, stop!'" Tears fell down the young girl's cheeks.

"That sounds scary. What did you do?" He held on to the poor thing as she dug her fingers into his collar.

"I hid with my stick-ums."

And she had probably stayed there all night, up until the time they found her, starving, soiled, and frightened out of her wits. She had hidden with her toys scattered all around her and the stick-ums board clutched tight to her chest. Ted felt he had pushed the child more than enough and didn't want to cause her any further suffering.

Carl took the silence as his cue and entered the room with the doctor behind him. "Who wants some ice cream?" Carl held up two Styrofoam cups. "I have chocolate, and I have strawberry."

Dawn looked up at the mention of the treat. "Strawberry." She held out her hand.

Ted placed her on the cushion of the examination table as the sheriff handed her the cup and gave the other one to him. "Here you go, Deputy. You deserve it." Carl watched as Ted and the young girl dug into the ice cream, and smiled.

Ted had handled the situation well, and Dawn revealed exactly what Carl suspected. That her brother, Tommy, had attacked and killed their parents. Somehow, the boy had overlooked the fact that his sister was still in the house.

Carl attempted to work out the exponential factors of the problem in his head. It was now evident that Felix Castillo had infected at least two others prior to his untimely introduction to the front bumper of the delivery truck. Tommy Negal and Jeff Campbell had gone missing for several hours Sunday afternoon, and it was becoming clear what had happened.

That chance meeting appeared to have resulted in the transmission of the contagion to not only the Campbell and Negal families but most likely to the Barnes family as well. In addition, the Tobin boys were missing along with a dozen other of the town's citizens. That brought the possible infection count close to thirty. Carl needed an immediate course of action and had no idea what he would say to the state police when he called them for backup. *Christ, I might need to call the National Guard.* "Deputy Lutchen, could you stay here with Dawn while the doctor and I go for a walk?"

Ted agreed through a mouthful of chocolate ice cream. It was hard to tell who was enjoying the snack more, the deputy or the five-year-old girl.

Ziegler led Carl down the hall and started to fill him in. "Christ, it isn't good, not good at all. I called Oswego. Not only did Dr. Malcolm never show up, but he never called and never scheduled the transfer of the children. I contacted every facility that deals with toxicology and infectious disease, and struck out on all of them. It's as if Dr. Malcolm and the children just vanished."

Carl removed his hat and rubbed at the bridge of his nose. It was just as he feared. Dr. Malcolm had been compromised. He wrestled with how this changed the exponential factor of the situation. *If Dr. Malcolm has been infected, then so are the children's parents. Dear God!* That was three children, Dr. Malcolm, and four more adults. With the exponential probability of transmission, there was no telling how many people in town had already been compromised.

"You think maybe you should have called me a bit sooner?" Carl rubbed at the dull ache in his temples.

"As you can see, we've been inundated with a rash of absenteeism and an increase in emergency room activity. Without Dr. Malcolm, it's all I can do to keep up with the cases as they come through the door, and I still have patients to attend to on the wings."

"I get it. We're all stretched thin. But we've got a real mess here. Have you thought about what may have happened last night in the MRI?"

"I have, but I don't have any real answers yet."

"Well, keep working on it. By my count, this may have already spread to thirty or forty so far. And every minute that passes sinks us that much deeper into shit's creek, and we're already up to our necks. I need answers, and I think that MRI machine has something to do with it."

"I'm doing the best I can, Sheriff." Ziegler had walked Carl to the Lab where Burt was working. They entered the room as the coroner looked up from a pile of reports.

"So, this is where you've been hiding." Carl nodded. "Don't get up. I'm in big trouble, old man, and I need all the help I can get. You probably heard the sirens this morning."

"I did." Burt furrowed his brow, preparing himself for the bad news.

"You know about the house fire last night. Well, it wasn't any old fire. Someone left the dinner burning on the stove, and there weren't any bodies discovered in the place. The upstairs bedroom window was busted out from the inside as if something jumped through it. I found blood outside the back door and seriously doubt if anyone was in the house when it caught. I believe they were infected by their neighbors, the Campbells."

"Isn't that one of the kids that was lost in the foothills?" Burt asked.

"Bingo. He and his friend Tommy were the ones who left their bikes in the woods. I think our guy Felix got to them sometime after he left your lab. The kids and both their families are missing. We found a hell of a lot of blood over at the Campbell place ... and again, no bodies."

"Jesus Christ!" Burt gasped.

"I'm afraid it gets worse," Ziegler added. "Dr. Malcolm and the children never made it to Oswego. At this point, we have to assume they're all infected and possibly still in Garrett Grove."

"Jesus Christ!" Burt repeated. "You saw what one of those things did. Can you imagine what twenty or more are capable of?"

"Unfortunately, I can," Carl said. "And that's why I'm counting on both of you to figure out what it was about that MRI machine that put the damn thing down."

"I didn't know we moved past trying to save people." Ziegler raised his voice. "For crying out loud, we're talking about children here. We're talking about our neighbors. I'm a doctor. I took an oath to do no harm. These are your people, Sheriff. Don't you care about that?"

Carl felt the pressure rise within him. He'd been trying to keep it together as best he could, but the situation was about to go critical; he could feel it. *Who the fuck does this guy think he is, anyway?* Carl grabbed the doctor by his lab coat and lifted him off his feet. "You don't think I know that?" he screamed into Ziegler's face. "I grew up in this town, for fuck's sake. I don't need you to tell me who these people are. If you can figure out a way to save them, then I'm all ears. But you need to pull your head out of your ass, Dr. Ziegler, because I don't think there's any coming back from this. It's your job to prove me wrong."

Burt put his hands on Carl's shoulders and pulled him off the doctor. "Whoa, easy, Carl. That's not helping."

Burt's presence seemed to snap Carl out of it.

He released Ziegler and took several deep breaths. "You're right ... I'm sorry, Doctor." He took his hat off and rubbed at his temples again. "I don't know what came over me."

"No, I'm the one who should apologize. I was out of line. Truce?" Ziegler held out his hand, and Carl took it and gave it a firm shake.

"I could leave if you guys want some alone time." Burt laughed. "I could get you a bottle of wine, maybe a Barry White album."

Carl replaced his hat and looked out the window of the lab to make sure no one was in earshot. "Here's what I'm looking at. We have no idea what we're dealing with. If there is a way of fixing it, we need to figure that out ... fast. We're beyond the whole 'that's not possible, dead people don't get back up' thing, so there's no point in wasting time on that conversation. Right now, I'm thinking triage, I'm thinking containment, and I am thinking about saving the rest of them. Because if we don't get a handle on this, we're gonna lose this town. Consider yourselves officially deputized."

"What about your other deputies?" Burt asked. "What are you going to tell them? They need to know what they're up against."

It was something Carl had been considering. He was already down one officer with no idea what might have happened to Gary Forsyth. At this point, it was safe to assume he had been infected as well. That left Ted, Kovach, Rainey, and the dispatchers. Rainey was up to speed, and Carl was confident that Ted, the department's youngest officer, savior to animals and small children, would fall in line without losing his mind. It was Deputy Kovach he was worried about. Kovach was a real by-the-book, logical officer and would probably have the most difficult time accepting the impossible.

"I didn't want to say anything until I was one hundred percent sure it was as bad as I suspected. But I guess it's time. I'm worried about Deputy Kovach; I don't see him dealing with it all that well. He doesn't have a very good imagination, and this isn't exactly your everyday situation."

"You're not the most imaginative guy on the planet either, but it's hard to argue when it's staring you in the face," Burt said. "If it walks like a duck and it talks like a duck, you know what they say."

"Okay, that doesn't even make sense, but thanks for trying. I'll take care of bringing my deputies up to speed. Do you still have what I gave you?"

The coroner pulled the .25 cal. from his jacket pocket and showed him.

"Good, although I might want you to have something with a little more stopping power, and I'd like you to carry as well, Dr. Ziegler."

"I'm not a cop; I'm a doctor. I wouldn't even know what to do with a gun." Ziegler held up his hand in a show of submission.

"Well, I saw what you did to my deputy at the morgue. If it wasn't for that arm of yours, I'd be dead right now. I'm not asking you to go shooting up the place; I just want you to be able to protect yourself if you need to. The one thing we do know is that a bullet to the head turns them off like a switch."

"Come on, Carl," Burt reasoned. "That might be easy for a guy who goes to the range twice a week, but I haven't shot a gun in a long time, and I was never a good shot anyway. Dr. Ziegler here probably doesn't have any hands-on experience." Ziegler shrugged his shoulders and shook his head. "You're talking about a headshot to a moving target. This isn't the movies. That's not easy for guys who aren't familiar with guns."

It was a valid point, but there wasn't much of a choice. "I'm just saying, it's better to have a gun and not need it than to need one and not have it."

"Fine, so let's say you give me a gun and you make me a deputy; I'm still a doctor, and I have a responsibility to my patients."

"Exactly, and if something horrible were to happen and you had to hit someone over the head with a stainless steel basin or, worst-case scenario, shoot something to protect one of your patients, then as a deputized member of the Sheriff's Department, I can protect you from any legal backlash that might come your way when the dust settles."

Ziegler nodded his head in agreement. "Okay, fair enough."

"You don't need to ask," Burt added. "I made a promise to your father before you were even born. Whatever you need from me, consider it done."

Carl put his hand on his friend's shoulder. "Thank you. Thank you both. I need to figure out how to brief my deputies, and even then, we may still need a few more hands on deck. Doctor, what's the prognosis on the girl?"

"Well, there isn't any sign of the infection; that much is certain. But I would recommend she spend the night for observation. Is there any next of kin?"

"We're working on that. My deputy will stick around for a little while. She seems to have taken to him. She'll be safe with him, at least until we find a family member to come get her."

"I hate to be talking about my own needs with all that's going on, but I need to get some lunch before I pass out. Anybody hungry?" Burt stood up and straightened his jacket, trying to adjust the weight of the gun in the pocket.

"I need to get back to the emergency room. I'll meet up with you in a little bit," Ziegler told them and turned for the door.

"Can't; I have to check back in with Ted before I leave. I'll try to return sometime this afternoon. We'll reconvene at that point. In the meantime, put some thought into that MRI machine. What happened, and why?"

"I'm on it."

The three men left the lab and headed in different directions. Carl repositioned his hat and prepared himself for the daunting task ahead of him.

CHAPTER 41

Father Kieran mulled around the emergency room, waiting for any news on the young man he had found on his doorstep. The center was busier than he'd ever seen in the past, and Kieran didn't think it was any coincidence. The staff appeared on edge and stretched too thin to handle the patient load, and the lack of available employees didn't strike him as coincidental either.

He walked in a slow circle past the nurses' station, through the emergency room, and then near the boy's bed, where the doctor was examining him. Most people were not allowed in the ER, but when you were dressed like a Catholic priest, you pretty much got to go wherever you wanted. Kieran made another pass and found himself in front of the boy's bed once again.

"Father," a faint voice called to him.

He looked at the bed next to the boy to see a young girl who belonged to the parish. He wasn't positive but thought her name might be Susan. She had a large bandage wrapped around her head that also covered one eye.

Fresh stitches ribboned throughout a laceration that extended the entire length of her cheek. Kieran offered his kindest smile and approached her bedside.

"Yes, child." He hesitated to call her by name.

"It's Susan, Father. Susan Smith. I know I haven't been to Mass lately, but do you have a minute?" The girl looked like she had lost a fight with a woodchipper and might be feeling the effects of a sedative, as her exposed eye drooped and hung heavy.

"Of course. How can I help, Susan?"

"We were in an accident. Me and Debbie Horne were on Route 3 early this morning. I was driving, and a mountain lion ran across the road." The girl closed her eye and looked as if she might fall asleep at any moment.

"You're going to be all right. Has anyone called your parents yet?" He pulled a chair beside her bed and sat down.

"Yes, they're on the way. I didn't see it till the last minute … the mountain lion. I-I swerved and crossed into oncoming traffic. I drove right into the other c-car. Is Debbie okay? Can you see her, Father?" Kieran looked over to where Susan pointed and saw the girl a few beds down. A flurry of nurses and doctors were at work; a basin was passed to one of the women, filled with scarlet-soaked bandages. Kieran had to stop his breath short to prevent himself from reacting in front of Susan.

"She looks as if she's resting, and that's what you should be doing as well." Kieran knew that Susan's friend would soon be with the Lord, but he wasn't about to tell Susan that. *Sometimes, an omission of truth is the merciful path.*

"Would you bless me, Father?"

"Of course." He made the sign of the cross and bowed his head. "In the name of the Father, and of the Son, and of the Holy Spirit, Amen. Through this Holy anointing may the Lord in His love and mercy help you with the grace of the Holy Spirit. May the Lord who frees you from sin save you and raise you up. Amen."

"Amen," Susan said and allowed her one exposed eye to close once again, then she looked up at him and smiled. "Thank you, Father."

"You're welcome, my child." He took her hand and comforted her. She had seen the animals coming off the mountain as well. He hadn't even imagined the problem it might create, having all those displaced animals running around town. Something had moved into their home, and the wildlife no longer felt comfortable there. The girl turned to look at the bed next to them and saw the doctor working on the boy.

"What's Billy doing here?" she asked.

Father Kieran gasped. "You know him?" He hadn't considered that the girl might recognize the mysterious boy that had shown up on his doorstep, though they both looked to be about high school age.

"That's Billy Tobin, Debbie's boyfriend. Is he okay?"

"Yes, he's going to be fine. Now get some rest, child. God bless you."

Father Kieran let go of the girl's hand and left her to sleep. Then, he walked to the nurses' station and spoke to the woman behind the desk. "I believe the boy's name is Billy Tobin."

Lois had been at Alice's house for about an hour before the phone rang. Will answered and ran into the living room, where the women sat on the sofa.

"They found Billy; he's in the emergency room."

"What about Eric? Is Eric with him?" Alice cried.

"They didn't say anything about Eric. They just said Billy was there, and he's unconscious."

Lois helped Alice to her feet and out the door. She followed them to the medical center in her Impala.

Father Kieran felt better after placing an identity on the mysterious boy. The child was under the care of physicians, which was far better than any he could offer himself. Feeling confident enough to leave the child's bedside for a moment, he followed the directory arrows down a long corridor and arrived at the cafeteria. The smell of coffee and fried food greeted him the second he stepped inside; his stomach reacted with a loud rumble. He hadn't had a moment to even think about food and couldn't recall when he had last eaten.

A friendly face looked up from a table in the back and waved him over. He approached the man and took a seat across from him.

"Father Kieran, what brings you here today?" Burt Lively took the priest's hand and shook it.

"Hello, Burt, it's a long story, really. How are you? I didn't see you at Mass on Sunday."

Burt made the sign of the cross on his forehead. "I know, Father, I was called to work. We had a bit of a problem, and I found myself at the lab most of the day."

Burt worked at the cheeseburger and large mug of coffee in front of him, which looked delicious. And when the waitress came to the table, Kieran told her he would have the same thing his friend was having. A few minutes later, she sat a mug in front of him and said his order would be out in a few minutes. He took a sip of the coffee, and his stomach made another lurching growl.

"I guess you're hungry, Father?"

"I seem to have neglected to eat breakfast this morning." He took another sip of coffee, and Burt raised his own mug as well.

"I'll drink to that," Burt said.

Kieran noticed the distinct aroma of blackberry brandy. He smiled and lowered his voice.

"My coffee is strong, but I'm afraid it isn't quite strong enough." He lifted his eyebrows and held out his mug. Burt looked around the cafeteria, reached into the breast pocket of his jacket, and removed a small flask. He unscrewed the cap and poured a generous helping of the liquor into Kieran's mug. "Bless you, my child." Kieran took a long sip and sighed.

The men sat in silence for a few minutes, sipping at their spiked coffees, until Kieran's order arrived. He tore into the burger without bothering to add any ketchup or mustard. It wasn't an uncomfortable silence, thanks to the brandy, but it was enough to allow Kieran a minute to consider what was going on in the woods behind the rectory. So much had happened in only a few days. He cleaned his plate and tipped back the rest of his mug before Burt was halfway done with his own. "Thank you, Lord. I certainly needed that."

"How are things over at the rectory, Father? Are they keeping you busy up there?" Burt asked.

Kieran looked back at the man and wondered if Burt had read it on his face. "I suppose," he said. "Burt, you've been a member of the parish since long before I came to Garrett Grove."

"Yeah, been here all my life."

"You know the area of the woods behind the church, the place they call the foothills?"

Burt straightened up in his chair and stared back at him. "Have you seen something, Father?"

Kieran glanced into his empty mug. "You've seen them as well?"

"I have, and too close for my liking. Look, if you need to talk to someone, I think you might have come to the right table."

"Are you asking me if I'd like to make a confession?" Kieran allowed an uneasy smile to cross his face.

"I'll tell you what. Why don't I start, and you can jump in anytime you want."

Kieran listen as Burt told him everything, explaining how the body of Felix Castillo had been found early Sunday morning, less than a mile from the steps of the rectory, and how the corpse had been depleted of nearly all its fluids. He told him how the body had disappeared from the morgue and then shown up at the far end of town the following morning. Burt paused only for a moment when the waitress approached the table to fill their mugs. After she left, he told Kieran about the three children who had been admitted to the medical center Saturday night and then signed out by Dr. Malcolm. And what he believed the situation implied: that Dr. Malcolm had been compromised and a percent of the population were now infected.

Father Kieran allowed Burt to top off his mug and sat for a moment without saying a word. He hadn't even considered that the aberrations he saw in the woods were members of his own parish. He'd been thinking in terms of demons and not demonic possession, certainly not on such a grand scale. "I've seen terrible things in the past few days, my son. I can confirm that your fears are accurate. There are a great many of these beasts. They have been traveling through the foothills by night. I've seen their shadows in the woods, but they don't look like people anymore. And despite how many you think there are, you should reconsider that number. There are far more than that."

"Sweet Jesus!" Burt gasped.

Father Kieran took another long sip from his coffee. "Amen." He shared his own story about how the boy had shown up at his doorstep, half-dead and in shock. And how he hadn't even known the child's identity until only a moment ago. "From what you told me about these creatures, how Abe was infected and how the deputy was possessed, it's a miracle the boy survived."

"There's something else, Father. When we put Abe into the MRI, it did something to him. Something came out of him. It looked like a cloud of smoke. I don't know ... it looked evil."

It was exactly what Kieran had seen that first day in the woods, and he knew Burt was right. *It is evil ... it is the fallen Angel.* "The Lord works in mysterious ways. But Satan's works are far more mysterious. There is a presence in Garrett Grove, and that presence is pure evil."

"How do you stop evil, Father?"

"The only way to fight the darkness is with the light of the Holy Spirit, the power of Jesus Christ." The men continued to talk and drink their spiked coffee. The brandy helped to loosen their tongues and allowed for an even exchange that might have otherwise been hindered by insecurities and customary expectations. And rather than meeting as priest and parishioner, the two men met as equals over a meal and a cup of coffee. "I'm glad I ran into you, Mr. Lively," Kieran said.

"So am I, Father. It's always good to have a man of God on the team."

CHAPTER 42

Billy Tobin remained unresponsive. He was in shock and suffering from acute blood loss as well as dehydration. His temperature was high, but he didn't appear to have sustained any head trauma. Dr. Freedman explained to the boy's family how Father Kieran had brought him in and that one of the girls involved in the auto accident identified him. Unfortunately, there was still no information to the whereabouts of his brother, Eric; Alice and Will were near hysterics.

Lois tried to console them but was distracted herself by the flurry of activity going on around them. Chilton was too busy for a Tuesday afternoon. Not only did the facility appear understaffed but there was an increase in emergency room cases. She looked toward the nurses' station just in time to see Carl approaching from the connecting hallway. "I'll be right back," she told her sister and brother-in-law, then marched up to Carl and intercepted him at the desk. She caught him off guard and ripped into him with guns blazing.

"Where the hell have you been, and why didn't you start looking for my nephews sooner? Eric is still out there, and Billy's unconscious! Just what the hell are your officers even doing, for Christ's sake?"

Carl backed up a step, clearly caught off guard by her assault. "Lois, slow down. My men are doing all they can to find your nephews. You know I can't report anyone missing until forty-eight ho—Wait, did you say Billy is here?"

"No thanks to you! Father Kieran brought him in less than an hour ago. He's in bad shape, and Eric is still missing."

"Where's Father Kieran now?"

"How the hell would I know? I can't believe you. My nephews are missing, and you make my sister wait. That's not the Carl I thought I knew. Not the man I—" She stopped talking for fear of what she might say next, feeling the steam rise within her like a kettle about to boil over.

"Look, Lois," he said, lowering his voice. "I'm doing everything I can, not just for your family but the whole goddamn town. There's a lot going on that you have no idea about. So, if you would please give me a break and let me do my job. And please stop yelling at me."

She hadn't planned on ambushing the guy but was out of her mind after what Ziegler told her last night. Not to mention, she had driven all over God's creation looking for Carl in an attempt to get to the bottom of it. At this point, she didn't know what to think.

"How could you treat my sister like that?"

"Walk with me." Carl took her by the arm and led her out the emergency room door. The fresh air did little to change the mood, and Lois felt the heat continue to simmer within her. "Goddammit, Lois. I'm trying to protect your family. You have no idea what's going on."

She folded her arms and pressed her lips together, considering whether her next attack should be a frontal assault or one a bit more tactical; she opted for the tactical approach. "Well, I talked to Dr. Ziegler last night, so why don't you try me. You might be surprised just what I have an idea about." *Bullseye.* Lois watched his jaw drop like she had hit him with a right cross. Still, Carl wasn't as easy to manipulate as most men and was far more intuitive. He stepped back and took a defensive pose.

"What exactly did he tell you?"

Lois balked and attempted to recover, but the man had called her bluff.

"He told me the children might be suffering from something a bit more serious than the flu." She scanned his poker face and could tell he was waiting to see what else she knew.

"Okay, what else?"

"Well, he suggested we take a family vacation. So why don't you tell me just what the hell is going on here. What happened to Rob and the Richards kids that has Dr. Ziegler so freaked out? And what's got your department so busy you can't find the time to look for my nephews? Eric's still out there somewhere."

Carl removed his hat and scanned the parking lot to the left and the right. Then he stepped in, just inches from her, and lowered his voice once again.

"Maybe you *should* consider leaving Garrett Grove for a week or two. Pick Troy up after school and take him upstate, just for a little while."

His words settled over her like a glacier as an icy frost took Lois's breath. Now she was the one who had been caught off guard. It was one thing to hear it from Dr. Ziegler, but Carl wasn't the type to jump to conclusions. If he was telling her to get out of town, it was a warning to be taken seriously. Lois covered her mouth with both hands, allowing a gasp to slip through her fingers.

"My God, Carl! What is it? Is it that contagious?" Tears pooled in the corners of her eyes.

He rested his hands on her shoulders and looked directly into her. "It's worse than I could even explain. I don't want to see anything happen to you or your family. I'm sorry about your nephews, but I'm really doing all I can. People are dying, more than a few. So please take your family and get the hell out of town."

Her tears swelled and overflowed their banks as Lois struggled to process the words. Then Carl pulled her to him and wrapped his arms around her; she hugged him back and cried into his chest. She tried to speak but found it difficult to accept the fleeting moment of comfort. It felt more than familiar to be wrapped in his arms with her head resting against his chest. It was a feeling she had never forgotten, even after all these years. Warm, safe, complete. *God, he still smells the same ... he still feels the same.* It was hard to describe, but if she had to, Lois would have said it felt a lot like coming home.

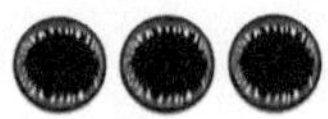

The trio of children cut through the ballpark, passed the outfield and the firehouse, crossed over the railroad tracks, and entered the Village where Janis lived. The pup's tail started wagging the moment she saw her master approaching. "How's my good girl?" Peanuts ran from one child to the next, unable to make up her mind whose face she wanted to lick first.

Janis's aunt met them at the door. "I don't think we have any cookies left, but there might be some Ring Dings. Are you guys hungry?" Which had been a silly question since the answer was obvious. Lynn went to the kitchen to rustle up a snack while the children scrambled up the stairs. They maneuvered around a stack of boxes and entered the room with Peanuts underfoot every step of the way.

Wendy sat on the bed and cut right to the chase. "If these things have been around for so long, how come we're just finding out about them now?"

"That's what my grandfather was working on. My mom doesn't tell me, but I know she knows more about it than she says. Wait right here." Janis walked into the hallway and proceeded to rummage through the stack of boxes until she located what she was looking for. "Here it is," she said, returning to the bedroom.

She held what looked like a photo album, put it on the bed, and opened it. The first page showed some very old black and white pictures of people wearing dated and funny-looking clothes. The next page showed a hole in the earth so deep the people were using ladders to climb into it.

Janis flipped to another page that contained the photos she was looking for. Various pictures of the small teeth were revealed, exactly like the ones she had in her case. There were labels above each of the photographs. One said Cahokia and showed several shots of the teeth and the jawbone they had come from.

"If you had to guess, do you think those things had a mouth like this?" Janis asked.

It was hard to tell what kind of an animal the jawbone belonged to. It looked canine, only much more dangerous. Troy hadn't gotten a good look at what chased him and could only imagine. "I guess so; I don't know, really. I was running so fast I didn't see. It's kind of hard to tell from looking at a picture."

"Yeah," Wendy said. "But do you think it's possible?"

"I guess it's possible."

"Good. So, maybe they're like bears and need to hibernate, only they hibernate for a *really* long time," Wendy continued. "Maybe it's like your mom said. I know she was just playing and trying to scare us, but maybe there's something true in her story that she didn't even know. Maybe there isn't anything called an Ojanox, but maybe there's something that only comes out after it's hibernated for a long time. Like the Ojanox coming out at Halloween. Maybe that's why no one knows about it. By time it comes back, everyone that was around is long gone."

Troy stared at the girl who had grabbed him in the haunted house, kissed him, and declared herself his girlfriend. *That makes a lot of sense.* At the moment, he felt like the maturity difference was a whole lot more than two years between him and Wendy. She was smart, everything she said made sense, and it just rolled off the top of her head. Troy sat there with his jaw open, searching for some intelligent remark to contribute ... He had nothing.

"That's got to be it," Janis said. "The Ojanox, or whatever you want to call it, shows up after a long sleep, goes into a town like Cahokia, or Garrett Grove, and kills everybody. Then goes back to sleep. After a hundred years or so, it just becomes one big mystery, and everyone is like, I wonder what happened to Garrett Grove."

Now they were both moving too fast for him to follow, almost as if they had rehearsed it. Troy suddenly felt like the stupid kid in the room and wanted more than anything to add to the conversation. "So, how do you kill them? It doesn't sound like anyone has ever been very good at that."

Both girls nodded as he spoke, making him feel somewhat relevant. Janis flipped to the next set of pictures, one that showed a few arrowheads and a spearhead. The others depicted a large dagger surrounded by several round objects worn into perfect globes. The tiny balls resembled bullets or musket balls. *That's it.* Troy focused on the picture of the weapons that looked to be made up of the same material and knew exactly what it was.

"Oh my God, that's lodestone!" Troy shouted as Janis's aunt entered the room carrying a tray of snacks.

Janis slammed the book shut, and all three of the children looked up at once.

"What's going on in here?" Lynn smiled and surveyed the room.

"Nothing, Aunt Lynn. You just scared us." Janis set the book on the floor behind her.

"Y-yeah ... scared us." Troy attempted to act like he hadn't been caught red-handed.

"Mmm-hmm, if you say so." Lynn set the tray of Ring Dings and juice on Janis's dresser, inciting Peanuts to lift her head up at the smell of food.

"Thank you," the children said nearly in unison, and Lynn left them to whatever it was that they had been doing.

Once she was gone, Wendy leaned in and punched Troy in the arm. "You almost blew it, dork."

He rubbed where she had hit him, trying not to show how much it had actually hurt. They each grabbed a cake, and the dog inhaled every crumb that fell to the floor.

"Now, what was this you were saying, lodestone?" Wendy asked as Janis opened the book to the page they had been looking at.

"Those little balls. My dad said the cave that he and your mom are working in is full of these things. They're all made of lodestone. It's magnetic and hard to work with, so they took a long time to make. That means that they must have really needed them."

"Do you think these are the same thing ... lodestones?" Wendy asked.

"I don't know for sure, but if I had to guess. What are the odds your mom studies these things and has pictures of the teeth and weapons? I'd say if your mom's job took her to that cave, then those weapons are *all* made from lodestones."

The girls nodded and appeared to agree with his line of reasoning, Wendy especially.

"Do you think it's like garlic for a vampire or kryptonite to Superman?" Janis asked.

"I guess the people from Cahokia and the Lenape thought so. I don't know, really." Troy had given up his wealth of information and needed the girls to take over again. Then it occurred to him. It had been at the tip of his mind, just waiting to come out. "My dad said the whole cave is made out of lodestone. He also called it magnetite, and if all of those bones up there are from the Ojanox ..." He shook his head. *Jeez, even I'm calling it Ojanox.* It was a stupid name his mother had come up with, and now they were all using it, which was more than just a little embarrassing.

Wendy nearly spit the cupcake out of her mouth. "That's it! Only maybe they weren't hibernating; maybe they were trapped in the cave. Maybe they couldn't escape because of the magnetite."

It sounded as right as anything else they had come up with so far. At least it didn't sound wrong to Troy. Still, he wondered about the bones. *If there's bones up there, then they died in the cave.* It didn't all make sense yet but felt like it was coming together.

"So, if you kill it with lodestone and you can trap it in a cave, how do we get some of that stuff? Because I'm not going out on Halloween without some protection," Janis said.

"That's a good question." Wendy squinted as she concentrated. "We have to get your dad to bring some home for us, or—" She looked at Janis. "Or you got to ask your mom to get some."

Both Troy and Janis looked doubtful at the possibilities of either idea being very successful. Then Wendy presented an alternate option. "Or ... we need to visit that cave and get some of it ourselves."

With the small opening to the unknown area blocked off and everyone made aware of the potential danger, Don, Stephanie, and the rest of the team moved on to the secondary chamber of the cavern. The murals in this section of the cave were even more elaborate than the ones they had photographed yesterday. There appeared to be exactly twelve individual scenes with a distinct chronology to them. Don still couldn't recall where he had seen it all before.

The first mural depicted a near entirely black landscape with a singular object set in the center that looked like a massive brown cloud. Shades of yellow sulfur and the most volatile green had been added to the shape, giving it the appearance of smog or swamp gas. The peculiar choice of color looked as if the artist had merely been experimenting with hue and technique and hadn't perfected either. At least Don thought so. But Stephanie and Gail focused a great deal of time and attention on this one mural alone. Stephanie pointed to the top right corner of the mural, where the only piece of vivid color entered the scene. It was white with accents of gold and crimson and looked like a secondary cloud sitting in the far distance. A polar opposite of the dark-colored haze that resembled pollution.

There was nothing ambiguous about the next mural. The scene was a fiery explosion of reds, yellows, and oranges. The scarlet was so red and the yellow so warmingly powerful, Donald could almost imagine the heat and force of the blast. He held his breath, staring at the dynamic piece of art. The flash from Gail's bulb accentuated the scene, bringing the mural to life and adding to the illusion that the explosion was currently happening.

"How were they able to capture such a vivid image?" he asked.

"It's beautiful, isn't it?" Stephanie said. He jumped, not realizing she was standing next to him. He'd been so enrapt by the mural he didn't notice she was practically on top of him. "They were quite advanced in culture and art. We could have learned much from them."

The murals continued to line the walls on the left side of the tunnel, which was now being referred to as "the secondary chamber." The flash of the camera splayed across the mural's surface, nearly triggering the memory within Don. And for a second, he could almost recall what it all reminded him of, but the moment passed without him latching on to it. He dismissed it, figuring it would eventually come to him.

The third painting was a picture of the earth sitting amongst the heavens. Donald stared in disbelief at the rendition of the blue planet sitting in its correct position in the cosmos, carefully nestled between the violet gasses of Venus and the red sands of Mars. *That's impossible.* There was no way the Lenape could have knowledge of the solar system like this. Sure, they would have known about the sun and the moon, but how could they have learned the positioning of all the other celestial objects? Orion was fixed in the furthest corner of the cave wall. Even the nebula located within the three stars of the constellation's belt were visible. And not only that, Cassiopeia, Ursa Major, and Minor were all located very close to where they would be, had they been gazing at this scene in a planetarium.

"How is this even possible?" Gail asked with her flashbulb clicking away at a feverish pace. "It's so vivid, and the accuracy is amazing."

"I get it," Don said. "This is a depiction of their creation story. It's the Big Bang, right? But how would they have known about that? This is incredible."

"Well." Stephanie cleared her throat. "Carl Jung had a theory called collective unconscious. The belief that the information we come to know as truth is not entirely organic. That all we know is derived from inherent knowledge, like code written into our DNA."

"You're saying that we know about the Big Bang because our ancestors knew about it and it was transferred in our genetic makeup?" Don tried to keep a straight face.

"It isn't the craziest theory if you think about it," Stephanie explained.

Somehow, the Lenape tribe had attained the knowledge. Was it possible they knew about the Big Bang because their ancestors knew about it, and the knowledge had become a part of their genes? Don doubted the possibility, but it was something to think about. No one could explain how infants made the connection when it came to developing the skills to put sentences together. In every culture, it was a phenomenon that baffled psychologists and physicians. One day, a baby struggled with the basics like mama and dada. Then almost overnight, they developed the ability to string words together and form coherent sentences. Oftentimes, they used words they had never been exposed to with complete cognitive understanding. Don had witnessed that himself with Troy. *Fill 'er up, Pop.* He remembered his toddling son standing in his crib.

That could be a form of what she was talking about, a collective unconsciousness lying dormant within our cells, just waiting to be triggered at the right time. For infants, the language trigger came somewhere between the ages of one and two. For the Lenape and most civilizations prior, maybe the need to understand their own creation was the springboard that ignited the creation story. Every culture had one, and it was crazy how they were all so similar.

"That's a pretty far-out theory. I don't know if I buy it, but it's definitely an icebreaker at the cocktail party." Don looked at the mural of the earth set in its proper quadrant of the solar system. It was uncanny. "Still, I can't explain how the Lenape could have gotten these details on their own. It's pretty damn amazing."

Stephanie pointed to the wall where the rendition of the universe had been painted centuries ago. "Is this lodestone as well?"

"Yeah. Crazy, isn't it? It's got to be one of the largest deposits ever recorded. This is definitely a cave for anomalies. I've never seen so much beauty in one place." He suddenly realized he was no longer looking at the mural; he had been staring at Stephanie. He offered a smile and watched her face flush crimson a second before she turned away.

"Yeah, you sure do know how to talk to women, Mr. Fischer," she said, and walked on to the next group of murals.

Lois pulled away from Carl and looked up at him through a haze of bloodshot tears. A million thoughts raced through her head, but not one of them made any damn sense. There was one that felt right, but she wasn't about to act on it. For a fleeting moment as Carl attempted to comfort her, she had thought about taking his face in her hands and kissing him right there in front of the emergency room entrance. Instead, she stepped back, wiped her eyes, and struggled to control herself enough to talk. "What's going on that's so bad?" He had confirmed everything that Ziegler said. "Who has died, Carl?"

He scanned the parking lot and hesitated as a man and woman exited from the doors behind them and headed to their car. "This really isn't the place. I promise I'll tell you everything, but you're not going to believe it. Christ, I don't believe it myself. I need to talk to Billy as soon as he wakes up, and I need to apologize to Alice and Will. Not to mention, I still have one missing deputy and a bitch of a headache. I will tell you, but I need to handle a few things first. Where can we talk?"

Lois thought about it for a second; it wasn't like he could just stop by and discuss it over dinner. She didn't want Troy to hear any of this ... or Don, for that matter. "Troy is at a friend's house." She checked her watch and noticed the time. She wanted to stay a little longer with Alice and Will, but she would have to call Troy and tell him that she was running a little late. *I could ask Janis's aunt if he could stay a bit longer.* That would give her enough time to hear everything Carl had to say. "Can you meet me at the house at five?"

He raised his eyebrows and offered a cautious look.

"Donald won't be home until seven, and Troy is at a friend's. It's not a public place, so there's no chance of anyone overhearing us."

"Fine, I'll be there around five. But first, I need to see if Billy is awake."

They walked back inside, through the emergency room, to the bed where Billy Tobin lay. He was still unconscious and looked pretty messed up. And he wasn't the only one. It had been a grueling day in the emergency room; at least one of the patients involved in the car accident had passed away, two others were critical.

Carl apologized to Alice and Will for not being more responsive. He explained how they had found the body on Sunday morning and were still following leads on Monday. Alice asked the obvious question: was there a connection between the murder and their son's disappearance? Carl told her no and that he wanted to be alerted as soon as Billy regained consciousness. The boy would be able to tell them where he and Eric had been, and that would be the best lead to help them find him.

"Deputy Lutchen will be here for the next few hours if you need him. He can reach me on the radio," he said before he left. Then Carl checked in on Ted. He entered the room to find Dawn fast asleep, sucking her thumb, on the examination table.

"I want you to stay here until we locate a next of kin."

"Sure, Sheriff. Um-I was wondering."

"What's that?"

"Well, the girl's dog is still in the pen and is probably hungry and thirsty again. I think someone should go take care of it?"

"Can't we just call the pound?" He had enough on his plate without having to worry about a dog.

"That's cruel, Sheriff. I'll take care of it. Besides, he seemed to like me anyway. Um, what if no one shows up for Dawn?"

Carl studied the rookie's face. Ted was practically a kid himself and looked as if he had just started shaving over the past year.

"We'll figure something out, Deputy." Carl put his hat on and started out the door.

"Sure thing, Sheriff."

Carl left the medical center with a great deal on his mind and even more on his plate. First, he needed to stop back at the station and go over things with dispatch and the rest of the officers. Then he intended to pay a visit to the armory and make a withdrawal. He promised both Burt and Dr. Ziegler something with a little more stopping power and had just the thing in mind. He checked his watch and ran to the cruiser—time was slipping away, and sunset was right around the corner. *Christ, I hope we're ready for this.* He had started to formulate a plan but had no idea if they'd be able to pull it together in time.

CHAPTER 43

Dawn Negal had eaten her ice cream and then fallen asleep while Ted remained at her bedside feeling helpless. His mind kept fixating on the child's dog, still left outside in its pen. They had fed the Shepherd enough food to nearly last it the rest of the week, but it was the water bowl that Ted was worried about. More than likely, Baxter had tipped it over again. He agonized over it, feeling responsible for the animal, and started thinking. Dawn was out like a light, and Ted figured she would sleep straight through. There was little chance she had slept the night before, curled up terrified beneath her bed.

He got up from his chair and looked out into the hallway to find two nurses passing by. "Excuse me," he said.

The girls, who couldn't be any older than Ted himself, turned on their rubber soles and stared at him. One flashed a wide Cheshire smile, and the other nurse bit her lower lip. "Yes, Officer, how can I help you?" the lip-biter asked.

"I was wondering if either of you ladies could do me a favor?" They looked at each other and giggled. "I have to step out for a moment and need someone to watch over my friend." The nurse that had spoken leaned her head into the room and saw the sleeping child.

"Oh my, she's adorable. I'm on break, so I can sit with her for a little while. How long do you think you will be?" She looked up at Ted and batted her eyes.

"Less than a half-hour; you're sure you don't mind? I really appreciate it."

"It would be my pleasure." She held out her hand and bounced on her toes once, then twice. "I'm Carole ... Carole Reiner." Ted shook her hand. "I'll be here when you get back."

Ted thanked her and sped off down the hall towards the exit. Becky Ramos, the nurse who hadn't thrown herself at the deputy, looked at her friend and slapped her arm. "Very subtle, Carole. I'm surprised you didn't just hike your skirt and ask him, 'do these panties make my ass look fat?'"

Carole laughed and watched Ted as he double stepped down the hall. She bit her lip and replied, "I think I'll try that when he comes back."

"Carole Reiner, you're terrible!"

Lynn worked in the kitchen, trying to get everything put away and the place in working order. She had gotten used to relocating and now considered herself a professional when it came to packing and unpacking. Since she moved in with Stephanie and Janis, they had changed houses, as well as states, three times in under two years.

Being born only eighteen months apart, Lynn and her sister had always been very close. Which helped when Stephanie separated from her husband, Brian. He had been a decent enough father but a terrible husband who respected only two things: his money and his libido.

Brian had been looking for a trophy wife and sat on the board of executives at the museum. Stephanie had studied ballet for years and still held her dancer's physique when she came to work for the MNH and, to put it mildly, was a knockout. Brian noticed her immediately and went after her like a shark. He swept Stephanie off her feet, married her in a whirlwind, and they were expecting Janis long before the honeymoon was over. At the time, he seemed like the perfect man. But it didn't take long for Brian Thompson to show his true colors.

He was neither violent nor an evil man; he just couldn't keep his dick in his pants. Brian messed around constantly and was horrible at keeping it a secret. He slept with half the interns at the museum, and the ones he wasn't sleeping with, he was working hard to do so. He had even propositioned Lynn once at a family event. Lynn had slapped him across the face and told her sister immediately. Which hadn't come as a surprise. Stephanie had seen the signs but tried to maintain the façade of a happy marriage for Janis's sake. But Brian had crossed the line by going after her own sister. Stephanie could no longer ignore his transgressions and confronted him.

The louse didn't even have the decency to deny it or try to hide the fact he was fucking every piece of ass that walked through the doors of his office. He threw the importance of his position on the board in her face, reminding her that the funding for her father's research had to go through him first. And Stephanie told him he could do the same with his funding as he did with the rest of his whores—he could *Fuck It!* The next day she contacted her lawyer and not only slapped Brian with divorce papers but filed a class-action suit against him and the museum for threatening her position as well as her funding. Most of the interns that Brian had been using as his own personal harem took the stand as witnesses to his professional misconduct. Girls he had manipulated into believing a position with the museum required they submit to a few positions of his own had been more than willing to testify. And the museum was just as willing to settle out of court. Brian was terminated, and Stephanie was offered the job of curator after her father retired. Brian was forced to pay a staggering wad in the divorce settlement along with pain and suffering compensation to not only Stephanie but every girl that had joined in the class action suit.

It hurt Brian's bottom line, but the guy had been born into money, so it didn't break him. He continued to treat Janis as if he could buy her love. But she was her mother's child, and the endless endowment of gifts didn't affect her. She was a pure soul.

Stephanie and Lynn's father passed away shortly after the divorce, and Stephanie had taken up his research. Lynn moved in to help raise Janis, which she considered a pleasure. She had never been married herself, and although she was only in her early thirties, she believed that ship had sailed. It certainly looked as if she would never have children of her own, and becoming Janis's surrogate while Stephanie was at work was the next best thing.

Lynn had tried to find her own direction and taken more than a few misguided steps along the way. She went to college for business, but after graduation, she realized she didn't have even a remote interest in it. Instead, she found work as a waitress and bartender, then spent some time on the road following the Grateful Dead. She'd always been a free spirit. And in the music and the lifestyle, she believed she had found the secret meaning to life. For a good year and a half, she'd been under the misconception that if you dropped enough acid and listened to enough Scarlet Begonias, you could attain enlightenment. Unfortunately, despite all the laughs and amazing sex she had while she was tripping, Lynn never became enlightened. Much like her heroes, she arrived at the realization that the great prophets of the late '60s and early '70s had been misinformed. Timothy Leary had been dead wrong. Jerry Garcia, Grace Slick, and Abby Hoffman had all been ill-advised. The only thing to be attained by ingesting handfuls of LSD was a brain full of mashed potatoes.

Lynn was thankful she made it through her Deadhead days with most of her brains intact. But she had wasted far too many years chasing an illusion. She had some great memories and a few foggy recollections. One that she would never forget was the trip she made to see Jerry and the boys at Woodstock. She and her friends had been stuck on the New York State Thruway in bumper-to-bumper traffic and thought it'd be fun to show their tits to all the vehicles traveling the opposite way. One of the cars they had given an eyeful to had been driven by a priest; the guy even flashed them the peace sign. It had been a crazy time, and for the most part, her wild days were behind her. However, even now, as she unpacked the last of the dishes and placed them in the cupboard, she thought it might be nice to have a few hallucinogenic mushrooms to help with the rest of the work.

The phone rang and broke her from her daydream. Lynn picked up on the second ring. "Hello."

"Hello, this is Lois Fischer, Troy's mom."

"Hi, Mrs. Fischer, this is Lynn, Janis's aunt. How are you today? Do you want to talk to Troy?"

"Um, no. I was just calling because I'm running a little late. My nephew's in the emergency room, and I'm here with my sister. Is there any way Troy could stay a little longer? I should be able to pick him up by seven."

"No problem, Mrs. Fischer. Is your nephew going to be all right?"

"Well, it's too soon to say, but the doctor seems to think so. He's still unconscious and needs his rest."

"I'm so sorry to hear that. Troy can stay here as long as you need. Is it okay if I feed him dinner? I'm baking a chicken."

"Don't go to any trouble. I'm sorry to impose."

"Nonsense, I look forward to meeting you later. Stephanie might be home by then, and I know she's looking forward to meeting you as well. I'll see you when you get here."

"That would be great, thank you. Goodbye."

"You're quite welcome, bye." Lynn checked in on the children and told Troy his mother was running late and he would be staying for dinner. She said nothing about his cousin, thinking it best for Mrs. Fischer to tell him herself.

Baxter paced back and forth, waiting for anyone to show up and remember he was still in his pen. On most days, he'd have already gone for several walks and been allowed back in the house, but it had been a very strange day and an even stranger night. He lay on the concrete with his muzzle resting between his front paws, allowing an occasional exaggerated sigh to speak for his frustration with the entire situation.

Then the man opened the gate and appeared on the side of the house. It was the same man from before, the one with the hose. Excited, he jumped at the fence, unable to contain himself.

"Hey, buddy, I didn't forget you." Ted grabbed the leash hanging on the pen. "Do you want to go for a walk?" Baxter started to yelp and dance as if he had been offered a hot roast beef sandwich. The answer was obvious.

Ted opened the pen, and Baxter pounced, landing his front paws against the deputy's chest. Ted fastened the leash, grabbed the empty bowls and the bag of food, then led the dog out the gate. He took Baxter for an extended walk to do his business, then opened the back door of the cruiser. The dog looked up at him as if unsure. "Get in," Ted said, which was all the assurance needed. Baxter hopped into the backseat, and together, they headed back to Chilton. Ted knew there was only one problem with his plan; he hadn't yet figured out what he would say when he got caught sneaking a German Shepherd into the medical center. He hoped something would come to him.

Carl pulled into the back lot of the sheriff's department, near the door that led to the holding cells and the hallway connected to the armory. He let himself in, proceeded to the secured area, and unlocked the steel door where the weapons were stored. He scanned the stockpile and decided on two .40 cal. semi-automatics and a .357 Smith and Wesson revolver. Placing the guns into a duffle bag, he added several extra magazines and two boxes of .40 cal. bullets. He continued to fill the bag with boxes of .38 ammunition for his own weapon, three boxes of 12 gauge shotgun shells, and two boxes of 30-30 Winchester rounds. With the bag slung over his shoulder, he grabbed two shotguns from the rack and the 30-30 lever-action Marlin 336, which had always been one of his favorites. He left the armory, locked the door behind him, and deposited the cache into the trunk of his cruiser next to the helmets and riot gear they had used at the morgue.

Feeling as confident as he could under the circumstances, Carl slammed the trunk and climbed the stairs to the main floor of the station. Andrea Geary had just arrived to relieve Tara Jefferies, who was ready to walk out the door. Carl barged in, surprising both women with his brisk entrance, and began to dictate the procedures he needed executed.

"I haven't much time, so please don't make me repeat myself. I want all hands on deck tonight. I will brief the entire department at seven p.m.

sharp. Tara, I know you just pulled a full shift, but I need you here. I want Deputy Kovach and Rainey here as well. Don't worry about Ted; he's still at Chilton and will probably be there most of the night." The women watched as he continued without stopping to take a breath. "Also, I need Chief Jones from the fire department and two of his men; I would prefer Koloski and Gomes. We can't count on Deputy Forsyth returning to work anytime soon, so I want you to call in Beau Jenkins and Tim Colbert." Carl finally stopped to take off his hat.

"Sheriff, you want Jenkins and Colbert; aren't they both retired from the department?" Tara wrote everything down and tried her best to keep up.

"They're about to be reinstated. Also, I want you to get in touch with the first aid squad and have a couple of paramedics here. Did you get all that?"

Both women stared at him with the same look, a cross between disbelief and concern. It had been a rough twenty-four hours for the whole department. Garrett Grove had seen more activity in one day than it usually saw in six months.

"What's going on, Sheriff?" Andrea asked.

"I'll fill you in at seven. Until then, I want you both to carry your sidearms." His words fell with the gravity of an avalanche.

CHAPTER 44

Lois hugged Alice and Will, told them she had to leave to pick up Troy and that she would return in a little while. She felt terrible lying to her sister, but telling her she was planning to meet Carl was out of the question.

She arrived home at ten to five and waited; Carl didn't pull up to the house until a quarter after. By then, Lois believed he wasn't going to show. She opened the front door before he even exited the cruiser, her eyes red with dark circles spreading beneath them. He walked straight into the house, took off his hat, and sat down in the kitchen. Lois immediately noticed how tired he looked and examined the crow's feet at the corners of his eyes and the grey in his hair that appeared to have doubled overnight.

Lois wrung her hands, waiting for him to begin.

"This is going to take a while," he said. "I could really use a cup of coffee and a few aspirins. Would that be possible?"

Making coffee gave Lois something to do with her hands that felt better than just fidgeting. She handed Carl a bottle of Bayer and a glass of water, and he proceeded to swallow three of the white pills and gulped down nearly half the glass. Soon the smell of coffee filled the kitchen and provided a small sense of familiarity to the uncomfortable weight of the moment. Lois pulled a pack of cigarettes out of her purse and lit one.

Carl waited while she stared at him through a grey cloud of smoke. "This is going to sound crazy. Christ, it feels crazy to even think it. First of all, whatever those three kids have, it's a lot more contagious than anyone believed. And no one knows what the hell it is. Maybe a parasite, maybe a bacterium." Lois opened her mouth to either speak or gasp but was unable to do either. She continued to stare instead. "You can't catch it like the flu, so don't worry about that. It's a bloodborne pathogen; that's the only way you can catch it ... as far as we know. A man was murdered sometime late Saturday night or Sunday morning. We found the body at the end of Foothills Drive."

"By Robert's house?"

"Right in front, to be exact. The man appeared to have died from acute blood loss, only there wasn't any found at the scene. There was a small wound on his neck. His name was Felix Castillo; he worked for Con Ed and was transported to the morgue for examination." Carl took a deep breath and paused. "Around three o'clock on Sunday, Mr. Castillo's body disappeared. At the time, we believed some kids had broken in and stolen it. Do you think that coffee is ready?"

Lois got up and walked to the counter. As she prepared the cups, she watched Carl lean across the table, grab her pack of cigarettes, and light one. She couldn't recall the last time she had seen him smoke and suddenly knew he hadn't even told her the worst of it yet. She returned to the table with the coffee and set a mug in front of him.

"Early Monday morning, a man was hit by a truck on Sunset Road. The guy's body was thrown into a drainage ditch. You know how those gullies fill up with water and muck. Well, he was dead, covered in mud, head to toe, and hadn't been carrying any identification. We didn't get a good look at him until we got him back to the morgue and washed him off. So, Burt gets him in the tub and starts hosing him down, then we see the wound on the neck. The guy in the tub—the guy who got hit by the truck ... It was Felix Castillo."

Wendy needed to be home shortly after five and informed Troy it was customary for him to walk her to the corner. He happily obliged and even offered to carry her books, but Wendy was having no part of it. He couldn't figure out why she wanted him to walk with her in the first place since she refused to talk and only replied with single-syllable grunts. They reached the corner where he knew they would part ways, and Troy prepared for the anticipated kiss that would follow. He leaned his head in to accept her affectionate peck on the side of his mouth and closed his eyes. After what felt like an eternity, he opened them to see Wendy already halfway down the block. There had been no kiss, no peck on the cheek, not even a *see ya later*—she just kept walking. Troy knew he had done something wrong—again—and figured he would find out what that was sooner than later. At the moment, he didn't have a clue and felt okay about it. He imagined his acceptance of the situation would also lead to further backlash. *This is impossible.* Wendy made his head spin, but somehow, he found it well worth it. He headed back to Janis's house, doing his best to forget about the whole thing.

Janis met him at the door; the smell of baked chicken filled the living room and caused Troy's stomach to growl. He followed the girl back up to her room with Peanuts trailing underfoot.

They sat on the floor once again with the photo binder spread out in front of them. Troy studied the pictures of the various weapons, trying to imagine how the Lenape had crafted them.

"You know, I was thinking," Janis said. "Maybe we don't need to go to the cave after all."

"What do you mean?"

"Well, you said it's called magnite."

"Magnetite," he corrected her.

"Right." She blushed and pushed a curl behind her ear. "Well, isn't it just a magnet?"

"Yeah, I guess so." He saw what she was getting at.

"Well, if magnetite can kill them, then maybe we could just get regular magnets and make weapons out of them. It's a lot easier to go to the toy store than the cave. Don't you think?" She offered a toothy grin that lit up her face.

"That's smart. We could buy those big magnets and make as many weapons as we need. If we make them sharp enough, they'll work better than little balls. We could get a few wrist rockets. I bet if you hit one of those things with a magnet from a wrist rocket, it would knock 'em right out."

"You're smart too, Troy. Wendy is lucky," she said, shifting her eyes down at the carpet.

"Yeah? Well, tell her that. I'm not doing very good at being a boyfriend. I make a lot of mistakes."

"No, you're doing fine. Girls are complicated. It's not you at all."

"You think so?"

Janis nodded and smiled again. "Can I ask you a question?"

"Sure, what is it?"

"Um ... what was it like when you and Wendy kissed?"

He noticed she wasn't looking at the carpet anymore; now she was looking right at him. Staring at him with eyes too blue to be real. His heart started pounding and felt like it was inside his throat, a big wet lump catching his breath. He hadn't seen the conversation taking this turn. Where the heck was all this coming from, anyway? *Dear God, they're working together. There is no way I can win if they keep changing the rules.* He gulped hard, forcing the lump down, and made a strange noise that sounded like a wheeze.

"Don't get all freaked out, man. I just want to know what it was like. I never kissed a boy before."

"Um ... good ... I guess," he said. He was sure he would pass out any minute. And even prayed that he would. Which might be the only way to get out of the awkward situation he was in. He thought about pretending to faint but knew he couldn't pull it off.

"What do you mean?" She sat cross-legged, rocking in place. "Tell me."

"I don't know ... It was kinda nice. Soft and, I don't know ... nice." He didn't know how to describe it any better than that. Wendy had caught him by surprise with the first kiss, and he hadn't really felt anything from that one. Then the second one happened, and he was a bit more ready for it. His stomach had felt funny, and he got a bit tingly all over. It was kind of like the way you felt when you stuck a paper clip in the electric outlet, only everywhere. Still, he was too nervous to put any of it into words. "Um ... it was nice."

"I want you to kiss me, Troy," Janis said, and he nearly threw up on her.

What? He couldn't breathe. *Dear God, get me out of here.* He prayed he might dissolve into the carpet.

"Just as friends, I won't tell anyone."

"I-um ... I-c—" There was nowhere to run; he could feel his legs cramping.

"If you don't kiss me, I'm gonna tell Wendy you said she was stupid." Janis folded her arms and glared at him. Troy felt like he had been kicked in the teeth. This one was even more evil than the other. *Where do these girls learn this stuff? Is it written in a book?* He figured their mothers must teach them witchcraft; it was the only explanation. Troy knew he had fallen for the worst type of treachery imaginable. Wendy had tricked him with bologna and surprise kisses, and Janis used Ring Dings and ultimatums.

"Hey, you can't do that." He squirmed as if it would help.

"I can, and I will," she said. "So don't be a big baby. Just close your eyes and stop making such a fuss."

He searched but couldn't see any way out of this mess. What made it even worse, Troy thought it might be kind of nice to kiss her. There was something exciting about being threatened by the little demon with the blonde hair. "Fine!" he shouted and closed his eyes. "Just don't say anything."

Troy leaned in, waiting for Janis to kiss him. He puckered his lips and clenched his eyes. His heart raced like a lunatic locomotive with the antici-pated feel of her lips against his. He felt her draw closer to him and realized he was smiling. Troy suddenly knew he had wanted to kiss her since she walked into class on Monday. He felt her breath close to his, sensed her lips just inches away, and then it happened.

A hot, wet tongue lapped him directly on the mouth and continued to work on his nose, his cheeks, and the entire rest of his face. He jumped at the feel of the strange sensation and opened his eyes. He looked up to find himself face-to-face with the snout of the beagle. Janis sat before him with Peanuts's muzzle zeroed in on him. The pooch continued to lap at him as if his cheeks were made of cheeseburgers.

"Gross!" he shouted.

Janis laughed and let go of the dog. "Oh my God. You should have seen your face. What a dork, ha-ha-ha." Tears streamed down her cheeks in a full deluge. She continued to bellow and point at him like it was the single funniest event of her young life.

Troy couldn't move, let alone think. He stared at her in delightful disbelief. *How could she? What the—?* That had been the greatest prank he had ever been a part of, even if he was on the receiving end. Troy knew he was dealing with a level of genius that was far superior. *Are all girls this evil? Are they all so twisted? Are they all so wonderful?*

Carl stubbed out his smoke and continued to tell Lois everything that had transpired over the past three days. "It was Felix Castillo in that tub, no doubt about it. He had died on Sunday, then got up and walked out the back door of the morgue. He'd been infected by the same thing that infected the children. Whatever it is, it changed him ... Christ." He downed the rest of his mug and walked to the counter to pour another, then returned to his seat. "Everything about him, his bones, his organs. God, his mouth—it was filled with all these damn teeth."

"He used this tongue thing to grab Abe Gorman, Burt's assistant. Tossed him across the room like a scrap of paper and killed him. I shot it three times in the chest, didn't even slow him down. Then I shot him in the head. That did it. But Christ, Lois, he had gotten up twice already. We had no idea if he was really dead. So, I secured it to the table with a roll of duct tape, and Burt cut it open." Carl let out an uncomfortable laugh that fell across the table and sat between them for a moment.

Lois held her breath, unable to recall a time when she had ever seen him so unraveled.

"We taped Abe down just to be safe, and Burt took blood samples from both men. He says it looks like a parasite with a bacterial signature. I don't understand it myself, so I called Chilton. Dr. Malcolm wasn't there; I spoke to Dr. Ziegler. Well ... he confirmed it; it's the same infection that they found in the children." He slugged back the rest of his coffee, checked his watch, and finished by telling her how the thing inside Abe had somehow controlled Deputy Rainey and what had happened when they tried to examine Abe in the MRI machine.

Lois felt the color draining from her face.

"Dr. Malcolm never made it to Oswego, he never called there, and the children were never transported. I have no reason to believe that any of them ever left town. The phones have been ringing off the hook with reports of missing persons, and I know of at least three families that were ... Well, let's just say they're gone."

"Billy and Eric were missing, and Billy has a temperature. You don't think—?" Lois clutched her pack of Parliaments in a white-knuckled death grip.

"I'll call Burt and Ziegler and have them keep an eye on him."

"Th-this isn't possible." Her hand trembled as she tried to light another smoke. She studied Carl's face and stared into his eyes, hoping to find the lie hiding somewhere beneath the surface. There was none to be found, not that she had ever known him to even bend the truth. "W-what should I do?"

"I told you. Pick up Troy and leave town as soon as possible. If tonight is anything like last night ..." He didn't finish.

"But Alice and Will are at the center with Billy, and Eric is still missing." Lois felt the room start to spin and found it impossible to think straight.

"If I can arrange to have Billy transported, will you go?" He dug into the pocket of his jacket. "Will you take your family and get the hell out of Garrett Grove? Will you please do this for me, Lois?"

"I doubt if Donald will leave the job site." She regretted saying it as soon as the words left her lips. Carl's eyes suggested he really didn't care what happened to Donald.

"Yes," she replied. "If I can't make it happen tonight, I will go first thing tomorrow. I promise."

Carl removed the object from his jacket and placed it on the table. The gun was a big nickel-plated revolver. "Take this. It's got some stopping power, and the kick isn't too bad. Remember, it's got to be the head; body shots won't do a thing."

"Tell me this isn't happening." She stared at him through a salty blur, but the look in his eyes suggested it was even worse than what he had told her. It was the first time she had ever seen him scared, and that terrified the life out of her.

Carl stood up, grabbed the gun from the table, and walked around to where she was sitting. He placed the cold steel in her hand, then set a box of .38 special ammunition in front of her.

"It's a .357, but if you use the .38s, you'll have better accuracy. Better chance at making headshots."

She knew he had put his career on the line by confiding in her and giving her one of the department's weapons. After all these years, he was still watching out for her. And how had she repaid him? By cheating on him and breaking his heart. All he ever wanted was to love her, and she had thrown it back in his face. And still, here he was ... standing in her kitchen.

Lois set the gun on the table, stood up, and threw her arms around him. She pulled him in tight and let the flood gates open. She buried her head against his chest and bawled like a child. The triggering scent of his Irish Spring wrapped around her like a warm blanket.

For a fleeting moment, time stood still. But it was already getting dark, and if Carl was right, trouble was coming. She didn't allow herself to think twice, knowing if she did, she would lose her nerve and probably never get another chance. She looked up into Carl's eyes and kissed him. Soft and slow at first, then bittersweet and intense, with a sense of urgency. She felt the blood rush to her face and throughout her arms and legs as their mouths moved in perfect synchronicity as if there weren't a mile of years between them. Before it could go any further, she took a step back, looked up at him, and smiled.

"I suggest you leave town tonight. If for some reason you can't, which would be a mistake, stay in the house and don't let anyone inside. I don't care if you know them or not. Your neighbors might not be who you think they are." He grabbed his hat and headed to the door.

"Carl," she said as he was halfway down the stairs. "I should have said no."

He looked back and tilted his head. "Huh?"

"All those years ago. You asked me if I was in love with him. I should have said no; I should have told you that I wasn't. But I knew what you would have done. And I couldn't let you take care of me and raise a child that wasn't yours."

He stared back for a moment as the silence and the magnetic pull between them intensified. "Yeah," he said. "You probably should have." Carl opened the door and stepped onto the porch, leaving Lois standing at the top of the stairs, alone with her laments.

CHAPTER 45

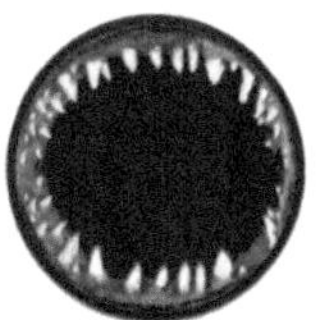

Deputy Ted Lutchen walked through the side entrance of the medical center with the large German Shepherd padding along beside him like they owned the place. Baxter looked up at him as they passed the waiting area and headed for the hall that led to the girl's room. Ted carried a box of Dawn's favorite toys with a doll under his arm and almost made it to the hallway before Nurse TenHove shouted at him.

"Pardon me, Deputy. You can't bring that dog in here."

He turned to her and offered the most serious face he could muster. "It's okay, ma'am, K-9 unit. Official business, Sheriff's orders." He continued on his way before she could say otherwise.

Ted escorted Baxter through the hallway and opened the door to Dawn's room. Nurse Carole jumped out of her chair as Baxter ran to her and started licking her hand. "Sorry I'm late, Nurse."

"Call me Carole," she said. "It was my pleasure; she slept the whole time." Baxter nuzzled up against her, and she obliged by rubbing his ears.

"Wow, a cop who likes kids and dogs. Can I buy you a cup of coffee, Captain America?"

"That would be nice, but I don't want to leave Dawn."

"Have a seat and I'll be right back. Milk and sugar?" He nodded. "Try not to miss me while I'm gone." Carole winked as she opened the door.

Ted knew he was probably blushing, but Nurse Carole appeared happy to see his reaction, as her smiled bloomed and she winked a second time before stepping into the hallway.

Carl Primrose climbed the steps of the sheriff's department and stopped for a moment to survey the parking lot. Judging by the excessive number of vehicles, Tara and Andrea had followed his instructions to the letter. He entered the building and was met by the throng of people clustered around the dispatch area. They stopped what they were doing and looked up; an unnerving hush fell upon the crowd.

Carl removed his hat and nodded. "Meet me in the briefing room in five minutes!" he shouted, then skirted past them toward his office and closed the door behind him. The large group stared at him as he passed without saying a word. Carl imagined they were all thinking the same exact thing: *What the hell is this all about?*

He sat at his father's old desk and picked up the phone. Nurse TenHove answered on the second ring. "Are you still there, Doris?"

"Is that you, Sheriff? What's the big idea bringing a dog in here?"

"Excuse me."

"Your deputy just came in here with a dog. Walked through the waiting room like he owned the place. Said it was police business."

"I see." Carl knew exactly what Ted had done. "Well, it kind of is. Look, I'll take care of it when I get there. The dog belongs to the little girl we brought in earlier. We thought it would help her since she just lost her family." Carl figured he would throw the deputy some bail; Ted had really proven his worth today.

"Oh, well in that case." Doris's tone appeared to soften.

He asked if he could talk with either Burt or Dr. Ziegler, and a moment later, the phone started ringing and a familiar voice answered.

"Yeah, I mean, hello, Lab."

"Hey, Burt, it's me. Looks like I'm gonna be a little late. I want you and Ziegler to sit tight and don't go anywhere. I mean it. Don't go anywhere!"

"Is that your gut talking, Carl?"

"Right now, it's singing like Donna Summer. If you see Deputy Lutchen, tell him the same thing and that I'll see him when I get there."

"You got it. Where are you now?"

"I'm at the station recruiting a little extra help. Be careful, old man."

"Don't I always?"

Carl shook his head and hung up, thinking it best to not say anything.

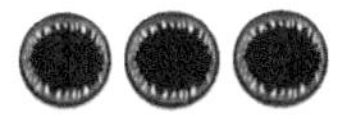

Its children had rested throughout the day, and now that the sun had once again begun to set, they were ready. It summoned the brood from their sleep cycle and instructed them. They began to stir and rose to their feet, the ones that still possessed them. While some of the creatures retained a glimmer of their human resemblance, most had already evolved beyond such. It dispatched them from the mountain and sent them into the town. Soon, it would possess all that stood in its way. The first objective was to destroy the

machine and the men who had used it. Then it would propagate and feast like never before.

Carl walked into the briefing room to find nearly every seat filled. Scanning the crowd, he noticed that everyone he asked for had shown up. He approached the front desk and took a seat. "Thank you all for coming."

There was a stirring and an overall look of confusion on the faces staring back at him. None of them had any idea why they were there or what he was about to say, except Deputy Rainey, of course.

"You're wondering why I asked you here, so let me cut to the chase. As some of you know, we found a body Sunday morning on Foothills Drive. Since then, there has been a house fire." He looked at Bob Jones, the fire chief, who nodded in agreement. "What you don't know is that since Sunday, there has been a spree of violent activity." The room erupted with a rash of questions and comments. Carl raised his hands to regain control and continued. "We have reason to consider the residences of both Fifteen and Sixteen Poplar to be crime scenes. We also suspect a violent crime to have taken place sometime yesterday on Stanhope Road."

A dark-haired man in the front row stood up; it was Nick Gomes, one of Bob's firemen. "Excuse me, Sheriff. You said, 'consider to be a crime scene.' Are you not sure?"

"We found bloodstains and evidence of foul play. But we didn't find any bodies. Also, we've had increased reports of missing persons." He scanned the room once again and focused on Deputy Rainey, who looked a bit green around the gills. *Stay cool, kid, and keep your mouth shut.* The last thing he needed was Rainey explaining what happened at the morgue and starting a full-blown panic in the process.

"I called you here tonight because I need your help. We're a bit low on manpower, and I plan to deputize those of you who are not already members of law enforcement. For those who are retired, consider yourselves reinstated." There was another stir of murmurs and questioning stares, but Carl sensed that a swell of camaraderie had begun to spread throughout the room as well. *This just might work.*

"Currently, Deputy Lutchen is at Chilton and will remain stationed there. Bob, thank you for coming; I see you brought two of your best men."

Bob Jones gestured to the men sitting on either side of him. "I believe you know Nick Gomes and Ed Koloski. I'd trust these men with my life."

"That's good enough for me." Carl offered a confident smile and prayed it passed for sincere. "This is what I am looking to do. I'm beefing up the force tonight as a preemptive move. More than likely, nothing will happen. But I want to be prepared for anything. Mr. Koloski, you'll partner with Deputy Kovach. You will, of course, follow his lead by the numbers." Both men nodded their heads in acknowledgment.

"Deputy Rainey, Mr. Gomes is with you. Bob, you're with me. Tim and Beau, I know it's been a while since either of you wore the uniform, but I need you both here to help secure the station with Tara and Andrea. There will be a squad car out back if we need to call for backup. Are you feeling up to it?" Carl was most concerned about retired deputies Beau Jenkins and Tim Colbert, who were damn near seventy and not as spry as they used to be. But once a cop, always a cop. He smiled when they stood up and saluted. "Great, thank you all for your help. I'm issuing sidearms. I've seen you all at the range and taught most of you myself. Mr. Gomes and Mr. Koloski, if you're ordered to holster or surrender your weapons, you are to do so on the spot. Comprende?"

"Yes, sir," the men replied in unison.

Carl waved to paramedics Michelle Marks and Joseph Santos sitting in the back row. "I'm glad you're both here. I hope we won't require your services, but I want you to be ready." They nodded in agreement.

Carl prayed he was doing the right thing and the effort would be enough. His only other option was to admit defeat and call either the state police or the Feds. At the moment, he had no idea how to do that without sounding like a raving lunatic. Best-case scenario, they would laugh and hang up the phone. But more than likely, he would be relieved of duty and placed under psychiatric observation.

"One last thing. I know it's going to sound strange, but I want you all dressed in riot gear tonight, helmets and all." This raised even more questions and concerns from the crowd, but time was running out. Carl didn't think explaining it further would help them understand any better. "Trust me on this. You are to exercise extreme caution, and I want you to wear your helmets. If anyone attempts to accost you in any way, you are authorized to use whatever means necessary to subdue them. I repeat, any means necessary. I know you have questions, but I don't have any answers now. Just be careful out there and don't take chances. Check in with dispatch regularly."

There were still questions, and Carl attempted to answer those he could. But the sun had already set and there was no time left to waste. The riot gear and weapons were distributed, and Carl instructed Tara and Andrea about what they should do in a worst-case scenario. He prayed it wouldn't come to that. Then he sent his deputies out with their new partners and climbed into his own cruiser with Bob Jones riding shotgun. Beau Jenkins and Tim Colbert stayed back with the dispatchers, locked the doors, and fastened the deadbolts once the last of the patrol cars left the parking lot.

Carl served in Vietnam, which had been an unconventional war. In a conventional war, there was a clear line between armies, as there had been in both World Wars. Army A on one side and Army B on the other, with a stretch of No-Man's-Land between them. Vietnam hadn't been anything like that. The Viet Cong created an elaborate tunnel system to ambush their enemies and used civilian decoys as weapons. They employed unconventional methods against their enemies, which had given them a tactical advantage. The American soldiers entered the jungles of Vietnam expecting a conventional war, and it had ended in a bloodbath.

Carl remembered; he had seen it firsthand. They had lost in Vietnam because they underestimated the enemy. It was a mistake his platoon had made that day on the Mekong Delta, and it was a mistake he repeated almost a decade later in Garrett Grove.

Lois walked up the front steps of Twenty-Two Village Road and rang the doorbell. A few moments later, an adorable little blonde girl opened the door with Troy standing behind her.

"You must be Janis," Lois said. "I'm Mrs. Fischer."

"Nice to meet you, Mrs. Fischer. We were just finishing dinner. Are you hungry?"

Not only was the girl striking but polite as well. Lois smiled, giving the child the once-over, and had to stop herself from gasping as her eyes focused on the front of the young girl's shirt. She couldn't believe what she was seeing; Janis had already begun to develop. Lois averted her eyes to stop from staring and was sure that her mouth had dropped to the floor. *How is that possible?* Lois herself hadn't started to develop until sixth grade. And if she had noticed Janis's breasts within the first few seconds of meeting her, it was a sure bet that Troy and the rest of the boys in the class had noticed as well. Lois was willing to bet that Janis's dance card would be quite full for the rest of her life; the girl was gorgeous.

Lois nearly forgot what she had been asked. "No, thank you," she replied.

"Nonsense." A woman entered from the hallway. "Hi, I'm Lynn, Janis's aunt. Come in and have something to eat. I insist." Lois stepped inside and maneuvered around several stacks of boxes. It was obvious the family was still in the process of moving in. A second later, a small beagle jumped out from behind one of the large boxes and greeted her. Lois reached down to pet the pooch, who eagerly accepted.

"Don't jump, Peanuts," Janis said, pulling the pup away by its collar.

Lois took one look at Troy and was overcome. All that had happened and all that Carl had told her hit her at once. She grabbed her son and hugged him tightly, then she kissed him on the forehead and messed his hair. Troy made a face and pulled away, obviously embarrassed by the motherly display of affection in front of his new friend.

Although the place was still cluttered with boxes, there was already a sense of warmth and home about it. Lois thought it probably had more to do with the family that lived here rather than the place itself. Janis and her aunt were clearly related, both blonde-haired and bright-eyed and awfully polite. Then it hit her. The aroma of baked chicken and buttery potatoes waltzed in from the kitchen, making Lois's mouth water. She had a vague recollection of heating up a bowl of clam chowder for lunch but wasn't sure if she had eaten any of it. So much had happened. And although she wanted to get home and not appear rude, she was famished and accepted the offer. Lois followed everyone into the kitchen, joined them at the table, and helped herself. Her taste buds reacted as if it were the first time they had ever tried food.

"Oh my, this is amazing. How on Earth do you get it to taste like this?" Lois was overwhelmed by the explosive flavor of the bird.

Lynn smiled with appreciation. "Thank you so much. The secret is beer. You take a can and shove it right up there." She motioned with her hand. "There's something about the yeast and the hops that brings out the flavor."

"I'm impressed. What brand?" Lois asked.

"Yuengling," Lynn answered. "It's a Pennsylvania brew; oldest brewery in the country."

"I went to Penn State. I can't tell you how much Yuengling I drank my first year in college. Probably had a lot to do with my freshman fifteen." Lois took another bite and swallowed. "How do you like school, Janis?"

"It's great! Troy and Wendy made me feel welcome. We eat lunch together every day." She put a spoonful of mashed potatoes in her mouth. Then, when she thought the adults weren't looking, she stuck her tongue out at Troy, showing him a wad of half-eaten spuds. He returned the compliment and displayed a mouthful of chicken. Lois had seen the entire exchange.

"Troy, that's not polite," she told him.

He apologized, then leaned over and whispered to Janis. "Why did you trade your sandwich if you don't like egg salad?"

Janis looked at the food on her plate and swirled the potatoes around with her fork for a minute. "I don't know. I could tell you didn't want to eat it, and I felt bad. Wendy took your peanut butter, and you looked sad. It made me happy to give you mine."

"Wow, that was really nice. You're so cool." He grinned and continued to eat his food.

Lois overheard every word of the conversation and bit her tongue. *Be careful, Troy, you are so close to the deep end, and you don't even know it.* She could see that Janis had a crush on her son and doubted if he even had a clue. Troy was growing up fast, but he was still quite innocent; it was clear that all this girl stuff was new to him. Lois was thankful that Troy and his two new friends were still just ten years old and she didn't have to worry too much, at least for a couple years. But how long would it be before Troy found himself torn between two women? How long before he broke one of their hearts? Would he marry the right one, or would he make a mistake he would regret the rest of his life? Lois realized she was projecting a bit.

"Can we, Mom?" Troy's voice startled her back from the place her mind had wandered.

"I'm sorry, honey. What was that?"

"Jeez, I asked if I could show Janis and Wendy Scream in the Dark, maybe tomorrow?"

She and Don had promised they would think about it, but that was before she had spoken to Dr. Ziegler. After that, the world had spun off its axis. Lois didn't plan on being anywhere near Garrett Grove this time tomorrow. But Troy's question made her think about the reality of that. Sharing dinner with Janis and her aunt made her question the possibility. How could they just leave town and say absolutely nothing? How could she just abandon everyone, the girls who were swooning over her son, their families? How could she just leave and not tell her friends or the boy who bagged her groceries at the A&P? But if she did open her mouth, people were likely to think she had gone crazy. Lois prayed it could be as simple as that. Surely, any minute, she would wake up in her kitchen with a cold bowl of clam chowder sitting in front of her, her conversation with Carl never to have taken place, and Dr. Ziegler had just been overexaggerating. Lois looked down at Troy, who was still waiting for a reply. "Sure, honey, that would be fine."

Charlie Silva and Darren Webb were pulling extra shifts in the wake of a rash of absenteeism due to a nasty flu bug going around. Charlie worked as a lineman for Con Edison, and Darren was a subcontractor for the phone company. With winter on the way, there were a lot of preparations that needed to be made. Garrett Grove and Parker Plains wouldn't stay up and running on their own. Tonight, the men worked together, checking the tensile strength of the mains at the substation on Route 3. All the electric and telephone lines for the Grove passed through the station, where they were relayed to the four sectors of town.

Last year's winter storms had cut power to the town for the better part of a week. Most people had fireplaces, but not everyone. And many had found themselves in the basement of the high school, which was a bomb shelter built at the start of the Cold War in case Russia decided to drop "The Big One".

Charlie and Darren started outside running diagnostics on the structural integrity of the housing units on the main high-voltage relays. Once that was completed, Charlie needed to check the transformers while Darren inspected the telecommunication relay.

The sun had gone down over an hour ago, and it was chillier now than it had been the past couple nights. Charlie zipped up his coat and rubbed his hands together as Darren exited the truck with a thermos and two Styrofoam cups. He poured one for Charlie and one for himself. "Feels like it's gonna be one cold winter."

Charlie took the offering and drank. "Hopefully, the power doesn't go down like last year. That was a fuckin' mess. It's one thing to lose a few lines, but if the station goes, this town is in deep shit."

"Good thing we're here." Darren puffed out his chest. "Should have a good month before the snow starts falling. We'll be right as rain by then."

"Hope so. They'll be a helluva lot of overtime for us." Charlie aimed his flashlight at one of the relays. "This fucker's in rough shape. Probably ain't been serviced since before last winter."

"Shit, they can give me as much overtime as they want. My kids are eating me out of house and home. Oldest one's growing so fast he needs new shoes every other month."

"How are the kids?" Charlie asked.

"Better than me. Doug's got a girlfriend. Probably getting laid right now."

"Speaking of getting laid, how's the wife? I imagine she's been missing me." Charlie laughed at himself, and Darren joined.

The sound of pebbles being scattered cut their laughter short. The entire area of the substation was covered with small stones rather than dirt or grass, which prevented weeds from growing around the transformers and relays. The men stopped laughing and looked in the direction the noise had originated.

"Probably just a raccoon or possum," Charlie said. They relaxed and focused their attention on the relay and the rest of their coffee.

The noise came again. Pebbles, not just being walked on but being scattered as if someone were throwing them by the handful.

"What the fuck?" Darren said. "Hey, who's out there?"

Another handful of stones was scattered. The noise came from the darkest part of the lot. Staring into the shadows, Darren froze as a handful of the tiny pebbles landed at his feet.

He pulled a screwdriver out of his tool belt and brandished the weapon.

"What the hell is it, Dar?" Charlie shrank back toward the truck.

"Some wise-ass kids, no doubt." Darren took a step forward. "You don't want to try me, asshole. I'm in no mood." He waved the tool to prove he meant business.

The noise came again, but no pebbles were thrown. Instead, it sounded as if someone had scooped up a handful.

"I'm getting tired of this bull—"

A golf ball-sized stone rocketed out of the shadows and struck Darren in the chest, knocking the wind out of him and nearly setting him off balance. Charlie watched it happen and recoiled as if he had been hit himself.

"Motherfucker!" Darren screamed and clutched his chest. "I'm gonna kick the shit out of you fucks." The second rock hit Darren square in the face. It had been thrown fast and hard and with incredible accuracy.

His nose erupted in a cascade of blood. It flowed from his nostrils and the newly formed gash running down the entire length of his schnozzola. He screamed through a blinding cloud of searing pain.

Charlie ran toward his friend and almost made it before the first figure darted out of the shadows. Luckily, Darren had been temporarily blinded and didn't see what was coming at them ... or how fast they were. Charlie, on the other hand, saw everything and had just enough time to realize they were in deep shit.

The creatures were small, but they weren't children, at least not human ones. The figure in front resembled something that could have been fished out of the river. Its face was bloated and dark purple in color. Large slits ran down the side of the thing's neck and looked an awful lot like gills. In a heartbeat, the strange slits flared open, exposing the muscles and veins lying underneath, making the creature appear as if its neck had been flayed open.

The second abomination was equally horrific. Its head listed to the right as if its neck had been broken. It took several lumbering steps forward, then charged the men at full speed. A blood-boiling shriek exploded from a mouth so massive and threatening, it couldn't possibly be real. At least two individual rows of jagged teeth snarled at the men as the beast descended on them.

The third creature resembled some type of primate, only far more hideous. It was covered in coarse, dark hair and wore what looked like a pair of children's pajamas. It approached on all fours, dragging its knuckles.

Torn between helping Darren and running in the other direction, Charlie froze, unable to move his feet. His bladder was a bit more decisive and let loose. He stood there, pissing himself, with just enough time to grasp what was happening. The beasts closed the distance and descended on Darren like a school of piranhas; they tore into him, ripping at his flesh and feasting on the extracted pieces. A second later, they focused their attack on Charlie. The last thing he saw was a cloud of black rushing toward him, smothering him, and forcing its way inside. A voice spoke from somewhere inside of him, but before he could make out the words ... Charlie Silva was gone.

CHAPTER 46

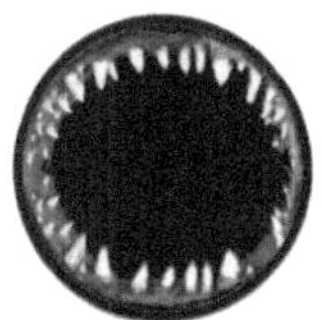

Dr. Ziegler and Nurse TenHove exhausted every possible resource trying to locate any of Dawn Negal's relatives in the area. With limited available options, Ziegler checked the child into a room on the second floor, where she could stay for the time being. He even made accommodations for her dog and the deputy. Ted Lutchen parked himself in a chair beside her bed and caught up on some much-needed rest himself.

The emergency room had finally quieted down, allowing Ziegler a little time to think. He made his final rounds, and on the way back to his office, he passed the lab where Burt was still hard at work. Next to the coroner sat the same priest who'd been mulling around the emergency room earlier. It made sense. Burt had been wearing the crucifix. Of course he was a Catholic. The man was probably having a good old heart-to-heart with the preacher. After everything they had been through, it wasn't surprising at all. *Good for you, Burt.*

Ethan Ziegler had never been very religious himself. His parents, on the other hand, were practically orthodox and tried to raise their son in the customs of the old country. It wasn't that young Ethan didn't follow the faith; he just wasn't as devout as his parents wanted him to be. He had gone to temple and become a man at his Bar Mitzvah, but as he got older, he drifted away from the practice like many young men did with every other religion. He discovered women, and that had been a significant diversion. And although his mother wanted him to marry a nice Jewish girl, they just didn't do it for him. Ethan had a thing for the Gentiles; they were a lot less frigid. It was his one weakness, which had gotten even more acute when he entered med school.

Deep down, Ziegler knew he wasn't a bad guy; he just loved women. More accurately, he loved having sex with them. He wasn't looking to settle down for any longer than a night or two, and the girls he was with didn't seem to mind. He was always honest and attentive to their needs, and he had even convinced himself that he was happy. It hadn't occurred to him until very recently that all the womanizing left him just a tad bit lonely. He watched the parents who brought their children in to be treated for strep throat, bronchitis, and chickenpox. And sometimes he thought ... it might be nice. Not to have chickenpox, but maybe, one day, it would be nice to have a kid of his own.

He wasn't getting any younger, and although it was different for men, he didn't want to look like a grandfather when he finally got around to settling down. *What the hell am I thinking?* he asked himself, not sure where all this was coming from. Possibly, it had been the sight of the priest talking to Burt, which had brought back memories of his mother and of his own faith—probably. Ziegler knew he had let his mom down with all his selfishness and skirt-chasing. She always said how proud she was of her son, the doctor, but deep down, he knew he had disappointed her.

Ziegler continued past the lab toward his office. Upon entering the room, he checked the time and decided it wasn't too late. He picked up the phone and dialed. A familiar woman's voice greeted him.

"Hi, Mom," he said.

"Ethan, is that you?"

"It's me. I wanted to see how you were. Is it hot in Florida today? How's Dad?"

"It was ninety degrees today. And your fathah's out of his mind. He thinks he's Arnald Palmah. He was out golfin' in the sun all day." The sound of her New York accent always made him smile.

"He was? Tell him he's got to take it easy. That Florida sun is no joke."

"How is my good-lookin' son, the doctah?"

"Good, Mom … I'm terrific." Ethan doubted if he had been all that good, and now that he thought about it, he figured he'd been fooling himself for a long time. He had believed he was happy, but listening to his mother talk about his "out of his mind fathah," he knew he had been sad, possibly for a long time.

"I miss you, Mom. I just wanted to call and tell you that."

"I miss you too, creampuff. Why don't you come down and visit your mothah? You should see Ellen Schumann's daughtah, Kim. What a knock-out. She's been asking about you, Ethan. Why don't you come down here and make an honest woman out of her."

"You know, I might just take you up on that." He let out a deep sigh.

"Who is this?" she asked. "What have you done with my son? Are you feeling all right? Usually, you want to give me a hard time. What's going on up there, Doctah Zieglah?"

"Nothing, Mom, really. I just thought it might be time for a vacation. I tell you what; I got a few patients I need to watch over for the next week or so, but I'm going to book a ticket and come visit you and Dad. How does November twelfth sound?"

"Be still my heart. You're gonna make your mothah cry."

"Aww, don't cry, Mom. It's been too long. I'm looking forward to seeing you and helping Dad with his golf swing."

"He'll be glad to have it. I wish he was here. He's across the street at Hank's house."

"That's all right. Tell him I called, okay?"

"Sure thing."

"I love you, Mom."

"Aww, you made my night, creampuff. I love you too."

"Okay, goodnight."

"Goodnight."

Ethan listened as his mother hung up. It'd been too long since he last saw his folks. It would be good to visit them and take some time off. And who knew, maybe he would even ask Kim Schumann out to dinner. He hung up the phone and ran his fingers through his hair. It was getting a little shaggy, and he would have to get it cut before leaving for Florida.

He leaned back in his chair and looked up at the bulletin board hanging on the wall. The red ladybugs sat there holding the papers in place. The big black dots on their backs looked like the eyes that had stared up at him from the gurney—Abe's eyes. Lost in thought, Ethan Ziegler stared into the big black dots on the backs of the red bugs, allowing what he had already been thinking to resonate and then register. *That's it!* He jumped up from behind his desk, nearly knocking his chair over in the process.

He scrambled to the bulletin board, pulled one of the bug magnets off, and held it an inch from the surface. Then he let it go and watched as it shot back and held in place. Doing it again, he imagined the invisible force that attracted the magnet to the board's surface like a bullet. The MRI machine was essentially a giant magnet that reacted to the electrons in the body. You couldn't enter the machine if you had any metal inside you or had tattoos with metal filings. The force of the machine would literally extract the alloys from your tissue. It all made perfect sense, and he cursed himself for not realizing it sooner. He shoved the magnet into his pocket, opened the door, and stepped into the hallway.

Ziegler almost ran right into the girl as she passed, pushing her cart. He stopped just in time to avoid colliding at full speed. She jumped with a start, then saw who it was and smiled.

"Dr. Ziegler, you scared me," the young candy striper said, making eye contact.

"I'm sorry." He scanned her name tag just to be sure. *Cyndi with an i.* "Cyndi ... I didn't mean to scare you like that. I was in a bit of a hurry, I guess."

"That's okay," she said. "I don't mind."

"Well, I'll be more careful in the future."

"I was hoping you wouldn't," she said, pressing up against him. "I kinda like it rough."

Ziegler felt the blood rush to nearly every part of his body, some areas more than others. He gasped as Cyndi lowered her hand and grabbed at the bulge that had started to grow in his pants. It felt good. Ziegler envisioned bending her over and taking the girl right there in the hallway.

Cyndi moved her lips close to his and squeezed once again. "Oh, Doctor, I think you need to take my temperature with this big thermometer."

He wanted her ... as much as he had ever wanted any woman. It would be easy to find an empty room and have his way with the girl; he had done it dozens of times in the past with Jackie Gilmartin, with others as well. *Like taking candy from a candy striper.* The thought resonated in his head and turned sour. It grew like a tumor, forcing all other thoughts to the side. Ziegler struggled to contain himself but was losing the battle as Cyndi backed him against the wall and squeezed. He latched on to the object in his pocket and forced himself to focus on anything else, anything more important than getting laid.

A clear image entered Ethan Ziegler's mind; he pictured himself getting on a plane and heading south. He could see the runway in Tampa, Florida, and could feel the warmth of the sun on his face. The warm spray of the salty Gulf was so vivid he could smell it. It fused with the scent of coconut oil and afternoon thunderstorms and tugged at him like a lasso. Ziegler thought about helping his father with his golf swing and the many ways he had let his mother down. Then he side-stepped away from Cyndi-with-an-i and smiled.

"I'm sorry, Cyndi. You're a beautiful girl, and I am very flattered. But I don't think it would be a good idea to do this. I don't want to use you, and I don't think I would respect either of us very much if I did. I'm sorry."

The girl's jaw dropped as if she was expecting to receive communion. Ziegler doubted she had ever been turned down in her life. Why would any guy in his right mind? For that matter, why was *he* turning her down, and what the *hell* was he thinking?

"I'm sorry, Cyndi. But I have to take care of something." He started off down the hallway when she called to him.

"Hey, Dr. Ziegler."

"Yes." He braced himself.

"Thank you. You're a real class act."

He nodded and smiled. "Thank you, Cyndi. So are you." Ziegler double-timed it down the hall. He finally knew what had happened to Abe and knew just how to prove it.

In a blinding whirl of sight and sound ... the world erupted. The explosion shook the building with the force of an atomic bomb, nearly knocking

Ziegler off his feet. His ears popped and started ringing, and the overhead fluorescents flickered on and off like strobes. He reached up and clutched the sides of his head, certain he had ruptured his ear drums. The lights flickered a second time and then went out completely. A moment later, the emergency generator kicked in, bathing the hallway in a dull amber glow. *Dear God, no!* Ziegler knew exactly where the explosion had originated. He ran down the hallway toward the back of the building, to the wing where the imaging department was located.

He tasted the smoke the second he entered the radiology wing, noxious and dark like burning plastic. Then he saw the carnage and debris. Ceiling tiles had been knocked loose and broken apart. Several light fixtures hung from the grid, suspended by their wires. Others had pulled free and smashed against the floor. The smoke grew thicker the further he progressed and nearly obscured the figure of the woman running towards him. She clutched her head like an over-inflated basketball, and the blood was everywhere. It ran down the sides of her face and through her fingers. She fixed Ziegler with a crazed stare as he approached, but the woman continued running, pausing only to snarl at him when he reached for her.

Shouts of pain and cries for help cut through the gonging inside his head; people were hurt, many were screaming, and the smoke was caustic. Ziegler did his best to navigate a path through the oppressive cloud, but his eyes burned and had started to tear. In a flash of understanding, he realized the ringing in his own ears wasn't just the residual effects from the explosion. It was the sound of an alarm ... The building was on fire.

Ziegler pressed forward, focused on helping the injured, but it was nearly impossible to see through the thick haze. It assaulted him like a stroke, causing him to choke and almost double over. He looked up to see the shadow emerge from the darkness; it stepped in front of him and stood there. There was something familiar about the figure. Ziegler squinted against the sting of smoke as the man approached him.

"You there!" he yelled. "Who is that?" By the time he saw the lab coat, it was too late.

Ziegler opened his mouth to scream, but the thing that had once been John Malcolm seized him by the throat and silenced him. It latched on to his neck with the strength of a tank and stared into his eyes. The former chief of medicine resembled little of his former self. He had lost most of his hair, though a few thin strands still clung to his scalp in random places. And his face was distorted, almost unrecognizable, and no longer looked human. Still, there was no mistaking the man beneath the monster.

Ziegler scratched at the claws wrapped around his throat as Malcolm lifted him off his feet. The air in his lungs sizzled and burned as he gasped to take a single breath. But the beast's hold on him was too powerful; its grip was inescapable. Ziegler flailed his legs and twisted his body while panic washed over him in a flood. The jet-black eyes of the monster stared into his own. Darker than midnight oil and larger than the spots on the backs of the ladybugs.

The ladybugs!

Ziegler suddenly remembered and plunged his hand into his coat pocket, grabbing for the tiny magnet within. He pulled it out just as Malcolm tightened his grip and twisted. Ethan Ziegler felt a momentary snap as his throat and spinal column were crushed.

A moment later, he felt nothing.

His feet stopped kicking, and his arms fell slack to the side; the item he had pulled from his pocket fell to the floor. The creature shook Ziegler one last time, then discarded the man like a wet dishrag, tossing his body against the wall, where it crumpled to the floor, limp, ruined, and lifeless.

In a fleeting moment, just before his world went dark, Ziegler's final thoughts had been of someone other than himself. Ethan Ziegler had been thinking about his mother.

CHAPTER 47

Before Donald Fischer left for the night, he instructed his men to secure the cave by roping it off and placing a barricade to impede trespassers. He also made plans with Mark Gold to have a few engineers accompany him tomorrow, the third chamber being the focal point of his concern. Don intended to take every possible precaution before he or anyone else stepped one foot in there. If it turned out to be a chasm, as he suspected, the entrance to the chamber would be permanently sealed off. And even though it was a remote possibility, the idea of someone slipping past his barricades and falling to their death sat in his belly like a handful of staples.

Stephanie was the last member of her team to leave for the night. She crossed the parking lot and approached Don where he sat in the front seat of his truck. "Hey, cowboy. So, about that invitation."

Don tilted his head and drew a blank. He had no idea what invitation she was referring to. "Huh?"

"Your son asked Janis to come over ... to see the haunted house."

"Oh! That's right. I completely forgot with all the talk of Big Bang and Collective Unconscious."

"Well, I just wanted to make sure that 'come over and look at my haunted house' wasn't code for 'I'll show you mine if you show me yours.'" They laughed for a quick second, but it was short-lived.

"They're only in fourth grade. I don't think we have to worry about that." Don hadn't had "the talk" with Troy and figured it could wait a couple years. He was pretty sure his son hadn't figured out the birds and bees on his own and was hoping Troy was just as clueless as he had been at ten years old.

"Well, maybe your son isn't there yet, but girls do mature a bit quicker; you know?"

She made a good point. Don had always felt about three or four years behind the girls his own age and spent most of his life trying to catch up.

"Why don't you come and help chaperone? The more adult eyes, the less hanky-panky."

They both laughed again and realized they were probably concerned over nothing; there was little chance that any of the kids would end up pregnant or with an STD. Neither of them had any idea they were being watched from the cliffside.

Strange dark eyes stalked the man and woman as they entered their vehicles and left the lot. Like a ravenous pack of jackals, they descended the rockface and bolted out of the darkness. They clamored over the fences, reaching the small building within seconds. Bold red letters were stenciled on the steel door and outside walls of the shed: DANGER EXPLOSIVES.

Burt and Father Kieran were sitting in the lab when the explosion shook the ground beneath them. The glass windows overlooking the hallway shattered, and the lights flickered and then went out. The roar of the concussion was deafening. Burt was thrust back into the memory of war as the very air in his lungs was stolen by the force of the blast.

Both men scrambled for cover underneath the lab table until the emergency lights turned on a moment later. Father Kieran was the first to rise to his feet, then helped steady Burt.

"Dear God. What was that?" Kieran shouted over the blare of the fire alarms. The first wisp of smoke made its way to the lab as a voice broke over the intercom system; it was impossible to understand a word being said. Staring back in confusion, Burt shook his head and shrugged. Father Kieran grabbed him by the shoulders and shouted, "I'm going to see if I can help. You stay here."

The priest opened the door and exited the lab. Burt didn't like the idea of staying behind and followed, only to find the smoke was considerably thicker in the hallway. Somewhere in the building, something was on fire. The suffocating fumes of burning plastic and toxic materials assaulted the men. Father Kieran removed his jacket and wrapped it around his face to shield him from the smoke, then instructed Burt to do the same.

Burt followed his lead, noticing the heavy object in his coat pocket. He felt around and found the gun Carl had given him. He removed it, shoved it into the waistband of his pants, then headed off behind Father Kieran, and they made their way down the hall. They hadn't gone more than a dozen steps before visibility was reduced to mere feet by the oppressive smoke.

A woman rushed at them from the haze, almost knocking Burt over as she plowed into them. Her head was bleeding, and she was in shock. With firm but compassionate hands, Father Kieran took the woman by the shoulders and stared into her eyes. She tensed up for a moment and then relaxed at the holy man's touch, allowing him to check her injuries and examine her. Burt watched as the priest removed his jacket and ripped off one of the sleeves. He carefully wrapped it around the woman's wounds and then made the sign of the cross above her forehead.

Other employees arrived to aid in the rescue effort. Father Kieran guided the woman and placed her hand in that of a large orderly, who led her away toward the ER. In a flash, Kieran was on the move and urging Burt to follow.

They pushed through the smoke, shielding their eyes as best they could from the bite of the fumes. Florescent lights that had been jarred loose hung by their wires from the ceiling. The floor was littered with broken glass and debris. Burt could tell they were close to where the blast had originated.

The temperature grew warmer as they approached the back of the building where the imaging wing was located. An orange glow at the end of the hallway was visible, and Burt could hear voices coming from the direction of the blaze. He followed Father Kieran through the smoke and around a corner that opened into a large hallway.

The dim silhouette of two figures appeared before them in the haze. The outlines of the shadows remained motionless, and even through the oppressive smoke, Burt could tell there was something wrong.

The two figures slowly came into focus, revealing the lab coats that both men wore. Burt recognized the one with his back to them as Dr. Ziegler. The coroner called out, but his voice was baffled by the drone of the fire alarms and the jacket wrapped around his mouth. Without warning, Dr. Ziegler was lifted off his feet by the other man, who had him by the throat.

Dear God, it's one of those things. It has Ziegler!

Time stood still. Burt was unable to react and could only watch the scene unfold. The doctor fought to free himself; a second later, his arms went slack and he stopped moving. The creature tossed Ziegler's body against the far wall, where it slumped in a most sickening way. Burt's stomach turned as he watched the man flop to the floor in a broken heap.

"No!" Burt screamed. He reached to remove the gun from his waistband and advanced on the creature. However, his feet were in motion long before he had control of the weapon. The beast drew a fix on him; an insectile grin flashed across its face.

Burt managed to free the weapon from his pants and raised it eye level. But the creature was faster and darted to the right, seizing Burt by the throat with one of its powerful arms. The gun flew from his hand as the creature tightened its grip around the coroner's neck.

Burt knew he had reacted without thinking; it was a mistake that would cost him his life. The creature tightened its grip, stopping the blood from reaching his brain. The jacket wrapped around his neck was the only reason he was still alive. Burt tried to draw a breath and looked up at the monster's face. *Dr. Malcolm!* Ice water ran through Burt's veins. There was no mistaking the man he had known and worked with for years, although his features had been altered considerably. The old doctor's face looked warped and distorted. His brow had grown thicker and protruded like a Neanderthal's. His nose had flattened into a defined look of brutality. And somehow, the man had grown nearly nine inches. *This isn't an infection,* Burt realized as he was lifted off his feet.

He clawed at the hand around his throat, but it was massive and so fucking strong. Burt's world grew dim as the Malcolm-beast clenched down on his throat, its hands encompassing the circumference of his entire neck. He wondered what would break first, his spine or his windpipe, then the world went black.

The thunder of an explosion roused him from the land of darkness. It was close and felt as if it had happened on top of him. It was followed by another loud concussion and then a third. The beast finally released him, and Burt fell to the floor, gasping for air. He looked up, half-dazed, as the muzzle flashed once more, hammering another explosion into the hallway. He struggled to focus on the face and looked into the eyes of the man holding the weapon.

Father Kieran stood firm with a steady hand and Burt's gun trained on the creature. The first bullet had hit the thing in the jaw and stunned it. The priest's second round hit the creature in the temple, causing it to release its grip.

Then Father Kieran stepped forward, took aim, and fired several more rounds into the monster's skull. It ceased to move, bleeding a thick black tar that spread out across the floor. Kieran raised the pistol and made the sign of the cross in the air before him. "I will fear no evil," he said. "For thy rod and thy staff comfort me."

Chris Wyatt was the only attendant working at Frank's Texaco on Route 3. The night shift typically wasn't busy, and tonight was no different, except for the occasional truck driver leaving from Wilson's diner down the street. The temperature had dropped considerably since sunset, and Chris had gotten tired of sitting in the little booth out by the pumps. He now watched the road from the comfort of the main office connected to the garage, where he could see approaching vehicles from either direction.

The radio was set to a rock station, and the King Biscuit Flower Hour had just come on. Chris turned up the small volume knob, giving Alice Cooper a bit more headroom as "Welcome to My Nightmare" crackled through the tiny speakers. A thick haze of cigarette smoke hung like a net from the Marlboro Reds Chris chained smoked. The fog permeated the air all the way into the connecting bays of the garage.

Chris was a senior and had been working at Frank's for the past four months. He didn't have any real aspirations for after graduation, but at least he would graduate. Which almost didn't happen due to his heightened infatuation for Diane Nathan, who had recently moved to town from Warren.

Diane was part German, part Polish, and exactly Chris's type. It wasn't so much the blonde hair and blue eyes that defined Chris's type as Diane's willingness to let him into her pants. He and Diane hit it off instantly, and it had been amazing. Chris had been with only one girl before meeting Diane, and it had been awkward at best. That girl was Abby Hamilton, the fire inspector's niece, who was nice enough to allow Chris to be her first. Chris didn't know what to expect, being his first time as well. But it had hurt like a bitch; it felt like Abby had clamped down on his pecker with a sandpaper vise. He didn't think it was supposed to hurt like that and had walked away with some serious road rash. Turned out, it had been even more uncomfortable for Abby, who bit her lip so hard she nearly lobbed it off.

They tried it again, but neither enjoyed it much, nor did they share any real connection. Chris liked that he was finally having sex but couldn't understand why everyone hyped it up so much. It wasn't all that great. After a month of failed attempts, Chris and Abby stopped seeing each other. Neither had taken it all that hard.

Then Diane moved to town, and Chris was knocked off his feet by her big blue eyes and long blonde hair. It was clear she was interested as well and let him steal third base the very first night. Chris noticed the difference right away and knew if Diane felt half as good on his dong as she did on his finger, his life was about to take a wonderful turn.

A week later, they were going at it like drunken rabbits. Chris had been right; Diane felt amazing and fit him like a glove. It had been a mind-numbing experience for both of them, and they proceeded to do it every chance they could. They'd run to his house after school and screw until his parents came home. Sometimes he'd sneak out in the middle of the night and climb the trellis outside her window. Then, with her parents sleeping in the room across the hall, they would attempt to stifle their sighs of desire as they humped each other's brains out. They did it in his car, in her parents' car, at the movies in the balcony, under the bleachers at the school, even in the graveyard.

It got to the point where neither of them thought it made any sense to stay at school during the day, not when they could be fucking. So, they cut class and spent their time in the park, naked and connected at the groin.

The only reason they showed up to school at all was so that they could meet at the front entrance and then walk out the back. It had come as a complete shock to Chris's mom when the principal called, telling her the boy had missed twenty-three days of school, and it was only October. His mother couldn't understand what was going on in her son's head, but his father sure did. He had met Diane and thought if Chris's mother looked like that back in high school, he never would have graduated either.

The principal agreed to give the kid another chance, and Chris promised he would buckle down and graduate. For some reason, Diane had been spared, and the principal hadn't noticed she'd skipped just as many days. It was a bullet she was glad to have missed; however, Diane had missed something else which was far more serious—her period. Diane was pregnant, and neither she nor Chris had fully wrapped their heads around the magnitude of it yet. They were still behaving as if nothing had changed, going at it like minks. Chris noticed once Diane got pregnant, she became hornier than before, which was hard to imagine. And if that was what it was like to have a pregnant girlfriend, then he was all for it. Chris Wyatt was just another guy who let the little head make all the big decisions. He wasn't the first, and he damn sure wouldn't be the last.

He lit another smoke and watched the car pull into the station from the north side of Route 3. Setting his Marlboro on the counter with the ash hanging off the edge, he stepped into the chilly October air and zipped his jacket up to his chin.

"Fill 'er up, regular," the guy said in a huff.

Chris turned on the pump, began filling, and walked back to the window to make small talk.

"Cold out tonight." Weather seemed to be the ultimate icebreaker when you had absolutely nothing to say.

The guy in the cab nodded and looked into the rearview to check the progress of the pump. "Yep, sure is."

"There was a line here during the day. Gas shortage has everyone freaking out. You picked a good time to come."

A horrible shriek pierced the night like an arrow. Chris instinctively turned in the direction from which it had come. The man in the car rolled up his window, almost as if he had been expecting it. Another cry ripped through the darkness and assaulted Chris's ears. He spun around again, completely freaked out by the inhuman noise.

There was movement on the far side of the highway; Chris froze as something broke from the shadows. The man in the car had seen it as well and started his engine. Chris tried to stop him, but it was too late.

"Wait, the pump is still running."

The guy put his foot to the floor and sped out of the station, ripping the hose from the pump. Gas poured freely from the broken nozzle and spread across the pavement in a flood.

There was movement again, this time from behind—something was coming. Chris started to run toward the office and nearly made it two complete steps before it hit him like a tank, spinning him around. Chris fell to the pavement in a lake of gasoline. He tried to get up, but before he could move, it jumped onto his chest and pinned him to the ground. He stared up at the monstrosity; it was straight out of a nightmare.

The face that loomed over him was grotesque and gargantuan, with huge cancer boils covering every inch of its skin. The massive cysts oozed yellow pus that reeked of decay and sickness. The odor invaded Chris's sinus cavity, causing him to gag and retch. One of the great boils erupted, spraying him in the face with a caustic solution that burned his skin like battery acid. Chris screamed through the pain, then the beast opened its mouth. The transfer was quick; it entered him, and the pain was gone. It was quite comfortable—in fact, it fit him like a glove.

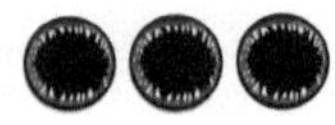

Deputy Kovach had been partnered with Ed Koloski, one of the volunteer firemen. Ed was just as surprised as everyone else when the sheriff deputized him, and from what he could tell, the man had overreacted. There hadn't been a single disturbance, and it didn't look like there was going to be. The streets were quiet, which was odd. Usually, there would be at least a few teenagers walking around. After all, it was only a couple days before Halloween; surely, some kids were bound to see how far they could push the limits of mischief. But so far, the night had been uneventful.

The men stopped at Wilson's for a quick cup of coffee. They took them to go and stood in the parking lot talking.

"I grew up in Rochester, and we always called it Mischief Night," Koloski said.

"What?" Deputy Kovach cinched his face into a grimace.

"The night before Halloween. We call it Mischief Night. But in different parts of the country, they call it other names."

"Oh, you mean Goosey Night," Kovach said.

"Exactly, like Goosey Night. I never heard it called that until I moved to Garrett Grove. That's a pretty odd name, don'tcha think? What the hell is a Goosey Night?"

"What the hell is a Mischief Night? That sounds a little soft. Like a buncha fruitcakes running around grabbin' each other's asses."

Koloski laughed. "What do you think Goosey Night sounds like? I've heard it called Devil's Night too. Now that sounds a bit more ominous."

"Mischief Night," Kovach repeated. "That's gotta be the dumbest thing I ever heard. Everyone knows it's Goosey Night."

Both men jumped as the initial sound of the explosion *Ka-Boomed* in the distance and then echoed off the brick wall of the diner behind them. A towering fireball vomited into the air across the highway from where they stood.

"Jesus Christ, that's Frank's Texaco!" Kovach shouted.

"Holy Fuck!" Koloski gasped.

"Get in!" Kovach jumped into the cruiser and grabbed the mic. "This is Deputy Kovach. There's been an explosion at Frank's Texaco on Route 3. I need backup, fire equipment, and paramedics. I repeat, Frank's Texaco on Route 3. The whole place just went up like a torch, over."

"Roger that, Deputy, responders are on the way."

Kovach put the cruiser in drive and raced toward the ball of fire. The flames stretched over a hundred feet into the air, billowing and churning in on themselves as if a bomb had been dropped on Garrett Grove.

The ash on Chris Wyatt's cigarette had gotten so long and heavy, it toppled from the counter, dragging the smoldering butt with it. By then, the endless rush of gasoline streaming from the broken pump found its way into the building and pooled on the office floor. For a second, it looked as if the gas had snuffed the smoldering butt, extinguishing it completely. Then suddenly, the smallest spark came to life, igniting a flame that erupted with a whoosh, sending a river of fire racing back toward the pump. The steady flow of fuel, combined with the massive lake that had already pooled on the pavement, propelled the initial blast several stories into the air. One moment, the October sky was dark and cold; the next, it blazed like the face of the sun and burned like the very bowels of hell.

CHAPTER 48

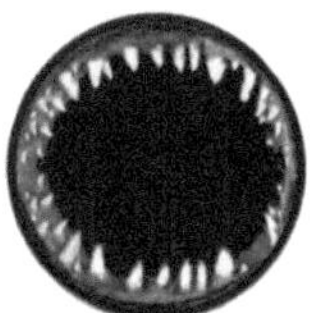

Lois thanked Lynn and Janis for dinner and for allowing Troy to stay late. She threw her coat on and was about to leave when the front door opened. The new arrival stepped inside, and Lois found herself face-to-face with one of the most beautiful women she had ever seen. She attempted to speak, but the words stagnated in her throat. Janis and Peanuts rushed forward and greeted the woman, saving Lois the embarrassment of looking like a fool.

"Hi, Mom." Janis hugged her as the dog whined and licked her hand. "This is my friend, Troy, and his mom, Mrs. Fischer."

Lois followed the woman's eyes as they looked her up and down. "I'm Stephanie. It's a pleasure to meet you."

"Call me Lois. It's nice to finally meet you too." Lois shook her hand and sized her up as well. Stephanie Thompson was gorgeous; she was petite and blonde and had the perfect little figure. *No wonder why he's been working late.* Looking at the woman, Lois was surprised Don bothered to come home at all and couldn't blame him. She was beautiful.

"And you must be Troy." Stephanie shook his hand.

"Hello, Dr. Thompson. My dad said you work for the museum."

"I do," she said. "I hear you're quite the explorer yourself. Did Janis show you her arrowheads?"

"Yes, she did." Troy nodded to Janis, then turned back. "What does it look like in the cave? I bet it's cool."

"It's very cool. I've never seen Lenape artifacts in such perfect condition. And we've only just begun to uncover their secrets."

An unbridled look of wonder spread across Troy's face, as if Luke Skywalker himself had just walked through the front door. "Really? What did you find so far?"

"Troy, that's not polite," Lois leaned over and whispered.

"That's all right. I love to talk about my work." Stephanie shrugged her shoulders, and Lynn chimed in.

"It's true, she does. But I warn you, once she gets started, it'll be difficult to get her to stop." Lynn tousled Janis's golden curls. "Like mother, like daughter, right honey?" Janis nodded in agreement.

Stephanie placed her bag down on a stack of boxes that hadn't been unpacked. "Why don't I make a pot of coffee? Then I can tell you anything you want to know about the Lenape tribe and what we found in the cave."

Troy hit Lois with a look she was all too familiar with; unfortunately, he wasn't going to get his way this time.

"We should probably be going, honey. Tomorrow is a school day." Lois had no intention of sending Troy to school tomorrow. All she could think about was getting him home safely and watching over him like a Doberman Pinscher. And the longer she stood there, trying to be polite, the more she was overcome by an urgency to leave the Thompsons' house.

Stephanie seemed to sense her apprehension and stiffened up as if suddenly put on the defensive. Lois prayed no one else could pick up on the tension between them and was now certain that Stephanie was just as uncomfortable as she was.

"Maybe some other time then." Stephanie offered a smile that could have been genuine.

"That would be nice," Lois lied.

"Yeah, like tomorrow night at our house," Troy blurted. "When the girls come over to see the haunted house." Lois wished he had kept his mouth shut, but that wasn't a skill Troy had fully mastered yet. "Remember, Mom, you said we could tomorrow."

She did say that, but Lois had no idea what tomorrow held. Carl had painted a vivid end-of-the-world scenario, and she was prepared to jump ship. But when it came down to the logistics of executing that plan, she found it to be more complicated. There were a million things she needed to take care of before she could just up and leave. And the more she thought about it, the more obstacles got in her way. *Maybe this is what happened to the people of Pompeii.* Lois couldn't help but wonder if the citizens who had seen the smoke lifting from the mountain and felt the earth tremble beneath them had also found a million reasons not to leave.

Not only did she have to think about Troy and herself but she had Alice, Will, and her nephews to worry about as well. And what about her friends? How could she leave them behind without saying anything? How could she run away thinking only of herself and her own family? *That's probably what happened to the people of Pompeii. The ones that were turned into human statues had probably been thinking the same exact thing.* Lois prayed the fear wasn't visible on her face.

"Yes, of course," she told Troy. "Tomorrow will be fine." She was thinking about the eruption of Mount Vesuvius and couldn't imagine what those poor people had been thinking when the top of the mountain exploded.

That's when it happened.

The darkness outside the Thompsons' picture window dissolved into a fiery orange blaze that heated into a burning red a second later. It was followed by a concussive blast that rattled the windowpanes and shook the house. The group watched in horror as a giant fireball rose in the distance. *Vesuvius.* It was all Lois could think of. She waited for the lava to rush in and turn them all into statues. She wondered if archeologists would find them one day and ask, "*Why didn't these people just leave town?*"

Ted sat in a chair next to Dawn's bed while she slept and had just started to nod off when Baxter began to whine and pace the floor. Not wanting to wake the child, he tried to calm the dog by scratching him behind the ears. But Baxter continued to carry on. "What's the matter, boy?" He had taken him out to do his business less than a half-hour ago and doubted if he needed to go so soon.

Still, Baxter continued to whine and began to pant like when Ted first found him in his pen, unattended and thirsty.

He reached for the dog, and Baxter reacted by running under the bed. A second later, the room shook as if a truck had crashed into the wall on the other side of the door. The chair he sat in lifted off the floor, and then he heard it ... an explosion, much louder than a gunshot.

Baxter howled from his position beneath the bed, waking the child, who immediately started crying. She scanned the room, not sure where she was until her eyes fixed on Ted. She stretched her arms out toward him and latched on to him as he picked her up and held her tight against his chest.

Ted poked his head out the door as the lights flickered and went dark. The emergency lighting kicked on a second later, revealing several employees scrambling about like yellow jackets swarming the nest, all of them trying to figure out what the hell had happened. Ted knew that the explosion hadn't occurred on the floor they were on and imagined it had taken place on one of the lower levels.

He could already smell smoke, and a moment later, an authoritative voice barked over the intercom system. *Code Redman, Code Redman, report to the imaging wing.* Ted knew Redman was the code for a fire.

Then the radio on his belt crackled, and a familiar voice shouted through the static. "This is Deputy Kovach. There's been an explosion at Frank's Texaco on Route 3."

What? That doesn't make any sense. Frank's was on the other side of town, and there was no way he could have felt the explosion at the medical center. Listening to the rest of Kovach's transmission, Ted realized there had been a second incident that had happened simultaneously. *That isn't any coincidence.*

He picked up his radio. "This is Deputy Lutchen. There is a fire at the medical center. I repeat, we have a fire at the medical center." His transmission was followed by a long period of silence. Then Andrea's voice broke up as she attempted to verify his call. Apparently, she couldn't believe the coincidence either.

Ted confirmed the information and requested backup as well as the fire department.

Carl and Bob Jones arrived at Chilton just as Deputy Kovach's call came in, immediately followed by Deputy Lutchen's. They looked up just in time to see the dark cloud erupt from the back of the building.

"Jesus Christ," Carl said. "We're too late."

Deputy Kovach and Ed Koloski arrived at the Texaco station to find the place engulfed in flames. The intense heat made it impossible to get anywhere near the front of the station itself, forcing Kovach to run to the back lot and hit one of the shut-off valves. The pumps had already discharged an incredible amount of gasoline onto the property, but the underground tanks had not gone up, and there was no way they could once they were shut off.

As Kovach ran for the switch, Koloski radioed the fire station and informed them what equipment was needed to fight the blaze. The chief was at the medical center, where there had been another incident, which left Koloski in charge at the gas station.

The blaze diminished considerably once the fuel supply was cut off, and the only thing left to do was wait for the trucks to show up and foam the place down. Kovach returned to the cruiser, popped the trunk, and removed two chemical extinguishers. He handed one to Koloski and took one for himself. They did what they could to soak the area near the road, as some of the gas had started to spill over onto Route 3. In the distance, the sound of sirens grew louder as the Garrett Grove Fire Department responded to the call.

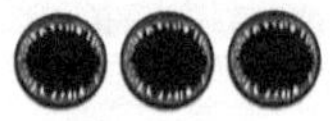

Father Kieran lowered the weapon and tucked it into his pocket just as the sprinkler system kicked on. He extended a hand to Burt, who stared back in disbelief. Somehow, he was still alive. The creature had had him by the throat, and Burt had been unable to breathe; the lack of blood to his brain had nearly turned off his light—permanently.

He'd been foolish to mistake his reflexes for that of a younger man. He had pulled the gun and dropped it without firing a single shot. It was Father Kieran who picked it up and ended the damn thing like he was Dirty Harry. The priest had saved Burt's life and killed the creature in a very badass fashion. Burt looked into the man's eyes as Father Kieran helped him to his feet. "I've never seen a priest do anything like that before," he said.

"I'm not your average priest." Kieran smiled.

The creature that had once been Dr. Malcolm lay dead on the floor. Bullet wounds now pierced its skull, allowing a thick, dark trail to seep from them. The black liquid mixed with the water from the sprinklers and ran through the halls like a river of ink. Father Kieran removed what was left of his jacket and threw it over the creature's face.

Burt rushed to where Dr. Ziegler had been thrown. The man's body lay twisted and broken against the wall. His neck had been crushed, and his head hung to the side at a most unnatural angle. Burt bent down and grabbed the man's hand and started to cry. "Jesus Christ," was all he could manage.

"Yes," Father Kieran said. "Jesus Christ, accept this child into your Kingdom. Forgive him of his sins and grant him everlasting life." Then he made the sign of the cross over the body.

"I think he was Jewish, Father," Burt said.

"I don't think he'll mind." Kieran offered the sign of the cross a second time.

Burt let go of Ziegler's hand and blessed himself. "No, I suppose not." He glanced down and noticed the small object that lay beside the doctor's body. He picked it up and studied the black and red ladybug magnet, turning it over in his hand, then grasped it tightly.

There was a commotion of voices from down the hall as two men rushed toward them. Burt looked up to see Carl and the fire chief.

"Burt," Carl yelled. "Oh, thank God. I thought that maybe you ..." Carl looked down at the doctor's body. "Oh God, not Ziegler."

"It got him, Carl. It was Dr. Malcolm; he came back." It was difficult to tell with the sprinklers raining down on them, but Burt was pretty sure that Carl had started to cry as well. Which was something he had never seen his friend do before.

Bob Jones approached the body of Dr. Malcolm and lifted the jacket, exposing the creature's face. "What the fuck is that?" he gasped.

"That's Satan's imp. An abomination of all things Holy," Father Kieran answered as Bob replaced the jacket and stepped backward.

"What happened to it?"

"I put it down. It killed the doctor and almost killed Burt."

Carl grabbed Burt and hugged him. "I'm sorry. I told you I would be right back. Are you all right?"

"Yeah, I guess so, but I wouldn't be if it weren't for Father Kieran here. He saved my life. We weren't in time to save Ziegler. It had him before we got here, dammit!" Burt and Carl stared at each other with the weight of a thousand suns between them. All their fears had been confirmed.

"Gentlemen." Bob stepped in. "I think it would be best if the father and Mr. Lively headed back to the emergency room. Carl, there's probably a lot of injuries, and we should keep moving." Years with the department had given the man a clear head under pressure. Even after seeing the impossible, he could pull it together and focus on the job.

Father Kieran assisted Burt to the emergency room while Carl and Bob headed toward the back of the building. They left the twisted body of Dr. Ethan Ziegler where it had landed, half propped against the wall with the sprinklers raining tears upon it. Burt had been right all along; there really was no dignity in death.

The medical center's fire suppression system extinguished the blaze quickly. And even without the inspector to verify, it was easy to conclude that the explosion occurred in the imaging wing. Several oxygen tanks had been placed in the same room as the MRI machine. Someone had then turned the instrument on and left. Once the machine began its cycle, the magnetic pull of the instrument became so great, it shot the tanks around the room like a couple of pinballs. It probably sucked them right into the chamber. The force would have been significant enough to shatter one or more of the valves, causing the gas to ignite. That was just Bob's theory, which seemed solid.

Carl figured Dr. Malcolm had let himself in through the back door, moved the oxygen tanks into the MRI room, and then started the machine.

There had only been three deaths and none of them caused by the explosion, at least not directly. Debbie Horne, who had made her first trip to the Mountainside Asylum just a few days ago and liked to think she looked like Crystal Gayle, passed away due to injuries she sustained from the car accident. Dr. Malcolm was the second fatality, although he had in fact died a long time ago. Dr. Ethan Ziegler was the third person to perish at Chilton Medical Center on Tuesday, October 27th. The man had saved Carl's life only yesterday, and he had been their best chance of figuring out how to save the town.

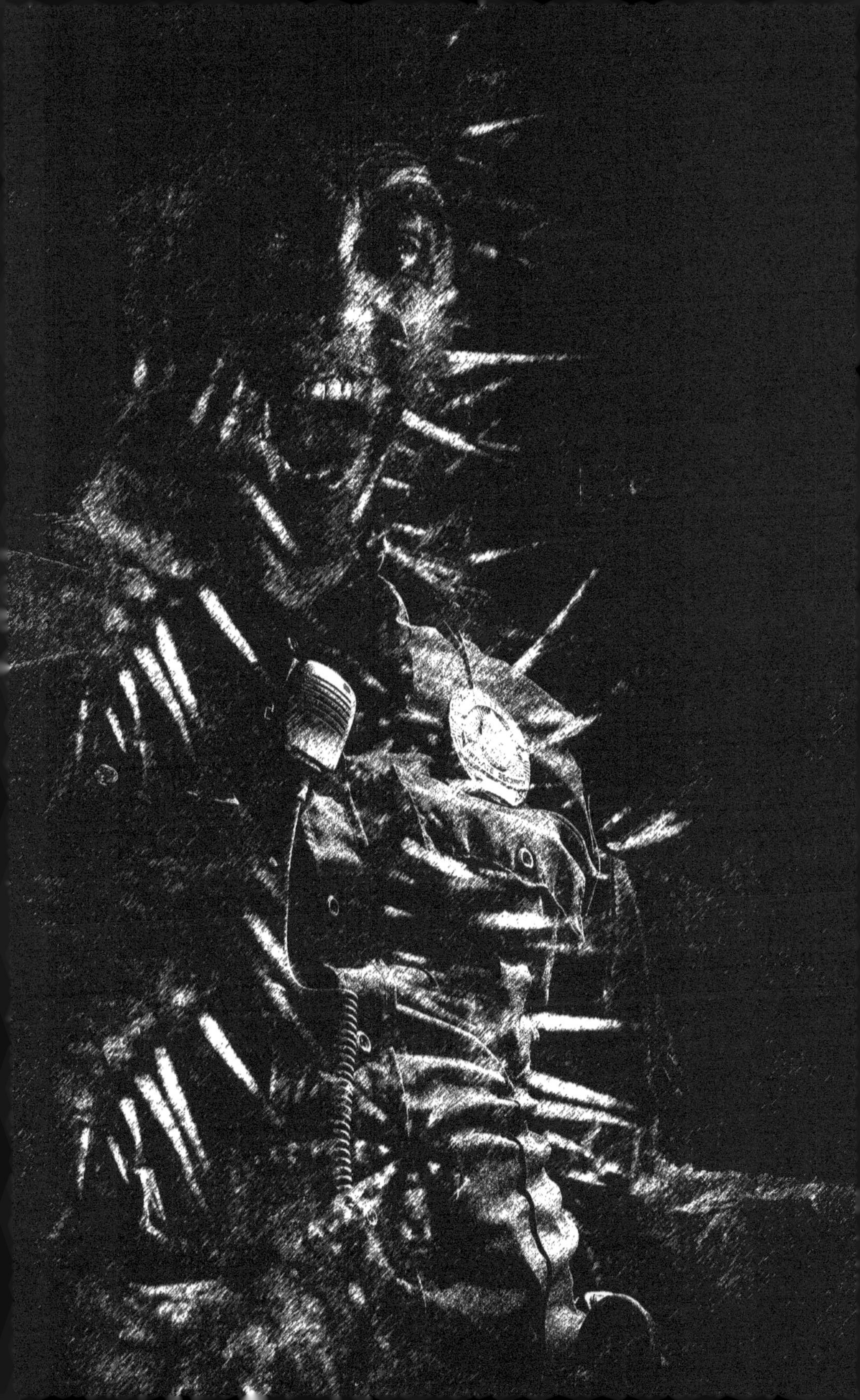

CHAPTER 49

Don Fischer was on his way home when the Texaco station went up like a Roman candle. He assumed the worst, thinking that a methane pocket had erupted at the quarry. They had run into several of them in the past and managed to avoid catastrophe every time. Still, the threat was always looming. He took his foot off the gas pedal, studied the blaze, and realized the explosion had originated on the south end of town and not at the quarry. He was more than relieved and continued on his way.

He nosed the old Ford into the driveway, noticing Lois's car was missing and the house was dark. Unable to imagine where they might be, he started to worry. It was unheard of for her and Troy to be out past eight o'clock on a school night. *What the hell?* He turned off the ignition, gathered his prints, and stepped out of the truck, expecting to find a note waiting for him on the kitchen table.

A quick rustling of leaves and the snapping of several branches caused Don to start. He spun on his heels toward the shadowed patch of woods along the far side of the driveway. The movement had been furtive and deliberate. He tensed up, holding his breath, half expecting someone to charge from out of the darkness. With his heart blasting cannon fire in his chest and his oiled palms growing slicker by the second, he waited, listening to the stillness of the night. Realizing it had probably been nothing more than a squirrel or a raccoon, he relaxed and exhaled a breath he had held too long. A second later, he found himself bathed in the yellow glow of headlights. Lois's Impala screamed into the driveway, almost hitting him in the process.

Troy bounced out from the backseat. "Hey, Dad, I just met Dr. Thompson. She's really cool."

"You did? That's nice, kiddo." Don struggled to relax, still tense from the sudden scare and nearly being hit by his wife's car. "Why are you guys home so late?" he asked as Lois jumped out of the vehicle and slammed the door.

She double-timed it across the lawn and made a beeline for the porch. "I'll tell you inside. Come on, Troy, get in the house."

"Did you see that?" Don stood for a moment, staring in the direction of the fire. "It looked like something blew up. I wouldn't be surprised if it was the gas station on Route 3."

"We saw it," she said. "Come on, Troy, in the house." She hurried him along.

"What the hell is going on?" He craned his head to the side, confused by her actions. "Are you all right, Lois?"

The snapping of a twig followed by the stirring of leaves caught their attention. Lois focused on the dark patch of woods near the driveway; her face faded to white as if it had been drained.

"Goddammit, Don! I said I would tell you inside. Now both of you get the *fuck* in the house!"

Neither of the Fischer men had ever heard that word come out of Lois's mouth and were bowled over by her outburst. Something had her rattled, and Don sure as hell didn't want to make it any worse. Troy appeared to get the message as well and ran straight across the lawn and into the house. Don followed his son's lead and kept his mouth shut.

Engine One and the ladder truck had been sent to battle the gas fire on Route 3 and were joined by retired Deputies Jenkins and Colbert. The blaze was snuffed out with a blanket of foam, revealing the broken pump as the source of the spillage. The fire had damaged part of the garage but not too severely. Fortunately, Deputy Kovach hit the shut-off valve in time to save the structure; otherwise, it would have been much worse.

Frank Palumbo, the station's owner, showed up ranting and raving and damn near hysterical. "That damn kid!" he screamed. "When I get my hands on him, I'm gonna kill him."

"I don't think you're going to have to do that, Frank," Kovach said. The deputy stood near the remains of at least two bodies lying on the concrete, covered in foam.

Frank approached the officer, joined by Koloski and several other men. It was difficult to tell what they were looking at until one of the firemen produced a water-dispensing extinguisher and proceeded to wash away the foam.

The cadavers were charred, the remains twisted and warped, but it was obvious there was something else wrong with one of the bodies. The burnt figure had curled into the fetal position, which was horrible enough. But what shocked the men were the features of the corpse's face. Its mouth was stretched to nearly three times the size of an average human's, as if it were made of plastic and had melted. An overcrowded row of jagged teeth resembling the maw of a shark snarled up at the men. And although the fire had rendered the body a cinder, it had not affected the lethal set of choppers in the least; they hadn't even turned black.

"What the fuck is that?" Kovach took a step back.

"Jesus Christ!" Koloski and the rest of the firemen moved in for a closer look.

It was impossible to be certain, but it was a good bet that one of the bodies belonged to Chris Wyatt, the boy who had been working at the time of the fire. No one could identify what the other one might be. It looked almost human—but not enough. The arms were too short to belong to a man, and the legs looked almost canine—back-jointed and powerful. Then there was the mouth and all those horrible teeth. The sheriff had tried to prepare them for what they might encounter tonight but hadn't mentioned anything even remotely like this. They all would have said he was nuts. But for the men who witnessed the discovery at the Texaco station, seeing was believing.

The fire was visible from the second-floor office of the Garrett Gazette, where editor-in-chief Milford Whitley watched the activities from the small window that overlooked Route 3. He'd been working late, as usual, when the pumps exploded less than a block away. Before he could gather his notepad and camera, he was alerted to the sound of someone entering the building through the back door on the basement level. Figuring it was either Ginny Gunderson, the paper's only full-time reporter, or Harry Veal, the staff photographer, Milford wasn't concerned at first. It wasn't every day the Texaco station caught fire, and he imagined both employees would want a piece of the story.

Moments later, the violent sound of destruction rose from the first floor. File cabinets were being turned over; desks were tossed about. From where Milford stood, it sounded as if someone was tearing the place apart. Then he heard it, the grunting snarls of wild animals. Aggressive like dogs, but far more vicious in a deep, guttural tone. Milford grabbed the closest thing he could find to protect himself, his Wilson putter, which he often used to practice when there was little to report. Brandishing it high above his head in his best defensive posture, Milford stood at the top of the staircase, listening to the chaos ensue below. Not wishing to commit himself to confronting the creatures, he remained as still as possible.

He nearly called out but thought better of it. Milford didn't have long to think before the raging destruction drew closer to the foot of the stairs and the creatures revealed themselves. There were two of them, dressed in the tattered clothes they had all but ripped out of. Ginny's dress, the same one she had worn before leaving work yesterday, hung in shreds from her mostly scaled and deformed torso. Large reptilian eyes stared up at Milford, frozen at the top of the stairs. When Ginny screamed, revealing a mouthful of razor-sharp incisors and hooked fangs, Milford soiled himself. A moment later, the second beast howled. Harry's camera still hung around his almost prehistoric-looking neck. It pendulumed to the left and right as he bolted up the stairs at his boss. Ginny joined in the hunt, and the two ripped into Milford, who never got to use his putter again.

No one from the Gazette ever made it to the fire at the Texaco station, and no one covered the explosion at the medical center. In fact, the small-town paper never released another issue.

Although there were only a few deaths at the medical center, there had been a mountain of injuries. Nurse TenHove, who'd been on the floor for over twelve hours, ran from bed to bed triaging patients and shouting orders to the rest of the staff. She was built for this. Some nurses learned how to deal with the pressure over time, others struggled and never got the hang of it, but Doris TenHove was a natural. That was the thing about her generation; they had been bred to survive and were born leaders. Doris was a born leader.

Father Kieran and Burt arrived in the ER soaking wet like most who had come from the back of the building. Doris rushed to Burt and began to examine his neck. "Who tried to choke you, old man?" She turned his head from side to side.

"It's a long story," he said.

She scowled and shook her head. "Well, you'll live, so get to work. You're officially a nurse. Go scrub up and make yourself useful."

"Yes, ma'am," he said with a grin as big as Texas spreading across his face, and headed to the sink to scrub up.

"How can I help?" Father Kieran offered.

"Give these people a friendly face to look at and help anyone who asks. Help the orderlies, help the nurses, whoever needs it." Although she was concentrating on a million things at once, Doris focused in on the job with microscopic precision. "Have you seen Dr. Ziegler?" she asked.

"I'm afraid the doctor didn't make it." Father Kieran lowered his eyes and blessed himself.

Doris pressed her lips and furrowed her brow, but with no time to grieve, the sentiment was quickly pushed aside. "That is a damn shame," she said. "He was a good man."

"Yes. Yes, he was," Kieran agreed.

Carl asked Bob Jones to help him deal with the bodies of Dr. Ziegler and Dr. Malcolm. He offered the chief a condensed version of the events that had transpired since Sunday morning. And although the man raised his eyebrows more than a few times during the sheriff's rundown, he took the news surprisingly well and maintained his composure.

They transferred the bodies into two impersonal-looking black bags, loaded them onto gurneys, and transferred them to the lab's cold storage freezer. After witnessing the resurrection of Abe Gorman, Carl was unsure what to expect from the body of Dr. Ziegler. Using similar leather bindings, he proceeded to tether both men to the gurneys and fastened steel basins over their faces.

The same agonizing thought repeated in Carl's head over and over. If he had arrived only ten minutes sooner, he could have saved Ziegler. At least he would have delivered the gun he had promised the man, which might have made all the difference.

The maintenance department had gone straight to shutting down the damaged parts of the building and resetting the rest of the breakers. A moment later, the main power kicked back on, illuminating the overhead lights that hadn't been damaged in the explosion.

As Carl and Bob stepped out of the freezer, they were met by Deputy Lutchen, who gave them a look of concern. "Is everything all right, Sheriff?" he asked.

"Not exactly, Ted." Carl knew he needed all his men on the same page and that he had made a terrible mistake tonight by holding back information. "I need to show you something."

He led Ted and Bob back into the freezer where the two body bags lay secured to their gurneys. Carl approached the body of Dr. Malcolm, removed the basin, then unzipped the bag, revealing its contents. Ted's reaction was nothing like the chief's. The deputy gasped and backed away from the grotesque deformity. It was obvious his brain couldn't interpret what his eyes were seeing, and it took him almost three full minutes before he could form a sentence. The figure that lay before them looked as if it had been transported from the Stone Age.

"I-I don't—Sheriff. What is that?" he finally asked.

"That's Dr. Malcolm. At least, it used to be. He's been infected by what we think is a bacterial parasite. It turns you into that or something worse."

The men stared at the thing on the table. Even with the bullet holes in the creature's skull and the dark fluid that had flowed from the wounds, it was easy to see the deformities and mutations caused by the infection. The doctor looked as if he had devolved.

"We can't be sure how many people have been infected already, but it's highly contagious, and as far as we know, there's no cure," Carl explained. "If you see anything like this, you need to stay the hell away from it. Shoot it in the head, and then shoot it again."

"Is this what killed the Negal family?" Ted asked.

"Something exactly like this."

Bob Jones had stayed quiet up till now. "Carl?" he finally asked. "How many of these things do you think are out there?"

"If I had to guess, over thirty."

"Sweet Jesus," Bob hissed.

"I'm sure you both have more questions than I have answers. I'm coordinating another meeting. People need to know what's going on. Tomorrow morning at the courthouse. Spread the word. In the meantime, you both need to try and get some rest. I got a feeling we're *all* gonna need it."

Don followed Lois and Troy into the house and closed the door. "You mind telling me what's going on?" he asked.

"Troy, it's late. Go wash up." Lois fixed him with a look to convey it was not a request and that she was in no mood.

Troy lowered his head and proceeded straight to the bathroom.

"What's going on?" Don asked again, entering the kitchen.

"Billy is in the emergency room, and Eric is missing." She stood with her hands on her hips.

"What? What happened?"

"They've been missing since Sunday night. Billy found his way to the rectory, where he collapsed. Father Kieran brought him to Chilton but had no idea who he was. They finally identified him this afternoon." Lois shook as she delivered the news. "Eric is still missing. I was at Alice's when they called."

"Dear God." Don reached out and hugged her. Lois allowed the gesture but refused to reciprocate. "Is Billy all right? Do they have any idea where Eric might be?"

"They think he'll be okay." She struggled to control the tears welling within her. "But he has a fever and is in shock. There's still no word about Eric." She wanted to tell him everything Carl said earlier but held her tongue. Don was practical and analytical; he understood science and facts and didn't possess an ounce of imagination. Especially not about things that sounded like they came out of a *Twilight Zone* episode. "I was picking up Troy from his friend's house and saw the explosion."

"I think it was the Texaco on Route 3. I'll bet one of the pumps caught fire." He rubbed her back. "Honey, I'm sure Eric will turn up, and Billy's a tough kid. They're both going to be fine."

"I hope you're right." She had been thinking about Pompeii when the fire started and was sure it was a sign. She pulled away and looked him in the eyes. "I think we should leave town for a couple weeks." She regretted saying the words as soon as they left her lips.

"What? What are you talking about? We can't leave. I have work, and the school year just started."

"I have a bad feeling. Carl said they still don't know what's wrong with Rob and the other kids. It might be bacterial. Billy's got a fever and has been unconscious since they found him. I just think it might be a good idea." It was as close as she could come to telling him.

"I thought the sheriff said we didn't have to worry about contagion. He said Dr. Malcolm had everything under control. If you want to keep Troy home for a day or two, fine. By then, this flu or whatever it is should be over."

She knew Don wasn't about to listen to anything she had to say, and she wasn't about to waste her breath trying to convince him. *Maybe I'll just keep Troy home from school tomorrow. And maybe while you're at work, I'll pack a couple suitcases and take Troy for a little drive upstate.* But first, she would call Alice. "You're right," she said. "The explosion just has me a little freaked out."

Don stared back at her with his mouth half open. "I get it." He smiled. "It looked like one hell of a fire. Probably looked a lot worse than it really was."

"I need to call Alice." She turned to the phone. "See if she's heard anything."

Lois picked up the receiver, depressed the button several times, and listened. There was no dial tone. She tried it again, but still there was nothing.

"What is it? What's wrong?" Don asked.

"It's dead." The receiver hung slack in her hand.

"Let me see that." He took the phone from her and tried himself. He pressed the button several times, then hung up. "The fire must have knocked out the lines. I'm sure they'll be up and running by morning."

I'm not so sure about that. Now she had no way to call Alice, or anyone else for that matter. *Dear God, I can't even get in touch with Carl.*

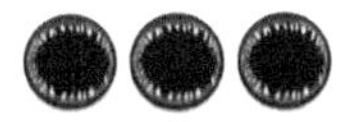

After the sun had set and its growing army had rested, it sent them out. The one called Malcolm was instructed to destroy the machine and had taken care of the one called Ziegler. Although Malcolm had been silenced in the process, the old doctor's consciousness continued to speak, revealing the secrets of the town and the people who lived there. Soon, it would have the numbers to terminate those who had hurt it. The one called sheriff, the one called Burt, and the clever one called priest. But first, there was work to do. It released its army and commanded them to hunt.

They crept through the shadows and found their way into the simple ones' homes. They entered through open windows and unlocked doors, making their way into the bedrooms of sleeping children and unsuspecting parents, where they consumed and multiplied. Then it dispatched the ones called Webb and Silva and set them loose on the substation.

After the dust had settled, there were eighteen staff members who sustained injuries due to the explosion in the imaging wing. Burt Lively suffered an acute whiplash, which was nothing compared to what Doris wanted to do to him. Nine people were treated for smoke inhalation, five suffered head injuries, seven received damage to their eardrums, some of whom had suffered multiple injuries. Then there had been Dr. Malcolm and Dr. Ziegler.

By the time the last of the patients were treated, it was late. Burt, who had been given a brace, sat in a chair drinking a ginger ale. Not only was his neck bothering him, but he had inhaled an awful lot of smoke, which made it difficult to swallow.

"What the hell happened back there, old man?" Doris asked, taking a seat next to him.

"You wouldn't believe me if I told ya." He took a hard sip from the can and grimaced.

"Why don't you try. I just might surprise you."

"I'm sure of that." He offered a sheepish grin. "The sheriff's called a meeting tomorrow. Why don't I pick you up in the morning? You can accompany me and hear for yourself."

"I tell you what, Mr. Lively." Doris met his stare. "Why don't *you* accompany *me* tonight. I can make you something to eat and take care of that neck of yours. Who knows … maybe I can take care of a few other things as well?"

"Nurse TenHove," he gushed. "You do surprise me."

"Wipe that stupid grin off your face before I change my mind. Now grab your coat, old man, and let's go."

Burt listened and followed her orders to the letter.

The head nurse and medical examiner left for the night and headed to her house on Fenwick Avenue. It had been years since Burt had been with a woman, and he was concerned that he might not rise to the occasion. But things worked out just fine, and he had been able to follow one of the golden rules that men his age lived by ... and he didn't waste it.

Alice and Will Tobin sat beside Billy's bed on the second floor, where he had been moved less than an hour before the explosion rocked the building. The lights had gone out for a little while, but the power was quickly restored, and the commotion appeared to subside. Rumors amongst the staff quickly circulated that an oxygen tank had exploded somewhere in the building. But one of the nurses assured them that it sounded worse than it had been, which didn't help ease their minds.

Alice tried to call Lois, but the lines had apparently been damaged in the explosion. That's when the nurse returned to the room carrying two coffees and asked if either of them would like something to eat. Alice was about to tell the girl she wasn't hungry when Billy started to moan. His fever was high, and he had been sweating profusely in his sleep.

She patted her son's face while the nurse checked his pulse. It was steady, but he was still burning up. Billy's eyes shot open and intently focused on them. Then he sat bolt upright and seized his mother by the arm.

"Oh, my God!" the nurse screamed.

The sheriff's station was busier than a fire ant mound. Patrol cars raced in and out of the parking lot, with the entire department pushed to the edge of exhaustion. Most men didn't return till after midnight, when they were informed about the meeting at the courthouse in the morning. There had been two separate instances, both explosions. The sheriff had been expecting some type of trouble, and he had been right.

The extra deputies made all the difference. There was far less damage to property and loss of life than if they'd been understaffed and unprepared. Deputy Rainey and Nick Gomes were the first to return to the station. They were told about the meeting, and both went home to get some well-deserved sleep. Tara, who had been on since early that morning, was relieved by Andrea, who resumed her regular position on the night shift. Kovach and Koloski stayed on duty and took turns napping in the basement, while the retired officers were thanked and sent home.

Carl was hesitant to dismiss them but believed they'd seen the worst of it. Tomorrow was another day, and he needed his deputies well-rested. Even though he already decided it was time to call in the state police. He still wasn't sure what he would tell them but knew he was in over his head and planned to make the call first thing in the morning.

He stepped out the back door of the station and opened the trunk of his cruiser. The bag of weapons containing the gun he intended to deliver to Dr. Ziegler stared up at him from the shadows. He removed the .40 cal. and tucked it into the back of his belt. Looking out across the empty parking lot, a strange sensation overtook him. The night was still and oddly quiet—too quiet. Carl knew he was being watched and scanned the darkness. He listened closely, but there was no movement—nothing at all. Slowly, he walked back into the station and ascended the stairs to his father's old office. He needed to channel the old man and quiet the screaming voice in his gut.

Tara Jefferies felt like she was running on fumes; she had been on duty since six a.m. and was dead on her feet. She pulled into her driveway and sat for a moment behind the wheel, collecting her thoughts. It had been one royally screwed-up day. The phone started ringing the moment she walked in the station, and it hadn't stopped. First, there'd been a report of a disturbance at the Campbell house on Poplar, then one at the Negal residence. Then, on top of that, the Tobin boys had gone missing. Thankfully, Billy had turned up, but poor Eric was still out there somewhere.

There were numerous other reports as well. Finally, the sheriff called the emergency briefing and put everyone on high alert. Good thing he did too, otherwise the fires at the medical center and the gas station would have been a whole lot worse.

Right now, the only thing Tara wanted was a hot bath and to forget this horrible day ever happened. It was more likely she would just pass out the minute she entered her apartment.

She walked to the front door, let herself in, and turned on the light. *God, it feels good to be home.* She climbed the stairs and entered the kitchen. Tara reached for the light switch. Then ... it grabbed her. Cold pressure seized her and dragged her into the kitchen with the force of a wrecking ball. She felt the pop in her teeth as her hand dislocated at the wrist. Blinding pain seared up the entire length of her arm, making it impossible to scream.

Sharp nails sunk into the flesh of her forearm as it yanked her towards him. There was just enough moonlight in the darkened kitchen to make out the distorted features of her assailant. It was Deputy Forsyth ... almost. At least the beast that lumbered before her was wearing his uniform, or what was left of it. Thorns protruded from the man's chest and torso. The face that sat atop the distorted mass of barbs had changed drastically. More of the sharpened spines appeared to have grown from the deputy's cheeks and forehead. Dark pus ran from his eyes and down his chin as he snarled and opened his mouth. Several rows of pointed teeth erupted from his gums like tombstones from the earth.

"No, Gary!" Tara cried as he pulled her against him. The thorns jutting from his body pierced her like a gourd, impaling her upon him as her breath stopped short. She stared up into his dark, black, horrible eyes.

The thing inside of Gary Forsyth screamed as it took the woman. A thick, oily vapor seeped out of the deputy and forced itself inside her. She felt the presence enter through her mouth and then through her eyes. She resisted it at first but was so tired, and ultimately, she welcomed it. Tara Jefferies closed her eyes, joined the collective, and was gone.

Father Kieran walked towards the room where he had been directed. The head nurse, who had been nice enough to offer Burt a ride home, told him where he could find Billy Tobin. Kieran made his way to the second floor, toward room 217. He approached the door and heard the woman scream from inside. "Oh my God!"

He immediately reacted and burst through the door. He still carried the coroner's pistol tucked beneath his shirt and believed there might be one bullet left.

The boy held his mother by the arm and pulled her towards him. *He's become one of those things.* Kieran reached for the gun. He wrapped his fingers around the cold steel and prepared himself.

"Look, Father, Billy's awake. It's a miracle." The woman looked up to him and smiled.

Billy slowly turned his head toward him, looking as if he had been run over by a lawnmower. "Hello, Father," his voice barely a whisper. "Thank you for helping me." He pulled his mother close and hugged her.

Kieran eased the weapon back into his waistband. Taking a slow breath, he relaxed and offered a friendly smile. It had been a long day and an even longer night. "It is truly a miracle. You're very welcome, Billy. I'm so glad to see that you're feeling better." Although the gun was empty and wouldn't have helped any, Kieran had been prepared to do whatever he needed and knew that, soon, he would need to again. There were more of those things out there and work to be done—God's work. He had been invited to attend the meeting at the courthouse in the morning and intended to be there.

Billy raised his hand and offered it to him. Kieran shook it. Despite his compromised state, the boy's grip was firm and strong. The child had been close to death yet still possessed the strength of Samson. Kieran knew the child was sent to his door for a reason. He was a soldier, a warrior. He had been sent to do God's work as well.

"Billy, where's Eric, honey? Do you know where your brother is?" Alice's voice wavered close to tears.

"We got separated. Something was wrong with Mick; he started fighting with Eric. I don't know—I can't remember."

"He needs his rest," the nurse said. "Give him a little time. He's been through an awful lot."

Billy laid his head against the pillow, struggling to keep his eyes open.

"I'm sorry, Mom. I can't remember ... Snakes," he said. "I remember snakes," Billy whispered and then passed out.

I bet you do remember snakes. Kieran looked down at him. *The serpent is in the garden, my son.*

"Thank you for all of your help, Father Kieran." Alice grabbed the man and hugged him. "Thank you so much."

"Of course. God bless you and your family," he told them and excused himself. He didn't know if it was safe to go back to the rectory or not, but he felt the presence of the Lord, and that was enough. He drove home, let himself in, and washed the soot from his body. Nothing tried to accost him as he exited his car and entered the rectory. And Father Kieran slept better than he had in the past two nights; he slept as if he had been given a coat of armor. *For thy rod and thy staff comfort me.*

Others had not been as fortunate as Father Kieran. Far more of the Grove's citizens met fates similar to that of Tara Jefferies. They had been ambushed in their homes as the creatures invaded like rapists and murderers, spreading its germ, allowing its consciousness to fester and propagate. It entered like an intravenous drip, filling their mouths and veins, consuming their thoughts, devouring their fears. When the sun rose on Garrett Grove the following morning, there were far fewer human eyes to witness it. Its autumn rays showed through broken windows into empty kitchens, bedrooms, and nursery floors, where dark crimson stains had dried brown throughout the night.

To be continued ...

The Ojanox Book III: All Fall Down

Coming 9/3/2024

Thank you for reading!

Please consider leaving a rating/review on Goodreads and Amazon.

CONTINUE READING THE OJANOX BOOK III: ALL FALL DOWN

Read an excerpt from All Fall Down

THE OJANOX SERIES: BOOKS 1 - 4

The Ojanox Series is now available at Amazon and Barnes & Noble.

ACKNOWLEDGEMENTS

If you ever find yourself in the town of Pompton Plains, New Jersey, and drive to the very top of Mountain Avenue, you will reach Mountainside Park, but you won't find an old road extension or an abandoned sanatorium. However, the inspiration for the old hospital comes from a place called the Overbrook, which wasn't all that far away. Neither is the real Garrett Mountain, for that matter. I took great liberties when writing this book, even changing the location to upstate New York, but many of the features are similar to the town I grew up in: Chilton medical center, the graveyard behind the Lutheran Church, even the hardware store at the corner of Jackson Ave. I just changed things a little to fit the story.

It's been four years since I first started writing this book, and there are many who helped bring this monster to life. Whether their assistance was inspirational, fact-checking, information gathering, or emotional support, I couldn't have done this without them. There are topics I touched on in *The Ojanox* that required the input of professionals and tons of research. When it comes to toxicology, lab work, virology, and bacteriology, I did my best to stick to the facts. When I got it wrong—when faced with serving the story or the hard medical facts, I chose the story. So that's on me.

First, I would like to thank Wendy Nastasi and my sister, Dawn Chiossi (Danielle), for a lifetime of inspiration, support, and for listening to me talk about nothing other than this damn book for the past three years. I would also like to thank them for lending their namesakes to this story, with written consent, of course.

There are several friends who read early versions of this book whose help was instrumental. Nick Gomes and Ed Koloski helped provide feedback and were my sounding board from the very start, back in the halfway house days. Greg Gillick and Mike Turrigiano have always had my back and were there to listen to my very first attempts at horror writing. And of course, Jack Wells. Jack has been my constant go-to guy with this project for years. He read it before the first rewrite, and he still came back for more. Now that's a true friend. In truth, *The Ojanox* wouldn't be half the book it is today without Jack's knowledge, skill, and literary prowess.

My editor, Lisa Lee Tone, took every page of this manuscript and made it better with her diligent attention to detail. I'm fortunate to have Lisa in my corner to call me out when I stray from the path, and I'm thankful she was always there to rope me back in.

I'd like to thank Ben Eads for his original developmental edits on *Scream in the Dark* and for the rigorous Jedi training and instruction. (Insert Yoda voice) Because of you, a better writer, I am.

Christy Aldridge has been so much more than a cover artist, or an illustrator, or even a contributor—she has been a partner, in every sense of the word. Without Christy's hard work and dedication, this project wouldn't be half of what it is today. For the past year or more, we have been joined at the hip. She took my vision and brought it to life. Thank you, Christy, I couldn't have done this without you. Now we need to start a new project.

Thank you, Don Noble and Jeff DeSantis for contributing your amazing illustrations and talents to this project.

Many thanks to my Alpha team and proofreaders for their time, input, and suggestions: Donna Latham, Heather Ann Larson, Jae Mazer, Kerrie Roylance, Bryan Moyer, Kristen Lynch, Susan Isenberg, John O'regan, Christina Marie, and Maryanne Pacheco Chappell.

And a huge thank you to Kira (Eagle Eyes) Seamon, for tirelessly hunting through these manuscripts, making sure that all the finishing touches were properly in place. It's the little things that make the difference, and had it been up to me, far too many little things would have slipped through the cracks. Thank you, Kira for squashing all those pesky little things into oblivion.

For all my friends who follow me on social media, for all the reviewers, bloggers, influencers who support the indie horror community, thank you. Also, thank you Tiffany Koplin, RJ Roles, and all the admins at the Books of Horror Facebook group for everything you do.

My life would have been very different if it hadn't been for my fourth-grade teacher, Mrs. Genevieve Smith, whose tutelage, undying devotion, and wealth of limitless stories molded not only myself but an entire generation. I especially would like to thank you for bringing my homework to the hospital when I broke my leg.

Thank you, Kelly Rainey, and all the fourth-grade classes of Pompton Plains school.

Anthony Lorraine helped by sharing with me his experiences in Vietnam. Without Anthony, the character of Carl Primrose would have been much different, as well as my knowledge of that moment in history. Sadly,

I learned of Anthony's passing when I was still in the halfway house. He was a good friend during a dark moment in my life. I miss you, Tony.

Thank you to my family and friends who helped contribute to the inspiration of this story through a lifetime of experiences, which I in turn felt compelled to fictionalize. And finally, for my mom, who told me my first ghost story, took me trick-or-treating, and allowed me to have a Halloween party at the house when I was ten years old. And for my dad, who let me build a haunted house and still reminds me periodically that I painted his garage walls black.

And thank you to the readers and horror fans who love this genre as much as I do. Thank you for taking this journey with me and thank you for allowing me to share this story with you. I hope you enjoyed it half as much as I enjoyed writing it.

Daemon Manx

About the Author

Daemon Manx is an American author with a backstory. He is a recovering addict who spent nearly a decade in the prison system where he focused on recovery and learned to perfect his horror writing craft. He has been featured in magazines in both the U.S., the U.K, and Germany. In 2021 he received a HAG award for his story *The Dead Girl* and was nominated for a Splatterpunk award that same year.

He was a bonus round winner on the gameshow *Wheel of Fortune* in 1999 and is infamously known for a motor vehicle accident he was responsible for, involving President Ronald Reagan's limousine.

After struggling with addiction and incarceration, Daemon now has over eleven years clean and sober. He uses his story to illustrate the positive outcome of sobriety and offer a glimpse at what life can be like when one receives a second chance.

He lives with his sister, author Danielle Manx and their narcoleptic cat, Sydney, where they patiently prepare for the apocalypse. There is a good chance they will run out of coffee far too soon.